PRIDE AND PLATYPUS:
Mr. Darcy's Dreadful Secret

Jane Austen and Vera Nazarian

Copyright © 2012 by Vera Nazarian
All Rights Reserved.

Cover Art Details: "Portrait of a Gentleman" by Daniel Dickinson, 1825; "Platypus" by John William Lewin, 1808; "A View of Norton Hall, near Daventry, North Hamptonshire, England" by Henry John Boddington, 1848; "A Lane In Headingley, Leeds" 1881, and "Au Clair de Lune" 1882, by John Atkinson Grimshaw; "Wolf" by Nicu Buculei & Tomasz W. Kozlowski (odder), 1-20-2007.

Interior Illustrations: "Appendix," courtesy of Pearson Scott Foresman. All other interior illustrations Copyright © 2012 by Vera Nazarian

Cover Design Copyright © 2012 by Vera Nazarian

ISBN-13: 978-1-60762-078-5
ISBN-10: 1-60762-078-2

FIRST EDITION
Trade Paperback

June 15, 2012

A Publication of
Norilana Books
P. O. Box 209
Highgate Center, VT 05459-0209
www.norilana.com

Printed in the United States of America

Pride and Platypus:
Mr. Darcy's Dreadful Secret

Curiosities

an imprint of

Norilana Books

www.norilana.com

The Collected Supernatural Jane Austen
by Vera Nazarian

(Series includes the following titles)

Mansfield Park and Mummies:
*Monster Mayhem, Matrimony, Ancient Curses,
True Love, and Other Dire Delights*

Northanger Abbey and Angels and Dragons

Pride and Platypus: Mr. Darcy's Dreadful Secret

Forthcoming:

Pagan Persuasion: All Olympus Descends on Regency

Emma Enchanted

Sense and Sanguine Sensibility

Lady Susan, Succubus

Pride and **Platypus**

Mr. Darcy's Dreadful Secret

ႜၐჂჄ႞ⴄ

Jane Austen

and

Vera Nazarian

ႜၐჂჄ႞ⴄ

With Scholarly Footnotes and Appendices

For Professor Anne H. Bages
with Love

And for Marian Crane
for reinforcing the Notion of the Platypus

Chapter 1

It is a truth universally acknowledged, that when the moon is full over Regency England, the gentlemen are all subject to its curse.

It is a peculiar monthly Affliction inducing them to take on various unnatural shapes—neither quite demon, nor proper beast—and in those shapes to roam the land; to hunt, murder, dismember, gorge on blood, consume haggis and kidney pie, gamble away familial fortune, marry below their station (and below their stature, when the lady is an Amazon), vote Whig, perform sudden and voluntary manual labor, cultivate orchids, collect butterflies and Limoges snuff boxes, and perpetrate other such odious evil—unless properly *contained*.

And thus, as the first pale rays of Selene's silver sphere illuminate the celestial velvet of the night, they *turn*—baronets and dukes, earls and marquises, counts and princes, lords and squires high and low, regardless of fortune—shedding skin and inhibitions, breaking bones and genteel habits (and fine china and porcelain), distending into strange unnatural musculature and contorting into bestial forms, growing nails and claws and teeth; fur, scales, feathers, gristle, hide, or peculiar additional appendages; becoming monstrous beings of savagery and grim wonder.

Woe to any who might encounter them thus! And woe a thousandfold to any who might in such a state encourage them!

Fortunately, as a rule, the gentlemen are safely restrained indoors for their transformation. They are locked up discreetly, in deep cellars or family crypts, caged behind thick iron bars and swaddled in heavy links of chain in custom bedrooms and parlors and hidden estate alcoves. Some are even bound and manacled to stone walls of ancient dungeons converted for just such use—while being closely observed and ministered to by their closest kin or loyal servants.

For as long as the devious pallid orb illuminates the night heavens, they remain thus. And only the golden rays of Helios, the bright luminary of morning, can return them to their human form. . . .

Alas! There is no antidote for this manly Affliction. There is no succor or respite, from month to month. And there are no exceptions. Indeed, even the regent himself is not immune.

All that remains is for the pious to pray, and for the ladies to speculate—for it is a rare amusement indeed to discuss the advantages of each gentleman based on the supposed nature of his Affliction (and manner of private confinement), in conjunction with the more pleasant expectations of his income and inheritance.

Now, it is also a truth universally acknowledged, that a single man in possession of a good fortune, bound by the usual gentleman's Affliction, must be in want of a wife.

However little known the feelings or views of such a man may be on his first entering a neighbourhood, this truth is so well fixed in the minds of the surrounding families, that he is considered the rightful property of some one or other of their daughters—even though, it is precisely such a man that must also harbor a Dreadful Secret.

"My dear Mr. Bennet," said his lady to him one day, "have you heard that Netherfield Park is let at last?"

Mr. Bennet replied that he had not.

"But it is," returned she; "for Mrs. Long has just been here, and she told me all about it."

Mr. Bennet made no answer. It was only a week till the full moon, and his customary leonine languidity was beginning to make its presence felt, foreshadowing other related symptoms.

"Do you not want to know who has taken it?" cried his wife impatiently, affronted more than usual by the sight of her excessively *absent*-seeming husband and the promise of what was yet to come.

"*You* want to tell me, and I have no objection to hearing it."

This was invitation enough.

"Why, my dear, you must know, Mrs. Long says that Netherfield is taken by a young man of large fortune from the north of England! He came down on Monday in a chaise and four to see the place, and was so much delighted with it, that he agreed with Mr. Morris immediately; he is to take possession before Michaelmas. Some of his servants are to be in the house by the end of next week. And in advance of his other possessions comes a very sturdy and generously proportioned *iron cage*."

"What is his name?"

"Bingley."

"Is he married or single?"

"Oh! Single, my dear, to be sure! A single man of large fortune; four or five thousand a year, and a grand impressive cage! What a fine thing for our girls!"

"How so? How can it affect them? Do you intend to incarcerate them monthly alongside this gentleman?"

"My dear Mr. Bennet," replied his wife, "how can you be so tiresome! You must know that I am thinking of his marrying one of them."

"Is that his design in settling here?"

"Design! Nonsense, how can you talk so! But it is very likely that he *may* fall in love with one of them, and therefore you must visit him as soon as he comes—and well before the Affliction takes its odious hold of the both of you."

"I see no occasion for that. You and the girls may go, or you may send them by themselves, which perhaps will be still better, for as you are as handsome as any of them, Mr. Bingley may like you the best of the party. In which case I will naturally have to call him out; fur will fly, and there will be all manner of sanguine unpleasantry."

"My dear, you flatter me. I certainly *have* had my share of beauty (and cage duels), but I do not pretend to be anything extraordinary now. When a woman has five grown-up daughters, she ought to give over thinking of her own beauty."

"In such cases, a woman has not often much beauty to think of."

"But, my dear, you must indeed go and see Mr. Bingley when he comes into the neighbourhood. Consider your daughters! Only think what an establishment it would be for one of them. Sir William and Lady Lucas are determined to go, merely on that account. Indeed you must go, for it will be impossible for *us* to visit him if you do not."

"You are over-scrupulous, surely. I dare say Mr. Bingley with his grandiose crate will be very glad to see you; and I will send a few lines by you to assure him of my hearty consent to his marrying whichever he chooses of the girls; though I must throw in a good word for my brave little Lizzy."

"I desire you will do no such thing! Lizzy is not a bit better than the others; and I am sure she is not half so handsome as Jane, nor half so good-humoured as Lydia. But you are always giving *her* the preference and letting *her* tend to the padlock and bars of your confinement room."

"Indeed! Lizzy is the only one who dares approach the confinement room when I am within. But—they have none of them much to recommend them," replied he; "they are all silly and ignorant like other girls; but Lizzy has something more of quickness than her sisters, and a great deal more courage."

"Mr. Bennet, how *can* you abuse your own children in such a way? You take delight in vexing me. It must be the odious moon, making you so *beastly* already. You have no compassion for my poor nerves."

"You mistake me, my dear. Unlike you, the moon is impotent in daytime. And I have a high respect for your nerves. They are my old friends. I have heard you mention them with consideration these last twenty years at least."

"Ah, you do not know what I suffer."

"Consider what I suffer in the moonlight behind two-inch thick iron bars. Now, I hope you will get over it, and live to see many young men of four thousand a year come into the neighbourhood, bringing with them enough sturdy metal enclosures to fill a zoo."

"It will be no use to us, if twenty such should come, since you will not visit them."

"Depend upon it, my dear, that when there are twenty, I will visit them all, if only to appraise the structural integrity of their containment. One learns a great deal from observation of other such contraptions to benefit one's own."

Mrs. Bennet could verily speak nothing to that, only open her mouth and wring her handkerchief.

Mr. Bennet was so odd a mixture of quick parts, sarcastic humour, reserve, and caprice, that the experience of three-and-twenty years had been insufficient to make his wife understand either his Affliction or his character.

Her mind was less difficult to develop. She was a woman of mean understanding, little information, and uncertain temper. When she was discontented, she fancied herself nervous. The business of her life was to get her daughters married; its solace was visiting and news.

Her single favorite nemesis was the dreadful luminary in the night heavens, the odious moon.

Chapter 2

Before the moon could fatten even by a sliver, Mr. Bennet was among the earliest of those who waited on Mr. Bingley. He had always intended to visit him, and timed it rather well (though, to the last, with a lion's distinctive indolence, always assuring his wife that he should not go). Indeed, till the evening after the visit was paid she had no knowledge of it, and fussed exceedingly at every window, making repeated adjustments to curtains against "that wicked illumination."

The visit was eventually disclosed in the following manner. Observing his second daughter employed in trimming a hat, he suddenly addressed her with an unmistakable hint of a rumble-purr:

"I hope Mr. Bingley will like it, Lizzy."

"We are not in a way to know *what* Mr. Bingley likes," said her mother resentfully, particularly displeased to hear the lion's familiar deep undertone, "since we are not to visit."

"But you forget, mamma," said Elizabeth, "that we shall meet him at the assemblies directly after the full moon, and that Mrs. Long promised to introduce him."

"I do not believe Mrs. Long will do any such thing. She has two nieces of her own. She is a selfish, hypocritical woman with a mangy boar or possibly hyena to tend to every month (so I am told, but of course *she* would never admit such a thing of her spouse), and I have no opinion of her."

"No more have I," said Mr. Bennet, continuing to rumble deeply (at which his wife reacted with rising discomfiture—of which he was no doubt perfectly aware—and thus they resonated off one another in perfect mutually-building dissonance, as only two perfectly un-tuned strings can, when forced by proximity to sound together); "and I am glad to find that you do not depend on her serving you."

Mrs. Bennet deigned not to make any reply, but, unable to contain herself, began scolding one of her daughters.

"Don't keep coughing so, Kitty, for Heaven's sake! Have a little compassion on my nerves. You tear them to pieces, worse than any large clawed creature in residence . . ."

"Kitty has no discretion in her coughs," said her father; "she times them ill, with little regard to the phases of the moon or her mother."

"I do not cough for my own amusement," replied Kitty fretfully. "When is your next ball to be, Lizzy?"

"To-morrow fortnight. As soon as the gentlemen are fully recovered from their Ordeal."

"Aye, so it is," cried her mother, "and Mrs. Long does not come back till the day before (since she has to mind some additional relation's odious cage); so it will be impossible for her to introduce him, for she will not know him herself."

"Then, my dear, you may have the advantage of your friend, and introduce Mr. Bingley to *her*."

"Impossible, Mr. Bennet, impossible, when I am not acquainted with him myself; how can you be so teasing?"

"I honour your circumspection. A fortnight's acquaintance is certainly very little. One cannot know what a man really *is* by the end of a fortnight—that is, one might observe the painful moments in the cage, followed by the usual glib recovery in the drawing room, but the true depths remain occluded from even the most discriminating eye and the most tattling tongue. But if *we* do not venture somebody else will; and after all, Mrs. Long and her daughters must stand their chance. Therefore, as she will think it an act of kindness, if you decline the office, I will take it on myself."

The girls stared at their father. Mrs. Bennet said only, "Nonsense, nonsense!"

"What can be the meaning of that emphatic exclamation?" cried he. "Do you consider the stressful art of introduction as nonsense? I cannot quite agree with you *there*. What say you, Mary? Come, have I grown my lion's coat and teeth a tad early that you stare so, child? Speak, for you are a young lady of deep reflection, read great books and make extracts."

Mary wished to say something sensible, but knew not how—particularly now that dire visions of her father's Affliction were presented so bluntly to her *sensible* mind.

"While Mary is adjusting her ideas," he continued, "let us return to Mr. Bingley."

"I am sick of Mr. Bingley!" cried his wife.

"I am sorry to hear *that*; but why did not you tell me that before? If I had known as much this morning I certainly would not have called on him. As I have actually paid the visit, we cannot escape the acquaintance now. Indeed, always a pleasure to make acquaintance with a fellow grand feline—a tiger, to be precise, for such, was revealed to me, is the gentleman's condition."

The astonishment of the ladies was just what he wished; that of Mrs. Bennet perhaps surpassing the rest. When the first tumult of joy was over, she declared she had expected it all the while, exclaiming, "A tiger, oh, what a fine thing! A tiger! Are you certain, Mr. Bennet? Did he admit to it outright? Indeed, how pleasantly direct of him!"

"If you recall, my dear, we have our ways of ascertaining such things without the uncouth bluntness of direct inquiry. But yes, rest assured, I *smelled* a tiger."

"Oh, Mr. Bennet!"

Her husband's chuckle was very much a rumbling purr.

"How good it was in you, my dear Mr. Bennet!" she continued. "But I knew I should persuade you at last. I was sure you loved your girls too well to neglect such an acquaintance. Well, how pleased I am! Such a good joke, too, that you should have gone this morning and never said a word about it till now."

"Now, Kitty, you may cough as much as you choose." And Mr. Bennet left the room, fatigued with the raptures of his wife.

"What an excellent father you have, girls!" said she, when the door was shut. "I do not know how we will ever make him amends for his kindness. Indeed, after this coming full moon, do take care to make your father's recovery as gentle as possible . . . At our time of life it is not so pleasant, I can tell you, to be making new acquaintances every day, feline or otherwise; but for your sakes, we would do anything. Lydia, my love, though you *are* the youngest, I dare say Mr. Bingley will dance with you at the next ball."

"Oh!" said Lydia stoutly, "I am not afraid; for though I *am* the youngest, I'm the tallest."

The rest of the evening was spent in conjecturing what manner and how much of a *tiger* he was, how soon he would return Mr. Bennet's visit, and determining when they should ask him to dinner.

Chapter 3

Whatever inquiries Mrs. Bennet, with the assistance of her five daughters, attempted, was insufficient to draw from her husband any satisfactory description of Mr. Bingley.

They attacked him in various ways—with barefaced questions, ingenious suppositions, distant surmises, and even feline wiles that were deemed most provocative for the lion. But he eluded their skill, and they were at last obliged to accept the second-hand intelligence of their neighbour, Lady Lucas.

Her report was highly favourable. Sir William had been delighted with Mr. Bingley (his own elderly panther nature finding immediate soothing familiarity in the youthful tiger). Mr. Bingley was quite young, wonderfully handsome, extremely agreeable, definitely in possession of a grandiose cage with most lordly and substantial iron bars, and, to crown the whole, he meant to be at the next post-moon assembly with a large party. Nothing could be more delightful! To be fond of dancing was a certain step towards falling in love; and very lively hopes of Mr. Bingley's tiger heart were entertained.

"If I can but see one of my daughters happily settled at Netherfield," said Mrs. Bennet to her husband, "and all the others equally well married, I shall have *nothing* to wish for."

Mr. Bennet refrained from uttering a triviality about *nothing but the moon*, his wife's source of constant aggravation, and would that it might at last elude her vigilant abhorrence in case of such a happy event. . . .

In a few days Mr. Bingley returned Mr. Bennet's visit, and sat about ten minutes with him in his library. Reportedly, feline gentlemen's sounds of ease and contentment in the form of grand purrs were soon heard to issue from behind closed doors. Mr. Bingley had entertained hopes of being admitted to a sight of the young ladies, of whose beauty he had heard much; but he saw only the father.

The ladies were somewhat more fortunate, for they had the advantage of ascertaining from an upper window that he wore a blue coat, and rode a black horse.

An invitation to dinner was soon afterwards dispatched. Mrs. Bennet set to planning the courses that were to do credit to her housekeeping, when an answer arrived which deferred it all. Mr. Bingley was obliged to be in town the following day, so close to the full moon and its inherent danger, and, consequently, unable to accept the honour of their invitation, etc.

Mrs. Bennet was quite disconcerted. She could not imagine what business he could have in town so soon after his arrival in Hertfordshire. What if he might be always flying about from one place to another, never settled at Netherfield as he ought to be?

Lady Lucas quieted her fears a little by starting the idea of his being gone to London only to get a large party for the ball. A report soon followed that Mr. Bingley was to bring twelve ladies and seven gentlemen with him to the assembly. Imagine the extravagance and the number of cages involved!

Never mind the cages—the girls grieved over such a number of *ladies*. But they were comforted right after the full moon and its resulting circumstances on the day before the ball by hearing, that instead of twelve he brought only six with him from London—his five sisters and a cousin. Some of the gentlemen apparently declined, as most preferred not to travel during, or even soon before or after the monthly Affliction. And thus, when the party entered the assembly room it consisted of only five altogether—Mr. Bingley, his two sisters, the husband of the eldest, and another young man.

Mr. Bingley was good-looking and gentlemanlike; he had a pleasant countenance in which the spirit of a noble tiger was easy to imagine, and easy, unaffected manners. His sisters were fine women, with an air of decided fashion. His brother-in-law, Mr. Hurst, merely looked the gentleman (but purportedly smelled a bit less savory, and a bit more doggish) . . .

But his friend Mr. Darcy soon drew the attention of the room by his fine, tall person, handsome features, noble mien, the report (which was in general circulation within five minutes after his entrance) of his having ten thousand a year—and a truly inscrutable and impenetrable *air of mystery* regarding his precise flavor of Affliction. It was as if a preternatural wall stood all about him, so that no one might sniff out what manner of supernatural creature commanded these delightful ten thousand—whether he were a noble feline, lupine, canine, ursine, or possibly porcine[1], lapine, or any other somewhat less notable beast.

Although unable to properly identify him as one of their own, the gentlemen pronounced him to be a fine figure of a man. The ladies meanwhile declared he was much handsomer than Mr. Bingley, and absolutely *had to be* one of the gallant Great Cat breed.

And thus he was looked at with great admiration for about half the evening . . . till his manners evoked a disgust which turned the tide of his popularity.

---

[1] It is unclear why mushrooms are referenced here. —Ed. *[Begging pardon of the reader, there are no "mushrooms" referenced here. "Porcine" refers to swine. —Ed. 2]*

For Mr. Darcy was discovered to be *proud;* to be above his company, and above being pleased. And not all his large estate in Derbyshire or his possible grand manner of Affliction could then save him from having a most forbidding, disagreeable countenance, and being unworthy to be compared with his friend.

Mr. Bingley had soon made himself acquainted with all the principal people in the room. He was lively and unreserved, danced every dance with the spring of a kitten, was outspoken as a vigorous tiger that the ball closed so early, and talked of giving one himself at Netherfield. Such amiable qualities must speak for themselves. What a contrast between him and his friend!

Mr. Darcy danced only once with Mrs. Hurst and once with Miss Bingley—showing neither feline grace nor lupine passion, only the icy precision of *extreme breeding.* He declined being introduced to any other lady, and spent the rest of the evening in walking about the room, speaking occasionally to one of his own party.

His character was decided and his Affliction disdained. He was the proudest, most disagreeable man in the world—likely, an uncouth Siberian bear whose enclosure required additional padlocks and much tedious cleaning afterwards. And everybody hoped that he would never come there again.

Amongst the most violent against him was Mrs. Bennet, whose dislike of his general behaviour was sharpened into particular resentment by his having slighted one of her daughters.

Elizabeth Bennet had been obliged, by the scarcity of gentlemen, to sit down for two dances. And during part of that time, Mr. Darcy had been standing near enough for her to hear a conversation between him and Mr. Bingley, who came from the dance for a few minutes, to press his friend to join it.

"Come, Darcy," said he, "I must have you dance. I hate to see you standing about by yourself in this stupid manner. You had much better dance."

"I certainly shall not. You know how I detest it, unless I am particularly acquainted with my partner. At such an assembly as this—a tawdry menagerie—it would be insupportable. Your sisters are engaged, and there is not another woman in the room whom it would not be a punishment to me to stand up with."

A few steps away, Elizabeth Bennet felt a sudden gust of heat envelop her, and listened, barely breathing. And immediately she could not help but imagine Mr. Darcy during the apex of the moon in a very dank and rotten, utterly dismal basement, transforming most *painfully* and *slowly* into a large mangy creature . . .

"I would not be so fastidious as you are," cried Mr. Bingley, "for a kingdom and a gilded cage! Upon my honour, I never met with so many pleasant girls in my life as I have this evening; and several of them are uncommonly pretty."

"*You* are dancing with the only handsome girl in the room," said Mr. Darcy, looking at the eldest Miss Bennet.

Nearby, the second-eldest Miss Bennet gave herself over entirely to her imaginary scenario, and now that dismal basement was thoroughly infested with rats . . .

"Oh! She is the most beautiful creature I ever beheld!" said Mr. Bingley. "But there is one of her sisters sitting down just behind you, who is very pretty, and I dare say very agreeable. Do let me ask my partner to introduce you."

"Which do you mean?" and turning round he looked for a moment at Elizabeth, till catching her eye, he withdrew his own and coldly said: "She is tolerable, but not handsome enough to tempt *me*."

Elizabeth's controlled breath stilled. Her cheeks, flaming only moments ago, were now numb. And her heart, just for an instant, was very, very cold. *In the basement, rats gnawed the thick rusted iron of his filthy cage, and inside, the unspeakable monster snarled, and, oh yes!—scratched himself furiously in unspeakable places . . .*

Meanwhile, Darcy continued; "I am in no humour at present to give consequence to young ladies who are slighted by other men. You had better return to your partner and enjoy her smiles, for you are wasting your time with me."

Mr. Bingley followed his advice. Mr. Darcy walked off; and Elizabeth remained with no very cordial feelings toward him, but with a thoroughly gratifying imaginary scene of moon-induced manly frenzy.

She told the story, however (indeed, both stories; and to the latter grotesque fantasy she added fleas), with great spirit among her friends; for she had a lively, playful disposition, which delighted in anything ridiculous—and was easily swayed to enhance the *merely ridiculous* into something truly *sublime.*

The evening altogether passed off pleasantly to the whole family. Mrs. Bennet had seen her eldest daughter much admired by the Netherfield party. Mr. Bingley had danced with her twice, and she had been distinguished by the tiger's sisters. Jane was as much gratified by this as her mother could be, though in a quieter way. Elizabeth felt Jane's pleasure. Mary had heard herself mentioned to Miss Bingley as "a proper lion's daughter" and the most accomplished girl in the neighbourhood. And Catherine and Lydia had been fortunate enough never to be without partners, which was all that they had yet learnt to care for at a ball.

They returned, therefore, in good spirits to Longbourn, the village where they lived, and of which they were the principal inhabitants. They found Mr. Bennet still up. With a book he was oblivious to the passage of time (indeed, with *any* book, scented with catnip or not, for the lion was a bibliophile); and on the present occasion he had a good deal of feline curiosity as to the events of an evening which had raised such splendid expectations. He had rather hoped that his wife's views on the stranger would be disappointed; but he soon found out that he had a different story to hear.

"Oh! my dear Mr. Bennet!" she cried as she entered the room, "we have had a most delightful, excellent evening and ball. I wish you had been there. Jane was so admired! Everybody said how well she looked; and Mr. Bingley thought her quite beautiful, and danced with her twice! And she was the only creature in the room that he asked a second time. First of all, he asked Miss Lucas. I was so vexed to see him stand up with her! But, however, he did not admire her at all; indeed, nobody can, you know, not with all that *pork*[2] in the family; and he seemed quite struck with Jane as she was going down the dance. So he inquired who she was, and got introduced, and asked her for the two next. Then the two third he danced with Miss King, and the two fourth with Maria Lucas, and the two fifth with Jane again, and the two sixth with Lizzy, and the *Boulanger*—"

"If he had had any compassion for *me*," cried her husband impatiently, "O that he had sprained his ankle in the first dance! For God's sake, say no more of his partners."

"Oh! my dear, I am quite delighted with him. He is so excessively handsome! One cannot help but think of the splendid roars that might issue from his enclosure every moon! And his sisters are charming women. I never in my life saw anything more elegant than their dresses. I dare say the lace upon Mrs. Hurst's gown—"

Here she was interrupted again. Mr. Bennet protested against any description of finery unless it included fur (in which case he attended, absentmindedly smoothing down his own thick head of hair—in particular the tufts behind the ears—and then adjusting his spectacles). She was therefore obliged to seek

---

[2] Alas! Gentle reader, Sir William Lucas was the sole panther in a long line of male boars. It was widely assumed that the somewhat dubious Affliction merely skipped a generation. In matters of the marriage mart, Miss Lucas was doomed.

another branch of the subject, and related, with much bitterness of spirit and some exaggeration, the shocking rudeness of Mr. Darcy.

"But I can assure you," she added, "that Lizzy does not lose much by not suiting *his* fancy; for he is a most disagreeable, horrid *beastly* man, not at all worth pleasing, and not likely to be anything more than a mangy housecat. So high and so conceited that there was no enduring him! He walked here and there, fancying himself so very great! *Not handsome enough to dance with!* I wish you had been there, my dear, to have given him one of your roaring set-downs. I quite detest the man."

Chapter 4

When Jane and Elizabeth were alone, the former, who had been cautious in her praise of Mr. Bingley before, expressed to her sister just how very much she admired him.

"He is just what a young man ought to be," said she, "sensible, good-humoured, lively, decidedly tigrine. And I never saw such happy manners!—so much ease and perfect good breeding!"

"He is also handsome," replied Elizabeth, "which a young man ought likewise to be, if he possibly can. His character is thereby complete."

"I was very much flattered by his asking me to dance a second time. I did not expect such a compliment."

"Did not you? I did for you. But that is one great difference between us. Compliments always take *you* by surprise, and *me* never. What could be more natural than his asking you again? He could not help seeing that you were about five times as pretty as every other woman in the room. Well, he certainly is very agreeable, and I give you leave to like him. You have liked many a stupider and *tamer* person."

"Dear Lizzy!"

"Oh! you are a great deal too apt to like people in general. You never see a fault in anybody. All the world are good and agreeable in your eyes. I never heard you speak ill of a human being in your life, not even when they are beastly."

"I would not wish to be hasty in censuring anyone; but I always speak what I think."

"I know you do; and it is *that* which makes the wonder. With *your* good sense, to be so honestly blind to the follies and nonsense of others! Affectation of candour is common enough—one meets with it everywhere, except during the full moon when cruel truth in its primeval form triumphs over artifice. But to be candid without ostentation or design or even the effects of Selene's pallid rays—to take the good of everybody's character and make it still better, and say nothing of the bad—belongs to you alone. And so you like this man's sisters, too, do you? Their manners are not equal to his. Indeed, I would venture to guess one lady's spouse barks at the moon."

"Lizzy! Oh, and certainly not—at first."

"Naturally not at first. Long before the man can howl or bark, he first crawls about on the floor of his cage in much discomfort—"

"Oh, Lizzy! you know very well of what I speak—his sisters' manners. But they are very pleasing women when you converse with them. Miss Bingley is to live with her brother, and keep his house. Surely we shall find a very charming neighbour in her."

Elizabeth listened in silence, but was not convinced. Their behaviour at the assembly had not been calculated to please in general. And with more quickness of observation and less pliancy of temper than her sister, and with a judgment too unassailed by any attention to herself, she was very little disposed to approve them.

They were in fact very fine ladies; good-humoured when they were pleased, agreeable when they chose it, but otherwise proud and conceited. They were rather handsome, had been educated in one of the first private seminaries in town, had a fortune of twenty thousand pounds, were in the habit of spending more than they ought, and of associating with people of rank and desirable Affliction—and were therefore in every respect entitled to think well of themselves, and meanly of others. They were of a respectable family in the north of England; a circumstance more deeply impressed on their memories than that their brother's fortune and their own had been acquired by trade.

Mr. Bingley inherited his feline Affliction and his property to the amount of nearly a hundred thousand pounds from his father, who had intended to purchase an estate, but did not live to do it. Mr. Bingley intended it likewise. But now, provided with a good house and the liberty of a manor, it was doubtful, considering the easiness of his temper, whether he might not spend the remainder of his days at Netherfield, and leave the next generation to purchase.

His sisters were anxious for his having an estate of his own. But, though he was now only established as a tenant, Miss Bingley was willing to preside at his table. And Mrs. Hurst, who had married a man of more fashion (and yes, more *bark*) than fortune, was disposed to consider his house as her home when it suited her. Mr. Bingley had not been of age two years, when he was tempted by an accidental recommendation to look at Netherfield House. He did look at it, and was pleased with the situation and the principal rooms, including not one but *three* very spacious and unyielding safe-room enclosures (each properly isolated and distanced from other quarters, and intended to host guests of nearly any Affliction) all reinforced with wrought-iron bars for the monthly Ordeal, and particularly clever locks which even Mr. Darcy approved. In short, Mr. Bingley was satisfied, and took it immediately.

Between him and Darcy there was a very steady friendship, in spite of great opposition of character. Bingley was endeared to Darcy by the easiness, openness, and malleability of his Great Cat temper, though no disposition could offer a greater contrast to his own, and though with his own he never appeared dissatisfied.

On the strength of Darcy's regard, Bingley had the firmest reliance, and of his judgment the highest opinion—whether it concerned padlocks or people. In understanding, Darcy was the superior. Bingley was by no means deficient, but Darcy was clever. He was at the same time haughty, reserved, and fastidious, and his manners, though well-bred, were not inviting, and indeed rather *mysterious*. In that respect his friend had greatly the advantage. Bingley was sure of being liked wherever he appeared; Darcy was continually giving offense.

The manner in which they spoke of the Meryton assembly was sufficiently characteristic. Bingley had never met with more pleasant people or prettier girls in his life; everybody had been most kind and attentive to him; there had been no formality, no stiffness—verily, the air around each gentleman was replete with pleasing wild forest creature scents, and he had soon felt acquainted with all the room. . . .

And, as to Miss Bennet, he could not conceive an angel more beautiful.

Darcy, on the contrary, had seen a collection of people in whom there was much *scent*, little beauty, and no fashion, for none of whom he had felt the smallest interest, and from none received either attention or pleasure. Miss Bennet he acknowledged to be pretty, but she smiled too much.

Mrs. Hurst and her sister allowed it to be so—but still they admired her and liked her, and pronounced her to be a sweet girl, and one whom they would not object to know more of. Miss Bennet was therefore *established* as a sweet girl, and their brother felt authorized by such commendation to think of her as he chose.

Chapter 5

Within a short walk of Longbourn lived a family with whom the Bennets were particularly intimate. Sir William Lucas had been formerly in trade in Meryton, where he had made a tolerable fortune, and risen to the honour of knighthood by an address to the king during his mayoralty—and the fortunate avoidance of a long-standing familial proclivity to a porcine Affliction which indeed had burdened the previous generations with endless boars.

The distinction had perhaps been felt too strongly by this only panther heir to bear the Lucas name. It had given him a disgust to his roots, his business, and to his residence in a small market town. And, in quitting the three, he had removed with his family to a house about a mile from Meryton, denominated from that period Lucas Lodge, where he could think with pleasure of his own decidedly *feline* importance, and, unshackled by business, or pig connections, occupy himself solely in being civil to all the world. For, though elated by his rank, it did not render him supercilious. On the contrary, he was all attention to everybody, and genuinely sympathetic to those with Afflictions less fortunate than others. By nature inoffensive, friendly, and obliging, his presentation at St. James's had made him courteous.

Lady Lucas was a very good kind of woman, not too clever to be a valuable neighbour to Mrs. Bennet. They had several children.[3] The eldest of them, a sensible, intelligent young woman, about twenty-seven, was Elizabeth's intimate[4] friend.

That the Miss Lucases and the Miss Bennets should meet to talk over a ball was absolutely necessary; and the morning after the assembly brought the former to Longbourn to hear and to communicate.

"*You* began the evening well, Charlotte," said Mrs. Bennet with civil self-command to Miss Lucas. "*You* were Mr. Bingley's first choice."

"Yes; but he seemed to like his second better."

"Oh! you mean Jane, I suppose, because he danced with her twice. To be sure that *did* seem as if he admired her—indeed I rather believe he *did*—I heard something about it—but I hardly know what—something about Mr. Robinson."

"Perhaps you mean what I overheard between him and Mr. Robinson; did not I mention it to you?" said Elizabeth. "Mr. Robinson's asking him how he liked our Meryton assemblies, and whether he did not think there were a great many pretty women in the room, and *which* he thought the prettiest? and his answering immediately to the last question: 'Oh! the eldest Miss Bennet, beyond a doubt; there cannot be two opinions on that point.'"

"Upon my word! Well, that is very decided indeed—that does seem as if—but, however, it may all come to nothing, you

---

[3] Here, the astute reader will naturally surmise that "they had several children" refers not to some dubious union between Mrs. Bennet and Lady Lucas but to Sir William and Lady Lucas. —Ed. *[This is absurdly unnecessary. The reader knows perfectly well whose children are being referenced. —Ed. 2]*

[4] This friendship, I hasten to add, is intended to be entirely chaste. [Who are you? —Ed.] *[Who is this? —Ed. 2]*

know. Gentlemen tigers can be as vigorous in their pursuits as they are likely to be swayed by new ones."

"*My* overhearings were more to the purpose than *yours*, Eliza," said Charlotte. "The inscrutable Mr. Darcy is not so well worth listening to as his friend, is he?—poor Eliza!—to be only just *tolerable*."

"I beg you would not put it into Lizzy's head to be vexed by his ill-treatment, for he is such a disagreeable man, entirely ursine (of the variety from the depths of wooded Russia where they all eat each other, I dare say), that it would be quite a misfortune to be liked by him—just think of tending the unspeakable soils of *that* cage! Mrs. Long told me last night that he sat close to her for half-an-hour without once opening his lips."

"Are you quite sure, ma'am?—is not there a little mistake?" said Jane. "I certainly saw Mr. Darcy speaking to her."

"Aye—because she asked him at last how he liked Netherfield, and he could not help answering her; but she said he seemed quite angry at being spoke to. No doubt he would have growled, had it been closer to the full moon."

"Miss Bingley told me," said Jane, "that he never speaks much, unless among his intimate acquaintances. With *them* he is remarkably agreeable. One doubts such a *controlled* gentleman might ever growl at all."

"I do not believe a word of it, my dear. A man is a man when the moon shines full, and *they all growl*—growl and roar and bite and drool and engage in other unspeakable behaviour, I assure you. Besides, if he had been so very agreeable, he would have talked to Mrs. Long. But I can guess how it was; everybody says that he is eat up with pride and sickened by his lofty Affliction, and I dare say he had heard somehow that Mrs. Long does not keep a carriage—what, with having to care for that hyena at home and all those cousins, it does not come cheap, I gather—and she had come to the ball in a hack chaise."

"I do not mind his not talking to Mrs. Long, or even any signs of growling," said Miss Lucas, "but I wish he had danced with Eliza."

"Another time, Lizzy," said her mother, "I would not dance with *him*, if I were you."

"I believe, ma'am, I may safely promise you *never* to dance with him."

"His pride," said Miss Lucas, "does not offend *me* so much as pride often does, because there is an excuse for it. One cannot wonder that so very fine a young man, with family, fortune, refined Affliction, everything in his favour, should think highly of himself. If I may so express it, he has a *right* to be proud."

"That is very true," replied Elizabeth, "and I could easily forgive all the mysteries of his Ordeal and yes, *his* pride, if he had not mortified *mine*."

"Pride," observed Mary, who piqued herself upon the solidity of her reflections, "is a very common failing,[5] I believe. By all that I have ever read, I am convinced that it is very common[6] indeed; that human nature[7] is particularly[8] prone to it, and that there are very few of us who do not cherish a feeling of

---

[5] Mary is entirely correct to note the common evils of pride, and furthermore to compare and contrast it with the somewhat different yet very similar evils of vanity. —Ed. *[This footnote is pointless and needs to be excised. —Ed. 2]*

[6] Once again, wise reader, it is suggested you ponder the astute commentary herewith. *[Again, needs to be excised. —Ed. 2]*

[7] There is no reason to remove necessary clarifications. I insist that Editorial 2 retract the previous comment to my commentary. —Ed. *[Your comments are pedantic and unnecessary restatements of text. Please desist, from this point forward. —Ed. 2]*

[8] I don't see why Editorial 2 is taking up such a tone with me. *[Editorial 1, please stop immediately. Your footnotes are inappropriate. —Ed. 2]*

self-complacency[9] on the score of some quality or other, real or imaginary. Vanity[10] and[11] pride[12] are[13] different things, though the words are often used synonymously. A person may be proud without being vain. Pride relates more to our opinion[14] of ourselves, vanity[15] to[16] what[17] we would have others think of us."

"If I were as rich as Mr. Darcy, and a grand and gruesome bear, or tiger—or, better yet, a wolf," cried a young Lucas, who came with his sisters, "I should not care how proud I was. I would keep a pack of foxhounds to keep myself occupied between the full moons, and drink a bottle of wine a day."

---

[9] Well, this is a doozy. I can certainly proceed to clarify texts wherever I find it necessary. And furthermore—

[10] You, sirrah,

[11] cannot

[12] stop

[13] me!!!

[14] Well, it is the occasional opinion of some other people that vanity and pride are both despicable vices— [Beg pardon, whoever you are, but you are in fact restating my very own opinion that I have already very clearly addressed in the previous contextual commentary of the text, just before I was so gracelessly interrupted by the other gentleman, though I hesitate to use the term "gentleman" to apply to such a —— in Editorial 2. —Ed.] *[Good grief! Who are you people? —Ed. 2]*

[15] *I hesitate to get drawn into this, since it is a blatant misuse of footnotes, but whatever does the "gentleman" in Editorial 1 imply by the reference to ——? —Ed. 2*

[16] PHTHththth!!!! That. sirrah, is what I imply; and also, Thou art a scoundrel and a cad, and an uptight ass. —Ed.

[17] **With our greatest apologies to the reader, footnotes are temporarily suspended. —Senior Ed.**

"Then you would drink a great deal more than you ought," said Mrs. Bennet; "and if I were to see you at it, I should take away your bottle directly—and get you clean of all those vermin that the lupine and ursine Affliction is so prone to breed on the gentlemen's skin."

The boy protested that she should not; she continued to declare that she would, and the argument ended only with the visit.

Chapter 6

The ladies of Longbourn soon waited on those of Netherfield. The visit was soon returned in due form.

Miss Bennet's pleasing manners grew on the goodwill of Mrs. Hurst and Miss Bingley. And though the mother was found to be intolerable, and the younger sisters not worth speaking to, a wish of being better acquainted with *them* was expressed towards the two eldest.[18]

By Jane, this attention was received with the greatest pleasure. But Elizabeth still saw superciliousness in their treatment of everybody, hardly excepting even her sister, and could not like them. Indeed, their dubious kindness to Jane was probably the effect of the influence of their brother's admiration.

It was generally evident whenever they met, by all the subtle feline details of his person (including the ghostly rumble-purrs and the swishing of a "phantom tail"—purportedly, a phenomenon manifest in feline gentlemen in-between full moons, somewhat akin to a *supernatural mirage*), that he *did* admire her and to *her* it was equally evident that Jane was yielding to the preference which she had begun to entertain for

---

[18] The eldest, both daughters, are Jane Bennet and Elizabeth Bennet. —Ed. *[What? Are we back to inane commentary? I cannot believe this! —Ed. 2]*

him from the first, and was in a way to be very much in love. But Elizabeth considered with pleasure that it was not likely to be discovered by the world in general, since Jane united, with great strength of feeling, a composure of temper and a uniform cheerfulness of manner which would guard her from the suspicions of the impertinent. She mentioned this to her friend Miss Lucas.

"It may perhaps be pleasant," replied Charlotte, "to be able to impose on the public in such a case; but it is sometimes a disadvantage to be so very *guarded*. If a woman conceals her affection with the same skill from the object of it (as a man might conceal the nature of his Affliction), she may lose the opportunity of fixing[19] him. And it will then be but poor consolation to believe the world equally in the dark. There is so much of gratitude or vanity in almost every attachment, that it is not safe to leave any to itself. We can all *begin* freely—a slight preference is natural enough. But there are very few of us who have heart enough to be really in love without encouragement—and distanced from the moon's brutal truth. In nine cases out of ten[20] a woman had better show *more* affection than she feels. Bingley likes your sister undoubtedly; but he may never do more

---

[19] The implication here is not to infer that a gentleman is broken and needs "fixing." Rather, it is gently suggested that fixing him (i.e. "affixing," "attaching," "sticking together," "aggregating," "uniting," et cetera) might refer to the delicate snares cast out by the ladies to attach eligible gentlemen to their own charming person—not by an adhesive substance such as horse glue or beeswax, naturally, but in the more delicate metaphorical and poetic sense of spiritual attachment of dainty souls. —Ed *[Oh, dear God! —Ed. 2]*

[20] Incidentally, noting to the numerically astute reader, mathematically and arithmetic-wise—that is, if one is to actually presume and endeavour to make a physical count using numbers (as opposed to some other means)—this fraction is the analogue equivalent of ten percent; which can furthermore be denoted and annotated as 10%. —Ed. *[Blatantly, factually incorrect. It is ninety percent! —Ed. 2]*

than like her, if she does not help him on. One must pet a tiger kitten to make it purr."

"But she *does* help him on, or pet, as you say, this beloved tiger, as much as her nature will allow. If I can perceive her regard for him, he must be a simpleton, indeed, not to discover it too."

"Remember, Eliza, that he does not know Jane's disposition as you do."

"But if a woman is partial to a man, and does not endeavour to conceal it, he *must* find it out."

"Perhaps he must, if he *sees* enough of her—or sees her *well* enough (an ability that might be enhanced next moontide). But, though Bingley and Jane meet tolerably often, it is never for long. And in large mixed parties it is impossible that every moment should be employed in conversing together. Jane should therefore make the most of every half-hour in which she can command his attention. When she is secure of him, there will be more leisure for falling in love as much as she chooses."

"Your plan is a good one," replied Elizabeth, "where nothing is in question but the desire of being well married, and if I were determined to get a rich husband, or any husband, I dare say I should adopt it. But these are not Jane's feelings; she is not acting by design. As yet, she is uncertain of her own regard. She has known him only a fortnight, and right after a full moon when gentlemen's earthly passions—such as affections—are liable to still run high. She danced four dances with him at Meryton, saw him one morning at his own house, and has since dined with him in company four times. This is not quite enough to make her understand his character."

"Not as you represent it. Had she merely *dined* with him, she might only have discovered whether he had a good appetite or if he had an indelicate beastly tendency to tear into his meat. But you must remember that four evenings have also been spent together—and four evenings may do a great deal."

"Yes; these four evenings have enabled them to ascertain that they both like Vingt-un[21] better than Commerce;[22] but with respect to any other leading characteristic, I do not imagine that much has been unfolded."

"Well," said Charlotte, "I wish Jane success with all my heart; and if she were married to him to-morrow, I should think she had as good a chance of happiness as if she were to be studying his character for a twelvemonth and observing him monthly in his cage. Happiness in marriage is entirely a matter of chance—and occasionally, of lunacy. If the dispositions of the parties are similar and well known to each other beforehand, it does not advance their felicity in the least. They always continue to grow sufficiently *unlike* afterwards to have their share of vexation. It is better to know as little as possible of the *defects* of the person with whom you are to pass your life."

"You make me laugh, Charlotte. But you know it is not sound, and you would never act in this way yourself. Especially if you had the opportunity to tend the gentleman's enclosure well in advance of matrimony."

Occupied in observing Mr. Bingley's attentions to her sister, Elizabeth was far from suspecting that she was herself becoming an object of some interest in the eyes of his friend.

Mr. Darcy had at first scarcely allowed her to be pretty. He had looked at her without admiration at the ball. And when they next met, he looked at her only to criticise.

But no sooner had he made it clear to himself and his friends that she hardly had a good feature in her face, than he

---

[21] A card game, "Twenty-One," taken from the French. O Erudite Reader, Thou needst ogle it. —Ed. *[The correct term is "Google it." However, it is unclear why we even know this term. We should not have any knowledge of this term. —Ed. 2]*

[22] Another card game? —Ed. *[Yes. —Ed. 2]*

began to find it was rendered uncommonly intelligent by the beautiful expression of her dark eyes. To this discovery succeeded some others equally mortifying—though, surely nothing was more *mortifying* than the *nature* of his Dreadful Secret. But—gentle reader, more on that anon—

Though he had detected with a critical eye more than one failure of perfect symmetry in her form, he was forced to acknowledge her figure to be light and pleasing. And in spite of his asserting that her manners were not those of the fashionable world, he was caught by their easy playfulness.

Of this she was perfectly unaware. To her he was only the man who made himself agreeable nowhere, and who had not thought her handsome enough to dance with.

The dreadful grotesque monstrosity howling in the darkness of a moldy, rat-infested basement . . .

He began to wish to know more of her, and as a step towards conversing with her himself, paid close attention to her conversation with others.

His doing so drew her notice, possibly because his usual impeccable *control* was now somewhat compromised by the approaching period of Affliction. For, it was at Sir William Lucas's, where a large party were assembled, just before the coming full moon. . . .

"What does Mr. Darcy mean," said Elizabeth to Charlotte, "by listening to my conversation with Colonel Forster?"

"That is a question which Mr. Darcy only can answer."

"But if he does it any more I shall certainly let him know that I see what he is about. He has a very satirical eye, and if I do not begin by being impertinent myself, I shall soon grow afraid of him, and of whatever is hidden beneath his mysterious demeanor. Indeed, is it not possible there is a hint of the wild owl in his undivided attention? Could he be—"

And unable to control her flight of fancy, she once again imagined the dank basement, and the rats, and the monster . . . Only this time it was shaped like a hideously overgrown avian with saucer eyes . . .

Alas! no; such a thing was quite unlikely.

On his approaching them soon afterwards (though without seeming to have any intention of speaking—indeed, not even issuing forth a hoot), Miss Lucas defied her friend to mention such a subject to him—which immediately provoked Elizabeth to do it.

That is, she did not question him *directly* on the subject of owlish (or any other such) Afflictions. That would have been unseemly even of Mrs. Bennet, much less a sensible and reasonably well-bred young female such as herself. Instead, she turned to him and said:

"Did you not think, Mr. Darcy, that I expressed myself uncommonly well just now, when I was teasing Colonel Forster to give us a ball at Meryton just after the moon's folly is past?"

"With great energy; but it is always a subject which makes a lady energetic."

"You are severe on us. We know far better than to take your gentlemanly *moon madness* lightly."

"I speak not of the luminary but of the female propensity to express great energy for a ball, for music and dance."

"It will be *her* turn soon to be teased," said Miss Lucas. "I am going to open the instrument, Eliza, and you know what follows."

"You are a very strange creature by way of a friend!— always wanting me to play and sing before everybody! If my vanity had taken a musical turn, you would have been invaluable. But as it is, I would really rather not sit down before those who must be in the habit of hearing the very best performers."

On Miss Lucas's persevering, however, Elizabeth added, "Very well, if it must be so, it must." And gravely glancing at Mr. Darcy, "There is a fine old saying: 'Keep your breath to cool your porridge or to howl at the stars'; and I shall keep mine to swell my song."

Her performance was pleasing, though by no means capital. At present the gentlemen's emotions were moon-elevated and moods sufficiently primed for preternaturally enhanced *perception*, which, fortune had it, she did nothing to offend.

After a song or two, and before she could reply to the entreaties of several less *attuned*, that she would sing again, she was eagerly succeeded at the instrument by her sister Mary, who being the only plain one in the family, worked hard for knowledge and accomplishments, and was always impatient for display.

Mary had neither genius nor taste. And though vanity had given her application, it had given her likewise a pedantic air and conceited manner. Elizabeth, easy and unaffected, had been listened to with much more pleasure, though not playing half so well. And Mary, at the end of a long concerto (which tranquillized the audience into an upright slumber), was glad to purchase praise and gratitude by Scotch and Irish airs, at the request of her younger sisters, who, with some of the Lucases, and two or three officers, joined eagerly in dancing at one end of the room.

Mr. Darcy stood near them in silent indignation at such a mode of passing the evening, to the exclusion of all conversation, and was too much engrossed by his thoughts to perceive that Sir William Lucas was his neighbour, till Sir William thus began:

"What a charming amusement for young people this is, Mr. Darcy! There is nothing like dancing after all. I consider it as one of the first refinements of polished society."

"Certainly, sir; and it has the advantage also of being in vogue amongst the less polished societies of the world. Every savage can dance—and every gentleman contorting in manacles, just before the *transformation* takes him."

Sir William only smiled. "Now, now, let us not speak of that dreaded curse tonight. Your friend performs delightfully," he continued after a pause, on seeing Bingley join the group; "and I doubt not that you are an adept in the science yourself, Mr. Darcy."

"You saw me dance at Meryton, I believe, sir."

"Yes, indeed, and received no inconsiderable pleasure from the sight. Do you often dance at St. James's?"

"Never, sir."

"Do you not think it would be a proper compliment to the place?"

"It is a compliment which I never pay to any place if I can avoid it—at *any* time of the month."

"You have a house in town, I conclude?"

Mr. Darcy bowed.

"I had once had some thought of fixing in town myself—for in a manner of all grand felines, as you know, I am fond of superior society—a *fellow sentiment* I dare say *you yourself* might possibly share—" Here Sir William paused meaningfully, waiting for the smallest hint from his companion, either in agreement or refutation of such a feline condition, and when none was forthcoming, continued, "but I did not feel quite certain that the air of London would agree with Lady Lucas."

He paused yet again in hopes of an answer. But Mr. Darcy was not disposed to make any. And since Elizabeth was at that instant moving towards them, Sir William did the very gallant thing, and called out to her:

"My dear Miss Eliza, why are you not dancing? Mr. Darcy, you must allow me to present this young lady to you as a very desirable partner. You cannot refuse to dance, I am sure when so much beauty is before you."

And, taking her hand, he would have given it to Mr. Darcy (who, though extremely surprised, was not unwilling to receive it) when she instantly drew back, and said with some discomposure to Sir William:

"Indeed, sir, I have not the least intention of dancing. I entreat you not to suppose that I moved this way in order to beg for a partner."

Mr. Darcy, with grave propriety, requested to be allowed the honour of her hand, but in vain. Elizabeth was determined; nor did Sir William at all shake her purpose by his attempt at persuasion.

"You excel so much in the dance, Miss Eliza, that it is cruel to deny me the happiness of seeing you; and though this gentleman dislikes the amusement in general, he can have no objection, I am sure, to oblige us for one half-hour."

"Mr. Darcy is all politeness," said Elizabeth, smiling.

"He is, indeed; but, considering the inducement, my dear Miss Eliza, we cannot wonder at his complaisance—for who would object to such a partner?"

Elizabeth looked archly, and turned away. Her resistance had not injured her with the gentleman, and he was thinking of her with some complacency, when thus accosted by Miss Bingley:

"I can guess the subject of your reverie."

"I should imagine not."

"You are considering how insupportable it would be to pass many evenings in this manner—in such *beastly* society; and indeed I am quite of your opinion. I was never more annoyed! The insipidity, and yet the noise—the nothingness, and yet the self-importance of all those people! A menagerie of the lowest sort! What would I give to hear your strictures on them!"

"Your conjecture is totally wrong, I assure you. My mind was more agreeably engaged. I have been meditating on the very great pleasure which a pair of fine eyes in the face of a pretty woman can bestow."

Miss Bingley immediately fixed her eyes on his face, and desired he would tell her what lady had the credit of inspiring such reflections. Mr. Darcy replied with great intrepidity:

"Miss Elizabeth Bennet."

"Miss Elizabeth Bennet!" repeated Miss Bingley. "I am all astonishment. How long has she been such a favourite?—and pray, when am I to wish you joy?"

"That is exactly the question which I expected you to ask. A lady's imagination is very rapid; it jumps from admiration to love, from love to matrimony, to tending splendid cages with properly thick bars, in a moment. I knew you would be wishing me joy."

"Nay, if you are serious about it, I shall consider the matter is absolutely settled. You will have a charming mother-in-law, indeed; and a tawdry old lion next to you in the moonlight quarters. And, of course, they will *both* always *be* at Pemberley with you."

He listened to her with perfect indifference while she chose to entertain herself in this manner. Gentle reader—he was contemplating a very *different* arrangement for a moonlit night.

And as his outer composure convinced her that all was safe, her wit flowed long . . . over rather deaf ears.

For, in his *thoughts*, he was far away.

Chapter 7

Mr. Bennet's property consisted almost entirely in an estate of two thousand a year, which, unfortunately for his daughters, was entailed,[23] in default of heirs male, on a distant relation. And their mother's fortune, though ample for her situation in life, could but ill supply the deficiency of his. Her father (purportedly, though rather dubiously, lupine) had been an attorney in Meryton, and had left her four thousand pounds.

She had a sister married to a docile and bearish Mr. Phillips, who had been a clerk to their father and succeeded him in the business, and a canine brother settled in London in a respectable line of trade.

The village of Longbourn was only one mile from Meryton; a most convenient distance for the young ladies, who were usually tempted thither three or four times a week, to pay their duty to their aunt and to a milliner's shop just over the way.

The two youngest of the family, Catherine and Lydia, were particularly frequent in these attentions. Their minds were more vacant than their sisters' (to the point of occasionally making hollow echoing sounds if struck with an accidental thought,

---

[23] That is, the estate itself, that venerable structure of masonry and wood, was not in any way implied to have a *tail*, or any other appendage, even though its male owner might have sported one during the full moon.

claimed Lizzy), and a walk to Meryton was necessary to amuse their morning hours and furnish conversation for the evening. And however bare of news the country in general might be, they always contrived to learn some from their aunt.

At present, indeed, they were well supplied both with news and happiness by the recent arrival of a militia regiment in the neighbourhood, and the consequent increase of manly beast aromas of all varieties. It was to remain the whole winter (that is, the *regiment* was to remain—though, the psycho-physical pheromone bouquet was naturally to linger also, and eventually to permeate *everything*), and Meryton was the headquarters. Oh, and what an endless parade of cages came with it! Regimental supply carts and wagons carrying glorious crates draped in military colors, with solid metal frames, many-inch-thick reinforcing beams of oak, everywhere bars of wrought iron, and all of it in so many splendid *manly* sizes! There were Great Cats here aplenty; and surely, ursine, porcine, lupine, and other mighty varieties well represented.

What a fine delight for the girls!

Their visits to Mrs. Phillips were now productive of the most interesting intelligence. Every day added something to their knowledge of the officers' names, connections, and Afflictions. Their lodgings were not long a secret, the cage enclosures readied for the monthly event (and properly admired in the manner of a carnival), and at length they began to know the officers themselves.

Mr. Phillips visited them all, in proper ursine fashion, and this opened to his nieces a store of felicity unknown before. They could talk of nothing but officers and the dimensions of the bars and padlocks on their crates in proportion to supposed gentlemanly attributes. . . . Mr. Bingley's large fortune, the mention of which gave animation to their mother, was worthless in their eyes when opposed to the regimentals of an ensign and the wonderfully frightful heft of the confinement chains at the bottom of his travel trunk.

After listening one morning to their effusions on this increasingly infernal subject, Mr. Bennet coolly observed:

"From all that I can collect by your manner of talking, you must be two of the silliest girls in the country. I have suspected it some time, but I am now convinced. If you are so fascinated by padlocks and chains and gentlemanly confinement, you ought to observe mine this month, alongside Lizzy. What, not so interested when it is your own father, are you?" And then he yawned widely in the telltale fashion of the lion, for the full moon was almost at hand.

Catherine was disconcerted, and made no answer, dreading the mere notion of her father's terrifying roars. But Lydia, with perfect indifference, continued to express her admiration of Captain Carter who was surely a wolf or at least a large dog, and her hope of seeing him in the course of the day, as he was going the next morning to London to be confined there for this immediate moontide.

"I am astonished, my dear," said Mrs. Bennet to her spouse, "that you should be so ready to think your own children silly, to think slightingly of them. It must be the horrid moon making you so *insensible*."

"If my children are silly, I hope to be always *sensible* of it."

"Yes—but as it happens, they are all of them very clever."

"This is the only point, I flatter myself, on which we do not agree. I had hoped that our sentiments coincided in every particular, but I must so far differ from you as to think our two youngest daughters uncommonly foolish."

Mrs. Bennet threw up her hands and went around the room furiously closing curtains, in the event that any moon *influence* was seeping through—even though it was the middle of day.

"My dear Mr. Bennet, you must not expect such girls to have the sense of their father and mother. When they get to our age, I dare say they will not think about officers any more than we do."

"Remarkable, for at my venerable age, I am now made to think of officers day and night. Furthermore, I also *hear* them, *smell* them; and, the other night, I am certain I *dreamt* them—two or three at least, maybe four, properly fighting each other, whether with regimental swords or natural teeth and claws I know not, but plenty of colorful fur was flying—"

"Oh, Mr. Bennet, you must stop! Now, I remember the time when I liked a red coat myself very well—and, indeed, so I do still at my heart. And if a smart young colonel, with five or six thousand a year and a proper feline condition, should want one of my girls I shall not say nay to him; and I thought Colonel Forster looked very becoming the other night at Sir William's in his regimentals. Could you not tell he was a wolf at the least?"

"My nose detected nothing of the sort; though, possibly a bit of rabbit or mutton. Wait, is it a fellow or a dinner roast we are discussing? Was I present at the happy affair?"

"Of course you were not there, Mr. Bennet! Must you always tease me so?"

"Mamma," cried Lydia, and went on about Colonel Forster and Captain Carter and their whereabouts.

Mrs. Bennet was prevented replying by the entrance of the footman with a note for Miss Bennet.

It came from Netherfield, and the servant waited for an answer. Mrs. Bennet's eyes sparkled with pleasure, and she was eagerly calling out, while her daughter read:

"Well, Jane, who is it from? What is it about? What does he say? Make haste and tell us, my love."

"It is from Miss Bingley," said Jane, and then read it aloud.

"MY DEAR FRIEND,—

"If you are not so compassionate as to dine to-day with Louisa and me, we shall be in danger of hating each other for the rest of our lives, for a whole day's *tête-à-tête* between two women can never end without a quarrel. Come as soon as you can on receipt of this. My brother and the gentlemen are to dine with the officers and prepare for the usual Moon Event.

—Yours ever,

"CAROLINE BINGLEY"

"With the officers!" cried Lydia. "I wonder my aunt did not tell us of *that*."

"Dining out," said Mrs. Bennet, "that is very unlucky. And with the horrid moon at near strength, what can they be thinking; leaving the premises!"

"Can I have the carriage?" said Jane.

"No, my dear, you had better go on horseback, because it seems likely to rain; and then you must stay all night."

"That would be a good scheme," said Elizabeth, "if you were sure that they would not offer to send her home, considering how *unsafe* it will be *this* night."

"Oh! but the gentlemen will have Mr. Bingley's chaise to go to Meryton to be confined there (however that might be), and the Hursts have no horses to theirs."

"I had much rather go in the coach."

"But, my dear, your father cannot spare the horses, I am sure. They are wanted in the farm, Mr. Bennet, are they not?"

"They are wanted in the farm much oftener than I can get them. And tonight, since I will be under padlock and key, roaring at the moon, I will neither want them nor care to get them."

"But still, if you have got them to-day," said Elizabeth, "my mother's purpose will be answered."

She did at last extort from her father an acknowledgment, in the form of a leonine rumble, that the horses were engaged. Jane was therefore obliged to go on horseback. And her mother attended her to the door with many cheerful prognostics of a bad day.

Her hopes were answered; Jane had not been gone long before it rained hard. Her sisters were uneasy for her, but her mother was delighted.

The rain continued the whole evening without intermission, while the *wicked moon* rose behind deep cover of clouds. . . .

Jane certainly could not come back in such *weather*.

"This was a lucky idea of mine, indeed!" said Mrs. Bennet more than once—as if the credit of making it rain were all her own—after having gone to make sure her husband was properly manacled and contained in his sturdy confinement chamber upstairs, leaving Lizzy as usual to observe the final moments of *transformation* and to make certain nothing was amiss.

No worries there; as the heavenly orb of night was revealed through clouds for a meager instant, Mr. Bennet *turned,* as always forgetting to remove his spectacles so they ended up flying off a lion's nose; grew his fearsome claws, teeth, lion coat; gave forth his usual thunderous roar that shook the very foundations of the building and sent the servants scuttling to their rooms; then promptly curled up into a great golden furball and fell into a lazy slumber for the rest of the night.

Till the next morning, however, Mrs. Bennet was not aware of all the felicity of her contrivance. Breakfast was scarcely over, Mr. Bennet newly released from his *special chamber* and recovering with a usual hearty meal, when a servant from Netherfield brought the following note for Elizabeth:

"MY DEAREST LIZZY,—

"I find myself very unwell this morning, which, I suppose, is to be imputed to my getting wet through yesterday. My kind friends will not hear of my returning till I am better.

They insist also on my seeing Mr. Jones—therefore do not be alarmed if you should hear of his having been to me—and, excepting a sore throat and headache, there is not much the matter with me.—Yours, etc."

"Well, my dear," said Mr. Bennet, cutting into a delightfully rare bit of steak, when Elizabeth had read the note aloud, "if your daughter should have a dangerous fit of illness— if she should *die*, it would be a comfort to know that it was all in pursuit of Mr. Bingley, and under your orders."

"Oh! I am not afraid of her dying. People do not die of little trifling colds. She will be taken good care of. As long as she stays there and does not go about wandering in the night, it is all very well. I would go and see her if I could have the carriage."

Elizabeth, feeling really anxious, was determined to go to her, though the carriage was not to be had. And as she was no horsewoman, walking was her only alternative. She declared her resolution.

"How can you be so silly," cried her mother, "as to think of such a thing, in all this dirt! You will not be fit to be seen when you get there."

"I shall be very fit to see Jane—which is all I want."

"Is this a hint to me, Lizzy," said her father, "to send for the horses?"

"No, indeed, I do not wish to avoid the walk. The distance is nothing when one has a motive; only three miles. I shall be back by dinner, well before darkness and any remaining danger of the moon's sway."

"I admire the activity of your benevolence," observed Mary, "but every impulse of feeling should be guided by reason. And, in my opinion, exertion should always be in proportion to what is required, especially on the nights before, during, and following the apex of the Affliction."

"We will go as far as Meryton with you," said Catherine and Lydia. Elizabeth accepted their company, and the three young ladies set off together.

"If we make haste," said Lydia, as they walked along, "perhaps we may see something of Captain Carter before he goes again into his *frightful* crate . . ."

In Meryton they parted. The two youngest repaired to the lodgings of one of the officers' wives, by long way of officers' row of cages, arranged in perfect splendor near the barracks, not unlike knightly tents before a medieval tourney.

Elizabeth continued her walk alone, crossing field after field at a quick pace, jumping over stiles and springing over puddles with impatient activity. She found herself at last within view of the house, with weary ankles, dirty stockings, and a face glowing with the warmth of exercise.

She was shown into the breakfast-parlour, where all but Jane were assembled, and where her appearance created a great deal of surprise. That she should have walked three miles so early in the day, in such dirty weather, and by herself, was almost incredible to Mrs. Hurst and Miss Bingley. And Elizabeth was convinced that they held her in contempt for it.

She was received, however, very politely by them. And in their brother's manners there was something better than politeness; there was—remarkably, in light of the recent wicked orb-influenced night—good humour and kindness.

The other gentlemen seemed to fare less well after that same night's effects. Mr. Darcy said very little, and Mr. Hurst nothing at all. The former was divided between *mysterious self-reflection*, admiration of the brilliancy which exercise had given to her complexion, and doubt as to the occasion's justifying her coming so far alone. The latter, in proper canine fashion, was thinking only of his breakfast.

Her inquiries after her sister were not very favourably answered. Miss Bennet had slept ill, and though up, was very feverish, and not well enough to leave her room. Furthermore, in her *state*, she had complained throughout the night of howls and roars and other effects of the Affliction heard around the house, which was entirely unseemly of *her* to *notice*.

Elizabeth was glad to be taken to her immediately. And Jane, fearing to cause undue alarm and withholding in her note how much she longed for such a visit, was delighted at her entrance.

She was not equal, however, to much conversation. When Miss Bingley left them, Jane only managed to express gratitude for the extraordinary kindness she was treated with. Elizabeth silently attended her.

When breakfast was over they were joined by the sisters. And Elizabeth almost began to like them herself, when she saw how much affection and solicitude they showed for Jane.

The apothecary came, and having examined his patient, confirmed that she had caught a violent cold, advised her to return to bed, and promised her some draughts. The advice was followed readily, for the feverish symptoms increased, and her head ached acutely.

Elizabeth did not quit her room for a moment. Nor were the other ladies often absent. The gentlemen being out (who knew where, preparing to confine themselves most likely yet again), they had, in fact, nothing to do elsewhere.

When the clock struck three, Elizabeth felt that she must go, and very unwillingly said so. Miss Bingley promptly offered her the carriage for safety against the remainder of the moon's folly.

She was about to accept it, when Jane showed such concern in parting, that Miss Bingley was obliged to convert the offer of the chaise to an invitation to remain at Netherfield for the present.

Elizabeth most thankfully consented, and a servant was dispatched to Longbourn to acquaint the family with her stay and bring back a supply of clothes.

Meanwhile, the moon was due to shine dangerously for yet another night.

Chapter 8

At five o'clock the two ladies retired to dress, and at half-past six Elizabeth was summoned to dinner.

To the civil inquiries which then poured in (and amongst which stood out the extraordinary tiger solicitude of Mr. Bingley), she could not make a very favourable answer.

Jane was by no means better.

The sisters, on hearing this, repeated three or four times how much they were *grieved*, how *shocking* it was to have a bad cold, and how excessively they *disliked being ill* themselves. And then they thought no more of the matter.

And their indifference towards Jane when not immediately before them restored Elizabeth to the enjoyment of all her former dislike.

Their brother, indeed, was the only one of the party whom she could regard with any complacency. His anxiety for Jane was evident. And his attentions to herself were most pleasing, preventing her feeling herself so much an intruder. She had very little notice from any but him.

Miss Bingley was engrossed by Mr. Darcy; her sister scarcely less so. And as for Mr. Hurst, by whom Elizabeth sat, he was an indolent dog of a man (in every sense of the word, short of sporting a tail in the daytime) who lived only to eat, drink, and play at cards; who, when he found her to prefer a plain dish to a ragout, had nothing to say to her.

When dinner was over, she returned directly to Jane, and Miss Bingley began abusing her as soon as she was out of the room. Her manners were pronounced to be very bad indeed, a mixture of pride and impertinence; she had no conversation, no style, no beauty. Mrs. Hurst thought the same, and added:

"She has nothing, in short, to recommend her, but being an excellent *walker*. I shall never forget her appearance this morning. She really looked almost wild—as though she *herself* might require a cage."

"She did, indeed, Louisa. I could hardly keep my countenance. Very nonsensical to come at all! Why must *she* be scampering about the country *alone*, at the moon's most dire time, because her sister had a cold? Her hair, so untidy, so blowsy!"

"Yes, and I hope you saw her petticoat, six inches deep in mud, I am absolutely certain; and the gown which had been let down to hide it not doing its office."

"Indeed! Do you know, it is spoken widely that she *single-handedly* tends her father's confinement, handles the padlock and bars like an uncouth servant, and then remains nearby to *observe!*"

"If so, her filial duty at the time of Affliction is admirable. And, while your picture of mud on petticoats may be very exact, Louisa," said Bingley; "it was all lost upon me. I thought Miss Elizabeth Bennet looked remarkably well when she came into the room this morning. Her dirty petticoat quite escaped my notice."

"*You* observed it, Mr. Darcy, I am sure," said Miss Bingley; "Indeed, surely you *sniffed* it. Gentlemen of breeding are capable of perceiving such natural scents as mud—or am I mistaken?— when the moon is at its wickedest? Thus, I am inclined to think that you would not wish to see *your* sister make such an exhibition."

"Certainly not."

"To walk three miles, or four miles, or five miles, or whatever it is, above her ankles in dirt, and alone, quite alone! What could she mean by it? It seems to me to show an abominable sort of conceited independence, and a countrified indifference to decorum and lunar danger."

"It shows an affection for her sister that is very pleasing," said Bingley.

At that point an upper servant arrived to discreetly inform Mr. Bingley that the gentlemen's *confinement areas* were ready for the night's Ordeal.

"Did you make certain to stock my room with the extra cuts of steak, preferably freshly trimmed?"

"I had indeed, sir."

"A stack of large bones to Mr. Hurst's?"

"Yes, sir, all in a trough."

"Splendid! And now, as I recall Darcy enjoys a hot soak afterwards, so did you have the tub delivered to the gentleman's enclosure directly?"

"It is done, sir. The tub is ready and will be filled, with the fresh linens at hand."

"Not *too* close at hand, I trust, or my most excellent fellow here will tear them to pieces, while still *not himself.* Is that not so, Darcy?" Bingley's tone was harmlessly teasing.

Mr. Darcy looked on with a closed expression, but then thanked his friend and host and nodded to the servant with utmost politeness.

"See, my good man, I remembered!" said Bingley with a rumble of feline delight. Then, added: "Even though, after all these years, you *still* will not tell me what manner of *beast* takes you during the moontide!"

"You know I prefer my privacy in this," replied Darcy evenly, without a blink, while the two ladies in the room painfully pretended not to listen, out of decorum.

"Yes, that you do. Well then, to each man his own experience. May we feel as little discomfort as possible when the Affliction takes us—wherever and *however* it does!"

Mr. Darcy was again all politeness; and a brief nod of acknowledgement was all that his friend could elicit at this yet another instance of the chronic monthly teasing to which he subjected the other gentleman—entirely to no avail.

After the servant had left, the conversation soon returned to the happy delight of abusing Elizabeth Bennet.

"I am afraid, Mr. Darcy," observed Miss Bingley in a half whisper, "that this adventure of hers has rather affected your admiration of her fine eyes."

"Not at all," he replied; "they were brightened by the exercise. And—as well you know—gentlemen of breeding are capable of perceiving *bright objects* entirely too well when the lunacy is nearly upon us."

A short pause followed this speech, while the gentlemen observed the clock for the approaching time when they must retire for the evening and regretfully confine themselves. The moon was due to rise within a few hours. . . .

Mrs. Hurst began again:

"I have an excessive regard for Miss Jane Bennet, she is really a very sweet girl, and I wish with all my heart she were well settled. But with such a father and mother, and such low connections, I am afraid there is no chance of it."

"I think I have heard you say that their uncle is an attorney in Meryton."

"Yes, supposedly a bearish one; and they have another, who lives somewhere near Cheapside . . . in a *kennel*."

Mr. Hurst started, with a choked barking noise.

"That is capital," added her sister, ignoring the stifled-bark reaction of her brother-in-law, and they both laughed heartily. (In case the gentle reader wonders at such an odd course of logic, it must be noted that Mr. Hurst's own condition was always set apart and considered a superior canine breed by his sisters. "A pedigreed wolfhound, never a dog," Louisa Hurst would insist with stiff decorum.)

Mr. Hurst cleared his throat and took a sudden interest in adjusting his sleeve.

"If they had uncles enough to fill *all* Cheapside," cried Bingley with a very tigrine roar (for that *time* was indeed drawing near), "it would not make them one jot less agreeable."

"But it must very materially lessen their chance of marrying men of any consideration in the world," replied Darcy. The only notice he gave of being in any way affected by the approaching Ordeal, was an even greater stiffening of his perfect posture, and a glance at the clock.

To this speech Bingley made no answer; but his sisters gave it their hearty assent, and indulged their mirth for some time at the expense of their dear friend's vulgar relations.

With a renewal of tenderness, however, they returned to the ailing Miss Bennet's room on leaving the dining-parlour, and sat with her till summoned to coffee. She was still very poorly, and Elizabeth would not quit her at all, till late in the evening, when she had the comfort of seeing her sleep, and when it seemed to her rather right than pleasant that she should go downstairs herself. On entering the drawing-room she found the whole party at loo,[24] and was immediately invited to join them[25]; but suspecting them to be playing high[26] she declined it, and making her sister the excuse, said she would amuse herself for the short

---

[24] Here, it is in no way implied that the party were all confined *en masse* to the privy or water closet! What an unseemly notion, dear reader, you must eradicate it from your mind's fragile visual center, the inner eyeball.

[25] Naturally, had this been a privy, there would be hardly any room for yet another personage.

[26] It is somewhat unclear what substances they might have had at their disposal to achieve a hallucinogenic state. —Ed. *[Fundamentally idiotic interpretation of an ordinary reference to wager amounts. But then, I am guessing, Editorial 1 is sloshed in absinthe, and has been partaking of belladonna. —Ed. 2]*

time she could stay below, with a book. Mr. Hurst looked at her with dog astonishment.

"Do you prefer reading to cards?" said he; "that is rather singular."

"Miss Eliza Bennet," said Miss Bingley, "despises cards. She is a great reader, and has no pleasure in anything else."

"I deserve neither such praise nor such censure," cried Elizabeth; "I am *not* a great reader, though I certainly aspire to be, and I have pleasure in many things."

Mrs. Hurst was heard to mutter something about padlocks and cages.

"In nursing your sister I am sure you have pleasure," said Bingley with another deep rumble; "and I hope it will be soon increased by seeing her quite well."

Elizabeth thanked him from her heart, and then walked towards the table where a few books were lying. He immediately offered to fetch her others—all that his library afforded—though possibly not all at once, not right this moment, considering the nature of the coming night.

"And I wish my collection were larger for your benefit and my own credit; but I am an idle fellow, and though I have not many, I have more than I ever looked into. Except for the few doused in catnip—" Mr. Bingley remembered himself and cleared his throat.

Elizabeth assured him that she could suit herself perfectly with those in the room.

"I am astonished," said Miss Bingley, "that my father should have left so small a collection of books. What a delightful library you have at Pemberley, Mr. Darcy!"

"It ought to be good," he replied, "it has been the work of many generations."

Many generations of what manner of unearthly creature? seemed to be the immediate unspoken question in the room.

"And then you have added so much to it yourself, you are always buying books," continued Miss Bingley.

"I cannot comprehend the neglect of a family library in such days as these."

"Neglect! I am sure you neglect nothing that can add to the beauties of that noble place. Charles, when you build *your* house, I wish it may be half as delightful as Pemberley."

"I wish it may."

"Indeed, make your purchase in that neighbourhood, and take Pemberley for a kind of model. There is not a finer county in England than Derbyshire."

"With all my heart; I will buy Pemberley itself if Darcy will sell it. What a marvel of a reinforced cellar it contains, a veritable dungeon of robust chains, suspension pulleys and cages for all manner of—Ahem!"

"I am talking of possibilities, Charles."

"Upon my word, Caroline, I should think it more possible to get Pemberley by purchase than by imitation."

Elizabeth was so much caught with what passed, as to lay aside her book. She drew near the card-table, and stationed herself between Mr. Bingley and his eldest sister, to observe the game, meanwhile noting the increasingly fretful *state* of the gentlemen.

"Is Miss Darcy much grown since the spring?" said Miss Bingley, in a delicate attempt to soothe the lunacy-heightened nerves all around; "will she be as tall as I am?"

"I think she will. She is now about Miss Elizabeth Bennet's height, or rather taller." Darcy spoke with more than usual reserve and a marked precision to his words. Holding himself with superhuman control, he did not display even a hint of sheen on his brow—unlike Bingley who was beginning to unconsciously growl every few moments, and Hurst who attempted to raise a leg up to his ear and then recalled himself in time and merely panted with enough breath to visibly stir the feathers in his spouse's elegant hair.

"How I long to see her again!" said Miss Bingley, markedly ignoring the rhythmically moving feathers on top of her sister's head. "I never met with anybody who delighted me so much. Such a countenance, such manners! And so extremely accomplished for her age! Her performance on the pianoforte is exquisite."

"It is amazing to me," said Bingley, fingers twitching like phantom cat claws on the cards in his hand, "how young ladies can have patience to be so very accomplished as they all are."

"All young ladies accomplished! My dear Charles, what do you mean?"

"Yes, all of them, I think. They all paint tables, cover screens, net purses, and decorate heirloom cage padlocks. I scarcely know anyone who cannot do all this, and never heard a young lady presented as anything but very accomplished."

"Your list of the common extent of accomplishments," said Darcy, "has too much truth. The word is applied liberally indeed whenever a woman nets a purse or stitches a cozy for a padlock. But I do not agree with your estimation of ladies in general. I cannot boast of knowing more than half-a-dozen that are really accomplished."

"Nor I, I am sure," said Miss Bingley, her gaze closely following the tapping movement of Mr. Bingley's finger-claws.

"Then," observed Elizabeth, "you must comprehend a great deal in your idea of an accomplished woman."

"Yes, I do comprehend a great deal in it."

"Oh! certainly," cried his faithful assistant[27] Miss Bingley, "no one can be really esteemed accomplished who does not greatly surpass what is usually met with. A woman must have a thorough knowledge of music, singing, drawing, dancing, cage

---

[27] It is in no way implied that Miss Bingley, at any point in the narrative, serves as Mr. Darcy's personal assistant or secretary. —Ed. *[No, it is not. That would be ludicrous and unsuitable. Only an idiot would presume to think so. —Ed. 2]*

containment, and the modern languages, to deserve the word; and besides all this, she must possess a certain something in her air and manner of walking, the tone of her voice, her address and expressions, or the word will be but half-deserved."

"All this she must possess," added Darcy, "and to all this she must yet add something more substantial, in the improvement of her mind by extensive reading."

"I am no longer surprised at your knowing *only* six accomplished women," said Elizabeth. "I rather wonder now at your knowing *any*."

"Are you so severe upon your own sex as to doubt the possibility of all this?" Darcy spoke, looking directly in her eyes, his own occluded in mystery.

Mr. Hurst chose the moment to stop panting momentarily in order to wipe the considerable drool from the corner of his mouth and the front of his cravat. He then observed the clock.

His spouse used discretion to adjust the now-stilled feathers in her hair.

"I never saw such a woman," said Elizabeth. "I never saw such capacity, and taste, and application, and elegance, as you describe united."

Mrs. Hurst and Miss Bingley both cried out against the injustice of her implied doubt—which set off Mr. Hurst again into rapid panting and consequent drool formation—and were both protesting that they knew many women who answered this description. It was then that Mr. Hurst could no longer hold back a full-bodied bark (which swiftly called them to order), and attempted to disguise the latter outburst by voicing bitter complaints of their inattention to what was going forward—bringing their attention to the clock, the lateness of the hour, and the proximity of the Ordeal.

As all conversation was thereby at an end, the gentlemen ready to depart to their padlocks, bars, and containment, Elizabeth soon afterwards left the room.

"Elizabeth Bennet," said Miss Bingley, when the door was closed on her, "is one of those young ladies who seek to recommend themselves to the other sex by undervaluing their own; and with many men, I dare say, it succeeds. But, in my opinion, it is a paltry device, a very mean art."

"Undoubtedly," replied Darcy (to whom this remark was chiefly addressed) in controlled haste as he prepared to depart, motioning to Bingley and Hurst to follow, "there is a meanness in *all* the arts which ladies sometimes condescend to employ for captivation. Whatever bears affinity to cunning is despicable."

Miss Bingley was not so entirely satisfied with this reply as to continue the subject. But there was nothing to be done, for the moon was rising and the gentlemen were not to be detained an instant longer. . . .

Elizabeth joined them again, right in that precise moment, only to say that her sister was worse, and that she could not leave her.

Bingley, halted in the process of rapidly ascending the stairs to his containment chamber, urged Mr. Jones being sent for immediately . . . at which point Darcy, ahead of him on the staircase, reminded Bingley that Mr. Jones would have to be contained likewise, by *female* staff, and was therefore not able to fulfill any duties at present.

Bingley's sisters, convinced in any case that no country advice could be of any service, recommended an express to town for one of the most eminent physicians—naturally as soon as the wicked moon was out of sight once again by dawn hour. Alas! What a terrible coincidence to require a physician now, on such a night!

This Elizabeth would not hear of. But she was amenable to their brother's suggestion. Thus it was settled that Mr. Jones should be sent for early in the morning once the sun was up and he was no longer Afflicted—but only if Miss Bennet were not decidedly better.

Bingley was quite uncomfortable. . . . But the moon would have it that he must now quit their fair company in all haste and be locked and contained.

Much slamming of heavy doors was heard for the next half hour; much scurrying about of female serving staff, from one gentleman's strong room to another, dragging lengths of chain, rope, padlocks and various weighted implements of the Ordeal. To Mr. Darcy's room a grand bathtub had been delivered earlier, and now buckets of steaming water were carried to fill it. Then the female servants locked *everything* and, as instructed, fled. . . .

While this went on, Mr. Bingley's sisters declared that they were miserable. They solaced their wretchedness, however, by duets after supper—which frequently served to drown out unidentifiable frightful *beastly noises* coming from the floors above and below.

Bingley, meanwhile, just before the moon took him, could find no better relief to his moon-heightened feelings than by giving his panicked housekeeper last-minute directions (delivered with roars from behind thick iron bars of his tiger enclosure), that every attention might be paid to the sick lady and her sister.

But now, gentle reader, we must leave Mr. Bingley to his rather ordinary Ordeal, and take you instead, beyond the doors of a far more interesting containment room next door.

At last we are permitted to observe Mr. Darcy and learn his Dreadful Secret.

When the last maidservant departed and the reinforced main door shut behind her with a tremendous slam, Darcy stood in the middle of the strange containment chamber which was stocked to his precise specifications.

The main area of the room was fitted with a great rectangular cage of many feet across, almost ceiling-high, and nearly equal to the chamber itself, and leaving only a narrow perimeter corridor of space between the inner three-inch thick bars and outside walls for servants to pass all around unaccosted. There was a single wrought iron door to the cage and it was locked with a row of deadbolts, padlocked in triplicate, and thick iron chains were wound between the bars to provide additional reinforcement.

Inside that cage, directly on the floor was a heavy wooden board laid out like a dining table with thick cuts of raw meats of different varieties (since Darcy never specified a preference) and in the center, a claw foot tub filled with steaming water. Next to it, sat a bucket filled with an unusual combination of small fish, mussels, worms, grubs, gravel, handfuls of grain and a few raw vegetables thrown in. Finally, nearby was a stack of fresh linen towels.

Mr. Darcy stood within this remarkable iron contraption and surveyed the contents. He was wearing only shirtsleeves, breeches and footwear, having refused, as usual on the night of Affliction, the assistance of a valet.

It must be added that there was a single small window in this chamber, situated high up near the ceiling, and through which might be observed a silvery glow. On cloudless nights the illumination took on the brightness of day, and tonight was no different.

Selene, the silver orb of night, began to shimmer through the lace of delicate cloud near the tops of trees, as she rose only minutes ago, and began her ascent into the clear heavens.

As the moon rose, full and wicked, the sky grew brighter. . . .

Darcy looked up, in long-suffering resignation, and observed the window fill with otherworldly pallid light, indicating the beginning of the *transformation*.

With the first stab of moonlight in his eyes, came an intense moment of sudden clarity and breathless pause, like the calm before the storm.

And then came rending agony.

With a single human cry the elegant gentleman doubled over, clutching his chest and abdomen, exhaling with a shudder, and falling forward on his hands and knees in a gesture of supplication to the supernatural force that had taken hold of him—and every other man in the realm.

From thereupon he made no sound. While beyond the walls issued bloodcurdling male cries and then terrifying roars of a tiger (or yapping dog barks—depending on which wall you attended) and the thunderous rattling of iron cage and shuddering of the floor and ceiling, here, in *this* chamber was a voiceless unimaginable sight. . . .

Mr. Darcy's shape rapidly contorted, and there was a soft snapping noise of shattering bones, then a strange malleable dullness as he seemed to have settled into a new form, and strangely *shrunk*.

Most of his bodily mass disappeared into nothing. His shirtsleeves fell loosely in a heap of fabric, as there were suddenly no more arms, only tiny protrusions at the sleeve holes.

The back collapsed, rounded, became like a smallish log wrapped in fine linen. The legs also disappeared, shortening into tiny flopping stumps until the breeches and stockings lay empty on the floor, next to the shoes that had clattered as discarded.

And the head . . . Oh, the demon horror that became Mr. Darcy's head!

Dissolving from a handsome and noble male countenance, the face extended and flattened. But then, instead of continuing to settle into a recognizable feline or canine, or any other beast muzzle, it seemed to have taken a wrong turn . . . and then simultaneously *lengthened* and grew into a blunt peculiar bill, somewhat resembling a duck's, while the top of his splendid human head shrunk and rounded, his elegant locks retreated into a short coat of dark brown fur, and became very much like the upper portion of the muzzle of a beaver or an otter.

For a moment the long-nosed *thing* on the floor wrapped in Mr. Darcy's clothing moved about, trying to break free of its fabric confinement, waving its bizarre limbs protruding from the sides of the log-body. Then it went around in a circle this and that way, stumbling and dragging the elegant eveningwear all over the floor of the cage and scattering cuts of meat in all directions. . . .

Finally, with either hellish purpose or absolute accident, it bumped against the edge of the tub, somehow sensed water, and then gave an amazing flop upward, springing powerfully from its hind appendages, and landed with a loud plop into the tub.

There was a thunderous splash as the cooling water sloshed everywhere, and then the thing resurfaced, free of the linen and lace and breechcloth at last, and made a loud sneezing sound.

The moon illuminated the chamber as the thing swam about the tub, paddling with its front webbed paws, in absolute dreamy silence, punctuated by occasional sneezes and gentle snorts. While elsewhere, hellish tigrine roars continued to rip the night, interspersed with occasional doggish yelps, barks, and howls from another direction, the strange aquatic creature finally climbed out of the tub. It moved, waddling like a peculiar mammalian lizard and retracting its webbed hands to reveal otter claws underneath in the front appendages and sharp heel spurs in its hind legs, not to mention a long beaver tail in the back.

The thing—being altogether a duck, an otter, a beaver, a lizard, and a snake all in one—finally found the bucket of fish and seafood and gravel. With a satisfactory sneeze it stuck its duck bill in the watery mess, and scraped the bottom of the bucket for all it was worth, filling its inner cheek pouches till they were stuffed.

It then rested on the floor of the cage, flat on its rounded tummy, rolling its sea bounty in the bill and mouth, happily and silently *feeding*. . . .

Thus, at last, before the gentle reader's stunned and unbelieving gaze, is harrowingly revealed none other than our proud hero, Mr. Fitzwilliam Darcy, gentleman and platypus.

Mr. Fitzwilliam Darcy, gentleman and platypus.

Chapter 9

While the esteemed reader is naturally still reeling from the shocking revelation of the bizarre and mortifying secret of Mr. Darcy's Affliction, it must be said that the remainder of the accursed night was spent by him rather uneventfully.

Mr. Darcy, as duckbill platypus[28], ate his fill of fish and grubs, then returned to the bathtub to loll and splash about in the water for hours, until the moon sank out of sight and the first light of dawn came to paint the window.

Immediately, the creature's tiny form began to contort once more, and grow in mass and regain human limbs. The face shortened and returned to its handsome gentlemanly proportions, brown fur was replaced with water-soaked stylish locks, and the man himself regained his reason and consciousness, lying with a bundle of his discarded wet clothing in the tub, and an unpleasant fishy taste in his mouth and on his lips.

The gentleman released a painful groan, spat out the last shrimp or mussel or maybe a bit of gravel, rose from the water

---

[28] A platypus is a fiendish beast both unnatural and impossible, made up of many other creature parts and hailing from a non-specified circle of hell. — Ed. *[Hailing from Australia. That is sufficient; a continent of uncouth savages, it is said. For if I do not say it, you most certainly will; hereby I save you the trouble. —Ed. 2]*

dripping—and a fine muscular form he made, it must be admitted—then fished out his shirt and breeches and quickly clad himself, since he had no intention of facing the serving staff in nothing but linen towels. For whatever unfortunate reason, he had once again forgotten to request a dry set of clothing to be laid out for himself—really, even a smoking jacket could have been a useful accessory.

Indeed, he must make a note of it for next time.

And then, until the first morning servants came, Darcy strolled about the cage noisily, rattling it a bit, scattering the last pieces of raw meat and making sure it smeared the floor and iron bars for best horrific effect. He also ripped his sleeves and collar for good measure, and then picked up the nearest steak and slapped it over the front and back of his shirt for an enhanced sanguine appearance.

When the valet arrived with a jangle of keys, cautiously opening the chamber door, then unlocking the padlocks of the cage, he was met with a scowling and fiercely bloodied gentleman, and the cage all a proper mess, as expected.

"Shall I discard the ruined clothing, sir? And will you be coming downstairs at present, or do you prefer to be served here?" he enquired politely.

"A thorough cleaning first, then I must join my host and company."

"Very well, sir. And—a ham or rare steak for breakfast, sir?" the servant continued.

The splendid answer issuing from Mr. Darcy was:

"Both."

While the gentlemen all over the domicile were tended to, it is time to return our attention to the ladies.

Elizabeth passed the chief of the night in her sister's room, shutting her ears to the roars and yaps coming from every direction. In the morning she sent a tolerable answer regarding Jane's condition to the inquiries which she had received from

Mr. Bingley (back in human form, after a fretful night of tearing apart steak and roaring at the moon) delivered by a housemaid, and some time afterwards from the two elegant ladies who waited on his sisters.

In spite of Jane's improvement, however, she requested to have a note sent to Longbourn, desiring her mother to visit Jane, and form her own judgment of her situation. The note was immediately dispatched, and Mrs. Bennet, accompanied by her two youngest girls, reached Netherfield soon after the family breakfast.

Had she found Jane in any apparent danger, Mrs. Bennet would have been very miserable. But seeing that her illness was not alarming, she had no wish of her recovering immediately, as her restoration to health would probably remove her from Netherfield.

She would not listen, therefore, to her daughter's proposal of being carried[29] home. The apothecary also did not think it advisable. After sitting a little while with Jane, on Miss Bingley's appearance and invitation, the mother and three daughters all attended her into the breakfast parlour.

The gentlemen, rather in high spirits after their night Ordeal, were all gathered at breakfast and fiercely partaking of a splendid cutting board of various lightly-cooked meats which the servants frequently replenished. Mr. Hurst picked at a bone long after it was stripped of every edible bit (a servant discreetly attempted to remove the plate, but was almost snapped at, before the gentleman remembered himself and cleared his throat with a yap). Darcy, impeccable as always, was methodically cutting into a ham.

Bingley, meanwhile, displayed a genuine devotion to Jane, instantly setting aside his grandiose lamb chop in order to

---

[29] Gentle reader, fear not on the kindly matron's behalf; this is a mere turn of phrase. Mrs. Bennet was naturally not expected to lift and carry Jane herself. —Ed. *[Naturally not. —Ed. 2]*

express hopes that Mrs. Bennet had not found Miss Bennet worse than she expected.

"Indeed I have, sir," was her answer. "She is a great deal too ill to be moved, particularly now, while the moon is still at its most horrid. Mr. Jones says we must not move her. We must trespass a little longer on your kindness."

"Removed!" cried Bingley with a near-roar. "It must not be thought of! My sister, I am sure, will not hear of her removal."

"You may depend upon it, madam," said Miss Bingley, with cold civility, "that Miss Bennet will receive every possible attention while she remains with us."

Mrs. Bennet was profuse in her acknowledgments.

"I am sure," she added, "if it was not for such good friends I do not know what would become of her; for she is very ill indeed, and suffers a vast deal. But she always has the greatest patience in the world, the sweetest temper. I often tell my other girls they are nothing to *her*. You have a sweet room here, Mr. Bingley, delightfully stocked, I see, as all you gentlemen require—for the Affliction takes its toll and must be compensated with rich and abundant feeding—I always tell Mr. Bennet to mind his manners afterwards and have his first steak in private, quite early in the morning, and well before descending to the parlor, for otherwise he tears it to bits dreadfully at breakfast table. . . . Oh, and what a charming prospect you have over the gravel walk! I do not know a place in the country that is equal to Netherfield. You will not think of quitting it in a hurry, I hope."

"Whatever I do is done in a hurry," replied he, recalling his passion for the lamb chop; "if I should resolve to quit Netherfield, I should probably be off in five minutes. At present, however, I am quite fixed here."

"That is exactly what I should have supposed of you," said Elizabeth.

"You begin to comprehend me, do you?" cried he, turning towards her, unwisely brandishing a fork and sending a bit of lamb projectile toward Mr. Hurst who nearly snapped his head in catch reflex, then fortunately controlled himself with a sheepish glance at his spouse.

"Oh! yes—I understand you perfectly."

"I wish I might take this for a compliment; but to be so easily seen through I am afraid is pitiful."

"Nevertheless, a deep, intricate character is no more or less estimable than such a one as yours."

"Lizzy!" cried her mother, "remember where you are, and do not run on in the wild manner that you are suffered to do at home, especially when the gentleman is still recovering and, I dare say, still feeling rather *wild* himself!"

"I did not know before," continued Bingley immediately, while cutting into another thick rare slice, "that you were a studier of character. It must be amusing."

"Yes, but intricate characters have the advantage of being the *most* amusing."

"The country," said Darcy, pausing his own rather dispassionate dissection of ham, "can in general supply but a few subjects for such a study. In a country neighbourhood you move in a very confined and unvarying society."

"But people themselves alter so much, even without lunar influence, that there is something new to be observed in them for ever."

"Yes, indeed," cried Mrs. Bennet, offended by his manner of mentioning a country neighbourhood. "I assure you there is quite as much of *that* going on in the country as in town."

Everybody was surprised, Mr. Hurst yelped, and Darcy, after looking at her for a moment as if she were a cut of ham, turned silently away. Mrs. Bennet, who fancied she had gained a complete victory over him, continued her triumph.

"I cannot see that London has any great advantage over the country, except the shops and public places. The moon shines with the same odious effect in both places, does she not? Really, the country is a vast deal pleasanter—is it not, Mr. Bingley?"

"When I am in the country," he replied, "I never wish to leave it; and when I am in town it is pretty much the same. I can be equally happy in either."

"Aye—that is because you have the right disposition. But that gentleman," looking at Darcy, "seemed to think the country was nothing at all."

"Indeed, Mamma, you are mistaken," said Elizabeth, blushing for her mother. "Mr. Darcy only meant that there was not such a variety of people to be met with in the country as in the town, which you must acknowledge to be true."

"Certainly, my dear, nobody said there were; but as to not meeting with many people in this neighbourhood, why, there are few larger. I know we dine with four-and-twenty families."

Nothing but concern for Elizabeth could enable Bingley to keep his countenance. His sister was less delicate, and directed her eyes towards Mr. Darcy with a very expressive smile.

Elizabeth, for the sake of saying something that might turn her mother's thoughts, now asked her if Charlotte Lucas had been at Longbourn since *her* coming away.

"Yes, she called yesterday with her father, just before he was to be locked up for the night, but kindly put himself at the disadvantage just to pay the visit. What an agreeable man Sir William is, Mr. Bingley, is not he? So much the man of Great Cat fashion! So genteel and easy; always with something to say to everybody. *That* is my idea of good breeding; and those persons who fancy themselves very important, and never open their mouths, quite mistake the matter."

"Did Charlotte dine with you?"

"No, she would go home. I fancy, after assisting her father's confinement she was wanted about the mince-pies for the next morning's rich feeding. For my part, Mr. Bingley, I always keep servants that can do their own work at any phase of moon; *my* daughters are brought up very differently. But the

Lucases are a very good sort of girls, I assure you. It is a pity they are not handsome! Not that I think Charlotte so *very* plain—but then she is our particular friend."

"She seems a very pleasant young woman."

"Oh! dear, yes; but you must own she is very plain. Lady Lucas herself has often said so, and envied me Jane's beauty. I do not like to boast of my own child, but—one does not often see anybody better looking. Everybody says it. When she was only fifteen, there was a wolfish man at my brother Gardiner's in town so much in love with her that my sister-in-law was sure he would make her an offer before we came away. But, however, he did not. Perhaps he thought her too young. However, he stood outside her window for a se'ennight and howled poetry for hours on end, very prettily."

"And so ended his affection," said Elizabeth impatiently. "There has been many a one, I fancy, overcome in the same way—except, thankfully, for the howling. I wonder who first discovered the efficacy of poetic or *other* serenades in driving away love!"

"I have been used to consider howling—that is, poetry—as the *food* of love," said Darcy, completely forgetting his ham.

"Of a fine, stout, healthy love it may. Everything nourishes what is strong already. But if it be only a slight, thin sort of inclination, I am convinced that one good howl or sonnet will starve it entirely away."

Darcy only smiled; and the general pause which ensued made Elizabeth tremble lest her mother should be exposing[30] herself again. She longed to speak, but could think of nothing to say.

---

[30] Here, it is never implied that Mrs. Bennet is in any manner going to disrobe— *[No! Do not even complete that sentence! —Ed. 2]*

After a short silence Mrs. Bennet began repeating her thanks to Mr. Bingley for his kindness to Jane, with an apology for troubling him also with Lizzy, at a time of Affliction, no less.

Mr. Bingley was unaffectedly civil in his answer, and forced his younger sister to be civil also, and say what the occasion required. She performed her part indeed without much graciousness, but Mrs. Bennet was satisfied, and soon afterwards ordered her carriage.

Upon this signal, the youngest of her daughters put herself forward. The two girls had been whispering to each other during the whole visit (there was frequent mention of "padlocks" and "cage dimensions"), and the result of it was, that the youngest should remind Mr. Bingley about his promise on his first coming into the country to give a ball at Netherfield.

Lydia was a stout, well-grown girl of fifteen, with a fine complexion and good-humoured countenance; a favourite with her mother, whose affection had brought her into public at an early age. She had high animal spirits—*"decidedly leonine, inheriting her father's tendencies, if such a thing had been natural in women,"* her mother always said—and a sort of natural self-consequence, which the attention of the officers, to whom her uncle's good dinners, and her own easy manners recommended her, had increased into assurance.

She was very equal, therefore, to address Mr. Bingley on the subject of the ball, and abruptly reminded him of his promise; adding, that it would be the most shameful thing in the world if he did not keep it. After all, the worst of the moon's *horridness* for this month was nearly over!

His answer to this sudden attack was delightful to their mother's ear:

"I am perfectly ready, I assure you, to keep my engagement. When your sister is recovered, and the effects of Selene upon us all are safely in the past, you shall name the very day of the ball. But you would not wish to be dancing when she is ill, nor when all these gentlemen are still not quite ourselves."

Lydia declared herself satisfied. "Oh! yes—it would be much better to wait till Jane was well, the lunacy behind us, and by that time most likely Captain Carter would be at Meryton again, with his oh-so-splendid engraved chains and padlocks. And when you have given *your* ball," she added, "I shall insist on their giving one also. I shall tell Colonel Forster it will be quite a shame if he does not. I might even tease him that I will steal in during the next moon, pry his cage unlocked—"

"Fie! Hush, Lydia, child, what a horrid thing to even say!" her mother interjected.

Mrs. Bennet and her daughters then departed, the gentlemen returned to their civilized savage breakfast, and Elizabeth returned instantly to Jane—leaving her own and her relations' behaviour to the remarks of the two ladies and Mr. Darcy; the latter of whom, however, was one again apparently engaged in ham and could not be prevailed on to join in their censure of *her*, in spite of all Miss Bingley's witticisms on *fine eyes*.

Chapter 10

The day passed much as the day before had done. There was only one more dangerous night remaining, which could call forth the manly Affliction, and the rest were expected to be past all serious transformational effects and beyond the moon's influence.

Mrs. Hurst and Miss Bingley had spent some hours of the morning with the invalid, who continued, though slowly, to mend. And in the evening Elizabeth joined their party in the drawing-room.

The loo-table,[31] however, did not appear. Mr. Darcy was writing, and Miss Bingley, seated near him, was watching the progress of his letter, his elegant handwriting (in a hand unshaken by any lunar wickedness, and revealing no demonic bestial tendency, not even chicken scratch) and repeatedly calling off his attention by messages to his sister. Mr. Hurst and Mr. Bingley were at piquet, and Mrs. Hurst was observing their game and listening (with some small concern) to occasional cat and dog sounds of excitement issuing from their direction.

---

[31] Once again, rest assured, such a table does not in any way contain a privy or relate to a privy. —Ed. *[Even if it did, would it stop you? —Ed. 2]*

Elizabeth took up some needlework, and was sufficiently amused in attending not to cats and dogs but to what passed between Darcy and his companion. The perpetual commendations of the lady, either on his handwriting (so precise!), or on the evenness of his lines (no hint of beastly exuberance, no fluctuation outside, above, or below!), or on the length of his letter (so thorough!), with the perfect unconcern with which her praises were received, formed a curious dialogue, and was exactly in union with her opinion of each.

Whatever beast lives inside him, thought Elizabeth, *admittedly, it keeps itself well hidden, despite provocation.*

"How delighted Miss Darcy will be to receive such a letter!" cooed Miss Bingley.

He—and his demon beast—made no answer.

"You write uncommonly fast."

"You are mistaken. I write rather slowly. Care must be taken to keep Selene's passion at bay."

"How many letters you must have occasion to write in the course of a year! Letters of business, too! How odious!"

"It is fortunate, then, that they fall to my lot instead of yours."

"Pray tell your sister that I long to see her."

"I have already told her so once, by your desire."

"I am afraid you do not like your pen. Let me mend it for you. I mend pens remarkably well, especially for *unsteady* gentlemen at moontide.

"Thank you—but, as you see, unsteadiness is not a concern. And I always mend my own."

"How can you contrive to write so even?"

He was silent. And yes, gentle reader, it can be admitted that the *demon platypus* within was nigh at breaking point, longing for the peace of a pond or watery tub, or even a large deep bucket in which to hide. . . .

"Tell your sister I am delighted to hear of her improvement on the harp! And I am in raptures with her beautiful design for a table—infinitely superior to Miss Grantley's."

"Will you give me leave to defer your raptures till I write again? At present I have not room to do them justice."

"Oh! it is of no consequence. I shall see her in January. But do you always write such charming long letters to her, Mr. Darcy?"

"They are generally long; but whether always charming it is not for me to determine."

"It is a rule with me, that a person who can write a long letter with ease, even on days of the Ordeal, cannot write ill."

"That will not do for a compliment to Darcy, Caroline," cried her brother with an excited yowl, "because he does *not* write with ease. He studies too much for words of four syllables. Do not you, Darcy?"

"My style of writing is very different from yours."

"Oh!" cried Miss Bingley, "Charles writes in the most careless way imaginable. He leaves out half his words, and blots the rest, as if his hands are great clawed paws even on ordinary days."

"My ideas flow so rapidly that I have no time to express them—by which means my letters sometimes convey no ideas at all to my correspondents. Though, there are occasional tufts of fur—"

"Your humility, and your inadvertent *enclosures*, Mr. Bingley," said Elizabeth, "must disarm reproof."

"Nothing is more deceitful," said Darcy, "than the appearance of humility. It is often only carelessness of opinion, neglectful shedding, and sometimes an indirect boast."

"And which of the three do you call *my* little recent piece of modesty?"

"The indirect boast; for you are really proud of your defects in writing—you consider them indicative of quick thinking. And you think that carelessness of execution is at least highly interesting, in particular when done by a tiger. All quickness is inherently prized by felines, often regardless of performance. When you told Mrs. Bennet this morning that if you ever resolved upon quitting Netherfield you should be gone in five minutes, you meant it to be a sort of panegyric, of compliment to yourself and your Great Cat nature. And yet—what is so very laudable in leaving necessary business undone?"

"Nay," cried Bingley, "this is too much, to remember at moon-night, just before the recurrence of the Ordeal, all the foolish things that were said in the morning. And yet, upon my honour, I believe what I said of myself to be true. At least I did not display needless precipitance merely to show off before the ladies."

"I dare say you believed it; but I am by no means convinced that you would be gone with such haste. If, as you were mounting your horse, a friend were to say, 'Bingley, you had better stay till next week,' you would probably remain—and at another word, might stay a month—even with moon in sky and you without a cage."

"You have only proved by this," cried Elizabeth, "that Mr. Bingley has an amiable disposition and a powerful regard for friendship."

"I am exceedingly gratified," said Bingley, "by your converting what my friend says into a compliment on the sweetness of my temper. But I am afraid you are giving it a turn which that gentleman did not intend. He would think far better of me if I gave out flat denials, and rode off as fast as I could."

"Would Mr. Darcy then consider the rashness of your original intentions atoned by your obstinacy in adhering to it?"[32]

"Upon my word, I cannot exactly explain the matter; Darcy must speak for himself," said Bingley, beginning to

---

[32] For the esteemed reader's elucidation, the "it" here in this sentence refers to "rashness." —Ed. *[By Jove, is it really necessary to "assist" the esteemed reader to such a degree? Why is this being footnoted? —Ed. 2]*

unconsciously tap his fingers in a nervous parody of flexing claws.

Darcy, noting his friend's twitching, glanced at the clock. He then spoke in an exceedingly controlled tone. "You expect me to account for opinions which I have never acknowledged. Even if such were the case, you must remember, Miss Bennet, that the friend who is supposed to desire his return to the house, and the delay of his plan, has merely *asked*, not insisted."

"To yield to the *persuasion* of a friend is no merit with you," said Elizabeth.

"To yield without conviction is no compliment to the understanding of either."

"You appear to me, Mr. Darcy, to allow nothing for the influence of friendship and affection," she replied, and then proceeded to make a convincing argument in favor of compliance based on such.

"Will it not be advisable, before we proceed on this subject, to account for the importance of a given request, as well as the degree of friendly intimacy between the parties?"

"By all means," cried Bingley, ending on an agitated roar; "let us hear all the particulars, including comparative height and size—for that will have more weight in the argument, Miss Bennet, than you may be aware of. I assure you, that if Darcy were not such a great tall fellow, in comparison with myself— though, to be sure, I have no notion how we might compare in our beastly forms, my demon tiger pitted against his *whatever monstrous beast*—I should not pay him half so much deference. I declare I do not know a more awful object than Darcy, on particular occasions, and in particular places; at his own house especially, and of a Sunday evening on a full moon, when he has nothing to do but have himself *contained*, with many a chain and padlock, for the safety of us all."

Mr. Darcy smiled *mysteriously*; but Elizabeth thought she could perceive that he was rather offended, and therefore checked her laugh.

Miss Bingley, meanwhile, warmly resented the indignity he had received, in an expostulation with her brother for talking such nonsense.

"I see your design, Bingley," said his friend. "You dislike an argument, and want to silence this, perhaps wisely, considering the nearing wicked hour."

"Perhaps I do. Arguments are too much like disputes, especially on nights we are drunk with the moon. If you and Miss Bennet will defer yours till I am out of the room and in my cage, I shall be very thankful; and then you may say whatever you like of me. That is, Darcy will roar it from beyond the bars of his own enclosure, and I would be too far in the throes of lunacy to hear."

"What you ask," said Elizabeth, "is no sacrifice on my side; and Mr. Darcy had much better finish his letter."

Mr. Darcy took her advice, and did finish his letter, well before it was time for the gentlemen to retire for their yet another night of the Ordeal.

But first, he applied to Miss Bingley and Elizabeth for an indulgence of some music. Miss Bingley moved with some alacrity to the pianoforte; and, after a polite request that Elizabeth would lead the way, which the other politely and earnestly refused, she seated herself.

Mrs. Hurst sang with her sister (Mr. Hurst periodically joined them in sudden howl outbursts, especially during the Neapolitan airs, but was soon restrained by frigid looks from Darcy and stunned feline hisses from Bingley). And while they were thus employed, Elizabeth could not help observing, as she turned over some music-books that lay on the instrument, how frequently Mr. Darcy's eyes were fixed on *her* (that is, when he was not giving Hurst basilisk stares).

She hardly knew how to suppose that she could be an object of admiration to so great a man. And yet that he should look at her because he disliked her, was still more strange—for assuredly, *she* was not the one howling during the chorus of *Santa Lucia.* . . .

She could only imagine, however, at last that she drew his notice because there was a something about *her* more wrong and reprehensible (and possibly more doggish?), according to his ideas of right, than in any other person present, including all those making mewling and barking noises (and here one does *not* speak of Bingley's sisters and the pianoforte).

The supposition did not pain her. She liked him too little to care for his approbation. Besides, thankfully soon, he and all the gentlemen will heed the moon's call and depart for the night. . . .

After playing some Italian songs, Miss Bingley varied the charm by a lively Scotch air. Immediately, Mr. Bingley started to purr and knead the sofa upholstery, then disguised it with a polite cough and flexed his fingers instead.

And Mr. Darcy, drawing near Elizabeth, said to her:

"Do not you feel a great inclination, Miss Bennet, to seize such an opportunity of dancing a reel?"

She smiled, but made no answer. He repeated the question, with some surprise at her silence.

"Oh!" said she, "I heard you before, but I could not immediately determine what to say in reply. One may never be too careful with a gentleman of heightened senses, on the verge of *transformation.* You wanted me to say 'Yes,' that you might have the pleasure of despising my taste, with the fierce passion that only Selene gives. But I always delight in overthrowing those kind of schemes, soothing a wild beast, and cheating a person of their premeditated contempt. I have, therefore, made up my mind to tell you, that I do not want to dance a reel at all— and now, rage with the moon, and despise me if you dare."

"Indeed I do not dare."

Elizabeth, having rather expected to affront him, was amazed at his gallantry. But there was a mixture of sweetness and archness in her manner which made it difficult for her to affront anybody; and Darcy had never been so bewitched by any woman as he was by her. He really believed, that were it not for the inferiority of her connections, he should be in some danger.

Gentle reader, it was at this exact moment that a danger appeared from an entirely different direction. . . .

The clock struck a late hour, and the moon began to rise, so the gentlemen regretfully excused themselves from the fair company and departed to their respective chambers to be duly contained. The household staff went into the customary hurried panic, in a repeat of the previous night, with maids carrying chains, padlocks and other implements. Finally, there was much slamming of deadbolts and locking of doors.

And then, the night was pierced like a fork by a stomach-rending human scream of abject terror. . . .

"Dear Heavens! has it started so soon?" said Miss Bingley from the sofa, with a tedious look at the door, followed by a longer glance at the curtained window through which no moonglow seeped as yet.

"I have not the faintest notion," replied Mrs. Hurst, still seated near the pianoforte.

"I thought tonight should be the last of it for the month, an easier Ordeal by far, with the moon's influence at its weakest. Sometimes, I recall, they can even control it somewhat, and do not necessarily *turn* . . . at least not for the entirety of the night."

"Well, *someone* has *turned* early," replied Louisa carelessly.

Elizabeth got up, taking the opportune moment to excuse herself and join her still-recovering sister upstairs for the rest of the evening—at which point the terrible scream came again.

"Oh!" started Miss Bingley. 'This is truly insupportable! Did they not take care to lock all the doors yet, and shut everything to reduce the usual *noises?*"

In that moment the parlor door opened in much greater haste than was normally deemed polite, and a frightened maidservant came rushing in, to say there was "a beast on the loose, and one of the masters has seen it, and has gone to chase and *turned* before they could lock him in, and *now he is loose also*, and—"

"Stop! What are you saying?" Mrs. Hurst was up from the chair in a rush. "*Who* is loose?"

"Oh, Oh! Mr. Hurst is, Ma'am! Your spouse!"

"What?"

"The gentleman, he has *turned* and—and—oh! There is a *monstrous flying creature*, Ma'am, right upstairs, in the house! It came flying as I was just locking the cage, but had not a moment to finish; for it came at me, fiendish-screeching, with great big wings, it did, and oh! And then the gentleman *saw* it, just as he started to disrobe in the cage, and he just *turned* immediately, in a blink, moon or no! Oh, gracious, and he barked and barked! And he ran from the cage in his demon skin—if I might be so bold—with not even his pants on, before I could shut the door! And the flying monster flew into the corridor, and to be sure the dog—that is, *hound*—the gentleman—went after it, and they are *both of them* upstairs, running loose, and the servants are all a'scream an' hiding, and I was told to fetch you, Ma'am!"

As the maid prattled on, there came horrible barking noises and thunderous pounding of feet from upstairs, intermingled with falling furniture, breaking glass, women's screams (one of them decidedly belonging to the housekeeper who never raised her voice in her life; so this was of some significance) until in moments the entire ceiling over their heads shook.

"Fetch *me?*" said Mrs. Hurst in a rising voice. "Whatever can *I* do, silly girl? You apparently let him loose through your own incompetence, and did not lock the cage properly, foolish idiot girl! And now what is to be done?"

"But Ma'am, there was a monster flying at me, a *monster thing!* I am so sorry, but it was about to strike me, it was—"

"Oh, gracious!" said Miss Bingley, rising also. "Whatever shall we do?"

Elizabeth took a few steps forward, when the door burst open again, this time with no attempt at gentility at all, and two more women servants ran within, screaming and begging the ladies to come assist, or run and hide, or both—it was somewhat difficult to understand precisely what was being said between the squeals.

"Pray do not go up there, Miss! There's a *monstrous duck*, Miss!" exclaimed one, addressing Miss Bingley.

"A what?"

"They call it the Brighton Duck,[33] forgive me, Miss, I tell no lie, but surely it is none other than the Brighton Duck! You might have heard of it spoken as far as Bath and Portsmouth, and mayhap London! A killer, born and bread to tear a man's head off, and it needs no moon to turn! That is, Miss, it is not *turned per se*, it just *is* what it is, a monster duck! A great big horrible humongous cannibal, it is!"

"A duck? A cannibal? Now, stop this nonsense, immediately!" Miss Bingley protested yet again, but taking no chances started to back away from the door. "I suggest we might find a safer room than this one, if indeed someone is loose as they say—"

In that moment, apparently the moon rose at last. . . . Because from upstairs, the newly forged roars of a tiger now joined the cacophony.

"Oh dear. And now Charles has quit us," said Mrs. Hurst.

"Yes, I can *hear* him." Miss Bingley was looking up at the ceiling, while the three maids in the room had gone entirely silent and cowered, uselessly wringing their hands.

"Well then. Just so that we might understand correctly," said Elizabeth, "is Mr. Hurst up there, running loose this

---

[33] A creature of nightmares, rumored to be first observed and harbored at a certain fine estate called Mansfield Park. Purportedly, there were also mummified Egyptians involved. —Ed. *[This is possibly the only relevant footnote in this entire volume. —Ed. 2]*

moment? With no restraints? And there is some kind of large flying *murderous* duck?"

"Yes, Miss!"

"And Mr. Hurst—pardon me for asking—he normally *turns* into a hound? Now, is it a particularly large and fierce hound?"

"Yes!" said Miss Bingley and Mrs. Hurst; while, "No!" said the maidservants simultaneously.

Elizabeth looked at them all, then continued, "What kind of breed of—ahem—hound, would you say it is?"

"A magnificent wolfhound!" Mrs. Hurst exclaimed.

"A bullish great dane at least!" added Miss Bingley.

"I am thinking, Miss," said the first servant, glancing discreetly at the floor to avoid the glares of the Bingley sisters, "maybe he is more like a fox hound—that is, a middling terrier of sorts . . ."

Elizabeth understood perfectly, and continued to enquire:

"So then, does Mr. Hurst—when in his hound form—does he bite?"

"Oh goodness, frightfully!" exclaimed Louisa, and Caroline added, "Gracious, yes, he is a terror! I am entirely certain he has eaten someone horridly, at least a few times over the years!"

Standing off to the side, one of the maids discreetly shook her head negatively, while the other two also addressed expressive looks to Elizabeth.

Once again, Elizabeth understood perfectly. "Will you be so kind as to take me there, upstairs?" she said bravely. "I am afraid my poor Jane, resting abed, might be in grave danger, and I would be at her side. That is, if you do not mind—"

"Yes, Miss, not at all, I will be happy to take you there."

"Miss Bennet, I expect that would be folly," said Mrs. Hurst. "I highly denounce such a course and do not recommend you move from this room, which is safe, at least for the moment."

"However, for the sake of my dear sister Jane, I insist."

"Well then, Miss Bennet, proceed at your own risk and discretion—or lack of such!" said Miss Bingley, and gave a superior smile when Elizabeth proceeded to do just that.

When the door clicked behind them, Miss Bingley added: "See, Louisa, what did I speak to you! Petticoats in mud, and now, chasing an Afflicted gentleman and an unknown monstrosity. She is the most vulgar example of a female I have ever seen!"

Overhead, the ceiling thundered in mayhem.

Elizabeth followed the maid out of the chamber, who, trembling, led the way, first carefully peeking outside the door, then stepping into the hallway.

They ascended the staircase past several harried maid staff, carrying candles to light the way, and the noise was deafening.

"You should know, Miss, it is the monstrous fowl that poses the greatest danger here, not the gentleman—Mr. Hurst is normally gentle as a mouse in his little cage, happy to have the bones and steak," said the maidservant. "If it were not for this Brighton Duck that came out of nowhere, he would be docile as anything; why, you can likely pet 'im outside his cage!"

"I see," said Elizabeth, encouraged even more by this news.

"But now he 'as likely lost all his senses and is giving chase to this frightful creature, as you know all terriers are liable to do when they see a bird or rabbit. Might you be able to corner him, Miss? Or at least speak to him, since he knows you, and is more like to heed you than me or Mary or Janet there?"

"I will do my best," said Elizabeth, thinking of all the times she had sweet-talked her father within his own cage back at Longbourn, to stop gnawing at the bars, or otherwise soothed his Ordeal.

They had reached the second floor and in the corridor Elizabeth saw a row of bedchambers, with several doors thrown open, and fortunately the doors to Mr. Bingley's and Mr.

Darcy's still intact and shut tight—however, with grandiose tiger roars issuing from one, and suspicious silence from the other.

The door of the containment chamber given to Mr. Hurst was flung wide open, and only candlelight and silence was streaming from within.

But it was from further down the hall that the most frightful noises were issuing—from another guest bedroom, supposedly unoccupied. These were not roars but the pounding sound of large objects crashing; the breaking of wood and china; yapping and barking and periodic screeches worthy of a banshee.

"Oh, do be careful, Miss!" cried a young girl servant who had come rushing out of that very room, armed with a broom handle in one hand and a large saucepan in another, somewhat like a Grecian Amazon swordmaiden, but mostly not. "I tired to corner the Brighton Duck before it kill me, I did! But the monster is flying every which way, on top of cabinets and wardrobe, and Mr. Hurst is gone all mad with barking and jumping up at it, and oh—"

Elizabeth braced herself and carefully entered past the warrior kitchen maid into a chamber that was revealed to be a mess of fallen chairs, a broken writing table, a disheveled poster bed, and broken knickknacks spilled all over the floor.

On top of a wardrobe sat a giant *hell-spawn creature* with indeed a grandiose wingspan, dove-grey in coloration, and rather well fattened for a duck, or else simply gargantuan in proportion. For the moment it calmly reposed, having perched on the tallest spot, its wings insolently folded. And it gazed down, with what likely amounted to amused disdain, upon a medium-small wiry-maned light brown dog that jumped around as if it were a bouncing ball upon a circus trampoline; and all the while the dog barked with rabid intensity, fierceness, and abandon.

"Dear lord . . ." whispered Elizabeth.

At the sound of her voice, the duck turned its head in her direction, fixing its frightful eye upon her, then turned calmly back.

The terrier did not even notice her, and continued bouncing and yapping, being entirely single-minded in its buoyant dark desire to reach and then tear the duck into infinite pieces.

Elizabeth cleared her throat. "Mr. Hurst," she said, "Might I have your attention?"

The dog ignored her.

The duck made a sudden loud squawk.

"Mr. Hurst? Here, good—uhm—Mr. Hurst! *Here, boy!*"

It was no use.

Elizabeth sighed. She then turned to the servants lined up behind her and out in the hallway, and said: "If someone would be so kind as to fetch me a bone?"

Moments later, a maid returned with a meaty, large bone in her apron, taken from Mr. Hurst's containment room.

"Be ready to shut this door upon my signal," said Miss Bennet, taking the bone in one hand and the broom handle in another, then turned back inside with renewed courage.

But before she could act, the monstrous duck suddenly lifted from its perch overhead. Flapping its great wings it hurtled above and past Elizabeth and out the door into the hallway, scattering both screaming servants and grey-tipped feathers.

Elizabeth dropped the broom handle, which clattered with a thunderous noise as it hit the floor.

Mr. Hurst gave a horrendous howling yap, and sprang, but was instantly distracted by Miss Bennet who in that moment spoke a silent prayer and threw the bone directly at him.

The terrier had just lunged at the doorway, barely missing the bone's airborne trajectory; then, just as quickly flung himself back at the irresistible temptation thrown his way, forgetting the duck in an instant.

"Now, shut the door!" cried Elizabeth, and when no one responded, she backed herself out and swiftly closed the door to the chamber. But indeed, there was no urgency now—Mr. Hurst, in his fox terrier form, remained within, growling in fierce delight and tearing at the bone to his canine heart's content.

An entirely different matter was transpiring in the corridor.

The door to Mr. Darcy's room suddenly opened from the inside—being in fact entirely *unlocked* and unsecured in any manner conceivable—and out stepped the gentleman himself, hastily clad in elegant breeches and dripping-wet shirtsleeves. He was in disarray, but entirely composed, and entirely *human*.

"Whatever is going on here?" he inquired in an icy manner and a powerful voice. And then his stern gaze fell upon Miss Elizabeth Bennet.

Elizabeth glanced in the gentleman's direction, only to meet his close perusal of her, and *saw* him.

"Oh! Mr. Darcy! You are—*yourself!*"

"Indeed, Miss Bennet, who else might I be?"

At the physical entirety of him—at the sight of his soaked condition—Elizabeth felt an uncontrollable horrid heat rising in her cheeks.

"But you are—that is, you are *unturned*."

"Miss Bennet, you are restating the obvious."

"I am merely admitting that you, sir, are not a present danger."

"That is entirely untrue. I may indeed be an immediate, wrathful, and inclement danger to the negligent serving staff who had failed to take the necessary measures with my containment—and, apparently, the containment of Mr. Hurst. Incidentally, where is he?"

Elizabeth took a step away from the closed door of the bedroom behind her, from wherein came canine snorts and growls. "I believe," she said, "He is safely locked in for the moment. And I provided him with a—means of occupation."

Darcy continued to look at her with an unreadable expression.

Elizabeth was not at all certain as to how to interpret its nature. Indeed, did he truly dislike her so much? Was he seeking whatever new and clever means to kindle his scorn? Therefore she countered his look with earnest words:

"Will you not say, 'Well done, Miss Bennet?' Have I not earned even a word of approbation for getting that door closed and even managing to drive off a monstrous duck?"

"What duck?"

Elizabeth parted her lips. But before she could explain, one of the maids (of those who had fled in all directions when the flying monstrosity shot past them through the hallway) now peeked from a narrowly opened door, and dared to speak. "Begging pardon, sir, it's the Brighton Duck, sir! I saw it go flying down the corridor, sir, around the corner, or possibly back down the stairs! I fear it has gone where the ladies are presently—"

"Oh, dear! Oh!" exclaimed Elizabeth, putting the back of her hand to her mouth. "What of—Jane? Jane!" She suddenly recalled her sister was not that far from them all, on the other wing of this very floor, at the far end of the same hallway. "Oh, I must go to her immediately!"

And forgetting all else, picking up her skirts, she sped past Mr. Darcy, past several servants hiding behind other doors and niches, and disappeared around the corner.

Darcy stared in her wake, in perfect amazement.

But he did not have more than a few moments to ponder, because a terrible banshee screeching, followed by an impossibly loud unrestrained roar, came from the same direction in which Elizabeth had gone.

The roar was the sound of a tiger—unmuffled by doors or walls—a decidedly *uncontained* tiger.

It was succeeded by two female screams. There was no doubt one of them belonged to Miss Elizabeth Bennet.

Without a moment of thought Darcy ran after her.

While all these dire events were taking place on the second floor of the manor at Netherfield, downstairs in the drawing room, Miss Bingley and Mrs. Hurst strolled fretfully, making rounds along the chamber, quietly conversing, often starting anxiously at various noises coming from above, and looking up at the ceiling.

"Should I ring the bell and call someone, Louisa? It has been half an hour at least, and I fear the worst."

"Do you think it prudent? To even open the door?"

As if precipitating Miss Bingley's thought, a maidservant knocked in some haste, then entered, saying, "Oh, madam and miss, it is dreadful! Just dreadful!"

"What is it?" Mrs. Hurst squeaked, turning quite pale.

"Speak up now! Quickly!" said Miss Bingley. "Is someone dead?"

"Why, not at all! 'Tis good news!"

"But—you just said 'it is dreadful!' Which is it?"

"Well, it is! Or at least it seems, begging pardon—the gentleman, Mr. Hurst is now locked up—at least I think he is, there with the nice bone, and with Miss Elizabeth Bennet—or is it the other poor Miss Bennet, bless her soul, the poor sickly dear—but, miss, madam, I think the monster duck is still out there, which is horrid, but out of sight, which is a blessing—we thought, maybe it had come down here, no? 'Tis a wonder! Well, in any case, it is the other gentlemen that are a bit of a problem. To be sure, a horrifying thing it may be, in all truth! They are *all uncontained* now, both Mr. Darcy and Mr. Bingley; supposedly both are on the loose, and not sure how they all got out of their cages—"

Miss Bingley gave a faint scream.

Mrs. Hurst fainted.

Elizabeth Bennet found herself in the hallway in front of the pleasant guest bedroom allocated so generously by Mr. Bingley to Jane for her sick stay.

She was about to knock and enter, gently calling out to her sister, to announce herself. But right then, from *inside* that bedroom came a fearful gasp—in Jane's dear voice!—then a truly ear-rending banshee screech, and finally, the unthinkable—a horrifying tiger roar.

Elizabeth screamed without thinking. She grabbed the handle and threw the door open, rushing within . . . and then froze, with her sister's name on her lips. . . .

Miss Jane Bennet was seated in bed, clutching a coverlet to her nightgown, with trembling fingers.

On top of a wardrobe, once again in the tallest spot of the room, sat the infamous Brighton Duck.

The window was flung wide-open, curtains pushed aside, with the moonlight pouring in, bright as day.

And just a few steps away, in the corner of the bedroom, illuminated by the slightly-waning but still round and swollen, wicked moon, softly growled a very large, orange-gold and black striped *tiger*.

"Sh-sh-sh! . . . Oh . . . My . . . Lizzy . . ." whispered Jane very quietly, very slowly, clutching the bedding, and not daring to breathe.

Elizabeth felt the coldest terror imaginable envelop her. Never had she felt so helpless to do anything, yet at the same time so indignant, and yet perfectly aware that *something* had to be done, and immediately—for the Afflicted gentleman in such a dangerous transformed shape was in no position to be reasoned with. Here was no terrier, and Jane's life was in very real peril.

"Bingley! Control yourself this instant. You must *turn*, immediately."

Mr. Darcy's commanding voice sounded from the doorway. He was standing out of the moon's direct light, just behind Elizabeth, so that she nearly felt a breeze where his hand brushed past her shoulder to rest on the doorframe, as he towered over her. And then, with surprising gentleness, he moved her out of the way, sweeping past her into the bedchamber.

If he were not so entirely dripping-wet, he would cut a dashing figure, she could not help but think—but only for an instant.

"Listen to me, Bingley," he continued, while the tiger growled louder, gathering itself to pounce, and started to part its teeth for a monstrous roar. "You must remember who you are. Think, now! The demon shape has no power over you. Control it! Do it for the sake of the eldest Miss Bennet whom you hold in such high regard. *Turn!*"

And, amazingly enough, the tiger started to roar (while Jane squeaked), but the timbre of it changed, and instead of attacking, the creature fell forward. The air around it seemed to dissolve as its outline blurred and there was the sound of grinding and breaking bones. . . .

Several painful moments later, there was Mr. Bingley, groaning on the floor, and entirely *en déshabillé*.

"Well done, my friend," said Darcy, then stepped into the room as though nothing was amiss, and quickly drew the curtains shut to block the moonlight. He then took a blanket from the nearest chair. "Here, cover yourself. You are in the presence of ladies."

On the bed, Jane gave a minor gasp, and reposed back on the pillow, shutting her eyes, then cautiously staring in front of her, so as not to look down beside the bed at the floor . . . and at the gentleman so scandalously in want of any manner of attire.

Elizabeth exhaled in relief, and rushed forward to embrace her sister. The two Miss Bennets held each other, shaking from the onrush of nerves, when all of a sudden the giant duck roosting on the wardrobe unfurled its wings. Everyone looked up as, with a trumpet squawk, it flew up, circled the tiny room, and then, disdaining the window, hurtled into the open doorway and disappeared out of sight. . . .

"What in blazes—" Mr. Darcy exclaimed, noticing the duck for the first time.

But the sisters no longer paid heed.

"Oh, Jane!" "Oh, Lizzy!" they cried to each other.

At the same moment, on the floor, Mr. Bingley had come fully to his senses. Clutching the blanket around himself, he coughed, sputtered; then managed to say, "Darcy! What on earth—Where am I? Why are you here? What—"

At which point with a side-glance he noticed Jane Bennet and her sister, seated on the bed. And Bingley froze in place, then turned as red as a gentleman could be, when in the presence of a young lady he is interested in, and when he also happens to be entirely lacking pants.

"Good God! Miss Bennet! Whatever is—that is, a thousand pardons!"

"It is quite all right, Mr. Bingley, we are unharmed," said Elizabeth, while Jane continued shaking, and then had a fit of coughing. "Mr. Bingley," she managed between coughs, "yes, we are both fine, please do not trouble yourself—"

"Trouble myself? Why, dearest Miss Bennet, I put you in terrible danger! I am not to be ever forgiven! I am—"

Bingley got up, dreadfully flushed in the face, covered in the blanket, and with Mr. Darcy leading him by the shoulders, they exited the bedchamber with much haste, and much embarrassed muttering and protestations on Bingley's part.

Once in the hallway, Mr. Bingley raised his voice dreadfully. He railed in anger at the servants who had come forth from their hiding, unused to hearing such passions from their mild-tempered master, not even at the height of the full moon.

"*Who* is responsible? Who had left the cages and the doors unlocked? Which one among you villains? I almost murdered Miss Bennet and her sister! Who dared—"

"Compose yourself," said Darcy calmly. "No harm was done, fortunately."

"What are you saying?" Bingley turned on his friend with passion, and almost dropped the blanket, then again recalled that he was not wearing any pants.

And then he noticed Darcy's own disarray. "And you! Why, my fellow, you are swimming wet! What is it with you? Why is it, that every time I see you, you are in wet shirtsleeves?"

"Speak for yourself, swaddled as a newborn babe." And Darcy added: "Fortunately, Hurst has been apprehended and safely contained—by a certain Miss Elizabeth Bennet. You can thank her later. Rest assured, we will deal with whoever it is responsible for this disaster in the morning; I am told we may have to go hunting ducks. For now, since we are both *under control*, I surmise we no longer pose a threat to anyone for the rest of the night, and likely it is over until next moon."

Mr. Darcy's assumption was correct. Even though the gentlemen diligently returned to their enclosures and made certain the window curtains were drawn tight, and the servants had properly turned all locks and shut all deadbolts behind them (excepting Mr. Hurst, the terrier, who was simply left where he was, harmlessly occupied with the destruction of the bone and one small pouf pillow), no one succumbed to the throes of Affliction for the rest of the night. And Mr. Hurst awoke near dawn, in his normal manly form, and with no memory of the incident.

The two Miss Bennet remained together in Jane's sickroom, since Elizabeth thought it prudent to not leave her sister's side.

And downstairs, Miss Bingley and Mrs. Hurst were both sufficiently calmed and, in the case of the latter, resuscitated. The ladies were informed of their present safety, and the evening was by-and-by deemed a success.

Indeed, even after everyone had retired for the night altogether, there was still no sign of the original instigator of the incident, that monstrosity called the Brighton Duck. . . .

In the morning, there were mild repercussions.

Mr. Bingley had the servants lined up in formation in the front parlor, and commenced an inquiry. And in the process it was revealed that someone had left a window open on the second floor early in the evening, and apparently the villainous duck must have flown in. Naturally, it started spreading mischief from room to room by *opening more windows* as it left each one, thus ventilating the corridor and scattering the terrified serving staff, so that none of the cages were properly locked and all other safety precautions were abandoned in favor of mindless panic.

It was for this precise reason, Mr. Bingley reasoned, that he himself had the terrible opportunity to climb outside through his own window—while in his tiger form—and navigate the narrow outer ledge from one window to another, and finally end up *somehow* in Miss Jane Bennet's bedroom.

"And thus, it all makes perfect sense," concluded Bingley; and after many more grim warnings he dismissed the servants.

"One may suppose it does," said Mr. Darcy, present for this inquest and observing the process with curiosity. "Only one thing eludes me. Why would this duck fly from room to room, opening windows? What purpose would that serve—for a *duck?* And how would a duck manage the intricate act?"

"What purpose? Why, pure mischief!" retorted Bingley. "Did you not hear it described how this fowl creature is *unnatural*, and a notorious villain, known for acts of senseless retribution from here all the way to London?"

"Yes, well; but *how* and *why* would this miraculous duck use its appendages to pry open a window? Does it not seem rather unlikely and impossible to you?"

"Darcy, you think too much!"

"Someone needs to. This is nonsensical."

Bingley's reply was never to be, for in that moment the ladies were seen descending, and among them, Miss Elizabeth Bennet.

Mr. Darcy's attention was immediately engaged, the duck forgotten. He observed her[34] as she earnestly assured Bingley that indeed "the dearest Miss Jane Bennet" was well on her way to full recovery and that all was perfectly amiable since last night.

And then Elizabeth turned to him directly, and said, looking him in the eyes, "I must thank you Mr. Darcy, for your timely assistance last night. Jane might not have fared so well—and I for that matter—had we remained in the room with the *tiger* alone without your intervention."

Darcy steeled himself. Because in that moment—seeing her expressive eyes and her clear gaze—there was an uncontrollable gathering of emotion within him; and his heart filled with such sentiment that it was in danger of overflowing. For that reason he bowed icily and replied in a lifeless, dispassionate voice, "No need. It is forgotten, and is of no consequence."

For a moment only their gazes held, and Elizabeth saw no inkling of human warmth, only pride—the one thing that he allowed her to see. And thus, her own moment of precarious warmth died inside her, and she turned away.

Darcy watched Miss Elizabeth Bennet and Mrs. Hurst make their way outside for a constitutional stroll, while Miss Caroline Bingley remained, in order to speak feelingly of the dreadful fright of the evening before. She asked her brother if any progress was made in apprehending the guilty party.

"Apparently the villain is an unnatural monstrous fowl," replied Bingley, and regaled his sister with the dire legend of the Brighton Duck. While he spoke at length and with much spirit, Miss Bingley paid little attention and instead carefully observed Mr. Darcy watch the departing Miss Bennet.

There was no doubt as to the intensity in his gaze, and the possible sentiments it implied.

---

[34] Miss Bennet, not the duck, was observed by Mr. Darcy. —Ed. *[Clearly someone out there needs to be reassured that such is the case. —Ed. 2]*

Miss Bingley saw, or suspected enough to be jealous. And her great anxiety for the recovery of her "dear friend Jane" received some assistance from her desire of getting rid of Elizabeth—as soon as possible.

It must be emphasized that Miss Bingley often tried to provoke Darcy into disliking her guest, by talking of their supposed marriage, and planning his "happiness" in such an alliance.

"I hope," said she, as they were walking together in the shrubbery later that morning, "you will give your mother-in-law a few hints (when this desirable event takes place) as to the advantage of holding her tongue. Next, you must cure the younger girls of running after officers, especially at the height of the full moon. And, if I may mention so delicate a subject, do endeavour to check that little something, bordering on conceit and impertinence, which your lady possesses."

"Have you anything else to propose for my domestic felicity?"

"Oh! yes. Do let the portraits of your ursine uncle and aunt Phillips be placed in the gallery at Pemberley. Put them next to your great-uncle the judge. They are in the same profession, you know, only in different lines and of different species. As for your Elizabeth's picture, you must not have it taken, for what painter could do justice to those beautiful eyes?"

"It would not be easy, indeed, to catch their expression, but their colour and shape, and the eyelashes, so remarkably fine, might be copied."

At that moment they were met from another walk by Mrs. Hurst and Elizabeth herself.

"I did not know that you intended to walk yet again since your earlier stroll," said Miss Bingley, in some confusion, lest they had been overheard. "But naturally, one must recall, Miss Bennet is a great walker."

"You used us abominably ill," answered Mrs. Hurst, "running away without telling us that you were coming out. And, of all things, with a wild monstrous flying *creature* on the loose!"

"Indeed, the duck could be anywhere," said Mr. Darcy. "Remind me to bring along a fowling piece on the next excursion."

"Oh! The mere notion that it is *out there* is insupportable! And—what if there is more than one? I do hope when you see it you shoot it immediately, Mr. Darcy."

Then, taking the disengaged arm of Mr. Darcy, she left Elizabeth to walk by herself (and be accosted by goodness knows what *unnatural* dangers flying out of the shrubbery). The path just admitted three. Mr. Darcy felt their rudeness, and immediately said:

"This walk is not wide enough for our party. We had better go into the avenue."

But Elizabeth, who had not the least inclination to remain with them, laughingly answered:

"No, no; stay where you are. You are charmingly grouped, and appear to uncommon advantage. The picturesque would be spoilt by admitting a fourth. Good-bye."

She then ran gaily off, giving no second thought to unnatural duck infestations, and rejoicing as she rambled about, in the hope of being at home again in a day or two. Jane was already so much recovered as to intend leaving her room for a couple of hours that evening—something that was going to lighten the heart of a certain concerned tiger.

"Bingley! Control yourself this instant. You must *turn*, immediately."

Chapter 11

When the ladies removed after dinner, Elizabeth ran up to her sister, and seeing her well guarded from cold and from uninvited gentlemen Afflicted by beastly form or lacking unmentionable portions of attire, attended her into the drawing-room, where she was welcomed by her two friends with many professions of pleasure.

"My dear Jane, you have been entirely too fortunate to miss some dreadful excitement this past night," said Mrs. Hurst. "Apparently it was the right thing to do to remain abed all evening, recovering—"

"You forget, Louisa," said Miss Bingley, "that our dear Jane hardly missed any of it at all, and was indeed visited by Charles in his most dreadful *state;* and if it had not been for Mr. Darcy's swift actions, I dare say she might have been—oh, but it is far too dreadful to pronounce!"

"Oh gracious, how could I forget such a thing indeed! It must have happened when I was senseless. Poor dear Jane!"

And they went on in this manner for quite some time, with Jane occasionally interrupting with gentle utterances of gratitude and insistences that it was "all quite well."

Elizabeth had never seen them so agreeable as they were during the hour which passed before the gentlemen appeared.

But when the gentlemen entered, Jane was no longer the first object. Miss Bingley's eyes were instantly turned toward Darcy, and she had something to say to him before he had advanced many steps. He addressed himself to Miss Bennet, with a polite congratulation and then a glance at Miss Elizabeth Bennet.

Mr. Hurst also made Jane a slight bow, and said he was "very glad" and then muffled the rest with a cough that managed to resemble a yap. Apparently Mr. Hurst was not entirely clear on the circumstances of the fateful night previous, but had been informed by Darcy that he himself had "behaved sufficiently well so as not to have caused any lasting harm—except to a certain bone and pillow."

But an intense crimson blush, followed by diffuseness and warmth remained for Bingley's salutation. The moment his gaze fell upon Jane, he was full of a delightfully odd mixture of apologies and self-reproach, coupled with joy and attention. The first half-hour was spent in piling up the fire, lest she should suffer from the change of room. Next, she moved, at his insistence, to the other side of the fireplace, that she might be further from the door. He then sat down by her, and made another thousand apologies and talked scarcely to anyone else. Elizabeth, at work in the opposite corner, saw it all with great delight.

When tea was over, Mr. Hurst reminded his sister-in-law of the card-table—but in vain. She had obtained private intelligence that Mr. Darcy did not wish for cards; and Mr. Hurst had therefore nothing to do, but to stretch himself on one of the sofas like a flopping hound and go to sleep. Darcy took up a book; Miss Bingley did the same; and Mrs. Hurst, principally occupied in playing with her bracelets and rings, joined now and then in her brother's conversation with Miss Bennet.

Miss Bingley's attention was quite as much engaged in watching Mr. Darcy's progress through *his* book, as in reading her own. She was perpetually either making some inquiry, or looking at his page. She could not win him, however, to any conversation; he merely answered her question, and read on.

At length, quite exhausted by the attempt to be amused with her own book, which she had only chosen because it was the second volume of his, she gave a great yawn and said, "How pleasant it is to spend an evening in this way, after all the dreadful excitement of yesterday! The moon's influence has waned, and you are all rid of it for another month, free to enjoy the *civilized* pleasures of an evening's leisure. I declare after all there is no enjoyment like reading! How much sooner one tires of anything than of a book! When I have a house of my own, I shall be miserable if I have not an excellent library."

No one made any reply. She then yawned again, threw aside her book, and cast her eyes round the room in quest for some amusement; when hearing her brother mentioning a ball to Miss Bennet, she turned suddenly towards him and said:

"By the bye, Charles, are you really serious in meditating a dance at Netherfield? I would advise you, before you determine on it, to consult the wishes of the present party; I am much mistaken if there are not some among us to whom a ball would be rather a punishment than a pleasure."

"If you mean Darcy," cried her brother, "he may go to bed or into a cage, if he chooses, before it begins—but as for the ball, it is quite a settled thing; and as soon as Nicholls has made white soup enough, I shall send round my cards."

"I should like balls infinitely better," she replied, "if they were carried on in a different manner. There is something insufferably tedious in the usual process. It would surely be much more rational if conversation instead of dancing were made the order of the day."

"Much more rational, my dear Caroline, I dare say, but it would not be near so much like a ball."

"Fie! Would you perhaps have it take place at high moontide, with all you gentlemen in your various dreadful *states*

and within cages lining the dance floor, roaring their admiration
to the ladies? It is no wonder Mr. Darcy despises the nonsense.
For, surely his own magnificent Ordeal is a severe drain on his
composure at any time of the month, as only the noblest of the
Afflictions can be. . . ."

Mr. Darcy made no answer, nor took the hint of yet another
probe into the nature of his Affliction, and soon afterwards Miss
Bingley got up and walked about the room. Her figure was
elegant, and she walked well; but Darcy, at whom it was all
aimed, was still inflexibly studious.

Desperate to engage his attention by any means, she finally
resorted to addressing Elizabeth:

"Miss Eliza Bennet, let me persuade you to follow my
example, and take a turn about the room. I assure you it is very
refreshing after sitting so long in one attitude."

Elizabeth was surprised, but agreed to it immediately. Miss
Bingley thus succeeded in the real object of her civility—Mr.
Darcy looked up.

He was as much awake to the novelty of attention in that
quarter as Elizabeth herself could be, and unconsciously closed
his book. When directly invited to join their party, he declined it,
observing that he could imagine but two motives for their
choosing to walk up and down the room together, and his joining
them would interfere with either.

"What can he mean? I am dying to know what can be his
meaning?" And Miss Bingley asked Elizabeth whether she could
at all understand him.

"Not at all," was Elizabeth's answer. "But depend upon it,
he means to be severe on us. Our surest way of disappointing
him will be to ask nothing about it."

Miss Bingley, however, was incapable of disappointing Mr.
Darcy in anything, and persevered in requiring an explanation.

"Well then," said he. "You either choose this method of
passing the evening because you are in each other's confidence,

and have secrets to discuss, or because you are conscious that your figures appear to the greatest advantage in walking. If the first, I would be completely in your way, and if the second, I can admire you much better as I sit by the fire."

"Oh! shocking!" cried Miss Bingley. "I never heard anything so abominable. How shall we punish him for such a speech?"

"Nothing could be easier," said Elizabeth. "Tease him— laugh at him. Intimate as you are, you must know how."

"But upon my honour, I do *not*. I assure you, my intimacy has not yet taught me *that*. How is one to tease calmness of manner and presence of mind, in a man who hides his *beast* so well that no one might encroach upon it? No, he may defy us there. And as to laughter, we will not expose[35] ourselves, if you please, by attempting to laugh without a subject. Mr. Darcy may hug[36] himself."

"Mr. Darcy is not to be laughed at!" cried Elizabeth. "That is an uncommon advantage! And, uncommon I hope it will continue, for it would be a great loss to *me* to have many such acquaintances. I dearly love a laugh."

"Miss Bingley," said he, "has given me more credit than can be. The wisest and the best may be rendered ridiculous by a person whose first object in life is a joke."

"Certainly," replied Elizabeth—"there are such people, but I hope I am not one of *them*. I hope I never ridicule what is wise and good—not even when I am startled out of my wits by a

---

[35] Miss Bingley, here, naturally does not refer to removing one's portions of or entirety of attire, but to revealing a surely delightful inner weakness. —Ed. *[Naturally; the reader is supremely grateful for having this being pointed out, for the "surely delightful" reader has no sufficient rational faculties to understand plain English vocabulary. —Ed. 2]*

[36] Hugging may be somewhat problematic, if Mr. Darcy attempts to embrace his own person with both hands and is unable to reach around fully. —Ed. *[What in Heaven's name are you about? Why is this a footnote? —Ed. 2]*

monstrous duck and must resort to "fowl" witticisms to regain my composure in the face of the absurd. On the other hand, follies and nonsense, whims and inconsistencies, *do* divert me. I laugh at them whenever I can. But these, I suppose, are precisely the qualities you are without."

"Perhaps that is not possible for anyone. But it has been the study of my life to avoid those weaknesses which often expose a strong understanding to ridicule."

"Such as vanity and secrecy and pride."

"Yes, vanity is a weakness indeed. But secrecy is nothing more than breeding coupled with discretion. And pride—where there is a real superiority of mind, pride will be always under good regulation."

Elizabeth turned away to hide a smile.

"Your examination of Mr. Darcy is over, I presume," said Miss Bingley; "and pray what is the result?"

"I am perfectly convinced by it that Mr. Darcy has no defect. He owns it himself without disguise. And as for his secret demon, why, he is no doubt a Great Cat, for none other would display such pride."

"Oh! Miss Bennet!" Miss Bingley exclaimed at such scandalous direct reference toward a gentleman's unspoken "secret" (which she herself had been regularly discussing with every confidante as though it were last night's lamb chop dinner; and furthermore, chipping away at Darcy's defenses on a daily basis, in his very company).

"No," said Darcy, "I have made no such pretension. I have faults enough, but they are not, I hope, of understanding. My temper I dare not vouch for. It is, I believe, too little yielding—certainly too little for the convenience of the world, or even Selene's wicked rays. I cannot forget the follies and vices of others so soon as I ought, nor their offenses against myself. My feelings are not puffed about by moonlight or with every attempt to move them. My temper would perhaps be called resentful. My good opinion once lost, is lost forever. And the nature of my demon beast, if you please, shall remain unspoken."

"*That* is a failing indeed!" cried Elizabeth. "Implacable resentment *is* a shade in a character. But no one can fault a gentleman of breeding for concealing his *beast* so well, against all provocation. Thus, you have chosen your faults well. I really cannot *laugh* at them. You are safe from me."

"There is, I believe, in every disposition a tendency to some particular evil—a natural defect, which not even the best education can overcome, and which the moon sometimes enhances."

"And *your* defect is to hate everybody."

"And yours," he replied with a smile, "is willfully to misunderstand them."

"Do let us have a little music," cried Miss Bingley, tired of a shocking conversation in which she had no share. "Louisa, you will not mind my waking[37] Mr. Hurst?"

Her sister had not the smallest objection, and the pianoforte was opened; and Darcy, after a few moments' recollection, was not sorry for it. He began to feel the danger of paying Elizabeth too much attention.

Fortunately, the wicked moon was on the wane, so that for the remainder of the month his feelings and his composure had some chance of being contained.

For the moment. . . .

---

[37] Gentle reader, it is indeed peculiar that Miss Bingley would consider walking Mr. Hurst, since he is certainly not in his beastly form; when a proper human gentleman, he does not require an assisted walk on a leash. —Ed. *[Why, this is not to be borne! The word is "waking" not "walking!" This worthless footnote needs to be excised immediately! How long must this editorial half-wit be allowed to continue? —Ed. 2]*

Chapter 12

Elizabeth wrote the next morning to their mother, to beg that the carriage might be sent for them in the course of the day.

But Mrs. Bennet, who had calculated on her daughters remaining at Netherfield till the following Tuesday, which would exactly finish Jane's week, sent them word that they could not possibly have the carriage before Tuesday. And if Mr. Bingley and his sister pressed them to stay longer, she could spare them very well.

Elizabeth was positively resolved against it. Impatient to get home, and fearful of intruding needlessly long upon Mr. Bingley's hospitality, she urged Jane to borrow Mr. Bingley's carriage immediately. And at length it was settled that their original design of leaving Netherfield that morning should be mentioned, and the request made.

The communication excited many professions of concern. Enough was said of wishing them to stay to convince Jane to defer their going till the morrow.

Miss Bingley was then sorry that she had proposed the delay, for her jealousy and dislike of one sister much exceeded her affection for the other.

The master of the house heard with real sorrow that they were to go so soon, and repeatedly tried to persuade Miss Bennet that it would not be safe for her—that she was not enough recovered. But Jane was firm where she felt herself to be right.

To Mr. Darcy their imminent departure was welcome intelligence—Elizabeth had been at Netherfield long enough. She attracted him more than he liked—and as a result, Miss Bingley was uncivil to *her*, and more teasing than usual to himself. . . .

Altogether, this was a dangerous combination that threatened to expose his Dreadful Secret.

Darcy wisely resolved to be particularly careful that no sign of admiration should *now* escape him, nothing that could elevate her with the hope of influencing his felicity. He knew that if such an idea had been suggested, his behaviour during the last day must have material weight in confirming or crushing it.

Steady to his purpose, he scarcely spoke ten words to Elizabeth through the whole of Saturday. And though they were at one time left by themselves for half-an-hour, he adhered most conscientiously to his book, and would not even look at her.

On Sunday, after morning service, the separation, so agreeable to almost all, took place. Miss Bingley's civility to Elizabeth increased at last very rapidly, as well as her affection for Jane. And when they parted, after assuring the latter of the pleasure it would always give her to see her either at Longbourn or Netherfield, and embracing her most tenderly, she even shook hands with the former. Elizabeth took leave of the whole party in the liveliest of spirits.

They were not welcomed home very cordially by their mother. Mrs. Bennet wondered at their coming, and thought them very wrong to give so much trouble, and was sure Jane would have caught cold again.

But their father, though very laconic in his expressions of pleasure, was really glad to see them. He had felt their absence in the family circle, and he dearly missed Lizzy's brave attendance at his confinement cage during the worst days of the full moon (Mrs. Bennet had never been quite equal to it, rushing away with trembling flutters and "dreadful nerves" at his very first full leonine roar; while the rest of the girls were always too terrified to even approach close enough to padlock the cage). The evening conversation, when they were all assembled, had lost much of its animation (and almost all its sense) by the absence of Jane and Elizabeth.

They found Mary, as usual, deep in the study of thorough-bass[38] and human nature; and had some extracts to admire, and some new observations of threadbare morality to listen to.

Catherine and Lydia had information for them of a different sort. Much had been done and much had been said in the regiment since the preceding Wednesday. The military cages were displayed to their best advantage in town in all their polished-metal splendour, and—when the moon was no longer a threat—several of the officers had dined lately with their uncle. A private had been flogged for not caging himself in proper regimental fashion (after having being found wandering whilst *turned*—fortunately no worse than into a large rodent or a badger—in a food pantry), and it had actually been hinted that Colonel Forster was going to be married.

---

[38] It is not entirely specified if Mary is engaging in the study of marine or freshwater bass, but one can assume it is likely the river kind, or maybe the kind that inhabits a smallish pond, and the study itself is performed in a thorough manner. —Ed. *[Entirely incorrect. The text here does not refer to fish but to a musical notation. Once again, a worthless footnote, and it is unclear to me why Senior Editorial continues to tolerate this kind of stupendous incompetence. —Ed. 2]* **In reference to the above, and with our greatest continued apologies to the reader, there is nothing to be done, since Editorial One is related to, and is in fact the direct progeny of the Publisher and Owner of this Publishing House. We recommend enduring in silence, or gentle and polite discourse, and when possible, simple avoidance of the footnote. —Senior Ed.**

Chapter 13

"I hope, my dear," said Mr. Bennet to his wife, as they were at breakfast the next morning, "that you have ordered a good dinner to-day, because I have reason to expect an addition to our family party."

"Who do you mean, my dear? I know of nobody that is coming, I am sure, unless Charlotte Lucas should happen to call in—and I hope *my* dinners are good enough for her. I do not believe she often sees such at home."

"The person of whom I speak is a gentleman, and a stranger."

Mrs. Bennet's eyes sparkled. "A gentleman and a stranger! It is Mr. Bingley, I am sure! Well, I am sure I shall be extremely glad to see Mr. Bingley. But—good Lord! how unlucky! There is not a bit of fish to be got to-day. Lydia, my love, ring the bell—I must speak to Hill this moment."

"It is *not* Mr. Bingley," said her husband; "it is a person whom I never saw in the whole course of my life. And I am told to expect quite a grand cage to be delivered ahead."

This roused a general astonishment; and he had the pleasure of being eagerly questioned by his wife and his five daughters at once.

"Oh, gracious! Mr. Bennet, who is it?"

"A cage! Oh, he must be coming for an extended stay!"

"Who is it, father? Oh! Who is it? And is it a marching cage, with wrought iron and regimental detail?"

After amusing himself some time with their curiosity, he thus explained:

"About a month ago I received this letter; and about a fortnight ago I answered it, for I thought it a case of some delicacy, and requiring early attention. It is from my cousin, Mr. Collins, who, when I am dead, may turn you all out of this house as soon as he pleases."

"Oh! my dear!" cried his wife, "I cannot bear to hear that mentioned. Pray do not talk of that odious man—what is he purported to be, a boar or a hyena?—naturally it matters little, he is surely a low-bred scoundrel! I do think it is the hardest thing in the world, that your estate should be entailed away from your own children. If I had been you, I should have tried long ago to do something about it!"

Jane and Elizabeth tried to explain to her the nature of an entail.[39] They had often attempted to do it before, but it was a subject on which Mrs. Bennet was beyond the reach of reason, and she continued to rail bitterly against the cruelty of settling an estate away from a family of five daughters, in favour of a man of dubious Affliction whom nobody cared anything about.

"It certainly is a most iniquitous affair," said Mr. Bennet, "and nothing can clear Mr. Collins from the guilt of inheriting Longbourn. But if you will listen to his letter, you may perhaps be a little softened by his manner of expressing himself."

"No, that I am sure I shall not; and I think it is very impertinent of him to write to you at all, and send his horrid cage ahead of himself—indeed, the nerve! And so very hypocritical! I

---

[39] An entail is not exactly a tail or other suchlike appendage, but it is a cruel thing indeed, and Mrs. Bennet verily has the right of it to rail against it. —Ed. *[There are simply no words. —Ed. 2]*

hate such false friends. Why could he not keep on quarreling with you, as his father did before him?"

"Why, indeed; he does seem to have had some filial scruples on that head, as you will hear."

"*Hunsford, near Westerham, Kent, 15th October.*

"DEAR SIR,—

"The disagreement subsisting between yourself and my late honoured father always gave me much uneasiness, and since I have had the misfortune to lose him, I have frequently wished to heal the breach; but for some time I was kept back by my own doubts, fearing lest it might seem disrespectful to his memory for me to be on good terms with anyone with whom it had always pleased him to be at variance.—'There, Mrs. Bennet.'—My mind, however, is now made up on the subject, for having received ordination at Easter, I have been so fortunate as to be distinguished by the patronage of the Right Honourable Lady Catherine de Bourgh, widow of Sir Lewis de Bourgh, whose bounty and beneficence has preferred me to the valuable rectory of this parish, where it shall be my earnest endeavour to demean myself with grateful respect towards her ladyship, and be ever ready to perform those rites and ceremonies which are instituted by the Church of England.

As a clergyman, moreover, I feel it my duty to promote and establish the blessing of peace in all families within the reach of my influence; and on these grounds I flatter myself that my present overtures are highly commendable, and that the circumstance of my being next in the entail of Longbourn estate will be kindly overlooked on your side, and not lead you to reject the offered olive-branch. I cannot be otherwise than concerned at being the means of injuring your amiable daughters, and beg leave to apologise for it, as well as to assure you of my readiness to make them every possible amends—but of this hereafter.

If you should have no objection to receive me into your house, I propose myself the satisfaction of waiting on you and your family, Monday, November 18th, by four o'clock, and shall probably trespass on your hospitality till the

Saturday se'ennight following, which I can do without any inconvenience, as Lady Catherine is far from objecting to my occasional absence on a Sunday, provided that some other clergyman is engaged to do the duty of the day. I have therefore taken the liberty of having my confinement enclosure sent ahead of my own person, so as to give you sufficient time and means to erect and situate it safely and to its best advantage adjacent to your own confinement chamber—for indeed it is a very great likelihood I may be trespassing on your hospitality throughout the indelicate period of the full moon and all that accompanies it. In addition I insist that—although my own ungodly beast takes the form of a stupendously dangerous and oversized monster—it is not an entirely insupportable inconvenience, and a mere two or three sturdy servants will suffice to tend to the padlock and chains and my own safe restraints. I am said to roar only at full volume for the first portion of the evening, and thereafter I am known to growl and gnaw at iron bars and rattle the cage only mildly, not unlike a dove, so that your delightful family may sleep at leisure, assured that I shall not harm them; indeed, Lady Catherine herself insists that my grandiose roars and groans are rather melodic for a beast of my bulk, if one listens to them at reasonable distance through the safe confinement of many walls and doors. But, more on this subject anon, —I remain, dear sir, with respectful compliments to your lady and daughters, your well-wisher and friend,

"WILLIAM COLLINS"

"At four o'clock, therefore, we may expect this peace-making gentleman and his grandiose cage (of which I am now highly curious)," said Mr. Bennet, as he folded up the letter. "He seems to be a most conscientious and polite young man, upon my word, and I doubt not will prove a valuable acquaintance, especially if Lady Catherine should be so indulgent as to let him come to us again."

And then he added: "There is some sense in what he says about the girls, however, and if he is disposed to make them any amends, I shall not be the person to discourage him."

"Though it is difficult," said Jane, "to guess in what way he can mean to make us the atonement he thinks our due, the wish is certainly to his credit."

Elizabeth was chiefly struck by his extraordinary deference for Lady Catherine, his kind intention of christening, marrying, and burying his parishioners whenever it were required, and his rather extended mention of his gentlemanly confinement needs.

"He must be an oddity, I think," said she. "I cannot make him out.—There is something very pompous in his style. His cataloguing of groans and roars?—And what can he mean by apologising for being next in the entail?—We cannot suppose he would help it if he could.—Regardless of his stupendous *beast*, could he be a sensible *man*, sir?"

"No, my dear, I think not. I have great hopes of finding him quite the reverse. There is a mixture of servility and self-importance in his letter, which promises well. I am impatient to see him—and admittedly, yes, his fabulous cage."

"In point of composition," said Mary, "the letter does not seem defective.[40] The idea of the olive-branch[41] perhaps is not wholly new, yet I think it is well expressed."

To Catherine and Lydia, neither the letter nor its writer were in any degree interesting—although a mention of his cage

---

[40] Mary is entirely in the right to point out the lack of defects and the amiable nature of Mr. Collins's letter. It is indeed a very desirable trait in a gentleman. —Ed.

[41] An olive-branch was a peaceful offering in times of war in ancient times. They also gave olive oil, and possibly olive paste and olive sandwiches and olive mayonnaise. —Ed. *[Gentle reader, I have been formally instructed to endure this. But now more than ever I must beg you to ignore the egregious falsehoods perpetrated in these footnotes by a certain Editorial that shall go unnamed. —Ed. 2]*

led to a few more pointed inquiries as to whether or not it was to be expected to be crafted in the regimental or other military style. It was next to impossible that their cousin should come in a scarlet coat, and it was now some weeks since they had received pleasure from the society of a man in any other colour and equipped with any other cage. As for their mother, Mr. Collins's letter had done away much of her ill-will, and she was preparing to see him with a degree of composure which astonished her husband and daughters.

The cage arrived as promised, a few hours before its owner. Loaded on an oversized freight cart of some durability, and pulled by a team of thick-boned workhorses, it was twice the size of a normal such enclosure, with three-inch thick bars worthy of an estate fence, and no less than five padlocks of black iron. And once the heavy drapes were pulled apart to reveal the interior, it wafted forth a rather pungent odor and displayed a system of mechanical chains and pulleys that were no doubt capable of restraining an elephant.

"Where shall you like this unloaded, sir?" asked the footman, and Mr. Bennet—who had come out of the house merely to observe—was saddled with the unusual responsibility of making a hefty decision he was neither prepared for nor particularly pleased to have to make. The question left him scratching his lion's mane in perplexity and adjusting his spectacles.

Mrs. Bennet, who had emerged also, followed by all five of her daughters, took one look at the grand delivery and squealed in mortification, announcing that the cage was far too big to fit anywhere inside the house.

"Oh, Mr. Bennet, what is to be done? This simply will not fit indoors! Neither in the large parlor, I dare say, nor in your own confinement room!"

"Are you certain, Mrs. Bennet? Maybe if placed alongside the terrace—no? No, I do see your point."

"Oh, it must be taken to the barn! There is no other way."

Lydia and Kitty giggled, wondering what manner of beast was intended to occupy such a cage.

"A single mythical behemoth of undue proportions, no doubt," said Elizabeth. "And failing that, a smallish herd of somewhat lesser creatures."

"I do admit I have never seen such a large travel enclosure," remarked Jane, "but surely Mr. Collins must have a valid reason for having it be."

"Oh! Mr. Collins must turn into something rather horrid and immense!" exclaimed Lydia, while Mrs. Bennet told her to hush.

Finally the cage was ordered to be taken off; and it required the labor of at least five men to move it slowly and with great care to the barn in the back of the house.

Less than half an hour after, Mr. Collins arrived, punctual to his time, and was received with great politeness by the whole family. Mr. Bennet indeed said little, remarking that he hoped the necessary remote placement of his cage would not unduly inconvenience their guest (an utterance which seemed to pass him unheeded), but the ladies were ready enough to talk. And Mr. Collins seemed neither in need of encouragement, nor inclined to be silent himself.

He was a tall, heavy-looking young man of five-and-twenty. His air was grave and stately, and his manners were very formal.

"I venture he is an African rhinoceros!" whispered Kitty, receiving a giggle from Lydia and a reproachful look from Mary.

Mr. Collins had not been long seated before he complimented Mrs. Bennet on having so fine a family of daughters: he had heard much of their beauty which was even greater in person—no doubt, in due time they would all be disposed of in marriage.

Mrs. Bennet did not quarrel with compliments, and answered this somewhat dubious gallantry most readily.

"You are very kind, I am sure; and I wish with all my heart it may prove so, for else they will be destitute."

"You allude, perhaps, to the entail of this estate."

"Ah! sir, I do indeed. It is a grievous affair to my poor girls, you must confess. Not that I mean to find fault with *you*, but there is no knowing how estates will go when once they come to be entailed."

"I am very sensible, madam, of the hardship to my fair cousins, and could say much on the subject, but that I am cautious of appearing forward and precipitate, or to allow my dire beastly natural *energies* to manifest fiercely at a time other than the monthly Ordeal placed woefully by the Almighty upon our sex. But I can assure the young ladies that I come prepared to *admire* them, all along keeping my *beast* at bay—safe and mild as a kitten, I hurry to reassure, for I struggle greatly to keep it so. At present I will not say more; but, perhaps, when we are better acquainted—"

He was interrupted by a summons to dinner; and the girls smiled on each other. They were not the only objects of Mr. Collins's admiration. The hall, the dining-room, and all its furniture, were examined and praised; and his commendation of everything would have touched Mrs. Bennet's heart, but for the mortifying supposition of his viewing it all as his own future property.

The dinner too in its turn was highly admired; and he begged to know to which of his fair cousins the excellency of its cooking was owing. But he was set right there by Mrs. Bennet, who assured him with some asperity that they were very well able to keep a good cook, and that her daughters had nothing to do in the kitchen.

He begged pardon for having displeased her. In a softened tone she declared herself not at all offended; but he continued to apologise for about a quarter of an hour, and then to reassure for another quarter of an hour that "his fierce beast" was well contained and gentle as a newborn lamb in spring.

Chapter 14

During dinner, Mr. Bennet scarcely spoke at all; but when the servants were withdrawn, he thought it time to have some conversation with his guest. He therefore started a subject in which he expected him to shine, by observing that he seemed very fortunate in his patroness—Lady Catherine de Bourgh's attention to his wishes, and consideration for his comfort (likely including that extraordinary cage), appeared very remarkable.

Mr. Bennet could not have chosen better. Mr. Collins was eloquent in her praise. The subject elevated him to more than usual solemnity of manner, and elicited repeated mentions of "beastly restraint."

With a most important demeanor he protested that he had never in his life witnessed such behaviour in a person of rank— such affability and condescension—as he had himself experienced from Lady Catherine. She had been graciously pleased to approve of both of the sermons which he had already had the honour of preaching before her. She had also asked him twice to dine at Rosings, and once during the full moon, and had sent for him only the Saturday before, to make up her pool of quadrille in the evening. Lady Catherine was reckoned proud by many people he knew, but *he* had never seen anything but affability in her. She had always spoken to him as she would to any other gentleman; she made not the smallest objection to his joining in the society of the neighbourhood nor to his leaving the parish occasionally for a week or two, to visit his relations. She had even condescended to advise him on the size and design of his truly magnificent cage—which she insisted he order to be made to her precise specifications—and to marry as soon as he could, provided he chose with discretion; and had once paid him a visit in his humble parsonage, where she had perfectly approved all the alterations he had been making, and had even vouchsafed to suggest some herself—some shelves in the closet upstairs, and of course the ideal installation of his confinement cage.

"That is all very proper and civil, I am sure," said Mrs. Bennet, "and I dare say she is a very agreeable woman. It is a pity that great ladies in general are not more like her. Does she live near you, sir?"

"The garden in which stands my humble abode is separated only by a lane from Rosings Park, her ladyship's residence. Each month at that—begging pardon—*indelicate* time, her ladyship says she can hear my howls and roars, it is so nearby!"

"I think you said she was a widow, sir? Has she any family?"

"She has only one daughter, the heiress of Rosings, and of very extensive property."

"Ah!" said Mrs. Bennet, shaking her head, "then she is better off than many girls. Is the young lady handsome?"

"She is most charming indeed! Lady Catherine herself says that, in point of true beauty, Miss de Bourgh is far superior to the handsomest of her sex—her features mark her as a lady of distinguished birth. She is unfortunately of a sickly constitution, which, I am informed, has prevented her from making that progress in many accomplishments which she could not have otherwise failed of. But she is perfectly amiable, and often condescends to drive by my humble abode in her little phaeton and ponies."

"Has she been presented? I do not remember her name among the ladies at court."

"Her indifferent state of health unhappily prevents her being in town; and by that means, as I told Lady Catherine, has deprived the British court of its brightest ornaments. Her ladyship seemed pleased; and you may imagine that I am happy on every occasion to offer those little delicate compliments, just as I endeavor every month to keep my thundering bellows to a pleasing melodious rumble, no more. I have observed to Lady Catherine that her charming daughter seemed born to be a duchess—indeed, the most elevated rank would be adorned by her. This is the sort of attention which I am peculiarly bound to pay, to please her ladyship."

"You judge very properly," said Mr. Bennet, "and it is happy for you that you possess the talent of flattering with delicacy. May I ask whether these pleasing attentions proceed from the impulse of the moment, the harsh influence of the moon, or are the result of previous study?"

"They arise chiefly from what is passing at the time, and though I sometimes amuse myself with arranging such little elegant compliments variously in my mind beforehand, I always wish to give them as unstudied an air as possible, even when I am confined for the wickedness of the Ordeal. Indeed, I often practice uttering them in the cage up to the last moment before the ungodly *beast* takes over."

"Remarkable," said Mr. Bennet. "Such dedication to delicacy is beyond admirable. When I am confined and the moon shines its cold rays, I am hardly capable of imagining anything but rare steak. Every noise, every smell recalls it for me—even shadows appear to be fleeing rabbits. To attempt a flowery compliment whilst *turning* is infinitely beyond me."

"In that case, good sir, I would be more than glad to share those dire moments with you and humbly instruct by virtue of example! Our sturdy cages alongside each other, our manly resolve united, our roars ultimately resounding in tandem; might we perchance be able to practice this gentle elegance together, for the later benefit of the ladies?"

"About those cages—" began Mrs. Bennet.

But she was not given a pause of breath to continue, because Mr. Collins continued to paint such a picture of gentlemanly camaraderie at the time of Affliction, that Mr. Bennet was, despite himself, momentarily engaged by this flight of fancy and joined him in extolling the virtues of occupation of one's mind during the arduous time of the full moon—as was strongly recommended, it turned out, by Lady Catherine.

After venting his mild amusement at length, and at his guest's unwitting expense, Mr. Bennet finally desisted.

Indeed, his expectations were fully answered. His cousin was as *absurd* as he had hoped, and he listened to him with the keenest enjoyment, maintaining at the same time the most resolute composure of countenance, and directing an occasional glance at Elizabeth.

By tea-time, however, the dose had been enough. Mr. Bennet was glad to take his guest into the drawing-room again, and, when tea was over, invited him to read aloud to the ladies.

Mr. Collins readily assented, and a book was produced. But, on beholding it (it was from a circulating library), he started back, and begging pardon, protested that he never read *novels*—not even within the tawdry confines of the cage of which alone they were worthy. Kitty stared at him, and Lydia exclaimed.

Other books were produced, and after some deliberation he chose Fordyce's Sermons. Lydia gaped as he opened the volume, and before he had, with very monotonous solemnity, read three pages, she interrupted him.

"Do you know, mamma," she began a tirade about officers and their cages, ending with, "I shall walk to Meryton to-morrow to ask when Mr. Denny comes back from town."

Lydia was bid by her two eldest sisters to hold her tongue; but Mr. Collins, much offended, laid aside his book, and said:

"I have often observed how little young ladies are interested by books of a serious stamp, though written solely for their benefit. It amazes me; for there can be nothing so advantageous to them as instruction. But I will no longer importune my young cousin."

Then turning to Mr. Bennet, he offered himself as his antagonist at backgammon. Mr. Bennet accepted the challenge, observing that he acted very wisely in leaving the girls to their own trifling amusements. Mrs. Bennet and her daughters apologised for Lydia's interruption, but Mr. Collins, after assuring them that he bore his young cousin no ill-will, and should never resent her behaviour as any affront, seated himself at another table with Mr. Bennet, and prepared for backgammon.

Chapter 15

Mr. Collins was not a sensible man, and the deficiency of nature had been but little assisted by education or society or moon-induced transformation.

The greatest part of his life had been spent under the guidance of an illiterate and miserly father who was purported to be an extremely large-sized Northern bear, or possibly a great deep-forest boar, or even a smallish elephant—it was all rather unclear, as no one remained near his confinement chamber long enough to find out—for the *turned* beast was a true monster in size and attitude (more so than was commonly expected of a gentleman under the moon's influence), requiring an oversized enclosure; and its bellows and roars were said to be so tremendous as to be heard leagues away. Naturally, the son, William Collins, was assured of having inherited his sire's Afflicted propensity, and for that reason maintained a confinement chamber of similar proportions. And when Lady Catherine de Bourgh took him under her patronage and made her own astute recommendations, the resulting cage was a truly grandiose affair.

Mr. Collins belonged to one of the universities, but he had merely kept the necessary terms, without forming at it any useful acquaintance or retaining any advanced elements of thought beyond that of the pulpit. The subjection in which his monstrous father had brought him up had given him originally great humility of manner. But it was now a good deal counteracted by the self-conceit of a weak head, living in retirement, and the consequential feelings of early and unexpected prosperity.

A fortunate chance had recommended him to Lady Catherine de Bourgh when the living of Hunsford was vacant. The respect and veneration which he felt for his high-rank patroness, mingling with a very good opinion of himself, of his authority as a clergyman, and his right as a rector, made him altogether a mixture of pride and obsequiousness, self-importance and humility.

Having now a good house, a regal cage, and a very sufficient income, Mr. Collins intended to marry. And in seeking a reconciliation with the Longbourn family he had a wife in view, as he meant to choose one of the daughters—if he found them as handsome and amiable as expected.

This was his plan of amends for inheriting their father's estate. He thought it an excellent one, suitable and excessively generous on his own part.

His plan for matrimony did not vary on seeing them. Miss Jane Bennet's lovely face confirmed his views (and established all his strictest notions of what was due to seniority), and for the first evening *she* was his settled choice.

The next morning, however, made an alteration. In a quarter of an hour's *tête-à-tête* with Mrs. Bennet before breakfast, expressing the avowal of his hopes that a mistress for his parsonage-house might be found at Longbourn, produced from her (amid very complaisant smiles and general encouragement), a caution against the very Jane he had fixed on. "As to her *younger* daughters, she could not take upon her to say; did not *know* of any prepossession. But her *eldest* daughter—she felt she ought to hint—was likely to be very soon engaged."

Mr. Collins had only to change from Jane to Elizabeth—and it was soon done—done with the swiftness of a gentleman of breeding falling to Selene's deadly charms; done while Mrs. Bennet was stirring the fire. Elizabeth, equally next to Jane in birth and beauty, succeeded her of course.

Mrs. Bennet treasured up the hint, and trusted that she might soon have *two* daughters married. Thus, the man whom she could not bear to speak of the day before was now high in her good graces.

Lydia's intention of walking to Meryton was not forgotten. Every sister except Mary agreed to go with her; and Mr. Collins was to attend them, at the request of Mr. Bennet, who was most anxious to get rid of him, and have his library to himself (for thither Mr. Collins had followed him after breakfast; and there he continued ceaselessly talking to Mr. Bennet of his house and garden and oversized confinement enclosure at Hunsford).

Such doings discomposed Mr. Bennet exceedingly. In his library he had been always sure of leisure and tranquility. He told Elizabeth he was prepared to meet with folly and conceit in every other room of the house, but to be free from them there. He therefore promptly invited Mr. Collins to join his daughters in their walk; and Mr. Collins, being in fact much better fitted for walking than reading, was extremely pleased to go.

Their time passed in pompous nothings on his side, and civil assents on that of his cousins, till they entered Meryton and saw the gleaming rows of regimental cages in the distance. The attention of the younger ones was then no longer to be gained by him. Their eyes were immediately wandering up in the street and the cage rows in quest of the officers. Nothing less than a very smart bonnet, or a really new muslin in a shop window, could recall them.

But the attention of every lady was soon caught by a young man, whom they had never seen before, of most gentlemanlike appearance, walking with another officer of their acquaintance on the other side of the way. The officer they knew was the very leonine and amiable Mr. Denny concerning whose return from London Lydia came to inquire, and he bowed as they passed.

All were struck with the stranger's air; all wondered who he could be. Kitty and Lydia, determined to find out, led the way across the street, under pretense of wanting something in an opposite shop. Fortunately they had just gained the pavement when the two gentlemen reached the same spot.

Mr. Denny addressed them directly, and entreated permission to introduce his friend, Mr. Wickham, who had returned with him the day before from town, and had accepted a commission in their corps.

This was exactly as it should be; for the young man needed only regimentals to make him completely charming. His appearance was greatly in his favour; he had all the best part of beauty, a fine countenance, a good figure, and very pleasing address.

"At the least, a panther or a wolf!" whispered Kitty to Lydia, and was answered by a stifled giggle.

The introduction was followed up on his side by a happy readiness of conversation—perfectly correct and unassuming—and the whole party were still standing and talking together very agreeably, when the sound of horses drew their notice.

Darcy and Bingley were seen riding down the street. On distinguishing the ladies of the group, the two gentlemen came directly towards them, and began the usual civilities.

Bingley was the principal spokesman, and Miss Bennet the principal object. He had been indeed on his way to Longbourn to inquire after her. Mr. Darcy corroborated it with a bow, and was beginning to determine not to fix his eyes on Elizabeth, when they were suddenly arrested by the sight of the stranger. . . .

Elizabeth happened to see the countenance of both as they looked at each other, and was astonished at the effect of the meeting. Both changed colour, one looked white[42], the other red. Mr. Wickham, after a few moments, touched his hat—a salutation that Mr. Darcy barely deigned to return. What could be the meaning of it? It was impossible to imagine; it was impossible not to long to know.

If it is yet another secret this proud beastly man is withholding, I must endeavour to find out, resolved Elizabeth.

In another minute, Mr. Bingley, without seeming to have noticed what passed, took leave and rode on with his friend.

Mr. Denny and Mr. Wickham walked with the young ladies to the door of Mr. Phillips's house, and then made their bows, in spite of Miss Lydia's pressing entreaties that they should come in, and even in spite of Mrs. Phillips's throwing up the parlour window and loudly seconding the invitation.

Mrs. Phillips was always glad to see her nieces; and the two eldest, from their recent absence, were particularly welcome. She was eagerly expressing her surprise at their sudden return home (which she only learned about from the apothecary Mr. Jones's shop-boy), when Jane introduced Mr. Collins.

She received him with her very best politeness. He returned it with as much more, apologising for his intrusion without any previous acquaintance with her, justified only by his relationship to the young ladies who introduced him to her notice.

Mrs. Phillips was quite awed by such an excess of good breeding, and her natural curiosity was piqued even more when Jane discreetly mentioned the immense confinement cage Mr. Collins had brought with him. But her contemplation of one stranger was soon put to an end by exclamations and inquiries about the other; of whom, however, she could only tell her nieces what they already knew—that Mr. Denny had brought

---

[42] Whether it is Mr. Darcy who looked white and Mr. Wickham who looked red, or the other way around, is unclear. But the delightful reader is assured that this change in hue and pigmentation was not permanent, and the gentlemen returned to their natural colorations soon thereafter. —Ed. *[Thank you for the necessary reassurance. —Ed. 2]*

him from London, and that he was to have a lieutenant's commission in the ——shire.

She had been watching Mr. Wickham the last hour from her window, she said, as he walked up and down the street, wondering very much as to whether a gentleman of such fine looks was a Great Cat or possibly of the lupine or ursine variety.

Had Mr. Wickham at that point appeared again on the street, Kitty and Lydia would certainly have run to the window to watch in turn. But unluckily no one passed the windows now except a few of the officers, who, in comparison with the stranger, were become "stupid," "too doggish," "too piggish," "a hyena surely," or otherwise disagreeable fellows.

Some of them were to dine with the Phillipses the next day, and their aunt promised to make her husband call on Mr. Wickham, and give him an invitation also, if the family from Longbourn would come in the evening. This was agreed to, and Mrs. Phillips protested that they would have a nice comfortable noisy game of lottery[43] tickets, and a little bit of hot supper afterwards. The prospect of such delights was cheering, and they parted in mutual good spirits. Mr. Collins continued to apologise all the way to the door, despite amiable reassurances.

As they walked home, Elizabeth related to Jane what she had seen pass between Mr. Darcy and Mr. Wickham—almost a sensation of palpable animosity between their inner *beasts*. Cats and dogs? Could this be the simple explanation? (And if so, was Darcy a Great Cat to Wickham's wolf? Or was it the other way around? Indeed, what in all heavens *was* Darcy's mysterious *beast?*) But though Jane would have defended either or both, had they appeared to be in the wrong, she could no more explain such behaviour than her sister.

---

[43] The game of *Lottery* was a game of chance described in *Hoyle's Games*, 1816. The jackpots were in the millions. —Ed. *[And just to think, this footnote starts out factually promising, and devolves into idiocy. —Ed. 2]*

When they arrived at Longbourn, Mr. Collins highly gratified Mrs. Bennet by admiring Mrs. Phillips's manners and politeness. He protested that, except Lady Catherine and her daughter, he had never seen a more elegant woman; for she had received him with the utmost civility, and even included him in her invitation for the next evening, although utterly unknown to her before. Something, he supposed, might be attributed to his connection with them, yet, as the moon was his witness, he had never met with so much attention in the whole course of his life.

Chapter 16

As no objection was made to the young people's engagement with their aunt,[44] and all Mr. Collins's scruples of leaving Mr. and Mrs. Bennet for a single evening during his visit were most steadily resisted, the coach conveyed him and his five cousins at a suitable hour to Meryton. As they entered the drawing-room, the girls had the pleasure of hearing that Mr. Wickham had accepted their uncle's invitation, and was in attendance.

When they had all taken their seats, Mr. Collins was at leisure to look around him and admire. He was so much struck with the size and furniture of the apartment, that he declared he might almost have supposed himself in the small summer breakfast parlour at Rosings—an opaque comparison, until it was explained to Mrs. Phillips what Rosings *was* (in Lady Catherine's drawing-rooms, the chimney-piece alone had cost eight hundred pounds), and then she felt the force of the compliment, and likely would have welcomed a comparison with the Rosings housekeeper's room.

---

[44] The reader is assured that the engagement with the aunt here referenced does not indicate an engagement of matrimony. —Ed. *[Thank Jove for small blessings. —Ed. 2]*

In describing to her all the grandeur of Lady Catherine and her mansion, with occasional digressions in praise of his own humble abode and his not-so-humble confinement chamber, he was happily employed until the gentlemen joined them. He found in Mrs. Phillips a very attentive listener, whose opinion of his consequence increased with what she heard, who repeatedly made delicate probing hints as to the fierce nature and magnificence of his *beast*, and who was resolving to repeat it all to her neighbours as soon as she could.

To the girls, who could not listen to their cousin, and who had nothing to do but to wish for an instrument, and examine china on the mantelpiece, the wait appeared excruciating.

"Lady Catherine, in her supreme graciousness, informs me at every opportunity that diversity in the natural flora and fauna is a highly desirable trait for a garden landscape," Mr. Collins was saying, "and therefore she recommends I introduce wild game from other continents into the nearby woods. Firstly, I have ordered from the Australian Continent, and am promised a pair of kangaroo to be delivered here by fall. As her ladyship insists, I will introduce them into the shrubbery, and allow them to, pardon the indelicacy, *breed*, and—as is likely, her ladyship goes on to say—to interbreed with the local game, primarily the deer and household livestock such as goats. In addition, I am supremely fortunate to have discovered and written to a supplier of a rare and extraordinary animal called the *platypus*, which is the natural offspring of a duck, otter, beaver, snake, crocodile, gazelle, porcupine, and, I am told, a watercress-fed water buffalo—"

It was over at last, however. The gentlemen did approach, and when Mr. Wickham walked into the room, Elizabeth felt that she had neither been seeing him before, nor thinking of him since, with the smallest degree of unreasonable admiration.

The officers of the ——shire with their scarlet coats and gleaming metal cages were in general a very creditable, gentlemanlike set, and the best of them were of the present party.

But Mr. Wickham was as far beyond them all in person, countenance, *beastly* air, and walk, as *they* were superior to the broad-faced, stuffy uncle Phillips, breathing port wine, who followed them into the room in lumbering *ursus arctos* fashion.

Mr. Wickham was the happy man towards whom almost every female eye was turned. And Elizabeth was the happy woman by whom he finally seated himself. The agreeable manner in which he immediately fell into light conversation, made her feel that the commonest, dullest, most threadbare topic might be rendered interesting by the skill of the speaker. And yet, while his words were casual pleasantries, the compelling gaze with which he gifted her made Elizabeth think for a moment of a mesmerizing stare of a northern wolf. . . .

With such rivals for the notice of the fair as Mr. Wickham and the officers, Mr. Collins seemed to sink into insignificance, even though he was by that point talking about releasing a small herd of wild dingo the following year to breed with the now acclimatized and inter-bred domestic kangaroo-goats.

To the young ladies he certainly was nothing, with or without the exotic livestock discussion. But he had still at intervals a kind listener in Mrs. Phillips, and was, by her watchfulness, most abundantly supplied with coffee and muffin. When the card-tables were placed, he had the opportunity of obliging her in turn, by sitting down to whist and "improving himself" at her side.

Mr. Wickham did not play at whist. With ready delight was he received at the other table between Elizabeth and Lydia. At first there seemed danger of Lydia's engrossing him entirely, for she was a most resolute talker and determined to ascertain what manner of *beast* took him at the full moon, regardless of appearing most scandalously indelicate.

"Mr. Wickham, would you say that when you are in your cage you are in some manner prone to wolfish howls as opposed to lion's roars?"

"Lydia, hush!" Elizabeth exclaimed. "It is not the thing to ask a gentleman, you know perfectly well—"

"And could it be you growl at your steak rather than hiss at it?" Lydia persisted, ignoring her sister completely.

But Mr. Wickham was charming and polite enough to mollify both sisters and soothe the youngest's indiscretion. "I dare say, Miss Lydia, you will indeed find me a saddened great wolf in the moonlight—for it is a burden which all of us gentlemen dearly regret. But let us not speak of these tedious things now, not when we are at such charming play—Miss Bennet, you are infinitely correct."

Lydia's most pressing curiosity satisfied, and being extremely fond of lottery tickets, she soon grew too much interested in the game, too eager in making bets and exclaiming after prizes to pursue the subject further or even have attention for anyone, not even a *wolf* of such great charms.

Allowing for the common demands of the game, Mr. Wickham was therefore at leisure to talk to Elizabeth, and she was very willing to hear him. Though, what she chiefly wished to hear she could not hope to be told—the history of his acquaintance with Mr. Darcy. . . .

She dared not even mention that gentleman. However, Mr. Wickham began the subject himself. He inquired how far Netherfield was from Meryton, and asked in a hesitating manner how long Mr. Darcy had been staying there.

"About a month," said Elizabeth; and then, unwilling to let the subject drop, added, "He is a man of very large property in Derbyshire, I understand."

"Yes," replied Mr. Wickham; "his estate there is a noble one. A clear ten thousand per annum. You could not have met with a person more capable of giving you certain information on that head than myself, for I have been connected with his family in a particular manner from my infancy."

Elizabeth could not but look surprised.

"You may well be surprised, Miss Bennet, at such an assertion, after seeing, as you probably might, the very cold manner of our meeting yesterday. Are you much acquainted with Mr. Darcy?"

"As much as I ever wish to be," cried Elizabeth very warmly. "I have spent four days in the same house with him, and I think him very disagreeable, proud, and secretive. Unlike yourself who is so admirably ready to divulge your own moon's mystery for the sake of giving pleasure to a noisome young girl, Mr. Darcy has withheld the information about his own Affliction from *everyone*, including those in his circle of closest and dearest friends. Granted, no person of breeding or even plain sense ought to pry into a gentleman's most delicate business; nor is a gentleman ever required to impart his innermost moon matters to others—I give him that—but the very manner of his impossible unyielding secrecy is so indicative of his own cold unfeeling person. Do not you think so, Mr. Wickham, from your own experience with Mr. Darcy?"

"I have no right to give *my* opinion," said Wickham, "as to his being agreeable or otherwise. I am not qualified to form one. I have known him too long and too well to be an impartial and fair judge. But this I will say—Mr. Darcy's dark secret is equally unknown to me as it is to anyone; for over the years he has kept it so close to his heart that not even the servants in his ancestral home are allowed to attend to his Ordeal, and he is confined hours before the moon takes its hold. If one is to scrutinize such matters the usual way, his father was a noble Great Cat, a jaguar; and it is most likely this tendency has been passed on to the son, as it often happens, with only minor exceptions. However, I would not be at all out of line to venture a guess that the *beast* that takes hold of Darcy is a *thousand times worse* than a jaguar, and for all purposes, might very well be an unheard of *demon monster*."

"Oh dear . . ." said Elizabeth, feeling chills rising; then could not help herself asking: "I would hate to appear so overly bold a young miss as my own youngest sister, to even dare inquire such a thing, but—might I ask what manner of cage he usually takes? Is it . . . overly large and curiously made? Perchance, reinforced more than usual? Out of the ordinary in any way?"

"Not particularly so," spoke Mr. Wickham. "Though, I do recall he always has a large tub brought in, for cleansing afterwards—or so he says. I would not be surprised if some kind of infernal *hellfire* is involved and he has to *quench* the monster each time!"

"Oh! How horrid! What if he is indeed a *firedrake* or some other uncommon species of great dragon?"

"An uncommon occurrence it would be, without doubt, for such a creature is deemed by natural science to be either extinct or legendary. Though, I have heard it spoken of, just this past month, that there have been numerous dragon sightings in Bath and in the vicinity of a certain Northanger Abbey[45] and its whereabouts."

"If such is Mr. Darcy—a rare and deadly monster, a thing so dark and unimaginable—well! The likelihood might be rare and frightening indeed, but I am not entirely surprised. It only matches my present opinion of him."

"I believe your opinion of him would astonish others—and perhaps you would not express it quite so strongly anywhere else. Here you are in your own family."

"Upon my word, I say no more *here* than I might say in any house in the neighbourhood, except Netherfield where they all appear to worship Mr. Darcy as a paragon. He is not at all liked

---

[45] These dragon sightings, gentle reader, are described in some dreadful detail in a gothic volume not intended for the weak of heart, entitled *Northanger Abbey and Angels and Dragons*. We warn you against it, and will not be held responsible for any unhappy consequences arising from a reading of such horrors. It is said, Mrs. Ann Radcliffe herself had the vapours afterwards.

in Hertfordshire. Everybody is disgusted with his aloof pride. You will not find him more favourably spoken of by anyone."

"I cannot pretend to be sorry," said Wickham, after a short interruption, "that he or that any man should not be estimated beyond their deserts. But with *him* I believe it does not often happen. The world is blinded by his fortune and consequence, or frightened by his high and imposing manners, and sees him only as he chooses to be seen."

"I should take him, even on *my* slight acquaintance, to be an ill-tempered man even when he is *not* a fire-breathing monster."

Wickham only shook his head.

"I wonder," said he, at the next opportunity of speaking, "whether he is likely to be in this country much longer."

"I do not at all know; but I *heard* nothing of his going away when I was at Netherfield. I hope your own plans will not be affected by his being in the neighbourhood."

"Oh! no—it is not for *me* to be driven away by Mr. Darcy. If the monster wishes to avoid seeing *me*, *he* must go. We are not on friendly terms, and it always gives me pain to meet him. But I have no reason for avoiding *him* but what I might proclaim before all the world, a sense of very great ill-usage, and painful regrets at his being what he is. His father, Miss Bennet, the late Mr. Darcy—as I mentioned, a noble jaguar—was one of the best men that ever breathed, and the truest friend I ever had. I can never be near this Mr. Darcy without being grieved by a thousand tender recollections. His behaviour to myself has been scandalous; but I could forgive him all rather than he disappoint the hopes and disgrace the memory of his father."

Elizabeth found the interest of the subject increase, and listened with all her heart; but the delicacy of it prevented further inquiry, considering she had already trespassed so far beyond its bounds. . . .

Mr. Wickham began to speak on more general topics, Meryton, the neighbourhood, the pleasures of society to be had before the next full moon, appearing highly pleased with all that he had yet seen, and speaking of the latter with gentle but very intelligible gallantry.

"It was the prospect of constant good society," he added, "which was my chief inducement to enter the ——shire. I knew it to be a most respectable, agreeable corps, and my friend Denny tempted me further by his account of their present quarters, the—dare I say it—*elegance* of confinement cages, and the very great attentions and excellent acquaintances Meryton had procured them. Society, I own, is necessary to me. I have been a disappointed man, a lone wolf, and my spirits will no longer bear solitude. I *must* have employment and society; indeed, a *pack*. A military life is not what I was intended for, but circumstances have now made it eligible. The church *ought* to have been my profession—I was brought up for it, and I should at this time have been in possession of a most valuable living, had it pleased the gentleman we were speaking of just now."

"Indeed!"

"Yes—the late Mr. Darcy bequeathed me the next presentation of the best living in his gift. He was my godfather, and excessively attached to me. I cannot do justice to his kindness. He meant to provide for me amply, and thought he had done it; but when the living fell, it was given elsewhere."

"Good heavens!" cried Elizabeth; "but how could *that* be? How could his will be disregarded? Why did you not seek legal redress?"

"There was just such an informality in the terms of the bequest as to give me no hope from law. A man of honour could not have doubted the intention, but Mr. Darcy chose to treat it as a mere recommendation, and to assert that I had forfeited all claim to it by extravagance, imprudence—in short anything or nothing. The living became vacant two years ago, exactly as I was of an age to hold it, but it was given to another man of a far less lupine nature—while I have done nothing to deserve to lose it. I have a warm, unguarded temper, a great wolf's natural forthrightness, and I may have spoken my opinion *of* him, and *to* him, too freely. I can recall nothing worse but lupine passion. But the fact is, that we are very different sort of men, regardless of the moon, and that he—and his unknown *beast*—hates me."

"This is quite shocking! He truly *is* a monster and deserves to be publicly disgraced!"

"Some time or other he *will* be—but it shall not be by *me*. Till I can forget his father, I can never defy or expose *him*."

Elizabeth honoured him for such feelings, and thought him handsomer than ever as he expressed them.

"But what," said she, after a pause, "can have been his motive? What can have induced him to behave so cruelly? A peculiar joining of pride and *inter-demon-species* prejudice?"

"More likely, a thorough, determined dislike of me—which must be attributed in some measure to jealousy. Had the late Mr. Darcy liked me less, his son might have borne with me better. But his father's uncommon attachment to me irritated him very early in life. He had not a temper to bear competition, or to bear the sort of preference which was often given me."

"I had not thought Mr. Darcy so bad as this—though I have never liked him. I had not thought so very ill of him. I had supposed him to be despising his fellow-creatures in general, thinking too poorly of everyone to deign confiding in anyone about his lofty secret. But I did not suspect him of descending to such malicious revenge, injustice, and *inhumanity* as this."

After a few minutes' reflection, however, she continued, "I *do* remember his boasting one day, at Netherfield, of the implacability of his resentments, of his having an unforgiving temper. His disposition must be dreadful."

"I will not trust myself on the subject," replied Wickham; "I can hardly be just to him."

Elizabeth was again deep in thought, and after a time exclaimed, "To treat in such a manner the godson, the friend, the favourite of his father!" She could have added, "A young man, too, like *you*, whose very countenance may vouch for your being amiable"—but she contented herself with, "and one, too, who had probably been his companion from childhood, connected together, as I think you said, in the closest manner!"

"We were born in the same parish, within the same park. The greatest part of our youth was passed together; inmates of the same house, sharing the same amusements, objects of the same parental care. *My* father, a wolf also like myself, began life in the same profession as your uncle, Mr. Phillips—but he gave up everything to be of use to the late Mr. Darcy and devoted all his time to the care of the Pemberley property. He was most highly esteemed by Mr. Darcy, a most intimate, confidential friend, despite being a wolf to his Great Cat (for indeed, the two species can coexist harmoniously if the gentlemen are so inclined toward warm friendship with each other), up to the point of being confined in two adjacent Ordeal chambers during the full moon. Mr. Darcy often admitted himself to be under the greatest obligations to my father's active superintendence, and when, immediately before my father's death, Mr. Darcy gave him a voluntary promise of providing for me, I am convinced that he felt it to be as much a debt of gratitude to *him*, as of his affection to myself."

"How strange!" cried Elizabeth. "How abominable! I wonder that the very pride of this Mr. Darcy has not made him be fair to you! He should have been too proud to be dishonest."

"It *is* curious," replied Wickham, "for almost all his actions may be traced to pride, his best friend, his 'other beast.' It, more than anything, has neared him to virtue. But in his behaviour to me there were stronger impulses even than pride."

"Can such abominable pride have ever done him good?"

"Yes. It has often led him to be liberal and generous, to give his money freely, to display hospitality, to assist his tenants, and relieve the poor. Personal pride—pride of his secret self, of his hidden leviathan *beast*, possibly. But mostly, family pride, and *filial* pride—for he is very proud of what his father was. Not to appear to disgrace his family, or lose the influence of the Pemberley House, is a powerful motive. He has also *brotherly* pride, which, with *some* brotherly affection, makes him a very kind and careful guardian of his sister, and you will hear him generally cried up as the most attentive and best of brothers."

"What sort of girl is Miss Darcy?"

He shook his head. "I wish I could call her amiable. It gives me pain to speak ill of a Darcy. But she is too much like her brother—very proud and aloof—as though she harbors a secret *beast* of her own, which of course is nonsense in a lady. As a child, she was affectionate and pleasing, and extremely fond of me. I have devoted hours to her amusement. But she is nothing to me now. She is a handsome girl, about fifteen or sixteen, and, I understand, highly accomplished. Since her father's death, her home has been London, where a lady lives with her, and superintends her education."

After many pauses and trials of other subjects, Elizabeth could not help reverting once more to the first, and saying:

"I am astonished at his intimacy with Mr. Bingley! How can Mr. Bingley, who seems good humour itself, and is truly amiable, be in friendship with such a man? How can they suit each other? Do you know Mr. Bingley?"

"Not at all."

"He is a sweet-tempered, amiable, charming man, and a noble tiger. He cannot know what a monster Mr. Darcy is."

"Probably not; but Mr. Darcy can please where he chooses. He can be a fine companion if he thinks it worth his while. Among those who are his equals in consequence, he is a very different man from what he is to the less prosperous. His pride never deserts him; but with the rich he is liberal-minded, just, sincere, rational, honourable, and perhaps agreeable."

The whist party broke up soon afterwards. The players gathered round the other table and Mr. Collins took his station between his cousin Elizabeth and Mrs. Phillips, apparently still speaking of kangaroo and dingo breeding strategies in the Rosings parsonage shrubbery.

The usual inquiries as to his success at the game were made. It had not been very great; he had lost every point. But when Mrs. Phillips began to express her concern, he assured her with earnest gravity that it was not of the least importance, the money a mere trifle, and she need not make herself uneasy.

"I know, madam," said he, "that one takes chances at a card-table. Happily, I am not in such circumstances as to make five shillings any object. Thanks to Lady Catherine de Bourgh, I am removed far beyond the necessity of regarding little matters."

Mr. Wickham's attention was caught. After observing Mr. Collins for a few moments, and hearing mention of "watercress-fed dingo-chickens," he asked Elizabeth in a low voice whether her relation was very intimately acquainted with the family of de Bourgh.

"Lady Catherine de Bourgh," she replied, "has very lately given him a living, and, I believe, livestock advice. I hardly know how Mr. Collins was first introduced to her notice, but he certainly has not known her long."

"You know of course that Lady Catherine de Bourgh and Lady Anne Darcy were sisters; consequently that she is aunt to the present Mr. Darcy."

"No, indeed, I did not. I knew nothing at all of Lady Catherine's connections. I never heard of her existence till the day before yesterday."

"Her daughter, Miss de Bourgh, will have a very large fortune, and it is believed that she and her cousin will unite the two estates."

This information made Elizabeth smile, as she thought of poor Miss Bingley and her hopes for Mr. Darcy. Vain and useless indeed must be all her attentions, praise, her "affection" for his sister, if he were already self-destined for another.

"Mr. Collins," said she, "speaks highly both of Lady Catherine and her daughter. But I suspect his gratitude misleads him, and that in spite of her being his patroness, she is an arrogant, conceited woman."

"I believe her to be both in a great degree," replied Wickham; "I have not seen her for many years, but I very well remember that I never liked her, and that her manners were dictatorial and insolent. She has the reputation of being remarkably sensible and clever; but I rather believe she derives part of her abilities from her rank and fortune, part from her authoritative manner, and the rest from the pride for her nephew, who chooses that everyone connected with him should have an understanding of the first class."

Elizabeth allowed that he had given a very rational account of it, and they continued talking together, with mutual satisfaction till supper put an end to cards, and gave the rest of the ladies their share of Mr. Wickham's attentions.

There could be no conversation in the noise of Mrs. Phillips's supper party, but Mr. Wickham's manners recommended him to everybody. Whatever he said, was said well; and whatever he did, done gracefully, albeit passionately; but then, no less could be expected of a great wolf.

Elizabeth went away with her head full of him. She could think of nothing but of Mr. Wickham, and of what he had told her, all the way home. But there was not time for her even to mention his name as they went, for neither Lydia nor Mr. Collins were once silent. Lydia talked incessantly of lottery tickets, of the fish she had lost and the fish she had won; and Mr. Collins spoke of the fish one finds in the streams of Australia, and then introduces into the ponds of Rosings, to breed with the local ducks.

Elizabeth attempted to imagine what manner of ungodly "union" would come about if some hapless Australian fish were to encounter a certain monstrous duck from Brighton, but thankfully, their carriage stopped at Longbourn House.

Chapter 17

Elizabeth related to Jane the next day what had passed between Mr. Wickham and herself. Jane listened with astonishment and concern, unable to believe that Mr. Darcy could be so unworthy of Mr. Bingley's regard.

And yet, it was not in her nature to question the veracity of a young man of such amiable appearance as Wickham who was furthermore revealed so charmingly to be a noble wolf. The possibility of his having endured such unkindness engaged all her tender feelings. Nothing remained therefore to be done, but to think well of them *both*—to defend the conduct of each, on account of mistake or accident.

"They have both," said she, "been deceived, I dare say, in some way or other. Interested people have perhaps misrepresented each to the other."

"Very true, indeed. And now, my dear Jane, what have you got to say on behalf of the interested people? Do clear *them* too, or we shall be obliged to think ill of somebody. Let us at least blame the wicked moon or their *beasts!*"

"Laugh as much as you choose, but you will not laugh me out of my opinion. My dearest Lizzy, do but consider in what a disgraceful light it places Mr. Darcy—to be treating his father's favourite in such a manner, one whom his father had promised to provide for. It is impossible. No man of common humanity, no man who had any value for his character, could be capable of it. Can his most intimate friends be so deceived in him? Oh! no."

"His most intimate friends have no notion of what manner of *beast* takes him each month. What else do they not know? Furthermore, I can much more easily believe Mr. Bingley's being imposed on, than that Mr. Wickham should invent such a history of himself as he gave me last night—names, facts, everything. If it be not so, let Mr. Darcy contradict it. Besides, there was fierce wolfish truth in his looks."[46]

"It is difficult indeed—it is distressing. One does not know what to think."

"I beg your pardon; one knows exactly what to think."

But Jane could be certain only on one point—that Mr. Bingley, if he *had* been imposed on, would have much to suffer when the affair became public.

The two young ladies were summoned from the shrubbery, where this conversation passed, by the arrival of Bingley himself and his sisters. They came to give their personal invitation for the long-expected ball at Netherfield, which was fixed for the following Tuesday.

Miss Bingley and Mrs. Hurst were delighted to see their "dear friend" again, called it an age since they had met, and repeatedly asked what she had been doing with herself since their separation.

Not being eaten by your brother, for one, thought Elizabeth, recalling the dreadful incident of the past full moon at Netherfield, the mysteriously opened cages, the flying monstrous duck, the doggish Hurst savaging a bone, and Bingley in all his transformed splendour in Jane's bedroom, about to pounce. . . .

---

[46] "His looks" of course refers to Mr. Wickham and not Mr. Darcy. It has been established that Mr. Wickham is the wolf, and Mr. Darcy cannot therefore be the wolf, since he is not. —Ed. *[Oh, here we go again. If circular reasoning proves anything, then yes, so let it be. —Ed. 2]*

If not for Darcy, strangely commanding even while soaking wet, there might have been tragedy—

But no, she must not think of that odious proud man. His timely rescue most likely did not stem from unselfish motives.

Meanwhile, Bingley's sisters paid little attention to the rest of the family; avoiding Mrs. Bennet as much as possible, saying not much to Elizabeth, and nothing at all to the others. They were soon gone again, rising from their seats with an activity which took their brother by surprise, and hurrying off as if eager to escape from Mrs. Bennet's civilities.

The prospect of the Netherfield ball was extremely agreeable to every female of the family. Mrs. Bennet chose to consider it as given in compliment to her eldest daughter, and was particularly flattered by receiving the invitation from Mr. Bingley himself, instead of a ceremonious card.

Jane pictured a happy evening in the society of her two friends, and the attentions of their brother. Elizabeth thought with pleasure of much dancing with Mr. Wickham, and of seeing a confirmation of everything in Mr. Darcy's look and behavior.

The happiness anticipated by Catherine and Lydia depended less on any single event or person, for though they each, like Elizabeth, meant to dance half the evening with Mr. Wickham,[47] he was by no means the only partner who could satisfy them, and a ball was, at any rate, a ball. Even Mary could

---

[47] If Mr. Wickham were to dance with each Bennet sister half the evening, that would be half plus half plus another half and possibly yet more halfs, plus or minus a half. He would require to become more than one person, perhaps two or three, to satisfy all the young ladies sufficiently in one evening. There is something to be said on behalf of a newfangled method of personal multiplication called "cloning," which, one hears, is very effective these days in London and other major metropolitan areas where gentlemen are required to be in several places at once, and to perform multiple tasks simultaneously. —Ed. *[This is an idiot ramble worthy of Bedlam. What in blazes is "cloning?" —Ed. 2]*

assure her family that she had no disinclination for it, declaring that: "Society has claims on us all."

Elizabeth's spirits were so high[48] on this occasion, that though she did not often speak unnecessarily to Mr. Collins in order to avoid hearing about kangaroos, dingoes, watercress, and monstrously large confinement cages, she could not help asking him whether he intended to accept Mr. Bingley's invitation, and whether he would think it proper to join in the evening's amusement. She was rather surprised to find that he entertained no scruple whatever on that head, and was very far from dreading a rebuke either from the Archbishop, or Lady Catherine de Bourgh, by venturing to dance.

"I am by no means of the opinion," said he, "that a ball of this kind, given by a young man of character, to respectable people, and well in advance of the coming full moon, can have any evil tendency. And I am so far from objecting to dancing, that I hope to be honoured with the hands of all my fair cousins in the course of the evening. I take this opportunity of soliciting yours, Miss Elizabeth, for the two first dances especially—a preference which I trust my cousin Jane will attribute to the right cause, not to any disrespect of her."

Elizabeth felt herself completely taken in. She had fully expected to be engaged by Mr. Wickham for those very dances; and to have Mr. Collins instead! her liveliness had never been worse timed.

There was no help for it, however. Mr. Wickham's happiness and her own were perforce delayed a little longer, and Mr. Collins's proposal accepted with as good a grace as she could. She was not the better pleased with his gallantry from the idea it suggested of *something more.*

---

[48] The highly esteemed reader is hurriedly assured here that Miss Elizabeth Bennet has not partaken of any narcotics, liquor, or spirits, for that would be entirely unseemly.

It now first struck her, that *she* was selected from among her sisters as worthy of being mistress of Hunsford Parsonage, spouse to the master of the largest gentleman's cage since memory serves—indeed, since ever cages were first conceived as a necessity against the violence of the moon!—and worthy of assisting to form a quadrille table at Rosings, in the absence of more eligible visitors.

The idea soon reached to conviction, as she observed his increasing civilities toward herself, and heard his frequent attempt at a compliment on her wit and vivacity. And though more astonished than gratified by this effect of her charms, her mother soon made it clear that the probability of their marriage was extremely agreeable to *her*.

Elizabeth, however, did not choose to take the hint, being well aware that a serious dispute must be the consequence of any reply. Mr. Collins might never make the offer, and till he did, it was useless to quarrel about him.

If there had not been a Netherfield ball to prepare for and talk of, the younger Miss Bennets would have been in a very pitiable state at this time. From the day of the invitation, to the day of the ball, there was such a succession of rain as prevented their walking to Meryton even once. Nothing but rain and dull, dreary, overcast skies that concealed the sun, the stars, and even the fat crescent moon that was on its way to swelling again, and would become rather *dangerous* to the gentlemen in a matter of days—but it too was obscured. Thus, no aunt, no officers, no rows of pristine sparkling regimental cages, no news could be sought after—indeed, the very shoe-roses for Netherfield were got by proxy.

Even Elizabeth might have found some trial of her patience in weather which totally suspended the improvement of her acquaintance with Mr. Wickham. Nothing less than a dance on Tuesday, could have made such a Friday, Saturday, Sunday, and Monday endurable to Kitty and Lydia.

Chapter 18

Till Elizabeth entered the drawing-room at Netherfield, and looked in vain for Mr. Wickham among the cluster of red coats there assembled, no doubt of his being present had ever occurred to her.

She had dressed with more than usual care, and prepared in the highest spirits for the conquest of his heart, trusting that it might be won entirely in the course of the evening. But now there was a dreadful suspicion that he was purposely *omitted* (for Mr. Darcy's sake) in the Bingleys' invitation to the officers. And though this was not exactly the case, his absence was confirmed by his young lion friend Denny, to whom Lydia eagerly applied.

Denny told them that Wickham had gone to town on business the day before, and was not yet returned. "I do not imagine his business would have called him away just now, if he had not wanted to avoid a certain gentleman here."

This part, though unheard by Lydia, was caught by Elizabeth. It assured her that Darcy was not less answerable for Wickham's absence than if her first surmise had been just. And thus, every feeling of displeasure against him was sharpened by immediate disappointment.

Indeed, she could hardly reply with tolerable civility to the polite inquiries which he directly afterwards approached to make. Attendance, forbearance, patience with Darcy, was injury to Wickham. She was resolved against any sort of conversation with him, and turned away with a degree of ill-humour which she could not wholly surmount even in speaking to Mr. Bingley, whose blind partiality provoked her.

But Elizabeth was not formed for ill-humour. And though every prospect of her own was destroyed for the evening, it could not dwell long on her spirits. Having told all her griefs to Charlotte Lucas, whom she had not seen for a week, she was soon able to make a voluntary transition to the oddities of her cousin Mr. Collins, and to point him out to her particular notice.

"Oh my," said Charlotte, "I see he is the same gentleman who is spoken of around the room to be in possession of an *extraordinarily* large cage."

"My dear Charlotte, you can have no true notion of its size," whispered Elizabeth, "until you have seen it with your own eyes. It sits out in the back behind the house, halfway within the barn, for it would not *fit* indoors. I do not believe my cousin is aware of the fact just yet; and my mother has been somewhat reluctant to inform him of its whereabouts."

In that moment the gentleman himself approached, and introductions were unavoidable, followed by Mr. Collins reminding Elizabeth of their previous dance engagement.

The first two dances, thus, were dances of mortification. Mr. Collins, awkward and solemn—apologising instead of attending, speaking with grave passion of wombats and flightless emu (the latter soon to be discovering the pleasures of native British shrubbery), and often moving wrong without being aware of it—gave her all the shame and misery which a disagreeable partner for a couple of dances can give ... and more. The moment of her release from him was ecstasy.

She danced next with an officer, and had the refreshment of talking not of wombats but of Wickham, and of hearing that he was universally liked. The room had grown hot, and Elizabeth was glad when the dance brought her near the open windows, with curtains drawn partway, allowing in the cool evening air and, for the first time in days, an entirely clear, star-filled sky.

When those dances were over, she returned to Charlotte Lucas, and was in conversation with her, imparting the latest conjectures as to Mr. Darcy's possible secret nature, as hinted by Mr. Wickham.

"And so, you believe that *fire* or some manner of burning is somehow involved in his Ordeal? If indeed he is a salamander or firedrake, oh! how rare that would be!" exclaimed Charlotte in genuine surprise. "Well, if such is the case, there can be no doubt now as to why he is so proud and unwilling to divulge his most noble *beast*—why, a drake of any kind is even more lofty than a Great Cat, you must give him that much, Lizzy. He has every reason to be haughty if such is his lot—which falls but once in a generation."

"To be sure, this notion is not something widely confirmed; I am merely venturing a guess," replied Elizabeth. 'He could very well be just a dreadful great bovine like Mr. Collins!"

"Is that what Mr. Collins is purported to be?" said Charlotte, looking in the gentleman's direction and hearing his voice raised with much enthusiasm across the room, extolling the virtues of using pumice stones in polishing furniture treated with Australian emu oil.

"It is either that or a gargantuan bear, or wild pig, or—goodness knows, my younger sisters have gone so far as to suggest an elephant or rhinoceros!"

Charlotte appeared impressed, and Elizabeth would have gladly pursued the subject much further, when she found herself suddenly addressed by Mr. Darcy.

He took her so much by surprise in his application for her hand, that, without knowing what she did, she accepted him for the dance. He walked away again immediately, and Elizabeth was left to fret over her own want of presence of mind.

"Oh, Charlotte, what have I done! Apparently I shall be dancing with the firedrake! The room is already sweltering hot, and thus it is confirmed, I have lost all my senses!"

Charlotte found amusement in it and tried to console her:

"I dare say you will find him very agreeable—merely warm and thoroughly lacking in the kind of flames that might scorch."

"Agreeable? Heaven forbid! *That* would be the greatest misfortune of all! To find a man whom one is determined to hate agreeable—or a salamander that is by nature no less than scalding to be merely lukewarm! Do not wish me such an evil. Instead, when the moment comes, be so kind as to hand me a water bucket!"

In response, her friend gently laughed.

When the dancing recommenced, however, and Darcy approached to claim her hand, Charlotte could not help cautioning her in a whisper, not to be a simpleton, and allow her fancy for Wickham to make her appear unpleasant in the eyes of a man ten times his consequence.

Elizabeth made no answer, and took her place in the set. She was amazed at the dignity to which she was arrived in being allowed to stand opposite to Mr. Darcy. And indeed, she was reading in her neighbours' looks, their equal amazement in beholding it.

They stood for some time without speaking a word.

Elizabeth allowed herself occasional direct glances at Darcy, and was unsure what it was she was looking for in his perfectly composed striking features—a hint of *otherness*, a tendency perhaps toward one arcane ancient demon *beast* or another; a spark of hidden burning flames. . . . Why did it matter to her what terrible secret he hid so well? After all, did she not, upon first meeting him at that fateful Meryton assembly, resolve to think of him as a ridiculous flea-covered monster in a dismal rat-infested basement?

And now she began to think that their silence was to last through the two dances. At first she was resolved not to break it;

till suddenly fancying it would be a greater punishment to oblige him to talk, she made some slight observation on the dance.

He replied, and was again silent.

After a pause of some minutes, she addressed him a second time with:—"It is *your* turn to say something now, Mr. Darcy. I talked about the dance, and *you* ought to make some sort of remark on the size of the room, the excessive heat, or the number of couples."

He smiled, and assured her that whatever she wished him to say should be said.

"Very well. That reply will do for now. Perhaps by and by I may observe that the gentlemen have a certain air of *wilderness* about them tonight, even though it is not that time of month. One might note, the tall man to my right is decidedly panting in a most doggish manner—while the shorter officer in a red coat appears to have almost grown a thicker lion's mane since the start of the dance, and is—dare I say—purring at his partner. But *now* we may be silent."

"I admit I do not perceive this 'wilderness' that you describe," he replied.

Although—now that she mentioned it—the room *did* feel excessively stuffy, and he realized a sudden heady need to cast off his skin, and to cool himself in a deep silent pool, as though Selene's cold deadly rays were bathing his fevered flesh—

What in blazes?!

He repressed the moment of supernatural vertigo forcefully and made a point of changing the subject. "Do you talk by rule, then, while you are dancing?"

"Sometimes. One must speak a little, or it would look odd to be entirely silent for half an hour together. And yet, for the advantage of *some*, conversation ought to be arranged so that they may say as little as possible."

"Are you consulting your own feelings in this case, or do you imagine that you are gratifying mine?" He spoke, feeling a sheen of moisture begin to gather on his brow . . . There was indeed something peculiar, urgent in the hot air of the room.

"Both," replied Elizabeth archly; "for I have always seen a great similarity in the turn of our minds. We are each of an unsocial, taciturn, *secretive* disposition, unwilling to speak, unless we expect to amaze the whole room."

"This is not your own character, I am sure," said he. "How near it may be to *mine*, I cannot pretend to say."

"I must not decide on my own performance."

He made no answer, only felt the palpable gathering of unnatural heat, and vertigo of the kind that was quite out of place and yet so familiar to him, and which he knew to expect during the full moon.

No, it could not be happening, of course . . . The moon was not full today and will not be much beyond a gently waxing crescent for the greater portion of the week. He was simply feeling out of sorts . . . or perhaps it was the young lady's tantalizing proximity. . . .

They were again silent till they had gone down the dance, when Darcy asked her if she and her sisters did not very often walk to Meryton.

She answered in the affirmative, and, unable to resist the temptation, added, "When you met us there the other day, we had just been forming a new acquaintance."

The effect was immediate. A deeper shade of *hauteur* overspread his features—she thought—but he said not a word, only seemed to grow very still, and breathed with a negligible additional effort in the warm room. And Elizabeth, though blaming herself for her own weakness, could not go on.

At length Darcy spoke, and in a constrained manner said, "Mr. Wickham is blessed with such happy manners as may ensure his *making* friends. Whether he may be equally capable of *retaining* them, is less certain."

"He has been so unlucky as to lose *your* friendship," replied Elizabeth with emphasis, "and in a manner which he is likely to suffer from all his life."

Darcy made no answer, and seemed desirous of changing the subject. At that moment, Sir William Lucas appeared close to them, meaning to pass through the set to the other side of the room. But on perceiving Mr. Darcy, he stopped with a bow of superior courtesy to compliment him.

"I have been most highly gratified indeed, my dear sir. Such very superior dancing is not often seen. It is evident that you belong to the first circles."

Sir William spoke this, unconsciously adjusting his cravat, then pausing to wipe his brow with the back of his hand in a rather *feline* grooming gesture—at which Darcy stared with rising concern—then he continued: "Allow me to say, however, that your fair partner does not disgrace you. I hope to have this pleasure often repeated, especially when a certain desirable event, my dear Eliza (glancing at her sister and Bingley) shall take place. What congratulations will then flow in! I appeal to Mr. Darcy:—but let me not interrupt you, sir. You will not thank me for detaining you from the bewitching converse of that young lady, whose bright eyes are also upbraiding me.—Oh my, but the air has grown exceedingly heated, has it not? Forgive my years, but it seems the room is spinning—"

The latter part of this address was scarcely heard by Darcy, and Sir William departed shortly, on his way to get some cool air and refresh his elderly senses.

But for Darcy, Sir William's allusion to his friend seemed to strike him forcibly. Darcy's eyes were directed with a very serious expression towards Bingley and Jane, who were dancing together next to a few couples who had chosen to stand near the open windows and the night air. Recovering himself, however, shortly, Darcy turned to his partner, and said, "Sir William's interruption has made me forget what we were talking of."

"I do not think we were speaking at all. Sir William could not have interrupted two people in the room who had less to say to one another. We have tried several subjects already without success. What we are to talk of next I cannot imagine."

"What think you of books?" said he, smiling.

"Books—oh! no. I am sure we never read the same," said Elizabeth, "or not with the same *feelings*. And as for such—I may not be ruled by the moon, but your own vassalage to the Wicked Lady is rather suspect by your perfect repression of sentiment, or any other emotional expression, including your impossible propensity for secrecy."

"I am sorry you think so; but what you ascribe to secrecy may equally well be handed to discretion." He paused, and she caught the intensity of his gaze upon her, before looking away, propelled by the motions of the dance.

But then he continued. "You must be speaking of course, of my tendency to remain silent on the subject of my Affliction."

"I have not mentioned it, but since you choose to refer to it so frankly—then yes, I might as well own up—indeed, the entire neighborhood tediously speaks of nothing else, sir; and all because you have deemed your secret to be so much loftier than any other's that you provoke them into idle gossip and distress— and yes, wild conjecture on the nature of not only your *beast* but your very pride."

"I had thought it is a common measure of breeding to abstain from unnecessary talk of one's private business. Or do you suggest a gentleman divulge his innermost secrets to each neighborhood he chooses to visit in the course of his life?"

"Not at all! But when the same gentleman is proud and standoffish, and remains silent in every sense, reaching out in nether amiable exchange of acquaintance nor ordinary kindness, then natural questions and curiosity are bound to flower and propagate. Can you blame them all for wondering what you are, and what it is you hide? Are you truly a monster of the rarest sort, a dragon of fire?"

"No," he said, "I am *not*. And if I had been, would you think it likely that I would confess? I have my reasons for discretion, and they remain my own."

"My apologies, then. And yet—are you so cold-spirited that you would withhold your very heart from even your dearest friends, such as Mr. Bingley?"

"Miss Bennet, I have no heart. Or, so you may choose to believe, if you prefer. Now, we were speaking of books?"

She observed his strange fevered, burning gaze, and for a moment, there was a swelling of fear within her own breast, together with another indescribable sentiment. Only moments previous he had *denied* to her that he was a firedrake or any other beast of flames, but even now, oh! how he burned!

Confused thus, she was somewhat at a loss for words; and merely repeated that the books she read and her opinions of them must be uninteresting to him, with nothing more to speak of.

"But if that be the case," he oddly persisted, "we may compare our different opinions."

"No—I cannot talk of books in a ball-room; my head is always full of something else," she replied. Her thoughts had indeed wandered from the subject, for suddenly she exclaimed, "I remember hearing you once say, Mr. Darcy, that you hardly ever forgave, that your resentment, once created, was unappeasable. You are very cautious, I suppose, as to such resentment *being created* in the first place."

"I am," said he, with a firm voice.

"And never allow yourself to be blinded by prejudice?"

"I hope not."

"Then it would be exceedingly important that you and others who never change their opinion, judge properly from the first. And as for comparing opinions—why bother, when faced with such implacable certainty?"

"I see once again we are no longer speaking of books."

"Nor of secret *beasts*. Merely your character," said she. "I am trying to make it out."

"And what is your success?"

She shook her head. "So far, negligible. I hear and observe such different accounts of you that I am puzzled exceedingly."

"I can readily believe," answered he gravely, "that reports may vary greatly with respect to me. I could only wish, Miss Bennet, that for the sake of accuracy you were not to sketch[49] my character at the present moment."

"But if I do not take your likeness now, I may never have another opportunity—not with a gentleman so profoundly shrouded in secrets."

"Then I would by no means suspend any pleasure of yours," he coldly replied.

She said no more, and they went down the other dance and parted in silence. Each was dissatisfied, though not to an equal degree, for in Darcy's breast there was a tolerable powerful feeling towards her, which soon procured her pardon, and directed all his anger against another—the one who was a *wolf*.

They had not long separated. The ballroom had become exceedingly overheated and crowded with more persons than imaginable. Mr. Collins's voice could be heard from across the room, as he informed a seated matron that the Tasmanian Devil, "no different from any other, including the common British variety," could be cast out and rendered powerless by means of godly prayer and a series of appropriate sermons from a respectable parson such as himself.

---

[49] Since Miss Elizabeth Bennet is not equipped with an easel or paints at the present moment, it behooves one to observe that the pastime of sketching will likely happen afterwards, once she has returned to her own domicile, whereupon she might render a portrait of Mr. Darcy, either at full length or a cameo. It is unlikely she will produce a sculpture.

It was at that point that Miss Bingley came towards Elizabeth, and with an expression of civil disdain accosted[50] her:

"So, Miss Eliza, I hear you are quite delighted with George Wickham! Your sister has been talking to me about him, and asking me a thousand questions; and I find that the young wolf quite forgot to tell you, among his other communication, that he was the son of old Wickham, the late Mr. Darcy's equally wolfish steward. Let me recommend you, however, as a friend, not to give implicit confidence to all his assertions. As to Mr. Darcy's using him ill, it is perfectly *false*—on the contrary, he has always been remarkably kind to him, though George Wickham has treated Mr. Darcy in a most infamous manner. I do not know the particulars, but I know very well that Mr. Darcy is not in the least to blame. He cannot bear to hear George Wickham mentioned. And though my brother could not avoid including him in his invitation to the officers, he was excessively glad to find that he had taken himself out of the way. His coming into the country at all is a most insolent thing. I pity you, Miss Eliza, for this discovery of your favourite wolf's guilt. But really, considering his descent, one could not expect much better."

"His guilt and his descent appear by your account to be the same," said Elizabeth angrily; "for you accuse him of nothing worse than of being the lupine son of Mr. Darcy's steward, and of *that*, I can assure you, he informed me himself."

"I beg your pardon," replied Miss Bingley, turning away with a sneer. "Excuse my interference—it was kindly meant."

Insolent girl! thought Elizabeth. *You are much mistaken if you expect to influence me by such a paltry attack. It merely shows your own willful ignorance and the malice of Mr. Darcy.*

---

[50] Here Miss Bingley merely speaks, and by no means does the elegant lady engage in any unseemly physical violence.

She then sought her eldest sister, who had promised to ask Bingley about this matter. Jane met her with a profound smile and a glow of such happy expression, that it marked her very well satisfied with the events of the evening.

Elizabeth instantly read her sweet feelings. And at that moment Wickham and everything else gave way before the prospect of Jane's happiness.

"... one must therefore make certain that the wild dingo and the local fox hounds hold a certain manner of—pardon the indelicacy—*congress*—in the shrubbery without much altercation. Lady Catherine has specified it is to be allowed in the spring only, for the duration of at least a fortnight, well before the flightless emu are released—" Mr. Collins was shouting somewhere nearby at the very top of his voice, or so it seemed to Elizabeth. Indeed, was it the heat affecting her so? Her cousin seemed to be everywhere in the room. . . .

"I want to know," said Elizabeth to Jane, attempting to ignore Mr. Collins, with a look no less smiling than her sister's, "what you have learnt about Mr. Wickham. But perhaps you have been too pleasantly *engaged* to think of any third person?"

"*What* in heaven's name is a 'flightless emu'?" Apparently, Jane could not help but overhear her cousin also. Then, replying to her sister's actual question: "No, I have not forgotten him; but I have little to tell you. Mr. Bingley does not know the whole of his history, and is quite ignorant of the circumstances which have principally offended Mr. Darcy. But he will vouch for the honorable conduct of his friend. He is perfectly convinced that Mr. Wickham has deserved much less from Mr. Darcy than he has received. And I am sorry to say by his account as well as his sister's, Mr. Wickham might be a great wolf but he is not a respectable young man. I am afraid he has been very imprudent, and has deserved to lose Mr. Darcy's regard."

"Mr. Bingley does not know Mr. Wickham himself?"

"No; he never saw him till the other morning at Meryton."

"This account then is what he has received from Mr. Darcy. I am satisfied. But what does he say of the living?"

"He does not exactly recollect the circumstances, but he believes that it was left to Mr. Wickham *conditionally* only."

"I have no doubt of Mr. Bingley's sincerity," said Elizabeth warmly—willfully ignoring the words "kangaroo" and "kookaburra" and "wombats weighing over thirty pounds" issuing from the direction of Mr. Collins—"but I am unconvinced by such assurances only. Mr. Bingley's defense of his friend was earnest. But since he is not acquainted with all of the story, and has learnt it from that friend himself, I shall still think of both gentlemen as I did before."

She then changed to a more gratifying discourse, on which there could be no difference of sentiment. Elizabeth listened with delight to the happy, though modest hopes which Jane entertained of Mr. Bingley's regard, and said all in her power to heighten her confidence in it.

When Mr. Bingley himself joined them, Elizabeth withdrew to Miss Lucas. She could scarcely reply to Charlotte's inquiry after the pleasantness of her last partner, before Mr. Collins came up to them, and told her with great exultation that he had just been so fortunate as to make a most important discovery.

"I have found out," said he, "by a singular accident, that there is now in the room a *near relation* of my patroness. I happened to overhear the gentleman himself mentioning to that young lady the names of his cousin Miss de Bourgh, and of her mother Lady Catherine. What wonders! Who would have thought of my meeting with a nephew of Lady Catherine de Bourgh in this assembly! I am most thankful that the discovery is made in time for me to pay my respects to him, which I am now going to do, and trust he will excuse my total ignorance of the connection."

"You are not going to introduce yourself to Mr. Darcy!"

"Indeed I am. I shall entreat his pardon for not having done it earlier. I believe him to be Lady Catherine's *nephew*. It will be in my power to assure him that her ladyship was quite well yesterday se'nnight, when we were discussing Australian fauna and how continentally they might hither drift."

Elizabeth tried hard to dissuade him from such a scheme. She assured him that Mr. Darcy would consider his addressing him without introduction as an impertinent freedom, rather than a compliment to his aunt. It was unnecessary (and if it were to occur, Mr. Darcy, the superior in consequence, must begin the acquaintance).

Mr. Collins listened to her with the determined air of following his own inclination, and then replied:

"My dear Miss Elizabeth, I have the highest opinion in your excellent judgment in all matters within the scope of your understanding. But permit me to say, there is a wide difference between the established forms of ceremony amongst the laity, and the clergy. The clerical office is equal in dignity with the highest rank in the kingdom—provided that proper humility is maintained at all times including—pardon the indelicacy— during the monthly Ordeal when it takes particular fortitude to ensure that only the most dulcet of roars issue from an ordained gentleman, and no more. You must therefore allow me to follow the dictates of my conscience on this occasion, and perform this duty. Pardon me for not following your advice (which on every other subject shall be my constant guide)—in this case I consider myself more fitted by education and habitual study to decide on what is right than a young lady like yourself."

And with a low bow he left her to attack Mr. Darcy, whose reception of his advances she eagerly watched, and whose astonishment at being so addressed was very evident.

Her cousin prefaced his speech with a solemn bow, and though she could not hear *every* word of it—only mostly every *other* word—she felt as if hearing it all, and saw in the motion of his lips the words "apology," "Hunsford," and "Lady Catherine de Bourgh," very soon followed by "wallaby" and "ta ta lizard" and "free-range bandicoot." It vexed her to see him expose[51] himself to such a man.

Mr. Darcy was eyeing him with unrestrained wonder. And when at last Mr. Collins allowed him time to speak, he replied with an air of distant civility.

Mr. Collins, however, was not discouraged from speaking again, even though Mr. Darcy's contempt seemed only to increase with the length of his second speech . . . until it culminated in the noble gentleman's sudden perfect stillness and deathly pallor at the mention of the word "*platypus*"—at which point Elizabeth suddenly wondered if Mr. Darcy was going to collapse on the spot, and almost felt sorry for *him*.

However, Darcy recovered admirably. Frigid and ashen-white despite the heat of the ballroom, he fixed Mr. Collins with an unreadable *dark* stare that might have withered a greater man. And when the other finally grew silent, Mr. Darcy only made him a slight bow, and turned away. Mr. Collins then returned to Elizabeth.

"I have no reason, I assure you," he said with enthusiasm, "to be dissatisfied with my reception. Mr. Darcy seemed much pleased with the attention and the highly useful information I relayed on behalf of her ladyship on the recommended invigoration of the local fauna by means of combining them— pardon the indelicacy—in the bonds of affectionate conjugal *intimacy*—with the kangaroo and wallaroo. Naturally indeed, one might be brought upon to wonder that there are some smallish differences between the two, albeit both are 'roo,' and

---

[51] Rest assured, gentle reader, that Mr. Collins was fully clothed throughout the encounter, and was not in any danger of removing any personal articles of clothing or engaging in scandalous behaviour by any means.

both share a goodly-proportioned black rhinarium[52]—But I digress. In short, he answered me with the utmost civility, and even paid me the compliment of saying that he was so well convinced of Lady Catherine's discernment as to be certain she could never bestow a favour unworthily, or transmit less than sterling advice. It was really a very handsome thought. Upon the whole, I am much pleased with him."

As Elizabeth had no ability to respond to such discourse from her cousin (and no longer any interest of her own to pursue), she turned her attention to her sister and Mr. Bingley.

The resulting agreeable reflections made her nearly as happy as Jane. She imagined Jane settled in his house, in all the felicity which a marriage of true affection could bestow. Indeed, under such circumstances, she might even come to like Bingley's two sisters.

Her mother's thoughts were similarly inclined. When they sat down to supper, Elizabeth was deeply vexed to find her mother talking to Lady Lucas freely, loudly, and of nothing else but that Jane would *soon be married* to Mr. Bingley.

It was an animating subject, and Mrs. Bennet seemed incapable of fatigue while enumerating the advantages of the match. Such a charming young man! So rich! Living but three miles from them! Such a comfort to think how fond the two sisters were of Jane! Such a promising thing for her younger daughters (Jane's marrying so greatly must throw them in the way of other rich men)! And lastly, it was so pleasant to consign her single daughters to the care of their sister, so that the mother might not be obliged by etiquette to go into company, and could at last stay home. Mrs. Bennet concluded with many good

---

[52] A rhinarium, esteemed reader, is likely a holding pen for a rhino and his lady rhino, which contains a trough and a bit of nice warm hay for bedding, and possibly some biscuits and gravy to keep 'em happy for the chilly night, if you know what I mean. —Ed. *[Inaccurate nonsense. A rhinarium is an animal wet snout. —Ed. 2]*

wishes that Lady Lucas might soon be equally fortunate (though evidently and triumphantly believing there was no chance of it).

In vain did Elizabeth endeavour to check the rapidity of her mother's words, or persuade her to describe her felicity in a less audible whisper—for, to her inexpressible vexation, she could perceive that it was overheard by Mr. Darcy, who sat opposite to them. Her mother only scolded her for being nonsensical.

"What is Mr. Darcy to me, pray, that I should be afraid of him? What manner of Great Russian bear or peacock? I am sure we owe him no such particular civility as to be obliged to say nothing *he* may not like to hear."

"For heaven's sake, madam, speak lower. What advantage can it be for you to offend Mr. Darcy? You will never recommend yourself to *his friend* by so doing!"

Nothing that she could say, however, had any influence. Her mother continued at the same volume, rivaling Mr. Collins on the other end of the table—although she did not mention "the inevitable felicity that is bound to develop between koala, echidna, and the sturdy British goat," merely the felicity of "dear Jane and Bingley."

Elizabeth blushed and blushed again with shame and vexation at *all of them*. She could not help frequently glancing at Mr. Darcy, though every glance convinced her of what she dreaded. To be sure, he was not always looking at her mother (the rest of the time he was looking at Mr. Collins), but she was convinced that his attention was invariably fixed between the two. The expression of his face changed gradually from indignant contempt to a composed and steady gravity. And whenever the word "platypus" was uttered—and uttered it was, frequently and with vigor—Mr. Darcy appeared practically sepulchral in demeanor.

At length, however, Mrs. Bennet had no more to say (and at his end, Mr. Collins was at last effectively silenced by nothing less than a lamb chop), and Lady Lucas (long yawning at the repetition of delights in which she could not share) was left to the comforts of cold ham and chicken which blessedly were not talking at her.

Elizabeth now began to revive. The many open windows in the supper room allowed in some pleasingly cool night air, and the starry heavens were soothing, deep velvet . . .

But not long was the interval of tranquility. When supper was over, singing was mentioned. And she had the mortification of seeing Mary preparing to oblige the company.

By many significant looks and silent entreaties, did Elizabeth endeavour to prevent this, but in vain—Mary would not understand them. Such an opportunity was delightful to her, and she began her song.

Elizabeth's eyes were fixed on her with most painful sensations. She watched her progress through the several stanzas of the song with an impatience that was poorly rewarded at their close—for Mary, on receiving polite thanks and negligible hints for an encore, after a short pause began another.

Mary's singing was entirely inadequate for such an extended display. Her voice was weak, and her manner affected.

Elizabeth was in agonies. She looked at Jane, to see how she bore it. But Jane was talking to Bingley—they were engrossed completely, and by all appearances the amiable tiger was on the verge of purring.

Elizabeth looked at Bingley's two sisters, and saw them making signs of derision at each other. She then glanced at Darcy, who continued, however, imperturbably grave.

At length, Elizabeth turned to her father with a look that bespoke despair, to entreat his interference, lest Mary should be singing all night. He took the hint, and when Mary had finished her second song, said aloud, "That will do extremely well, child. You have delighted us long enough. Let the other young ladies have time to exhibit."

Mary, though pretending not to hear, was somewhat disconcerted. And now Elizabeth was sorry for her, and for her father's speech, fearing that her anxiety had done no good. Others of the party were now applied to.

"If I," said Mr. Collins, "were so fortunate as to be able to sing, I should have great pleasure, in obliging the company with an air. To be sure, my speaking voice is sufficient, but Lady Catherine herself admits to some gratification at the melodious timbre of my *beastly* snarls and the gentle—one might say delightful—roaring tonality that is produced by the natural echoing, that sweetest pitter-patter mechanism of sound within the cage, as they reach a certain crescendo when the moon's forces are at their highest. I consider music an innocent diversion quite compatible with the profession of a clergyman—"

And then Mr. Collins proceeded to digress slightly and speak at length about parish duties and the duties of a rector in general, and then the care and improvement of his dwelling, and the introduction of Australian aboriginal fauna into the nearby shrubberies, concluding with, "Having cultivated such vigorous enriched livestock due to splendid advice, one should then cultivate an attentive and conciliatory manner, especially towards those to whom he is obliged for the cultivation advice and to whom he owes his preferment, and anybody connected with their family."

And with a bow to Mr. Darcy, he concluded his speech, which had been spoken so loud and in such a bellowing voice as to be heard by half the room. Many stared—many smiled (and a few, including Mr. Darcy, paled). But no one looked more amused than Mr. Bennet himself, while his wife seriously commended Mr. Collins for having spoken so sensibly. Mrs. Bennet then observed in a half-whisper to Lady Lucas, that he was a remarkably clever, good kind of young man, even if he did possess an *astonishingly* large cage.

To Elizabeth it appeared that, had her family made a common pact to expose themselves[53] as much as they could during the evening, they could not have surpassed this effort. Fortunately, Bingley did not notice, and was unlikely to be distressed by the *utter folly* which he might have seen. It was bad enough that his two sisters and Mr. Darcy should have such an opportunity of ridiculing her relations. She could not determine whether the silent contempt of the gentleman, or the insolent smiles of the ladies, were more intolerable.

The rest of the evening brought her little amusement. There was a certain air of high-strung nerves prevalent among the company—a sensation of *wilderness* indeed, as many of the gentlemen seemed to exhibit a more than usual tendency to bristle, twitch, scratch, drum fingers against the nearest surfaces, or otherwise move about in a discombobulated animal fashion, even during the dignified dance sets. Truly, seeing red coats with twitching legs standing up with young ladies—or even the few older gentlemen who had surely forgotten themselves and made inappropriate scratching motions despite the scandalized looks of their matronly dance partners—was a disturbing sight.

It was all so decidedly odd that, indeed, Elizabeth was not the only female to glance with some frequency at the open windows, the parted curtains, the entirely safe starlit night sky (with not even a crescent moon in sight), and to wonder. . . .

In addition to the strangeness, she was also tormented by Mr. Collins, who continued most perseveringly by her side, speaking very enthusiastically about the "happy unions" to be soon achieved, with her ladyship's blessings, amongst the pygmy possum, the bilby, and the British hare in the Rosings parsonage shrubbery.

---

[53] Rest assured once again, gentle reader, that no unseemly removal of attire was perpetrated by any of the Bennets. —Ed. *[And once again the long-suffering reader does indeed rest assured. —Ed. 2]*

At some point Elizabeth thought to interrupt him with an inquiry as to "why, pray tell, must this be done; and why must it be spoken of?" and "why combine precisely this pygmy possum, the bilby, and the hare; and furthermore, what exactly *was* a 'bilby?'" but thought better of it, and remained silent while Mr. Collins continued to inform her.

This went on for quite some time. And although her cousin eventually recalled he was not in the shrubbery but in a ballroom and spoke again of dancing, he could not prevail on her to dance with him again. Unfortunately this also put it out of her power to dance with *others*.

In vain did she entreat him to stand up with somebody else (*anybody* else!), and offer to introduce him to any young lady in the room, suggesting that, for example, Miss so-and-so, the young lady in the rose-colored dress was rather enchanted with the notion of British domesticated kangaroos; or that the equally elegant Miss K—— next to her, with a handsome demeanor and dowry, was not adverse to learning about shearing and lubrication methods for fine wood surfaces . . . or was it sheep?

He assured her, that as to dancing, he was perfectly indifferent to it. His chief object was by delicate attentions to recommend himself to *her* and that he should therefore make a point of *remaining close to her the whole evening.*

There was no arguing upon such a project. Elizabeth owed her greatest relief to her friend Miss Lucas, who often joined them, and good-naturedly engaged Mr. Collins's conversation to herself, bravely enduring the wombats and Lady Catherine and the shearing of sheep . . . or was it kangaroos?[54] Oh dear, it was the shearing of something or other.

----

[54] It must be pointed out that the shearing was very likely that of Australian sheep, and not the wooden mantels. Wood does not require shearing, only gentle polishing with an oiled cloth. Likewise, the shearing was not intended for Lady Catherine, since that would be a peculiar endeavour, and one has not heard of such a thing. It is to be reiterated, her ladyship is not a sheep.

If there were to be any positive to be gained from all this, at least Elizabeth was free from the offense of Mr. Darcy's further notice. Though often standing within a very short distance of her, quite disengaged, he never came near enough to speak—it was the probable consequence of her allusions both to his secret Affliction and to Mr. Wickham. And she rejoiced in it.

But alas! this brief respite was not to last.

For indeed, her two youngest sisters, Lydia and Kitty, had not yet had their turn at providing a fool exhibition—and hence advancing the Bennet family as a foremost source of ridicule among the present company. . . .

Now, Lydia had ended a dance, and with much giggles paused together with her partner near the windows, alongside Kitty and her own gentleman in a red coat. The curtains moved in the breeze, but the breeze was insufficient, and so Lydia turned and pulled the fabric aside. The drapery snagged on something, and, with a ripping tear, exposed much of the window to public view.

Heads turned at the tearing sound; those closest stared, and Kitty put her hands to her mouth; while Lydia said "oh!" and merely continued to giggle. She then turned her face to enjoy the cool air and the velvet darkness.

Elizabeth saw all this, was duly mortified yet *again*, and was about to call out to her sister in reproach. But in that moment, Kitty, looking at the window and the starry night outside, exclaimed:

"Oh, look how bright it is! Oh! What is that? Is that a *second* moon?"

At this point, dear Reader, it becomes rather necessary to interrupt our narrative with an explanation for such an impossibility, before one is left wondering whether the Author is discounting all the physical laws of science and nature and monthly lunar phases in favor of wild dramatization.

Blessedly, the answer is: not at all.

No, indeed—it was *not* another moon that Lydia revealed beyond the curtain and Catherine so keenly spotted.

What it was instead, riding the dark heavens with a brightness of many stars, was a *comet*.

The comet had appeared in the heavens but a few weeks earlier, having swept past the sun to unfurl its wondrous tail. And with each week it gained brightness as it approached the earth's sphere—appearing first to ride low on the horizon and then higher and higher, eventually visible to the eye of the earthly observer in the evenings and during clear nights.

With each passing hour its tail gained length and prominence, sparkling like an ancient dragon of Nordic ice . . . until this very night when it made a brilliant streak of illumination across the star-sprinkled expanse of darkness.

It was now a Great Comet, the greatest one seen in centuries. In its own burning heart, it bore no part of the deadly Curse that Afflicted the gentlemen, and *on its own* was quite harmless as a luminary of night.

However, rising alongside the moon's swelling crescent, it posed an unexpected danger.

The moon itself was far from full; far from its time of wickedness; and *on its own*, it too bore no immediate threat, no source of danger to any man who might observe and bathe in its cool rays.

But this night, for the first time, the comet and the crescent *together* in the heavens with the stars, made the precise amount of light—the precise *unholy* combination necessary—to evoke the fullness of the moon, and thus to simulate its wickedness, and call forth the effects of the monthly Curse upon the world.

And *tonight* not a single gentleman was properly contained.

"How strange indeed! Can it really be the moon and its twin? *Is* there such a thing as another moon?" Lydia echoed Kitty's outcry, forgetting her laughter and the torn curtain.

The two youngest Miss Bennets stared in curiosity and silent growing confusion, while the two officers next to them, bathed by the *wicked* potent light of all the multiple luminaries, were suddenly behaving in an altogether different manner. One's breath was caught, and his heartbeat quickened, while the other exhaled with an unusually deep *growl*, as he observed the bright heavens.

"What? What is it?" said Lady Lucas, who found herself closest the window and had heard this exchange. "Did you say the moon? Goodness, what is wrong? Is it *full?*"

"No, of course not," replied the elderly Mrs. G—— next to her, "What nonsense; we have nothing to worry about for at least a se'nnight."

But another gentleman warily approached the window together with Sir William, and he took one look outside and muttered that, "well, it *was* exceedingly bright" and that "it felt somewhat *peculiar*, did it not?"

But, "Look!" Kitty and Lydia both continued exclaiming, and thus Sir William trained a quizzing glass upon the skies, and squinted, and declared, "By Jove! There is indeed something else out there, I say! Right there, next to the crescent moon!"

The gentlemen and ladies crowded near the windows, dancing forgotten, and at some point one of the older gentlemen who had been to London, and had taken an astronomy lecture there just this past week, ventured a wild guess that this was "indeed another heavenly body akin to a meteor or a falling star, called a 'comet,' and it had been spotted and catalogued, and was even now being observed by gentlemen of science, as it made a rare visit to our skies."

"Thus indeed, nothing to fear," he concluded smartly, putting away his own quizzing glass, "For a comet such as this is a harmless visitor, and may be observed for pleasure and enrichment of the mind."

And having spoken thus, the gentleman cleared his throat politely . . . and suddenly emitted a very loud *howl*.

It was decidedly a *beastly* howl. There was simply no circumstance upon which it might have been mistaken for a post-supper belch.[55] Furthermore, he was echoed immediately by the two officers who had been standing longest near the windows with Kitty and Lydia, as they raised their faces to the night, and barked and bayed in a most canine fashion . . . while their teeth had grown quite long, and their eyes lost all humanity.

Lady Lucas and Mrs. Bennet both screamed immediately, and Kitty and Lydia drew back and shrieked—

And thus the ballroom turned to panic and Bedlam.

Elizabeth, standing a few feet away, felt herself jostled against the wall, as gentlemen everywhere started to collapse and double over, grunting, groaning, yelping, roaring, howling, bellowing, yowling, chirping, honking, screeching like banshees—no, that was Miss Bingley, or possibly Mrs. Hurst near the card table—snarling, yodeling, growling, and making an unspecified number of other impossible, terrible, beastly and demonic noises that normally accompanied the monthly Ordeal, and normally were heard muffled by thick walls, locked doors, and thick iron cages.

At the same time all the ladies present started to cry and run about the ballroom, while musicians abandoned their instruments and fled; menservants dropped decanters and platters, collided with each other, and ran from the chamber, also in the dark throes of *transformation*, accompanied by shrieking and scattering maids.

"Dear Lord! Get the ladies out of here!" exclaimed Sir William Lucas, and bravely stood aside and situated himself

---

[55] A howl has a certain determined, focused quality to it, and is in some ways far more civilized than a belch; for indeed the hound or wolf must use the howl to communicate his intent to other hounds and wolves, in particular, the *ladies* of the species.

behind a potted plant—in vain hopes that it might serve as barrier between his terrifying panther self and the public.

"Run, my dears, run!" cried Mr. Bennet to his wife and daughters, feeling the lion coming upon him; but whatever else he was about to say was dissolved into a thunderous grandiose *roar*, and he was down on the parquet floor, golden and bristling, and ripping out of his dinner jacket. . . .

Mr. Bingley and Jane had been at the other end of the ballroom, engrossed in a pleasant conversation. Therefore, the opened curtain and the discovery of the comet followed by the activation of the Curse had the taken them both entirely by surprise.

As the gentlemen *turned* all around them, Bingley grasped Jane's hands and desperately tried to pull her away with him toward a nearby alcove, then recalled himself, and released Jane—and the eldest Miss Bennet whimpered and wrung her hands and backed away from her lover. "By all that is holy, for as long as I am in control of my spirit, reason, and faculties, I will never harm you, Miss Bennet!" he roared, "and yet I beg you to get as far away from me as you can, and hide! Hide, my dearest Miss Bennet!"

"What is happening? Oh, Mr. Bingley!" Jane was saying, continuing to shrink back against the wall, until Elizabeth (having pushed past an unspeakable mess of gentlemen in all beastly stages of transformation; evening clothing flying every which way, waistcoats and pants and jackets in shreds, and rushing ladies gone mad from terror and airborne muslin and lace) had come upon her, and grabbed her sister's hand, and pulled her to herself, with an exclamation, "We must get out, Jane! Come with me if you would prefer to live!"

And holding hands tightly, the two eldest Miss Bennets attempted to fight their way toward the nearest exit.

Mr. Darcy had been *aware* all evening of something being inexplicably wrong, but was unable to put it into words, and attributed it to worry, nerves, and his new obsessive intensity when it came to all matters regarding a certain Miss Elizabeth Bennet.

But now, as the fateful drapery was torn by her youngest sister (precisely as a small pug might ravage a toss-pillow in unsupervised play) and the window revealed the comet blazing in the skies alongside the moon, he knew with an inevitable horror and certainty that, out of nowhere, the Affliction was upon him—upon them all.

It was in the quality of the cold wicked light that now streamed from the window, and *quickened* him.

Standing in the center of the ballroom, Mr. Darcy knew he had only moments before his perfect control would give way before the *transformation.* . . . Only moments before he would shrink to a tiny fraction of his proud human self, and scramble out of his clothing, and require a large tub filled with water for his useless and humiliating *platypus demon* to sink and glide in its cooling depths. . . .

But first—he was surrounded by helpless women about to be torn to shreds! And a room filled with other men in the process of becoming violent *monsters.*

And somewhere a mere few steps away, *she* was there, Elizabeth Bennet, vulnerable like every other female, and in the greatest danger of her life!

What was a gentleman of courage and breeding to do?

Darcy turned around swiftly, his gaze sweeping the room, and saw her, as Elizabeth had taken Jane by the hand, and both of them, filled with determination, were moving away—just as Bingley had fallen on all fours and was in that terrible fluid halfway stage of becoming a tiger. He would be upon them in two strides!

"Miss Elizabeth Bennet!" Darcy exclaimed, rushing after her, and just barely *not tripping* and instead stepping over what had been a regimental officer and now was a large prickly hedgehog, crawling out of its coat and breeches on the floor, "You must come this way, hurry! No, not *this* way! Do not come *toward* me; rather, move away, yes, back! Go back! No, not *that* way—"

Elizabeth and Jane both turned in his direction, somewhat confounded, but were immediately diverted by a trio of very large, very brown wolfhounds, or possibly two hounds and one huge golden-tan lion (formerly Mr. Denny) who were growling (hounds) and yowling (Denny) at each other, as felines and canines (natural adversaries) are wont to do.

Darcy—still human, thanks to unbelievable self-control—was gesturing wildly at them to *move!*

The large double doors were about twenty feet away, leading to the hallway. Oh, to reach it!

"**M**r. Darcy! Help! Oh, surely you of all people must command someone to contain this outrage—all of it—immediately!"

Behind him, sounded the keening voice of a somewhat disheveled Miss Bingley, followed by several ladies bunched close together for protection like the membership of a ladies sporting league. "Fie! This is altogether in poor taste, unnatural, and it cannot be happening! There is *no* full moon; I refuse to believe that you gentlemen cannot control yourselves with a silly comet—"

She was interrupted by a piercing shriek behind her as Mrs. Hurst was attacked by her own terrier spouse. Mr. Hurst had transformed swiftly and, tongue lolling, now vigorously jumped up at her, waist-level, then attempted to hump her leg, while Louisa screeched and fought him off with her silk fan in one gloved hand and a hastily snatched buffet chicken wing in the other.

"Miss Bingley, I regret—I am afraid I am not in any position to assist, only recommend dearly that you get away as far as possible, immediately!" replied Darcy through tightly squeezed teeth, and then turned away from them resolutely and headed toward the smaller exit.

Around him was a sea of raging beasts, and screaming ladies. . . .

He was feeling the vertigo sensation, the *transformation* coming over him—

"Gentlemen! All of you who can hear, attend me!" exclaimed Darcy, gathering his last force of personality and reason. "We must get outside, all of us! Run! Run to the nearest doors and corridors and windows! Hasten *outside!* Do it now, gentlemen, who are able to call themselves real men! Come now! No time to contain ourselves! There are no chains or cages for us here! Out! Get thee out!"

And with hands that were now trembling, he herded a few of the beasts nearest himself—discounting their rabid snarling—and turned now to the nearest window, seeing that some of the gentlemen—fortunately having come to the same conclusion as himself—were dutifully throwing themselves out the doors, windows, and other openings in the galleries and hallways, to the night gardens outside the Netherfield estate. . . .

Darcy ran, and swept open the French doors to the grand terrace which yielded the largest opening—and picking up a fallen walking-cane (which for some reason had a slim *shovel* attached[56] to its tip) he used it to poke and prod and swat a few wolves, mid-sized bears, one oversized (and frankly confused) ostrich, and a herd of dogs, beavers, foxes, steer, wild pigs, and lord knows what other four-legged mixed cattle—so that they poured out onto the terrace, roaring, yowling, barking,

---

[56] The walking-shovel is a recent and highly exclusive new gentleman's fashion accessory from Bath, described in much glaring detail in the notorious tome *Northanger Abbey and Angels and Dragons.* One cannot imagine how this particular specimen ended up at the Netherfield ball, except that it had to have been carried here by a supremely fashionable gentleman, naturally.

screeching, mooing, hissing, and rather remarkably leaving each
other largely unsanguined, as though having taken a lesson of
wisdom from the denizens of Noah's Ark. . . .

Others behind him started to leap and jump off the
terrace—panthers, lions, pumas, jaguars, leopards; more and
more Great Cats, it seemed, were now coming—and Darcy
momentarily saw the flashing stripes of a great gold and black
tiger, as he recognized the familiar beast shape that was Bingley
take a leaping dive off the balcony into the gaping night
darkness.

There was not another moment left to lose! Mr. Darcy
dropped the cane, and took a running leap—feeling in that
precise instant his own humanity receding at last; feeling himself
turn mid-air—and dove into the Netherfield shrubbery.

While the greater portion of the *beastly* demon menagerie
was emptying into the terrace in a stampede, off to the
side, near the buffet table, a very loud new commotion was
taking place, involving familiar wailing female voices, with *one*
voice reigning uppermost in pitch and intensity.

Gentle Reader, you have fathomed it correctly; it was the
high-pitched screech of Mrs. Bennet!

Elizabeth clutched her breast in alarm. She then pulled Jane
behind her (like one does with a small child), away from the
hounds and Denny-lion (thankfully occupied with each other),
and saw, in the distance, her own mother holding a large silver
platter up as a Grecian shield between herself, Mary, and Lady
Lucas on one side—and *something* smallish and furry, black and
white-striped on the other (which was leisurely waddling around
on the parquet floor before them). And all along, the goodly
matron was screaming at the top of her voice for Mr. Bennet,
Mr. Bingley—anyone!

The beast, mostly black, with a double long white stripe
running along its back, and a fluffy tail, had paused between
Mrs. Bennet and the buffet spread, and made short threatening

hisses, stomping motions with its front feet, and then the entire hind area, as the matron exclaimed in horror, "Please, no! Oh no! I beg of you, Mr. Collins, please remember yourself, no—"

But in vain did Mrs. Bennet brandish the platter. The *creature from hell* that had been their cousin poised itself, then lifted its bristling fluffy tail, aiming its backside directly at the three ladies . . . and suddenly let forth a powerful quick jet spray of some incredibly *foul* smelling liquid substance from the deepest bowels of the lower intestine of the sewers of Tartarus.

It was followed by three simultaneous screams of pure, white-hot agony, issuing out of Mrs. Bennet (direct in line of the attack), Mary Bennet, and Lady Lucas, in a single chorus of despair.

And then—

Oh, the odor! It swept the room with the speed of universal mortification, and reached gargantuan proportions and the pungency of uncorked ghastly spirits of constipated Hades himself.

"God help us! What is it?" cried someone on the opposite side of the ballroom where the musicians had played. "It is sulfur and brimstone, surely! It is the Apocalypse come upon us!"

"Dear heaven, Lizzy! Did you know—had you any idea that Mr. Collins is a *skunk!?*" exclaimed Jane in a theatrical whisper, as they tiptoed carefully behind a grunting six-foot bear (still partly wearing the regimental red coat, having retained a portion of his upper jacket, but entirely missing the breeches) and two young Miss R——s as they attempted to toss ribbons and a plate of buffet cold cuts at the bear, to distract it from its decidedly murderous intent.

"Our cousin being a skunk? I had not the faintest notion," Elizabeth replied, "but it certainly explains the absurd size of his cage—'tis a vain attempt to distance one from the odorous inhabitant—"

"Get the women away from here! Now! Woe to us! I must be chained immediately!" some belatedly still-human gentleman was yelling as he stumbled about, one of the last to *turn;* as those that had stood farthest from the window appeared most fortunate to have suffered the slowest effects of the Affliction.

Mr. Darcy was nowhere to be seen, Elizabeth noted (and neither was anything resembling his discarded clothing). She also noted the wide-open terrace doors, and the many windows into which the monster beasts were escaping in a demon great flood. . . .

They should flee also; but first, their mother and sisters—

Elizabeth, followed by Jane, bravely pushed past some kind of quadruped canine (heedless of its growling and long bared teeth, which fortunately were occupied with ravaging a dropped cold ham from the buffet); and, gathering air in her lungs beforehand, approached the grouping near the buffet tables— which had now become the epicenter of the unspeakable odor.

"Forgive me, I am simply unable to draw any closer, Lizzy!" exclaimed Jane behind her, in a sudden fit of coughing, as the pungent air entered her lungs, eliciting an immediate choking response—it had been too soon since Jane's illness.

"A handkerchief may be of some assistance, Jane!" her sister replied, pulling out her own lacy bit of fabric and applying it to her nose as a mask. Jane quickly followed suit, and they reached their mother and sisters, only to observe a most dejected sight that rivaled Napoleon's upcoming[57] rout at Waterloo.

In a thick miasma of malodorous fury, Mrs. Bennet was coughing and swatting at her own clothing, tears running down her cheeks. Mary was doing the same and bawling at the top of her voice about "the loss of reason and innocence." Lady Lucas,

---

[57] The Battle of Waterloo happened four years later, on June 18, 1815, but the erudite reader is assured that Mr. Collins was not present for the event, either in his human or skunk form. The rout took place entirely without him.

on the other hand, was instead very *still* and very blue from holding her breath, her eyes bulging from the effort.

The *demon-skunk* that had once been Mr. Collins was calmly walking around in circles among his own discarded attire, tail raised high, and apparently marking his territory around the buffet table with some other glandular excretion.

"Oh Lizzy! Oh Jane!" wailed her mother, between gasping breaths, "where have you been? Oh, I have lost all hope, and now, I am marked and horridly despoiled—"

"Mr. Collins!" exclaimed Elizabeth down at the skunk, "for shame! How could you, sir?"

She did not expect an answer, and indeed did not receive one. Instead, from underneath the long tablecloth draping the buffet table issued a small stifled cough, followed by a very faint voice belonging to Miss Charlotte Lucas.

"Is that you, Lizzy?" her friend whispered, venturing forth mostly unscathed from the relative safety of her hiding place, adjusting her gown and holding a dining napkin to her face. "I dare say, it is not so bad—"

The skunk regarded her silently, rendered harmless by the act of having sprayed once already. And thus, Miss Lucas stood next to him without any fear, and gently admonished him.

The same could not be said about Mrs. Bennet.

"Oh! Mr. Bennet! Oh! Our Holy Savior in Heaven! Oh, my nerves! This will never wash out! Not in ten, not in *ten dozen* washes! We are doomed to be pariahs in our own house and neighborhood!" cried Mrs. Bennet, alternating between wrenching her hands, beating her own breast, and choking on the miasma from her own clothing.

"Whilst it may behoove some people to assume that an odor produced under any other dire circumstances is any less pernicious," stated Mary with dignity, despite having shrieked but a moment ago, "a water soluble soap might accomplish much in way of dissolving any offending traces of it, in no less than a hundred regular boilings followed by an equal number of washings—"

"*Enough!* Hush, idiot child!" shrieked Mrs. Bennet, "you have no notion of my nerves in this foul moment; it will be the death of me!"

"Madam, I beg you yet again to compose yourself," said Elizabeth, "for, you forget, the wicked *beasts* are all around us, and we must endeavour to *not* draw their attention upon our own persons! And now, you—and Mary, Charlotte, and Lady Lucas, if you please—you must come with me if you aspire to live!"

The Bennets, matron and daughters, Miss Lucas, and Lady Lucas (still attempting to hold her breath), battled their way with great care to the end of the emptying ballroom, having picked up Kitty and Lydia on the way, and were out the doors at last, having avoided at least one giant boar and what seemed like the running bulls of Pamplona in the corridor.

"Oh, what is happening! The entire world has gone mad!" Mrs. Bennet bewailed, "first the odious moon, then an even more odious comet, and now, odorous *this*"—pointing at the front of her dress—"Oh, my wretched nerves! And where, someone pray tell me, is Mr. Bennet? How are we to take the carriage home without him?"

"I am certain," said Elizabeth, in an attempt to console, periodically putting the handkerchief to her nose, "he is unharmed and somewhere quite safe."

"Yes, father is perfectly safe," added Jane, also holding a handkerchief to her face and giving Elizabeth a private look that bespoke otherwise, and suggested quietly that a carriage home was the least of their worries.

"I am entirely at a loss as to what has happened to the gentlemen," mused Elizabeth, as they hurriedly descended the stairs. She meant of course, the general situation with the comet.

"Well! I dare say they are afraid to even approach us now, due to the ghastly *smell*," said Lydia, giving her mother and Mary and Lady Lucas horrid stares.

"And so it is! Why, yes indeed!" Mrs. Bennet exclaimed with sudden realization, almost cheerfully. "Lydia, my dear, you are so clever! If there is a good thing that has come of it, the wicked *beasts* are not so willing to attack us now, are they! I suppose we must thank Mr. Collins—we owe him that much! The dear young man surely meant well, intending to shield and rescue us all along by his action; so clever of him! Goodness, I was so terribly wrong about him, oh dear!"

The Longbourn party were thus among the last of all the company to depart Netherfield. Since no one wanted to share an enclosed equipage with the aromatic Mrs. Bennet, they had to wait for their carriage a quarter of an hour after everybody else was gone—the transformed gentlemen having hopelessly scattered all over the grounds of the estate; and the ladies huddled together for protection in great numbers, squeezing into thickly packed carriages, bravely carrying those among their rank who had fainted, all escaping to their own domiciles. And all this transportation detail was handled by harried, terrified women servants who—since the entire male staff[58] was indisposed—had to handle horses and drive.

The wait gave the Bennet ladies time to consider and wonder how fared the host and his family in this disaster. Mr. Bingley, the last that Jane saw of him, had become the tiger and had surely flown outside through a window or door. Mrs. Hurst and her sister had hidden away in the mayhem, and goodness only knows whatever had happened to them after Mr. Darcy had turned his back on Miss Bingley.

---

[58] Good heavens! I pray the gentle reader abstains from such unseemly thoughts.

At least, thought Elizabeth with bitter absurdity, they were spared from having to attend to the long speeches of Mr. Collins, who would have been complimenting Mr. Bingley and his sisters on the elegance of their entertainment, and the hospitality. . . .

Fortunately, for the time being, he was now a small, furry malodorous hell creature, and entirely incapable of holding a discourse about anything, including Australian wombats, or even Lady Catherine de Bourgh.

But—whatever has happened to Mr. Darcy? Elizabeth wondered, while stress-induced stupor and weariness had come upon them all, and even Lydia was too much fatigued to utter more than the occasional exclamation of "Lord, how tired I am!" accompanied by a violent yawn, followed by a sputter for air and a grasp of a handkerchief to her nose.

When at length they arose to take leave, and follow a terrified suffocating maidservant (discreetly holding a dishtowel to her face and keeping as far away from Mrs. Bennet as possible) to the carriage, Mrs. Bennet suddenly recalled a certain happy impending situation, and was most vocal in her hope of seeing the whole Bingley family soon at Longbourn, and too bad she could not address herself directly to Mr. Bingley, if it had not been for the odious comet, to assure him how happy he would make them by eating a family dinner with them at any time—as long as he was not being a tiger—without the ceremony of a formal invitation. . . .

"No doubt, madam," said Elizabeth, "Mr. Bingley, once he is himself again, would be all grateful pleasure, and would readily take the earliest opportunity of waiting on us, after his return to human form."

Mrs. Bennet was perfectly satisfied with such imaginings, and quitted the present house of horrors under the delightful persuasion that she should undoubtedly see her daughter settled at Netherfield in due course, regardless of all this comet-induced *wickedness*.

Of having another daughter married to Mr. Collins—skunk or no—she thought with equal certainty, and with considerable, though not equal, pleasure. Elizabeth was the least dear to her of all her children; and though the man and the match were quite good enough for *her*, the worth of each was eclipsed by Mr. Bingley and Netherfield.

And, speaking of Bingley and Netherfield, dear Reader—the next morning, the bright rays of Helios dawned, and all around the estate, dozens of partially or entirely unclothed or disheveled gentlemen found themselves awake in the shrubberies, along garden paths, and—in the case of Mr. Darcy—in the large duck pond in the middle of the grounds.

When the demonic Ordeal had finally taken him, Darcy had managed to reach the safety of the foliage, and then *transformed* in safe anonymity into the platypus. The unique creature then found its way by simple instinct (and likely some measure of electrolocation) toward fresh water, and dove into the pond, where it spent all night gliding in the moonlight and starlight and the light of the infernal comet.

With the first light of the sun, however, Darcy regained his human shape, and swam with powerful strokes from the center of the verdigris pond to its sloping shore, where he located some of his discarded clothing floating in the water among the reeds, and dressed himself quickly. He was thus dripping wet, but in complete command of himself.

A few hundred feet away up a grassy knoll he found his dear friend Bingley, sleeping in the thicket, and missing all of his garments, as usual.

Mr. Bingley woke up, saw his friend standing above him, infernally composed, fully dressed and offering a hand to help him up.

"Good Lord, Darcy!" he exclaimed, clambering up sheepishly, then remembered, "is everyone alive? Has anyone been harmed? Miss Jane Bennet?"

"I presume, all is as satisfactory as could be, considering the impossible circumstances of last night," Darcy replied.

They contemplated this in thoughtful, grim silence.

At length, the two gentlemen looked at each other closely, in that moment taking in the immediate details of one another.

There was an extended moment of pause.

"Wet shirt," said Bingley.

"No pants," said Darcy.

And thus—after searching and finding on the ground a discarded something or other in the way of clothing to provide Bingley with some decency—they returned to the house.

"I beg of you, Mr. Collins, please remember yourself, no—"

Chapter 19

The next day opened a whole new scene at Longbourn, Netherfield, and countless other locales.

First and foremost, there was now *that* horrid comet to contend with.

The gentlemen had woken up in various compromising situations all over Regency England to the awful knowledge that they had *turned* while uncontained and unrestrained, and therefore had surely eaten their loved ones—or at least put their lives in mortal danger and *someone else* had eaten them instead.

Fortunately, and rather remarkably, all throughout the realm there had been almost no casualties, and only a few minor scratches, bites, tears, cracked ribs, broken limbs, and marks of sanguined scuffle. A few ladies had gone missing, it was true, but most had been safely recovered in unusual hiding places, or else found in a dead faint while in plain sight—which in fact saved them by keeping them well away from the roaming and frankly disoriented demon *beasts* that left alone the *motionless* sort of prey in favor of the running kind. . . .

A miracle of fortune, indeed!

Among those at the ball at Netherfield, both Mr. Bennet and Sir William Lucas had *turned*, roared a couple of times, yawned, and had immediately gone to sleep right where they had been—

the former on top of a lounge sofa, and the latter in the corner of the ballroom adjacent to a potted plant. They were found the following morning by Darcy and Bingley, who had just returned from outdoors, and in both cases were swiftly provided their own garments.

Mr. Bennet promised Mr. Bingley to send a servant with a letter immediately upon arriving home and ascertaining that Miss Jane Bingley and the others were unharmed.

Mr. Collins was discovered by three horrified maids who approached to clean the remainders of last evening's supper buffet and instead found overturned plates and decanters, fallen ham and chicken, a dark miasma of unspeakable lingering odor, and a large resting gentleman. Upon being woken and handed pants, Mr. Collins excused himself profusely, and apologized endlessly, all the while expressing all hope that he had roared with sufficient delicacy during the night, and that he had not torn anyone to shreds.

After being reassured that all was under control, he joined Mr. Bennet in a suffocating carriage ride home to Longbourn.

Upon arrival, Mr. Bennet was greeted by his panicked spouse and daughters (who had all spent the majority of the night in a laundry-induced terror and had not had a wink of sleep), and inquired if they were all hale and unharmed. Next, after reassuring them in turn he was equally well, and embracing his gratefully sobbing wife, he inquired discreetly, "Mrs. Bennet, whatever is that putrid *smell?* It is the same that accompanied us in the carriage, and I do believe it comes from *Mr. Collins!* How did it happen to be on you?"

In reply, Mrs. Bennet only wailed more bitterly and started to cry for the maid, insisting that she must have a third bath drawn immediately, and that the laundry needs to be run through yet again, with a boiling and three additional scrubbings to be given to *that* odious dress. . . .

"What in heaven's name is going on, Lizzy?" her father asked, taking her aside, seeing he was not likely to get any reasonable answer from anyone else.

Elizabeth told him in a whisper about the skunk incident, adding, "I dare say, I do not think Mr. Collins has any idea what he turns into! He must have been spared the truth once by someone well-meaning, and now believes himself an oversized and imposing bear . . . what, with that giant cage, and with no one to tell him otherwise—"

Upon hearing this, Mr. Bennet was far more amused than he was ever going to admit. He therefore chuckled to himself, fully satisfied, and then asked for breakfast to be served.

And as for Mr. Collins himself—upon entering the parlor soon after Mr. Bennet (and profoundly affecting the breathable air in the room), he immediately made his profuse and endless apologies to the ladies and the entire Bennet household, invoked Lady Catherine, invoked his giant cage and asked for it to be readied in case there was to be a repeat of last night . . . and soon after, made a not entirely unexpected *declaration of another sort*.

The gentle Reader might wonder about the nature of this declaration; therefore, it needs be told that Mr. Collins—having had plenty of time to ponder the more agreeable portions of last evening before the comet's fateful illumination had had its infernal effects—was about to propose matrimony.

He resolved to do it promptly, since his leave of absence extended only to the following Saturday. And feeling no diffidence or distress, he set about it in a very proper manner.

After being successfully persuaded by Mr. Bennet to take a "refreshing morning bath" and change of clothing; and thereafter, upon finding Mrs. Bennet, Elizabeth, and one of the younger girls together, soon after breakfast, Mr. Collins addressed the mother in these words:

"May I hope, madam, for the honour of a private audience with your fair daughter Elizabeth in the course of this morning?"

Mrs. Bennet was still somewhat sensitive in regard to Mr. Collins's "certain *behaviour*"—as she now referred to the skunk incident—but the settling of her daughters was ever uppermost.

Thus, before Elizabeth had time for anything but a blush of horror, Mrs. Bennet answered instantly, "Oh dear!—yes—certainly. I am sure Lizzy will be very happy! Come, Kitty, I want you upstairs." And, gathering her work together, she was hastening away, when Elizabeth called out:

"Dear madam, do not go, I beg you! Mr. Collins can have nothing to say to me that anybody need not hear. I must go—"

"No, no, nonsense, Lizzy. I desire you to stay where you are." And upon Elizabeth's seeming about to escape, she added: "Lizzy, I *insist* upon your staying and hearing Mr. Collins."

Elizabeth could not oppose such an injunction. Instead, she realized it would be wisest to get it over with as soon as possible.

Therefore she sat down again and pretended to work at something with a needle. Mrs. Bennet and Kitty walked off, and as soon as they were gone, Mr. Collins began.

"Believe me, my dear Miss Elizabeth, that your modesty rather adds to your other perfections. But allow me to assure you, that I have your respected mother's permission for this address." And then Mr. Collins went on at length, mentioning "natural delicacy," "this little unwillingness," and concluding with, "my attentions have been too marked to be mistaken. Almost as soon as I entered the house, I singled you out as the companion of my future life."

Elizabeth was about to speak, but Mr. Collins was not done. "But before I am run away with by my feelings on this subject," he said, "perhaps it would be advisable for me to state my reasons for marrying—and for coming into Hertfordshire with the design of selecting a wife."

The idea of Mr. Collins being run away with by his feelings, made Elizabeth so near laughing, that she could not speak yet again.

And thus he continued about "a clergyman setting an example of matrimony in his parish," and "I am convinced that it will add very greatly to my happiness," and "it is the particular advice and recommendation of the very noble patroness."

Mr. Collins became ardent at this point, saying, "Twice has she condescended to give me her opinion (unasked too!) on this subject! It was the very Saturday night before I left Hunsford— between our pools at quadrille, while Mrs. Jenkinson was arranging Miss de Bourgh's footstool, that Lady Catherine said, 'Mr. Collins, you must marry. A clergyman like you must marry. Choose properly, choose a gentlewoman for *my* sake; and for your *own*, let her be an active, useful sort of person, not brought up high, but able to make a small income go a good way. Find such a woman as soon as you can, bring her to Hunsford, and I will visit her.'"

And Mr. Collins was almost rendered speechless by his own delight (but it did not stop him). "Allow me to observe, my fair cousin, that I do not reckon the notice and kindness of Lady Catherine de Bourgh as among the least of the advantages in my power to offer. You will find her manners beyond anything I can describe. And your wit and vivacity, I think, must be acceptable to her, especially when tempered with the silence and respect which her rank will inevitably excite."

And then for endless minutes more he went on (so that Elizabeth began to wonder if she was being persuaded to marry her ladyship instead of her cousin), explaining his reasons for looking in Longbourn instead of his own neighbourhood, since he was to inherit this estate after the death of her honoured father, and he "resolved to choose a wife from among his daughters, that their loss might be as little as possible, when the melancholy event takes place."

He concluded with, "And now nothing remains for me but to assure you in the most animated language of the *violence* of my affection—but not the *beastly* violence, to be sure, for begging pardon, my roars are quite delicate; and each full moon you will be pleasingly soothed by the lullaby of the timbre of—"

Elizabeth felt a smothering inability to breathe; then glanced with longing at the open window and its fresh air.

But yet again Mr. Collins was not done. "I am perfectly indifferent to fortune (or lack of such), and well aware that one thousand pounds in the four percents, (after your mother's decease), is all that you may ever be entitled to. To be sure, no ungenerous reproach on this subject shall ever pass my lips when we are married—"

It was absolutely necessary to interrupt him now.

"You are too hasty, sir!" she cried. "You forget that I have made no answer. Without further loss of time—my thanks for the compliment you are paying me, and for the honour of your proposals. But it is impossible for me to do otherwise than to *decline* them."

"I am pleasingly aware," replied Mr. Collins, with a formal wave of the hand, "that it is usual with young ladies to reject the addresses of the man whom they secretly mean to accept—when he *first* applies for their favour. Sometimes the refusal is repeated a second, or even a third time. I am therefore by no means discouraged, and hope to lead you to the altar ere long."

"Upon my word, sir!" cried Elizabeth, "I do assure you that I am *not* one of those young ladies who would risk their happiness on the chance of being asked a second time. I am perfectly serious in my refusal. You could not make *me* happy, and I am convinced that I am the last woman in the world who could make you so. Indeed, your friend Lady Catherine would find me in every respect ill qualified for the situation."

"Were it certain that Lady Catherine would think so—" pondered Mr. Collins very gravely, for a moment given some pause. "—But no, I cannot imagine that her ladyship would disapprove of you. When I have the honour of seeing her again, I shall speak in the very highest terms of your modesty, economy, and other amiable qualification."

"Indeed, Mr. Collins, all praise of me will be unnecessary. You must pay me the compliment of believing what I say. I wish you very happy and very rich—and by refusing your hand, do all in my power to prevent your being otherwise. In making me the offer, you have satisfied the delicacy of your feelings with regard to my family, and may take possession of Longbourn without any self-reproach. This matter may be considered, therefore, as finally settled." And rising as she spoke, she would have quitted the room, had Mr. Collins not thus addressed her:

"Naturally I hope to receive a more favourable answer *next* time I speak to you on the subject. I know it to be the established custom of your sex to reject a man on the first application—"

"Really, Mr. Collins!" cried Elizabeth with some warmth, "if what I said can appear as encouragement, I know not how to express my refusal in such a way as to convince you!"

"You must give me leave to flatter myself, my dear cousin, that your refusal of my addresses is *merely words*, of course. My hand is worthy of your acceptance, and the establishment I offer is highly desirable. My situation in life, my connections with the family of de Bourgh, and my relationship to your own, are circumstances highly in my favour—"

May heaven strike me if this goes on for much longer, she thought in agony.

"—Furthermore, in spite of your manifold attractions, it is by no means certain that another offer of marriage may ever be made you. Your portion is so small that it will undo the effects of your amiable qualifications. I must therefore conclude that you are not serious in your rejection of me—"

Dear merciful Lord, now would be a good time . . .

"—Why, yes! I see it clearly now! You wish to increase my love and passion by suspense—according to the usual practice of elegant females."

"Oh, I do assure you, sir, that I have no pretensions to the kind of *elegance* which consists in tormenting a respectable man. I would rather be paid the compliment of being believed sincere. I thank you again for the honour of your proposals, but to accept them is absolutely impossible. Can I speak plainer? I am not an 'elegant female' intending to plague you, but a rational creature, speaking the truth from her heart."

"You are uniformly charming!" cried he, with an air of awkward gallantry; "and I am persuaded that when sanctioned by the express authority of both your excellent parents, my proposals will not fail to be acceptable—"

In that moment, just as Elizabeth was considering what sins she might have committed that heaven remained so deaf to her pleas, a loud noise sounded at the window.

Then, a curtain blew. . . . A shutter banged. . . .

Mr. Collins went silent in his tirade and stared.

And the next instant, with a wild beating of wings, an enormously large, *monstrous* flying shape hurtled in through the open window from the outside, and trumpeted a thunderous war cry—just before it plummeted directly at Mr. Collins.

He bellowed once, twice[59], putting his hands up to defend his face, while the monster screeched like a thousand banshees and pecked at the top of his head, while simultaneously fanning its wings wide and sending a hail of duck feathers flying all about the room. . . .

"Good—Lord! What—what is this *fiend?* Fear not, dearest cousin Elizabeth, surely if I send up a prayer, as Lady Catherine

---

[59] The reference here is to Mr. Collins and not the duck. In other words, the gentleman was the one engaging in the act of bellowing, and not the monstrous fowl, which is generally not known to bellow, whereas gentlemen, upon occasion, do; though it is not altogether all that common.

always says to me, 'send up a prayer, Mr. Collins, verily, at all times of trial, you must send up a prayer'—as she did the other day in the shrubbery, and likewise when I was examining the parsonage goats—for as I have described previously, as you are aware they will be considered for—pardon me—*intimate relations* with the Australian kangaroo and wallaroo—and as such, with all due prayers, amen! The good Lord will protect us!" her cousin roared, the latter portion of his speech coming out in a fumble, and indeed exhibiting a minor loss of rational thought . . . while the duck circled the room and came back in for another pass.

And Elizabeth, who had risen up from her seat and moved back in startled amazement, recognized it—the horrifying airborne *hell-creature*, the same one she had seen that fateful night at Netherfield when Jane was lying sick abed—for, yes indeed, it was none other than the Brighton Duck!

Where had it come from? Heaven only knew.

Why was it here? It mattered not in the least.

Elizabeth gave up a silent prayer of thanks (both to heaven *and* to the duck), and then, before her cousin could resume his amorous address, and before the duck left them *tête-à-tête* again, requiring her to formulate yet another pointless refusal, she carefully backed away, and immediately and silently withdrew from the room.

The last she knew, Mr. Collins was entirely at his leisure to propose to the monstrous duck!

Chapter 20

M r. Collins was not left long to fend off the flying *monstrosity*—which curiously sped off, just moments after Elizabeth departed, right through the same window it came in—and then back to the silent contemplation of his interrupted proposal of marriage.

No sooner did Mrs. Bennet (dawdling about in the vestibule) see Elizabeth open the door and with quick step[60] pass her towards the staircase, than she entered the breakfast-room.

The duck had just gone, and all that remained as proof of its unholy visitation were piles of dove-grey feathers. . . .

Mr. Collins was still somewhat shaken, but hale and unharmed, and only displaying tufts of down in his hair and on his jacket lapels. Mrs. Bennet gave them no notice (just as she bravely gave no notice to the remnants of the pungent skunk

---

[60] The reader is begged to comprehend, despite what it may appear, that here Elizabeth Bennet was not dancing the quickstep, but walking in little quick steps perfectly appropriate to a delicate female such as herself, and in all haste. —Ed. *[I have given up here quite some time ago. But, upon occasion I do find it impossible not to "step" in and, if not to correct this profusion of idiocy, then at least to express my utmost woe to the reader, and to remind that, this too shall pass. —Ed. 2]*

odor still lingering about his person), and congratulated him in warm terms on the happy prospect of their nearer connection.

Mr. Collins received and returned these felicitations with equal pleasure. He then related the particulars of the interview— briefly mentioning the untimely interruption by the duck, at which Mrs. Bennet merely raised some brows but again expressed no particular surprise, being rather inured by the events of the previous night to *anything*. In short, Mr. Collins trusted he had every reason to be satisfied, since the "refusal" which his cousin had steadfastly given him was the natural result of her bashful modesty and genuine delicacy of character.

This information, however, startled Mrs. Bennet. She dared not believe her daughter had meant to encourage him by protesting against his proposals, and could not help saying so.

"But, depend upon it, Mr. Collins," she added, "that Lizzy shall be brought to reason. I will speak to her about it directly. She is a very headstrong, foolish girl, and does not know her own interest but I will *make* her know it."

"Pardon me for interrupting you, madam," cried Mr. Collins; "but if she is really headstrong and foolish, I know not whether she would be a very desirable wife to a man in my situation. If she persists in rejecting my suit, perhaps it were better not to force her into accepting me. With such defects of temper, she could not contribute much to my felicity."

"Sir, you quite misunderstand me," said Mrs. Bennet, alarmed. "Lizzy is only headstrong in such matters as these. In everything else she is as good-natured a girl as ever lived. I will go directly to Mr. Bennet, and we shall very soon settle it with her, I am sure."

She would not give him time to reply, but hurrying instantly to her husband, called out as she entered the library, "Oh! Mr. Bennet, you are wanted immediately; we are all in an uproar!"

"What, is there another comet? Need I sequester myself?"

"No! Gracious heavens, no! You must come and make Lizzy marry Mr. Collins, for she vows she will not have him, and if you do not make haste he will change his mind and not have *her*."

Mr. Bennet raised his eyes from his book, and fixed them on her face with a calm unconcern as to her communication.

"I have not the pleasure of understanding you," said he, when she had finished her speech. "Of what are you talking?"

"Of Mr. Collins and Lizzy! Lizzy declares she will not have Mr. Collins, and Mr. Collins begins to say that he will not have Lizzy."

"And what am I to do on the occasion? It seems a hopeless business," Mr. Bennet observed in his leonine drowsy manner, which so frequently provoked his spouse.

"Speak to Lizzy about it yourself. Tell her that you insist upon her marrying him!"

"Let her be called down. She shall hear my opinion."

Mrs. Bennet rang the bell, and Miss Elizabeth was summoned to the library.

"Come here, child," cried her father as she appeared. "I have sent for you on an affair of importance. I understand that Mr. Collins has made you an offer of marriage. Is it true?" Elizabeth replied that it was. "Very well—and this offer of marriage you have refused?"

"I have, sir. Repeatedly. Until we were interrupted by a duck."

"Very well—A *duck*, you say? What manner of duck?"

"I am not entirely certain, but it flew in through the window, and it was exceedingly large. I do recall having seen it elsewhere before."

"Fascinating," Mr. Bennet said. "And was this duck merely flying about the room or, doing what, precisely?"

"It flew at Mr. Collins," said Elizabeth with a very controlled expression. "It seemed, to me, sir, it was—attacking."

"I see! Curious indeed. And would you say it was attacking yourself also, or merely your cousin—"

"Mr. Bennet!" exclaimed Mrs. Bennet with a wail.

Her husband cleared his throat. "Ah yes, the proposal of matrimony.—We now come to the point. Your mother insists upon your accepting it. Is it not so, Mrs. Bennet?"

"Yes, or I will never see her again!"

"An unhappy alternative is before you, Elizabeth. From this day you must be a stranger to one of your parents. Your mother will never see you again if you do *not* marry Mr. Collins, and I will never see you again if you *do.*"

Elizabeth could not but smile at such a conclusion of such a beginning. But Mrs. Bennet, who had persuaded herself that her husband regarded the affair as she wished, was excessively disappointed, and furthermore, vexed.

"What do you mean, Mr. Bennet, in talking this way? You promised me to *insist* upon her marrying him!"

"My dear," replied her husband, "I have two small favours to request. First, that you will allow me the free use of my understanding on the present occasion; and secondly, of my room. I shall be glad to have the library to myself as soon as may be, for apparently my reading pleasure is to be cut short prematurely *every day* now, not merely during the full moon. Even now, the hour draws near when the moon and that dastardly comet together shall rise like vultures and wreak more havoc upon us. . . ."

And finishing up with a mutter, Mr. Bennet returned to his book.

In spite of her disappointment in her husband, Mrs. Bennet did not give up. She talked to Elizabeth again and again; coaxed and threatened her by turns, and even pressed upon Jane who declined interfering. And Elizabeth replied to her mother with unvarying determination.

Mr. Collins, meanwhile, was meditating in solitude on what had passed. He had early in the day inquired about the whereabouts of his confinement cage, since it needed to be readied for the evening's moon-and-comet showing. And now the servants were told to attend it, and no one had the nerve to impart to Mr. Collins its unusual placement in the shed in back of the house. . . .

As he waited, he pondered. Since he thought too well of himself to comprehend why his cousin could refuse him; and though his pride was hurt, he suffered in no other way. His "love" was quite imaginary; and the possibility of her deserving her mother's reproach prevented his feeling any regret.

While the family were in this confusion, Charlotte Lucas came to spend the day with them. She was met in the vestibule by Lydia, who, flying to her, cried in a half whisper, "I am glad you are come, for there is such fun here! What do you think has happened this morning? Mr. Skunk—I mean, Mr. Collins!—has made an offer to Lizzy, and she will not have him! And there was a giant duck!"

Charlotte hardly had time to answer, before they were joined by Kitty, who came to tell the same news; and no sooner had they entered the breakfast-room, where Mrs. Bennet likewise began on the subject (minus the duck), calling on Miss Lucas for her compassion, and entreating her to persuade her friend Lizzy to comply with the wishes of all her family.

"Pray do, my dear Miss Lucas," she added in a melancholy tone, "for nobody is on my side, nobody takes part with me. I am cruelly used, nobody feels for my poor nerves, and now, what with that horrid *comet* hanging outside—"

Charlotte's reply was spared by the entrance of Jane and Elizabeth.

"Aye, there she comes!" continued Mrs. Bennet, "looking as unconcerned as may be, while the world is falling apart, the gentlemen all gone *beastly* mad, and caring nothing, provided she can have her own way. But I tell you, Miss Lizzy—if you go on refusing every offer of marriage, you will never get a husband at all—and who is to maintain you when your father is dead? I shall not be able to keep you—and so I warn you. I have done with you from this very day. I told you in the library, you know, that I should never speak to you again, and you will find me as good as my word." And Mrs. Bennet went on at length about "undutiful children," "rare suffering," and "ailing nerves."

Her daughters listened in silence to this effusion, sensible that any attempt to reason or soothe would only increase the irritation. Thus, she talked on without interruption; till they were joined by Mr. Collins, who entered the room with an air more stately than usual, and a delicate whiff of *skunk*.

Seeing him, Mrs. Bennet said to the girls: "Now, I do insist that all of you hold your tongues, and let me and Mr. Collins have a little conversation together."

Elizabeth passed quietly out of the room, Jane and Kitty followed, but Lydia stood her ground, determined to hear all she could. And Charlotte, detained by curiosity and the civility of Mr. Collins, who attentively inquired after herself and all her family, walked to the window and pretended not to hear.

In a doleful voice Mrs. Bennet began the projected conversation: "Oh! Mr. Collins!"

"My dear madam," replied he, "let us be forever silent on this point. Far be it from me," he presently continued, in a voice that marked his displeasure, "to resent the behaviour of your daughter. Resignation to inevitable evils is the evil duty of us all." And Mr. Collins elaborated on the subject, mentioning "the duty of a fortunate young man" and "early preferment" and "positive happiness" and "blessed resignation."

He then concluded: "You will not, I hope, consider me as showing any disrespect to your family, my dear madam, by thus withdrawing my pretensions to your daughter's favour."

And for at least another interminable hour, Mr. Collins volubly apologised.

Chapter 21

The discussion of Mr. Collins's offer was now nearly at an end, and Elizabeth had only to suffer from the uncomfortable feelings necessarily attending it, and occasionally from some peevish allusions of her mother.

As for the gentleman himself, there was no embarrassment or dejection, only stiffness of manner and resentful silence. He scarcely ever spoke to her, and his assiduous attentions were transferred for the rest of the day to Miss Lucas, whose civility in listening to him was a relief to all, and especially to her friend.

The evening arrived, and now Mr. Bennet was faced with informing his guest about the whereabouts of his confinement cage (since Mrs. Bennet markedly refused this frightful duty).

"I am afraid my dear fellow," he began, "that we were unable to have your cage brought indoors due to its frankly heroic dimensions. And thus, with all our apologies, if you will make your way after me, I will gladly show you where it sits; and I believe they even put a nice warm tent around it . . . so now, it can be hoped that, tonight, the moon and silly comet together will have as little effect as possible. But, just to be safe—"

"My dearest Mr. Bennet," Mr. Collins interrupted. "My profuse apologies on behalf of all the trouble, but do you mean to say that I must be contained tonight *outside*, in the chill? What a rather unfortunate circumstance! My roars are, to be sure, grandiose, but quite melodious, and I assure you a thousand times that they will not keep you and your dear wife and daughters from your rest! Indeed, Lady Catherine herself says they remind her of a tinkling stream—"

"Yes, yes, well," said Mr. Bennet, "that is all rather well, and I am certain it is all so; but the fact is, the cage is just so extraordinarily proportioned, that we have no *doors* through which it might be made to *pass*. And the shed is rather warm, so it will not be altogether an unpleasant night for you."

"An infinite number of most sincere pardons for this—one might say—*difficulty* of positioning and delivery," continued Mr. Collins, "but I do want to reassure and confirm that the charming levels of hospitality in your sweetest domicile have been unmatched by even far more—dare one say—*loftier*—dwellings and estates than this one. And indeed—with only the magnificent nonpareil estate of Rosings aside—this exquisite Longbourn house has been the singlemost hospitable residence I have ever had the pleasure of stepping in for a delightful stay and sojourn. Were it at all to be made even more infinitely delightful, and a fount of veritable pleasures for a humble guest and connection such as myself—though one naturally recalls that as a member of the clergy one is eminently fit to be a guest at most domiciles—it would be merely to allow the necessary containment cage and mechanism its due place *inside* the residence—"

As he listened, Mr. Bennet slowly felt his reason and all rational thought slipping away on gentle wings, while in vain he attempted to comprehend what was being said to him. Then he replied:

"I assure you, Mr. Collins, were it at all in my power, I would bring your contraption in myself, but it simply is too large to fit! How else to say it? It *exceeds* the dimensions of the largest front entryway!"

"Oh, you flatter me, my dear Mr. Bennet! What a generous heart you possess; a true noble gentleman, to observe such niceties; but then indeed one cannot expect any less from such a charming man and his delightful family, of which close connection I am truly honoured to be reminded on a daily basis—"

"Really now, Mr. Collins!" cried Mr. Bennet, taking off his spectacles to wipe them with much energy against a handkerchief and thus relieve the brunt of his frustration. "It is not at all a matter of flattery, but of physics!"

"Now, now, I see where you are going with this, good sir!" continued Mr. Collins, as though not hearing, his voice rising with an effusion of delight. "You mean to speak thus merely because of your rare nobility of person and deepest generosity as a splendid host! I see that you intend to join me in this *en plein air* endeavour and have your cage and mine placed alongside so that we can contemplate the tremendous awe of the night and its wicked luminaries as we *turn* together, side by side, in our masculine Ordeal that the grace of heaven alone can alleviate and elevate our souls!"

And thus, Mr. Bennet found himself in a most unusual conundrum, and then, regretfully found himself accompanying his guest outside. And even more regretfully later that evening, for the first time in his life, he was forced to endure being locked in an older inconvenient cage that had been carried outside and situated near that of Mr. Collins—but not too near, and well out of range of a powerful jet spray. . . .

"I see now, Lizzy, what you had to contend with," said her father to Elizabeth in a loud whisper as he was heading into the cage, settling down on the one stool, and letting his daughter padlock it after himself. "I dare say, this cousin of ours is not staying long in this house, if I can help it!"

"What a magnificent evening!" meanwhile came the voice of Mr. Collins, who stood in the middle of his own great cage (that echoed his voice threefold) then periodically strolled like a peacock back and forth, graciously allowing Elizabeth to close and lock his padlocks also (since no one else would), but *not looking* at her even once throughout the process, and speaking his for-once terse thanks in a doleful tone of gravity.

"Dear child, well and bravely done," said Mr. Bennet. "Now, begone before the comet rises! And may this unhappy night be over in all haste, for it has not even quite begun and I am already exhausted." And he once again forgot to remove his spectacles before the Affliction took him, so that his daughter had to gently remind him.

Elizabeth did not need to be told twice; and after a peck on Mr. Bennet's check through the bars, she hurried as far away as possible and returned into the house, to be greeted by a very ill-humoured and sulking Mrs. Bennet.

The morrow produced no abatement of Mrs. Bennet's ill humour or ill health. Mr. Collins was also in the same state of angry pride, having transformed briefly, and—according to her father—harmlessly, into the *demon skunk*, and spending the greater part of the night roaming the perimeter of his great cage, tail held high, while the lion Mr. Bennet roared once, ignored his *beastly* neighbor, and slept as usual.

Elizabeth had hoped that his resentment might shorten his visit, but he still intended to stay until Saturday.

After breakfast, the girls walked to Meryton to inquire if there had been any casualties since the night of the comet (there were none, but one lady had been dreadfully bitten on the foot by a gentleman of the canine persuasion, and all manner of *dire consequences* were now expected and spoken of, in regard to her)—and to inquire if Mr. Wickham were returned, and to lament over his absence from the events of the Netherfield ball.

"I declare it would have been a rare wonder to see Mr. Wickham in his *wolf*, running about the ballroom, chasing the ladies!" giggled Lydia.

"Hush, silly!" retorted Jane, "speak not of that awful night and what other disaster might have come to pass!"

Wickham joined them on their entering the town, and attended them to their aunt's where his regret and vexation, and the concern of everybody, was well talked over. To Elizabeth, however, he voluntarily acknowledged that the necessity of his absence *had* been self-imposed.

"I found," said he, "as the time drew near that I had better not meet Mr. Darcy; that to be in the same room and party with him for so many hours together, might be more than I could bear, and unpleasant scenes might arise. And now it appears the actual situation was even more unfortunate, what with the *comet*, and it is a good thing I was absent, for my uncontained *wolf* might have caused undue harm—"

She highly approved his forbearance, and they discussed it and the strange effects of the comet at leisure, as Wickham and another officer walked back with them to Longbourn. During the walk he particularly attended to her. His company offered her a compliment, and was an occasion to introduce him to her father and mother.

Soon after their return, a letter was delivered to Miss Bennet; it came from Netherfield. The envelope contained a sheet of elegant, little, hot-pressed paper, well covered with a lady's fair, flowing hand. Elizabeth saw her sister's countenance change as she read it, and saw her dwelling intently on some particular passages.

Jane recollected herself, put the letter away, and tried to join with her usual cheerfulness in the general conversation. But Elizabeth felt an anxiety which drew off her attention even from Wickham. No sooner had he and his companion left, than a glance from Jane invited her to follow her upstairs to their room.

Jane took out the letter and said: "This is from Caroline Bingley. The whole party have left Netherfield and are on their way to town—without any intention of coming back again."

She then read the first sentences aloud, of their having just resolved to follow their brother to town directly, and of their meaning to dine in Grosvenor Street, where Mr. Hurst had a doghouse. "I do not pretend to regret anything I shall leave in Hertfordshire, except your society, my dearest friend; but we will hope, at some future period, to continue the delightful relations, and now to maintain a frequent correspondence."

To these high-flown words Elizabeth listened with distrust. Though the suddenness of their removal surprised her, she saw nothing in it to lament—their absence from Netherfield need not prevent Mr. Bingley's being there. And as to the loss of their society, Jane must cease to regard it, in the enjoyment of his.

"It is unlucky," said Elizabeth, "that you should not see your friends before they leave the country. But I hope that the period of future happiness to which Miss Bingley looks forward may arrive earlier than she is aware, and 'friends' will become 'sisters.' Surely Mr. Bingley will not be detained in London?"

"Caroline decidedly says that none of the party will return into Hertfordshire this winter. I will read it to you:"

> "When my brother left us yesterday, he imagined that the business which took him to London might be concluded in a few days. But we are certain it cannot be so—not with the dreadful comet situation, and the need to be caged every night as precaution. We are convinced that when Charles gets to town he will be in no hurry to leave it again. We will be following him thither, that he may not be obliged to spend his lonely Ordeal hours in a comfortless hotel and a stranger's rented cage.
>
> Many of my acquaintances are already there for the winter; I wish that you, my dearest friend, could join the happy crowd—but of that I despair. I sincerely hope your Christmas in Hertfordshire may abound in seasonal gaieties, and that your beaux will be so numerous as to prevent your feeling the loss of the three of whom we shall deprive you."

"It is evident by this," added Jane, "that he comes back no more this winter."

"It is only evident that Miss Bingley does not mean that he *should*."

"Why will you think so? It must be his own doing. He is his own master. But you do not know *all*. I *will* read you the passage which particularly hurts me. I will have no reserves from *you*."

> "Mr. Darcy is impatient to see his sister; and, to confess the truth, *we* are scarcely less eager to meet her again. I really do not think Georgiana Darcy has her equal for beauty, elegance, and accomplishments; and the affection she inspires in Louisa and myself is heightened into something still more interesting, from the hope we dare entertain of her being hereafter our sister. I do not know whether I ever before mentioned to you my feelings on this subject; but I will confide—my brother, with his fierce *tiger* nature, *admires her* greatly already, and will have frequent opportunity now to see her on the most intimate footing. Her relations all wish the connection as much as his own; and without a sister's partiality I call Charles most capable of engaging any woman's heart. With all circumstances to favour an attachment—and nothing to prevent it—am I wrong, my dearest Jane, in indulging the hope of an event which will secure the happiness of so many?"

"What do you think of *this* sentence, my dear Lizzy?" said Jane as she finished it. "Is it not clear enough? Does it not expressly declare that Caroline neither expects nor wishes me to be her sister; that she is perfectly convinced of her brother's indifference; and that if she suspects the nature of my feelings for him, she means (most kindly!) to put me on my guard? Can there be any other opinion on the subject?"

"Yes, and my opinion is totally different! Miss Bingley sees that her brother is in love with *you*, and wants him to marry Miss Darcy. She follows him to town in hope of 'caging' him there, and tries to persuade you that he does not care about you."

Jane shook her head.

"Indeed, Jane, you ought to believe me. No one who has ever seen you together can doubt his affection. Miss Bingley, I am sure, cannot. She is not such a simpleton. Could she have seen half as much love in Mr. Darcy for herself, she would have ordered her wedding clothes. But the case is this: We are not rich enough or grand enough for them; and she is the more anxious to get Miss Darcy for her brother, from the notion that when there has been *one* intermarriage, she may have less trouble in achieving a second—her own!—and I dare say it would succeed, if Miss de Bourgh were out of the way."

Jane looked at her in silence, and Elizabeth went on:

"But, my dearest Jane, you cannot seriously imagine that because Miss Bingley tells you her brother greatly admires Miss Darcy, he is in the smallest degree less sensible of *your* merit, or may be persuaded that, instead of being in love with you, he is very much in love with her friend."

"This is somewhat unjust," replied Jane, "I know Caroline is incapable of willfully deceiving anyone. And all that I can hope in this case is that she is deceiving herself."

"A happy idea! Believe her to be deceived, by all means. You have now done your duty by her, and must fret no longer."

"But, dear Lizzy, can I be happy in accepting a man whose sisters and friends are all wishing him to marry elsewhere?"

"You must decide for yourself," said Elizabeth; "and if you conclude that obliging his two sisters is preferable to the happiness of being his wife, then, by all means, refuse him."

"How can you talk so?" said Jane, faintly smiling. "You must know that though I should be exceedingly grieved at their disapprobation, I could not hesitate."

"I did not think you would. And that being the case, I cannot consider your situation with much compassion."

"But if he returns no more this winter, my choice will never be required. A thousand things may arise in six months!"

"Yes indeed; we may have more comets and another Mr. Collins come to visit!"

"Dear Lord, no! Though, if pressed to choose, I would take a comet!"

But, all jesting aside, Elizabeth treated the idea of Bingley's returning no more with the utmost contempt. It was merely Caroline's wishes, and she could not for a moment suppose that those wishes, however artful, could influence a young man so totally independent of everyone.

She soon convinced her sister, to happy effect. Jane's temper was not desponding, and she was gradually led to hope that Bingley would return to Netherfield and answer every wish of her heart.

They agreed that Mrs. Bennet should only hear of the departure of the family, without being alarmed with the details. But even this partial communication gave her a great deal of concern. Mrs. Bennet bewailed it as exceedingly unlucky that the ladies should go away just as they were all getting so intimate together; and oh, if it had not been for that *odious* comet!

After lamenting it, however, at some length, she had the consolation that Mr. Bingley would soon return and be dining at Longbourn.

Chapter 22

The Bennets were engaged to dine with the Lucases. And again, during the chief of the day, Miss Lucas was so kind as to listen to Mr. Collins—and listen, and listen, and *listen*.

Elizabeth took an opportunity of thanking her. "It keeps him in good humour," said she, "and I am more obliged to you than I can express."

Charlotte assured her friend of her satisfaction in being useful, and that it amply repaid her for the little sacrifice of her time. But Charlotte's kindness extended farther than Elizabeth imagined—its object was to engage Mr. Collins's addresses towards *herself!*

Such was Miss Lucas's scheme; and appearances were so favourable, that when they parted at night, just before he departed to his grandiose cage (followed by the very reluctant Mr. Bennet who was obliged as good host to keep him nightly company outdoors), she would have felt almost secure of success if he did not have to leave Hertfordshire so very soon.

But here she did injustice to the fire and independence of his character, for it led Mr. Collins to escape out of the Longbourn yard storage shed the next morning with admirable slyness—immediately, upon being liberated from his monstrous cage by a nervous maid holding a handkerchief to her nose, to tiptoe past the fretfully napping Mr. Bennet in his own adjacent enclosure—and hasten to Lucas Lodge to throw himself at her feet.

He was anxious to avoid the notice of his cousins, from a conviction that if they saw him depart, they would know his reasons, and he was not willing to have the attempt known before assured success. For though feeling almost secure (Charlotte had been tolerably encouraging), he was comparatively less confident since the adventure of Wednesday.

His reception, however, was of the most flattering kind. Miss Lucas perceived him from an upper window as he walked towards the house, and instantly set out to meet him accidentally in the lane. But little had she dared to hope that so much love and eloquence (and wombats) awaited her there.

In as short a time as Mr. Collins's long speeches would allow, everything was settled between them to the satisfaction of both. They entered the house and advanced to the parlor, with the gentleman carrying on an impassioned monologue and frequently digressing to mention Lady Catherine, twenty-pound koalas in the Rosings Parsonage shrubbery, and his plans for a rosy future. At one point, as Mr. Collins was declaring the very substance of his love, there was a familiar noisy beating of wings, and a large monstrous duck-shaped *object* hurtled through the open window. It made a violent aerial pass around the room, scattering feathers and forcing Mr. Collins to cover his head in a now familiar defensive gesture of distress, while Charlotte merely gave one mild exclamation and held on to her bonnet with a steady hand and observed the duck overhead in some amazement.

In seconds, however, the *hell creature* was gone, retreating back out the window, after letting forth one horrific banshee screech. After it was over, Mr. Collins straightened, adjusted his jacket, cleared this throat, and proceeded with his declaration as though nothing untoward had occurred.

After hearing her delightful answer in the affirmative, he earnestly entreated her to name the day that was to make him the happiest of men—and the lady felt no inclination to trifle with his happiness.

The stupidity with which he was favoured by nature, and the recent addition of the all-permeating *eau de mouffette* aroma, must guard his courtship from any charm that could make a woman wish for its continuance (unless the lady was suffering a loss of both the olfactory and common sense). Miss Lucas, who accepted him solely from the desire of a secure establishment, cared not how soon that establishment were gained.

Sir William and Lady Lucas were speedily applied to for their consent; and it was bestowed with a most joyful alacrity. Mr. Collins's present circumstances, regardless of his *beastly* nature, made it a most eligible match for their daughter, to whom they could give little fortune; and his prospects of future wealth were exceedingly fair.

Lady Lucas began directly to calculate how many years longer Mr. Bennet was likely to live.[61] And Sir William opined that once Mr. Collins was in possession of Longbourn, both he and his wife should make their appearance at St. James's.

The whole family was overjoyed. The younger girls formed hopes of *coming out* a year or two sooner; and the boys were relieved that Charlotte would not die an old maid.

Charlotte herself was tolerably composed. She had gained her object, and her reflections were satisfactory. Mr. Collins, to be sure, was neither sensible nor agreeable. His society was irksome, his cage grandiose and ridiculous, his speeches and his scent overpowering, and his attachment to her must be imaginary. But still he would be her husband.

Without thinking highly either of men or matrimony, marriage had always been her object. It was the only provision

---

[61] One wishes in all haste to assure the delicate reader that Lady Lucas was by no means planning a murder or assassination, or at least one hopes not.

for well-educated young women of small fortune, and however uncertain of giving happiness, must be their pleasantest preservative from want. This preservative[62] she had now obtained; and at the age of twenty-seven, without having ever been handsome, she felt all the good luck of it.

The least agreeable circumstance in the business was the surprise it must give Elizabeth Bennet, whose friendship she valued beyond that of any other person. Elizabeth would wonder, and probably blame her. And despite Charlotte's resolve, her feelings must be hurt by her friend's disapproval.

She resolved to give her the news herself, and therefore charged Mr. Collins, when he returned to Longbourn to dinner, to speak of this to no one.

A promise of secrecy was of course dutifully given, but it was difficult to keep; for the curiosity excited by his long absence elicited questions and required some ingenuity to evade. In addition, he was exercising great self-denial, for he was longing to publish[63] his prosperous love.

As he was to begin his journey too early on the morrow to see any of the family—and quite some time would be required for the servants to load his monstrous cage onto its freight cart—the ceremony of leave-taking was performed when the ladies moved for the night, just before the gentlemen headed outside

---

[62] A preservative is a noxious chemical substance that is periodically added to foods to make them less palatable, so that they can last for generations in the pantry, while preventing the growth of bacteria, trilobites, crocodiles, mushrooms, fungi, and infestations of vermin. A highly effective deterrent against the temptation of hunger, and an eventual reducer of any nutritive value. Wonderful diet aid for the ladies intent on slimming their figures, their chances of fertility, and, at some juncture, achieving mummification.

[63] It is rather unclear whether Mr. Collins was going to publish it as brochure or circular or an actual bound tome for the lending library. One can assume any or all of the above. It is recommended the erudite reader use their imaginary faculties and venture an educated and informed guess.

for their one last sojourn together in the confinement cages. Mrs. Bennet cordially emphasized how happy they should be to see him at Longbourn again.

"My dear madam," Mr. Collins replied, "this invitation is particularly gratifying. You may be certain I shall avail myself of it as *soon* as possible."

They were all astonished. Mr. Bennet—counting down the hours to his guest's departure, and dolefully about to spend yet another drafty night alongside his aromatic guest underneath the open skies and infernal illumination of both crescent moon and comet—could only imagine with horror such a speedy return.

"But is there not danger of Lady Catherine's disapprobation here, my good sir?" said Mr. Bennet. "You had better neglect your relations than run the risk of offending your patroness."

"My dear sir," replied Mr. Collins, "I am particularly obliged to you for this friendly caution. Depend upon it, I do not take so material a step without her ladyship's concurrence."

"You cannot be too careful. Risk anything rather than her *probable displeasure*. Stay quietly at home, and be satisfied, *we* shall take no offence."

"Believe me, my dear sir, my gratitude is warmly excited by such affectionate attention. You will speedily receive my letter of thanks for every mark of your regard during my stay in Hertfordshire. As for my fair cousins, though my absence may be short, I shall now take the liberty of wishing them health and happiness, not excepting my cousin Elizabeth—And now, I fear, the comet is rising and we must hurry to our masculine Ordeal, good sir! One more glorious night of communion—"

Not wishing to hear much more of this, the ladies withdrew in civil haste, leaving the men to their Affliction. All were surprised that Mr. Collins planned a quick return. Mrs. Bennet hoped he planned to pay his addresses to one of her younger girls—Mary might have been prevailed on to accept him.

Indeed, impressed by his "solid reflections," Mary rated his abilities much higher than any of the others. Though not as clever as herself, she thought that, with encouragement, reading, and disavowal of Australian fauna, he could improve himself by her example, and might become a very agreeable companion.

But the following morning, all such hope was shattered. Miss Lucas called soon after breakfast, and in a private conference with Elizabeth related the *event* of the day before.

The possibility of Mr. Collins's fancying himself *in love with her friend* had once occurred to Elizabeth. But that Charlotte could *encourage* him seemed almost as impossible as if she encouraged him herself. Her astonishment was greater than the bounds of decorum. And she could not help crying out:

"Engaged to Mr. Collins! My dear Charlotte—impossible!"

Miss Lucas's steady countenance gave way to a momentary confusion at such a direct reproach. But she expected it, and soon regained her composure.

"Why should you be surprised, my dear Eliza? Do you think it incredible that Mr. Collins should be able to procure any woman's good opinion, because he did not succeed with you?"

"I admit, I do have some difficulty in conceiving that you would choose to spend your life with a skunk."

"Oh, fie!—"

"And now, say 'fi-fo-fum,' and it would be complete."

There was quite more to be said. But Elizabeth had now recollected herself. With a strong effort she was able to wish her friend all imaginable happiness.

"I see what you are feeling," replied Charlotte. "You must be very much surprised—so lately as Mr. Collins was wishing to marry you. But when you think it over, I hope you will be satisfied with what I have done. I am not romantic. I ask only a comfortable home; and considering Mr. Collins's character, connection, and situation in life, I am convinced that my chance of happiness with him is as fair as any."

Elizabeth quietly answered "Undoubtedly." And after an awkward pause, they returned to the rest of the family.

Charlotte did not stay much longer, and Elizabeth was then left to reflect on the turn of events. It was a long time before she became at all reconciled to the idea of so unsuitable a match.

The strangeness of Mr. Collins's making two offers of marriage within three days was nothing in comparison of his being now accepted.

Maybe it too was the effect of the comet?

She had always felt that Charlotte's opinion of matrimony was not exactly like her own, but had not supposed her friend would sacrifice every better feeling to worldly advantage. Charlotte the wife of Mr. Collins was a most humiliating picture!

Charlotte had disgraced herself and sank in her esteem. It was impossible for her to be happy in the lot she had chosen.

Chapter 23

Elizabeth was sitting with her mother and sisters, reflecting on what she had heard, and doubting whether she was allowed to mention it, when Sir William Lucas himself appeared, sent by his daughter, to announce her engagement to the family.

With many compliments to them, and much self-gratulation on the prospect of a connection between the houses, he unfolded the matter to an incredulous audience—for Mrs. Bennet protested he must be entirely mistaken; and Lydia, always unguarded and often uncivil, boisterously exclaimed:

"Good Lord! Sir William, how can you tell such a story? Do not you know that Mr. Skunk—oh!—Mr. Collins wants to marry Lizzy?"

Nothing less than the complaisance of a courtier could have borne such treatment without anger. But Sir William's good breeding carried him through it all. He politely insisted he was correct, and listened to all their impertinence with the most forbearing grand feline courtesy.

Elizabeth mercifully confirmed his account by mentioning her prior knowledge of it from Charlotte herself. To stop the exclamations of her mother and sisters, she earnestly congratulated Sir William, and was readily joined by Jane. They both remarked on the happiness that might be expected from the match, the excellent character of Mr. Collins, and the convenient distance of Hunsford from London.

Mrs. Bennet was in fact too much overpowered to say a great deal while Sir William remained. But no sooner had he left them than her feelings found a rapid vent. She persisted in disbelieving the whole of the matter—no doubt, Mr. Collins had been taken in; they would never be happy together, and the match might be broken off.

Two things were undeniable—Elizabeth was the real cause of the mischief; and Mrs. Bennet herself had been barbarously misused by them all. And on these two points she principally dwelt during the rest of the day.

Nothing could console and nothing could appease her. A week elapsed before she could see Elizabeth without scolding her, a month passed away before she could speak to Sir William or Lady Lucas without being rude, and many months were gone before she could at all forgive their daughter.

Mr. Bennet's emotions were much more tranquil on the occasion. Indeed, bliss had come upon him, for there was no further need to particularly oblige Mr. Collins, no chance of becoming his father-in-law, and no more nights under the stars spent caged together. Thus he pronounced the results most agreeable, and was gratified to discover that Charlotte Lucas, whom he had assumed to be tolerably sensible, was as foolish as his wife, and more foolish than his daughter!

Jane confessed herself a little surprised at the match, but expressed her earnest desire for their sure happiness—Elizabeth could not persuade her otherwise. Kitty and Lydia did not envy Miss Lucas, for Mr. Collins was not only "*beastly* malodorous," but only a clergyman; and it affected them in no other way than as a piece of lurid news to spread at Meryton.

Lady Lucas was not insensible of her triumph. She could now regale Mrs. Bennet with the pleasures of having a daughter well married. She called at Longbourn more often than usual to do just that, though Mrs. Bennet's sour looks and ill-natured remarks might have been enough to drive happiness away.

Between Elizabeth and Charlotte there was a restraint which kept them mutually silent on the subject. Elizabeth felt persuaded that no real confidence could ever subsist between them again.

Her disappointment in Charlotte made her turn with fonder regard to her sister, for whose happiness she grew daily more anxious—Bingley had now been gone a week and nothing more was heard of his return.

Jane had sent Caroline an early answer to her letter, and was counting the days till she might reasonably hope to hear again. The promised letter of thanks from Mr. Collins arrived on Tuesday, addressed to their father, and written with all the solemnity of gratitude which a twelvemonth's abode in the family might have prompted.

After discharging his conscience on that head—precisely as a skunk would discharge the *demonic* contents of its anal scent glands, causing regret and temporary blindness—he proceeded to inform them, with many rapturous expressions and digressions about Lady Catherine and Australian livestock breeding programs, of his happiness in having obtained the affection of their amiable neighbour, Miss Lucas. He explained that it was merely with the view of enjoying *her* society that he was so ready to return to Longbourn, on Monday fortnight. Lady Catherine heartily approved his marriage, and wished it to take place as soon as possible—which he trusted would induce his amiable Charlotte to name an early day for making him the happiest of men.

Mr. Collins's return into Hertfordshire was no longer a matter of pleasure to Mrs. Bennet. On the contrary, she complained of it as much as her husband. "That hateful comet" was still wreaking havoc with the gentlemen's nightly routine, causing everyone to be caged *every night* regardless of the fullness of the moon; and hence, what were they to do, yet again, with that dreadful cage, which was nigh impossible to unload from the cart by three or four strapping servants! It was very strange that he should come to Longbourn instead of to Lucas Lodge (where he could deliver as many odious cages as he liked, bemoaned Mrs. Bennet). It was also very inconvenient and exceedingly troublesome for poor Mr. Bennet and his obligation as a host to keep their cousin company outdoors. Furthermore, she hated having visitors in the house while her health was so indifferent, and *lovers* were of all people the most disagreeable.

Such were the gentle banshee murmurs of Mrs. Bennet, and they gave way only to the greater distress of Mr. Bingley's continued absence.

Neither Jane nor Elizabeth were comfortable on this subject. Day after day passed without bringing any other tidings of him. Even Elizabeth began to fear—not that Bingley was indifferent—but that others would succeed in keeping him away. The united efforts of his two unfeeling sisters and overpowering friend, the attractions of Miss Darcy, and the amusements of London might be too much for the strength of his attachment.

As for Jane, *her* anxiety was, of course, more painful than Elizabeth's, but she concealed her feelings, and the subject was never alluded to.

But no such delicacy restrained her mother—an hour seldom passed in which she did not talk of Bingley, express her impatience for his arrival, or even require Jane to confess that if he did not come back she would think herself very ill used. Only Jane's steady mildness could endure these attacks.

Mr. Collins returned most punctually on Monday fortnight—this time together with his gargantuan cage, which followed him on its slow-moving freight cart like an oversized demonic familiar. But his reception at Longbourn was not quite so gracious as it had been on his first introduction. Mr. Bennet gravely directed the servants to bear *that object* to the back yard, and Mrs. Bennet silently wrung her hands.

Mr. Collins was too happy, however, to need much attention. And luckily for the others, the business of love-making relieved them from a great deal of his scented company. To be fair, the pernicious skunk odor was gradually dissipating, but it would take weeks for it to be gone entirely. And there could be no certainty that, on any given night, with the odious comet and swollen crescent working their concerted evil in the heavens, he might not let loose another such powerful *demon jet spray*, most likely in unhappy lion Mr. Bennet's direction.

The chief of every day was spent by Mr. Collins at Lucas Lodge. Sometimes he returned to Longbourn only in time to apologise for his absence before the family went to bed, and then to head outside with his reluctant host into their respective cages.

"Would that he but stay the night at Lucas Lodge," mused Mr. Bennet in wistful despondence. "Just one night! Mayhap, if he stays overlong and forgets the need to return here and contain himself for the evening's Ordeal, they would be forced to keep him locked up *over there?*"

"Oh, but I do hope he sprays them all!" exclaimed Mrs. Bennet in a subdued burst of fury. "Especially the mother—in her violet muslin gown with the border lace that she clucks over so much—and the scheming daughter—directly in the bonnet!"

Mrs. Bennet was really in a most pitiable state. The very mention of anything concerning the match threw her into an agony of ill-humour. The sight of Miss Lucas was odious to her. As her successor in that house, she regarded her with jealous abhorrence.

Whenever Charlotte came to see them, she concluded her to be anticipating the hour of possession. And whenever "that Lucas Whore of Babylon" spoke in a low voice to Mr. Collins, Mrs. Bennet was convinced that they were talking of the Longbourn estate, and resolving to turn herself and her daughters out of the house, as soon as Mr. Bennet were dead. She complained bitterly of all this to her husband.

"Indeed, Mr. Bennet," said she, "it is very hard to think that Charlotte Lucas should ever be mistress of this house, that I should be forced to make way for *her*, and live to see her take her place in it!"

"My dear, do not give way to such gloom. Let us hope for better things. Let us flatter ourselves that I may be the survivor."

This was not very consoling to Mrs. Bennet. However, the evening was at hand, with Mr. Collins likely on his way here even as they spoke.

No doubt, the comet was rising in the heavens, the moon was nearly full, and the lethal combination was naturally making her husband say such odious things before growing his fur and claws.

Chapter 24

Miss Bingley's letter arrived, and put an end to doubt. They were all settled in London for the winter, and her brother conveyed regret at not having had time to pay his respects before he left the country.

Hope was entirely over.

And when Jane could attend to the rest of the letter, she found little that could give her any comfort. Miss Darcy's praise and her many attractions occupied the chief of it. Caroline boasted joyfully of their increasing intimacy, and predicted the fulfillment of the wishes mentioned in her former letter. She wrote also with great pleasure of her brother's being an inmate[64] of Mr. Darcy's house, and mentioned with raptures his plans with regard to new furniture, including the most modern welded steel reinforcements for the confinement rooms. . . .

---

[64] It is assumed here that, because of the precarious comet situation, Mr. Darcy wisely kept Mr. Bingley incarcerated and confined round the clock, fearful that the gentleman might lose control of his *beastly* nature, *turn* tiger, and perhaps consume the delicate Miss Georgiana Darcy in a ghastly, horrid fashion, by his actions causing the most unfortunate accident since the tragic Fall of Rome and Juliet. Indeed, a loving sibling could not be too careful, one dares hope. —Ed. *[One dares hope that there is a known difference between the Fall of Rome and the tragedy of Romeo and Juliet. On the other hand, hope is such a fickle strumpet. —Ed. 2]*

Elizabeth, to whom Jane very soon communicated all this, heard it in silent indignation. Her heart was divided between concern for her sister, and resentment against all others. To Caroline's assertion of her brother's being partial to Miss Darcy she paid no credit. She still had no doubt that he was really fond of Jane. But, much as she had always like him, she could not think without angry contempt on his lack of resolve, which now made him the slave of his designing friends.

If only his own happiness had been the only sacrifice and not her sister's! She could think of nothing else.

A day or two passed before Jane had courage to speak of her feelings to Elizabeth; but at last, on Mrs. Bennet's leaving them together, after a longer than usual irate monologue about Netherfield and its master, she could not help saying:

"Oh, that my dear mother had more command over herself! She can have no idea of the pain she gives me by her continual reflections on him. But I will not repine. It cannot last long. He will be forgot, and we shall all be as we were before, and speak of nothing but the comet and Mr. Collins."

Elizabeth looked at her sister with incredulous solicitude, but said nothing.

"You doubt me!" cried Jane, slightly colouring; "indeed, you have no reason. He may live in my memory as the most amiable man of my acquaintance, but that is all. I have nothing either to hope or fear, nothing to reproach him with. Thank God! I have not *that* pain. No more than an error of fancy on my side."

"My dear Jane," exclaimed Elizabeth, "you are too good! Your sweetness and disinterestedness are really angelic. But nay, this is not fair. *You* wish to think all the world respectable, and I only want to think *you* perfect. There are few people whom I really love, and still fewer of whom I think well. The more I see of the world, the more am I dissatisfied with it. And every day confirms my belief of human inconsistency, and the scarcity of merit or sense—one such instance I shall not speak of, and the other is Charlotte's marriage."

"My dear Lizzy, do not give way to such feelings as these. You do not make allowance enough for difference of situation and temper. Consider—all *beastly* skunk nature aside—Mr. Collins's respectability, and Charlotte's steady, prudent character. Remember that she is one of a large family, and it is a most eligible match. She may indeed feel something like regard and esteem for our rather *unique* cousin."

"To oblige you, I would try to believe almost anything, but I should only think worse of her, if such is the case. My dear Jane, Mr. Collins is a conceited, pompous, narrow-minded, silly man long before he *turns* into a *demon skunk* or attempts to crossbreed all of England with Australia. You know he is, as well as I do. The woman who marries him cannot have a proper way of thinking. You shall not defend her, though it is Charlotte Lucas. You shall not, for the sake of one individual, change the meaning of principle and integrity, nor persuade anyone that selfishness is prudence, and insensibility of danger is security for happiness."

"I think your language is too strong in speaking of both," replied Jane; "and I hope you will be convinced by seeing them happy together. But—enough. You alluded to *two* instances. I entreat you, dear Lizzy, not to pain me by thinking *that person* to blame, and saying your opinion of him is sunk. Women often think admiration means more than it does."

"And men take care that they should."

"If it is intentional, they cannot be justified; but it is not!"

"Yes; to the last. But if I go on, I shall displease you by saying what I think of persons you esteem."

"You persist, then, in supposing his sisters influence him?"

"Yes, in conjunction with his secretive proud friend, the same one we assume to be a *fire dragon*."

"I cannot believe it. Why should they all try to influence Mr. Bingley? They can only wish his happiness; and if he is attached to me, no other woman can secure it."

"They may wish many things besides his happiness—such as his increase of wealth and consequence, or marriage to a girl who has all the importance of money, connections, and pride."

"Beyond a doubt, they *do* wish him to choose Miss Darcy," replied Jane; "but they have known her much longer than they have known me; no wonder they love her better. It is unlikely they should oppose their brother's wishes. If they believed him attached to me, they would not try to part us, nor could they succeed. Do not distress me by the idea of thinking ill of him or his sisters."

Elizabeth could not oppose such a wish; and from this time Mr. Bingley's name was scarcely ever mentioned between them.

Mrs. Bennet still continued to wonder and repine at his no longer returning. Elizabeth at last endeavoured to convince her that his attentions to Jane had been merely the effect of a common and transient liking, which ceased when he saw her no more. Mrs. Bennet's best comfort was that Mr. Bingley must be down again in the summer.

Mr. Bennet treated the matter differently. "So, Lizzy," said he one day, "your sister is crossed in love. I congratulate her. Next to being married, a girl likes to be crossed a little in love now and then. When is your turn to come? You will hardly bear to be long outdone by Jane. Here are officers enough in Meryton to disappoint all the young ladies in the country. Let Wickham be *your* man. He is a pleasant fellow, and would jilt you creditably, as an honest *wolf* is bound to do, both in society and in the wilderness. And, I venture a guess, *his* cage would readily fit indoors and cause me no undue inconvenience."

"Thank you, sir, but a less agreeable man would satisfy me. We must not all expect Jane's good fortune."

"True," said Mr. Bennet, "but it is a comfort to think that whatever of that kind may befall you, you have an affectionate mother who will make the most of it."

It must be noted, dear Reader, that throughout these events and the days that followed, the *comet* continued to rise every night. And when it rose at the time of the *real* full moon, with both luminaries fiercely burning in the heavens, it was discovered that gentlemen were so direly affected by the dual full force of the wicked illumination, that some even had to be contained during the *daytime*, due to an inexplicable propensity to *turn* and succumb to their specific Affliction at any given moment, including elegant dinner, constitutional walks in the countryside, use of the privy, and Sunday services.

The incidents were many and various. Family members were bitten or scratched or otherwise traumatized (though none were eaten outright). Dinner parties was ruined when doors were open to allow the gentlemen, after their brandy, to rejoin the ladies in the main parlor, and instead admitted packs of roaming wild *beasts*. And one matron was kept prisoner in her own bedchamber, for two solid days, by her own ursine spouse who roamed the hallway, slathering the mahogany paneling with honey, and fending off all servants with his roars—fortunately the dear lady escaped starvation by consuming bonbons, rosewater, and biscuits intended for her pug.

Things had become so unpredictable that containment cages were kept readied all throughout the realm, to be used at a moment's notice.

"Will we ever again get to sleep in our own beds?" many gentlemen complained.

"Will we ever sleep at all?" wondered the terrified ladies.

As for the rest—those men who somehow maintained a strict control over their Affliction—they often found themselves irritable, or with otherwise heightened *emotions* and senses.

Mr. Wickham was one such gentleman. He did not succumb to the Ordeal at inordinate times of day; and yet, his manners, his whole demeanor, bespoke of much unbridled *energy* and unusual excitement during the *daytime* of the full moon. Mr. Wickham's society was thus of material service in dispelling the gloom which the late perverse occurrences had thrown on many of the Longbourn family.

They saw him often, enjoyed his seeming positive excitement, and to his other recommendations was now added that of general *unreserve*. If most gentlemen of the lupine variety were deemed to be open and forthcoming, then this particular *wolf* undoubtedly suffered from logorrhea. The whole of what Elizabeth had already heard, his claims on Mr. Darcy, and *all* that he had suffered from him, was now openly acknowledged and publicly canvassed—over and over and over and over and over and over and *over* again—and everybody was pleased to know how much they had always disliked Mr. Darcy before they had known anything of the matter.

Only Miss Jane Bennet allowed the possibility of any extenuating circumstances in the case, unknown to the society of Hertfordshire. Her mild and steady candour (without being wolfish in the least, unlike *some* people) always pleaded for allowances, and urged the possibility of mistakes.

But everybody else—aggravated by moon and comet—condemned Mr. Darcy as the worst of men.

Chapter 25

After a week spent in professions of love and schemes of felicity, Mr. Collins was called from his amiable Charlotte by the arrival of Saturday.

The pain of separation, however, was alleviated by preparations for the reception of his bride. He had reason to hope that, shortly after his return into Hertfordshire, the day would be fixed that was to make him the happiest of men. He took leave of his relations at Longbourn with as much solemnity as before; wished his fair cousins health and happiness again, and promised their father another letter of thanks, together with comprehensive instructions on the care and feeding of dingoes.

His cage was loaded for yet another time from the shed in the back yard, and the cart rolled out of Longbourn like an elephant on parade. Mr. Bennet waved it a not-particularly-fond farewell from the window of his library and whistled a tune of triumph.

On the following Monday, Mrs. Bennet had the pleasure of receiving her brother and his wife, who came as usual to spend the Christmas at Longbourn. Mr. Gardiner was a sensible, gentlemanlike man who, when the moon took him, *turned* into a distinguished and well-behaved great dane, and was greatly superior to his sister, as well by nature as education.

The Netherfield ladies would have had difficulty in believing that a man who lived by trade, and within view of his own warehouses, could have been so well-bred and agreeable. Mrs. Gardiner, several years younger than Mrs. Bennet and Mrs. Phillips, was an amiable, intelligent, elegant woman, and a great favourite with all her Longbourn nieces. Between the two eldest and herself, there subsisted a particular regard. They had frequently been staying with her in town.

Since the moon was raging-full, the first part of Mrs. Gardiner's business on her arrival was to assist her spouse into his reasonably sturdy, unimposing cage that was easily delivered upstairs into a guest bedroom. Then—while the road-weary Mr. Gardiner, who could barely hold on to his human shape, *turned* in relief, then napped—she distributed her presents and described the newest fashions.

When this was done, it became her turn to listen. Mrs. Bennet had many grievances to relate, and much to complain of. The *odious comet* was an abomination, their cousin dreadfully taken in by a scheming strumpet, and they had all been very ill-used since she last saw her sister. Two of her girls had been upon the point of marriage, and after all there was nothing in it.

"I do not blame Jane," she continued, "for Jane would have got Mr. Bingley if she could. But Lizzy! Oh, sister! It is very hard to think that she might have been Mr. Collins's wife by this time, had it not been for her own perverseness. He made her an offer in this very room, and she refused him. Admittedly, his *beast* is a skunk, and he makes speeches for hours, but what of it? As a consequence, Lady Lucas will have a daughter married before I have, and the Longbourn estate is just as much entailed as ever. The Lucases are very artful people indeed, sister. They are all for what they can get. It makes me very nervous and poorly, to be thwarted so in my own family, and to have selfish neighbours. However, your coming is the greatest of comforts, and I am very glad to hear what you tell us in way of fashion, of long sleeves, and those curious walking-shovels."

Mrs. Gardiner, to whom this news had been given before, in Jane and Elizabeth's letters, made her sister a slight answer, and, in compassion to her nieces, turned the conversation.

When alone with Elizabeth afterwards, she said: "It seems likely to have been a desirable match for Jane. I am sorry it went off. But these things happen so often! A young man, such as you describe Mr. Bingley, so easily falls in love with a pretty girl for a few weeks, and easily forgets her."

"An excellent consolation in its way," said Elizabeth, "but it will not do for *us*. We do not suffer by *accident*—neither when the moon is full, nor when the comet flies. The interference of friends should not persuade a young man of independent fortune to think no more of a girl whom he was violently in love with only a few days before."

"But that expression of 'violently in love' is so hackneyed that it gives me very little idea. It is as often applied to feelings which arise from a half-hour's acquaintance, as to a real, strong attachment. Pray, how *violent was* Mr. Bingley's love?"

"He is a *tiger*."

"And ought that prove something?"

"Once I observed him hold his *beast* back for the sake of Jane's safety. Not many who profess to love can manage that."

"It does speak well of Mr. Bingley indeed," said Mrs. Gardiner with some thought.

"If I may add even more—" continued Elizabeth, "he was growing quite inattentive to other people, and wholly engrossed by her. Every time they met, it was more remarkable. At his own ball he offended several young ladies by not asking them to dance; I spoke to him twice, without receiving an answer. Could there be finer symptoms? Is not general incivility the very essence of love?"

"Oh, yes!—of that kind of love which I suppose him to have felt. Poor Jane! With her disposition, she may not get over it soon. It had better have happened to *you*, Lizzy; you would have laughed yourself out of it sooner. But do you think she would be prevailed upon to go back with us? Change of scene—and a little relief from home—might be of service."

Elizabeth was exceedingly pleased with this proposal, and certain of her sister's ready acquiescence.

"I hope," added Mrs. Gardiner, "that no expectations in regard to this man will affect her. We live in a different part of town, with other connections. We go out so little. It is not likely that they should meet at all, unless he comes to see her."

"And *that* is quite impossible; for he is now in the custody[65] of his friend, and Mr. Darcy would no more suffer him to call on Jane in such a part of London! My dear aunt, how could you think of it? Mr. Darcy may have *heard* of Gracechurch Street, but he would hardly think a month's ablution enough to cleanse him from its impurities—likely still wearing his *shirt* every time he dunks himself—were he once to enter it; and depend upon it, Mr. Bingley never stirs without him."

"So much the better. I hope they will not meet at all. But does not Jane correspond with his sister? *She* might call."

"She will drop the acquaintance entirely."

But in spite of her own words, Elizabeth did not consider the situation completely hopeless. It was possible that Bingley's affection might be restored by the influence of Jane's attractions.

Miss Bennet accepted her aunt's invitation with pleasure, and only hoped that Caroline did not live in the same house as her brother, so that she might visit her and not have to see him.

The Gardiners stayed a week at Longbourn; and what with the Phillipses, the Lucases, the officers, the full moon, and the

---

[65] As previously mentioned, Mr. Darcy is possibly holding Mr. Bingley under house arrest, as a safety precaution. It is unclear if Mr. Darcy possesses a law enforcement badge, but one might expect that such is the case.

comet, there was not a day without its engagement and without its bizarre proliferation of day and evening confinement cages. Indeed, at one dining event at Meryton, two officer gentlemen with a particular tendency to *turn* at any moment, had to have their regimental cages brought into the parlor and dining hall, and were served all the dinner courses through the slots between the thick iron bars—with the one benefit, of course, being that they could at least partake of the dining table conversation.

Mrs. Bennet had so carefully provided for the entertainment of her brother and sister, that they did not once sit down to a family dinner. And when the engagement was for home, Mr. Wickham was always made part of it.

Mrs. Gardiner, noting Elizabeth's warm commendation, narrowly observed them both. She did not suppose they were seriously in love, but their preference of each other was plain enough to make her a little uneasy. She resolved to speak to Elizabeth that it was imprudent to encourage such an attachment.

To Mrs. Gardiner, Wickham had one means of affording pleasure. Before her marriage, she had spent much time in that very part of Derbyshire to which he belonged. They had many acquaintances in common; and though Wickham had been little there since the death of Darcy's father, he could still give her news of her former friends.

Mrs. Gardiner had seen Pemberley, and known the late Mr. Darcy by character perfectly well. Here consequently was an inexhaustible subject of discourse.

In comparing her recollection of Pemberley with the minute description which Wickham could give (for hours on end, unless stopped), and in bestowing her tribute of praise on the character of its late possessor, she was delighting both him and herself.

On being described the present Mr. Darcy's treatment of him, she tried to remember some of that gentleman's reputed disposition when quite a lad which might confirm it. She was confident at last that she recalled having heard Mr. Fitzwilliam Darcy formerly spoken of as a very *proud*, ill-natured boy.

But not once did anyone mention the nature of his *beast*.

Chapter 26

Mrs. Gardiner's caution to Elizabeth was punctually and kindly given on the first opportunity of speaking to her alone:

"You are too sensible a girl, Lizzy, to fall in love merely because you are warned against it. Seriously, I would have you be on your guard. Do not involve yourself or him in an affection which the want of fortune would make so very imprudent. I have nothing to say against *him*; he is a most interesting young *wolf*; and if he had the fortune he ought to have, I should think you could not do better. But as it is, you must not let your fancy run away with you. You have sense, and we all expect you to use it. You must not disappoint your father."

"At present I am not in love with Mr. Wickham. But he is, beyond all comparison, the most agreeable man I ever saw—and if he becomes really attached to me—I believe it will be better that he should not. I see the imprudence of it. Oh! *that* abominable Mr. Darcy! My father's opinion of me does me the greatest honour, and I should be miserable to forfeit it. My father, however, is partial to Mr. Wickham. In short, my dear aunt, I should be very sorry to make any of you unhappy. But how can I promise to be wiser than so many of my fellow-creatures if I am tempted, or how can I resist? All I can promise is not to be in a hurry to believe myself his first object."

"Perhaps you ought to discourage his coming here so very often. At least, do not *remind* your mother to invite him."

"As I did the other day," said Elizabeth with a conscious smile: "very true, it will be wise to refrain from *that*. But it is on your account that he has been so frequently invited this week. You know my mother's ideas as to the necessity of constant company for her friends, and he is one of the few officers who may be relied upon not to *turn* into a slobbering dog or bear in the middle of the afternoon. But upon my honour, I will try to do what I think to be the wisest. And now I hope you are satisfied."

Her aunt assured her that she was, and on parting, Elizabeth thanked her for her kind hints, without resenting the advice.

Mr. Collins and his stupendously proportioned cage returned into Hertfordshire soon after it had been quitted by the Gardiners and Jane. But since he took up his abode with the Lucases, his arrival was no great inconvenience to Mrs. Bennet—or to her spouse who felt only relief and a bit of fluff amusement at the notion.

Mr. Collins's marriage was now fast approaching, and Mrs. Bennet was at length so far resigned as to think it inevitable. She even repeatedly said, in an ill-natured tone, that she "*wished* they might be happy" and "may the *skunk* pass their children by."

Thursday was to be the wedding day, and on Wednesday Miss Lucas paid her farewell visit. When she rose to take leave, Elizabeth, ashamed of her mother's ungracious and reluctant good wishes, and sincerely affected herself, accompanied her out of the room. As they went downstairs together, Charlotte said:

"I shall depend on hearing from you very often, Eliza."

"*That* you certainly shall."

"And I have another favour to ask you. Will you come and see me? I am not likely to leave Kent for some time. Promise me, therefore, to come to Hunsford."

Elizabeth could not refuse, though she foresaw little pleasure and much *odor* in the visit.

"My father and Maria are coming to me in March," added Charlotte, "and I hope you will consent to be of the party. Indeed, Eliza, you will be as welcome as either of them."

The wedding took place; the bride and bridegroom set off for Kent from the church door; the monstrous cage on a newly decorated cart drawn by festooned horses followed thereafter.

Elizabeth soon heard from her friend; and they corresponded as regularly and frequently as ever. But that they should be equally unreserved as before was impossible.

Elizabeth felt that all the comfort of intimacy was over, and corresponded for the sake of what had been. Charlotte's first letters were eagerly received—it was curious to know how she fared in her new home, how she liked Lady Catherine, and how happy she was. And Charlotte expressed herself exactly as foreseen. She wrote cheerfully, seemed surrounded with comforts, and mentioned nothing that she could not praise. The house, furniture, neighbourhood, roads, even her husband's outrageous cage, were all to her taste (and no *smell* was ever referenced), and Lady Catherine's behaviour was most friendly and obliging. It was Mr. Collins's picture of Hunsford and Rosings rationally softened. Elizabeth perceived that she must visit to know the rest.

Jane had already written to announce their safe arrival in London. And when she wrote again, Elizabeth hoped it would be something of the Bingleys.

Her impatience for this second letter was as poorly rewarded. Jane had been a week in town without either seeing or hearing from Caroline. She supposed that her last letter to her friend must have been accidentally lost.

"My aunt," she continued, "is going to-morrow into that part of the town, and I shall take the opportunity of calling in

Grosvenor Street. The moon is now again but a sliver, so with the comet still on high there is at least no danger in the *daytime*."

Jane wrote again when the visit was paid, and she had seen Miss Bingley. "I did not think Caroline in spirits, but she was glad to see me, and reproached me for giving her no notice of my coming to London. My last letter must have never reached her. I inquired after their brother. He was well, but so much engaged[66] with Mr. Darcy that they scarcely ever saw him. I found that Miss Darcy was expected to dinner. I wish I could see her. My visit was not long, as Caroline and Mrs. Hurst were going out—Mr. Hurst (unclear whether *hound* or gentleman) needed a walk. I dare say I shall see them soon here."

Elizabeth shook her head over this letter; convinced that only accident could reveal to Mr. Bingley that Jane was in town.

Four weeks passed, the comet still rode the heavens, and Jane saw nothing of him. She told herself that she did not regret it; but could no longer be blind to Miss Bingley's inattention. After waiting at home every morning for a fortnight, and inventing every evening a fresh excuse for her, the visitor did at last appear. But her short stay, and changed manner no longer allowed Jane to deceive herself, and she wrote to her sister.

> "My dearest Lizzy, do not triumph at my expense. I confess to have been entirely deceived in Miss Bingley's regard for me. But, my dear sister, though the event has proved you right, I still assert that, considering what her behaviour was, my confidence was as natural as your suspicion. I do not at all comprehend her reason for wishing to be intimate with me. Caroline did not return my visit till yesterday; and not a note did I receive in the meantime. When she did come, it was very evident that she had no pleasure in it. She made a slight, formal apology, for not

---

[66] To be sure, it is an impossibility that Mr. Bingley and Mr. Darcy were engaged to be married to each other; begging pardon of the delicate reader's sensibilities, but it is prudent to point out that both of them are *gentlemen*, and neither one is Oscar Wilde—though there is nothing wrong with that.

calling before, said not a word of wishing to see me again, and talked only of the comet and the various gentlemen *scandalized* by its illumination, in her social circles. She was in every respect so altered a creature, that when she left I was perfectly resolved to discontinue the acquaintance.

"I both pity and blame her. She was very wrong in singling me out as she did; I can safely say that every advance to intimacy[67] began on her side. But she must feel that she has been acting wrong. Surely, anxiety for her brother is the cause of it. Though *we* know this anxiety to be quite needless, yet it will easily account for her behaviour to me—so deservedly dear as he is to his sister, whatever anxiety she must feel on his behalf is natural and amiable.

"I cannot but wonder, however, if he had at all cared about me, we must have met, long ago. He knows of my being in town, I am certain, from what she said. And yet it would seem as if she wanted to persuade herself that he is really partial to Miss Darcy. I cannot understand it. There is a strong appearance of duplicity in all this. But I banish every painful thought, and only think of your affection, and the kindness of my dear uncle and aunt. Let me hear from you soon! Miss Bingley said something of his never returning to Netherfield, of giving up the house. But we had better not mention it. I am glad that you have such pleasant accounts from our friends at Hunsford. Pray go to see them. I am sure you will enjoy the visit.—Yours, etc."

This letter gave Elizabeth some pain. But her spirits returned as she considered that Jane would no longer be duped, by the sister. All expectation from the *tiger* brother was now

---

[67] Oh dear, yet again! What a scandalous notion to assume there might be something untoward going on between Miss Bennet and Miss Bingley of the romantic sort. One begs the reader to not dare think such outrageous notions, and to clear their filthy mind by closing their eyes and thinking of England, not Lesbos. Not two ladies together, but England. No, indeed. Never that. England. Absolutely not that fair Grecian isle of Lesbos where Sappho sung her immortal poetry. No, never that.

absolutely over. She would not even wish for a renewal of his attentions. His character sunk on every review of it. And as a punishment for him (and an advantage to Jane), she seriously hoped he might soon marry Mr. Darcy's sister—by Wickham's account, she would make him regret what he had thrown away.

Meanwhile, Mrs. Gardiner reminded Elizabeth of her promise concerning Mr. Wickham, and required an update.[68] And Elizabeth imparted that his apparent *partiality* had subsided. His attentions were over; he was the admirer of someone else.

Elizabeth could mention it without pain. Her heart had been but slightly touched, and her vanity was satisfied that *she* would have been his only choice, had fortune permitted it.

The sudden acquisition of ten thousand pounds was the most remarkable charm of the young lady to whom he was now rendering himself agreeable. But Elizabeth (less clear-sighted in his case than in Charlotte's) did *not* quarrel with him for his wish of independence. On the contrary, it seemed natural; and if it cost him a few struggles to relinquish her, she allowed it was wise and desirable for all, and sincerely wished him happy.

All this was acknowledged to Mrs. Gardiner:

> "I am now convinced, my dear aunt, that I have never been much in love—for had I really experienced that pure and elevating passion, I should now detest his very name, and wish him all manner of evil. But my feelings are cordial towards *him*; and impartial towards Miss King. I do not hate her, and am willing to think her a very good sort of girl.
>
> There can be no love in all this; thus I am not an interesting object of pity to all my acquaintances. Kitty and Lydia take his defection much more to heart than I do. They

---

[68] Mrs. Gardiner has been operating in the same outdated version for too many months, and now required to be updated to the latest release with more user-friendly features and advanced security. [Who is this, again? And what in blazes does it mean? —Ed.] *[Exactly how I feel when reading your imbecile commentary. —Ed. 2]*

are young in the ways of the world, and not yet open to the mortifying conviction that handsome young men with fine regimental cages must have something to live on as well as the plain."

Chapter 27

With no greater events than these in the Longbourn family, and the walks to Meryton, sometimes dirty and sometimes cold, did January and February pass away, with the comet still rising every night.

March was to take Elizabeth to Hunsford. At first, she did not seriously think of going. But Charlotte was counting on her visit, and she gradually began to look forward to it. Absence had increased her desire of seeing Charlotte again, and weakened her disgust of Mr. Collins.

There was novelty in the scheme. And with such a mother and such uncompanionable sisters at home, a little change was not unwelcome. The journey would moreover give her a peep at Jane. And as the time drew near, she would have been very sorry for any delay. Everything, however, went on smoothly, and was finally settled. She was to accompany Sir William, his dignified antique cage, and his second daughter. And with the addition of spending a night in London, the plan became entirely perfect.

The only pain was in leaving her father, who would certainly miss her. Indeed, *who* would now lock and secure his cage every night? He so disliked her going, that he told her to write to him, and almost promised to answer her letter.

The farewell between herself and Mr. Wickham was perfectly friendly—on his side even more. His present pursuit could not make him forget that Elizabeth had been the first to excite and deserve his *lupine* and manly attention, the first to listen and pity, the first to be admired. And in his manner of bidding her adieu—wishing her every enjoyment, reminding her of what she was to expect in Lady Catherine de Bourgh, and trusting their opinion would always coincide—there was a solicitude, an interest which must ever attach her to him with a sincere regard. She parted from him convinced that, whether married or single, he must always be her model[69] of the amiable.

Her fellow-travelers the next day were not of a kind to make her think him less agreeable. Sir William Lucas, and his daughter Maria, a good-humoured girl, but as empty-headed as himself, had nothing to say that could be worth hearing, and were listened to with about as much delight as the rattle of the chaise or the *voice* of Mr. Collins.

It was a journey of only twenty-four miles, and they began it so early as to be in Gracechurch Street by noon. As they drove through the streets of London, it was apparent that the predominance of gentlemen's travel cages of all dimensions was severely constricting traffic. It was but a healthy precaution that had forced so many men of breeding to take their chains, padlocks, and containment along with them even when making ordinary social calls among their circles of acquaintance. Such was the new norm of daily routine among the *ton*, evolved from an admirable aversion for any unpredictability that could arise from the lingering effect of the comet in the skies.

This effect of traffic congestion was observed all the way to Mr. Gardiner's door. Jane was at a drawing-room window

---

[69] Mr. Wickham did not at any time endeavour to model gentlemen's attire or work at a house of fashion as a mannequin, human or lupine. Were he ever to be engaged in such unspeakable behaviour, we would be duly informed of it.

watching their arrival on the street below, among the wrought-iron-and-varnished-wood sea of morning caller cages.

When they entered the passage she was there to welcome them, and Elizabeth, looking earnestly in her face, was pleased to see it healthful and lovely as ever. The day passed most pleasantly; the morning in bustle and shopping, and the evening at one of the theatres.

Elizabeth then contrived to sit by her aunt. She was more grieved than astonished to hear, in reply to her inquiries about her sister, that though Jane always struggled to support her spirits, there were periods of dejection. Mrs. Gardiner gave her the particulars of Miss Bingley's visit in Gracechurch Street, and repeated conversations between Jane and herself, which proved that the former had, from her heart, given up the acquaintance.

Mrs. Gardiner then rallied her niece on Wickham's desertion, and complimented her on bearing it so well.

"But, my dear Elizabeth," she added, "what sort of girl is Miss King? I should be sorry to think our *wolf* mercenary."[70]

"Pray, my dear aunt, what is the difference in matrimonial affairs, between the mercenary and the prudent motive? Last Christmas you were afraid of his marrying me, because it would be imprudent; and now, because he is trying to get a girl with ten thousand pounds, you want to find out that he is mercenary."

"If you will only tell me what sort of girl Miss King is, I shall know what to think."

"She is a very good kind of girl. I know no harm of her."

"But he paid her not the smallest attention till her grandfather's death made her mistress of this fortune. There seems an indelicacy in directing his attentions towards her so soon after this event."

---

[70] Despite what Mrs. Gardiner might think, the gentle reader is reassured in all haste that at no time has Mr. Wickham ever served as a mercenary, domestic or foreign, and was never employed in a Foreign Legion.

"A man in distressed circumstances has not time for all those elegant decorums which other people observe, in particular if he is a lone *wolf*. If *she* does not object to it, why should *we?*"

"*Her* not objecting does not justify *him*. It only shows her being deficient in sense or feeling—and possibly proficient in wearing a red riding hood."

"Well," cried Elizabeth, "fairy tale attractions aside, have it as you like. *He* shall be mercenary; *she* shall be foolish in red."

"No, Lizzy, that is what I do *not* like. I should be sorry to think ill of a young man who has lived so long in Derbyshire."

"Oh! if that is all, I already have a very poor opinion of young men who live in Derbyshire; and their intimate *tiger* friends who live in Hertfordshire are not much better. I am sick of them all. Thank Heaven! I am going to-morrow where I shall find a man who has not one agreeable quality, a powerful skunk odor, and neither manner nor sense to recommend him. Stupid men are the only ones worth knowing, after all."

"Take care, Lizzy; that speech savours strongly of disappointment."

Before they were separated by the conclusion of the play, she had the unexpected happiness of an invitation to accompany her uncle and aunt in a tour of pleasure which they proposed taking in the summer.

"We have not determined how far it shall carry us," said Mrs. Gardiner, "but, perhaps, to the Lakes. Traveling these days is a cumbersome affair of bringing those dour cages everywhere one goes, and such necessity does not appear to decrease any time soon; one supposes, not until that pesky comet departs the night skies conclusively once and for all. And even then—who knows what might follow, and how long the dire effects might linger on. . . . But, even with such additional cargo to bring along on the journey, the delights of that locale are worth the effort, would you not agree?"

No scheme could have been more agreeable to Elizabeth. "Oh, my dear aunt," she rapturously cried, accepting the invitation, "what delights indeed! what felicity! You give me fresh life and vigour. Adieu to disappointment and spleen. What are young men to rocks and mountains? Oh! what hours of transport we shall spend! Indeed, the nuisance of Mr. Gardiner's cage shall amount to nothing!"

Chapter 28

Every object in the next day's journey was new and interesting to Elizabeth. Her spirits were uplifted; for she had seen her sister looking so well, and the prospect of her northern tour was a constant source of delight.

When they left the high road with its proliferation of freight carts and other Affliction cage traffic—even this far outside the city few gentlemen of breeding dared to travel without one—and were now moving on the less traveled lane to Hunsford, every eye was in search of the Parsonage, and every turning expected to bring it in view.

The palings of Rosings Park was their boundary on one side. Elizabeth smiled at the recollection of all that she had heard of its inhabitants.

At length the Parsonage was discernible. The garden sloping to the road, the house, the green pales, and the laurel hedge—where likely the following year Mr. Collins was planning to enact his intimate *introduction* of Australian and British species—everything declared they were arriving.

Mr. Collins and Charlotte appeared at the door, and the carriage stopped at the small gate which led by a short gravel walk to the house. In a moment they were all out of the chaise, rejoicing at the sight of each other.

Mrs. Collins welcomed her friend with the liveliest pleasure, and Elizabeth was more and more satisfied with coming when she found herself so affectionately received.

She also saw instantly that her cousin's manners were not altered by his marriage. His formal civility, incessant loud discourse, and just the lightest whiff of *skunk*, was just as it had been. He detained her some minutes at the gate with inquiries after all her family. They were then (with no other delay than his pointing out the neatness of the entrance) taken into the house. In the parlour, he welcomed them a second time, with ostentatious formality to his humble abode, and punctually repeated all his wife's offers of refreshment.

A this point, Elizabeth cautiously inhaled, and was relieved to find the all-permeating skunk odor that, as she expected, filled the domicile, was decidedly tolerable.

Elizabeth was prepared to see Mr. Collins in his glory. She could not help imagining that in displaying the fine elements and furnishings of the room, he addressed himself particularly to *her*, as if wishing to make her feel what she had lost in refusing him.

But though everything seemed neat and comfortable, she was not able to gratify him by any sigh of repentance. Rather, she looked with wonder at her friend that she could have so cheerful an air with such a companion.

When Mr. Collins said anything of which his wife might reasonably be ashamed, she involuntarily turned her eye on Charlotte. Once or twice she could discern a faint blush. But in general Charlotte wisely did not hear.

After sitting long enough to admire every article of furniture in the room, from the sideboard to the fender,[71] to give an account of their journey and London, Mr. Collins invited them to take a stroll in the garden.

---

[71] It is uneasy and bewildering to imagine how either a guitar or the front portion of a horseless carriage ended up in the Collins parlor. Begging the reader's pardon, this is surely a mistake of the negligent Author.

It was large and well laid out, and its cultivation attended by Mr. Collins himself. To work in this garden was one of his most respectable pleasures. Elizabeth admired the command of countenance with which Charlotte talked of the healthfulness of the exercise, "the pleasures of the shrubbery and its future Australian residents," and owned she *encouraged it* as much as possible.

Here, leading the way through every walk, and scarcely allowing them an interval to utter the praises he asked for, every view was pointed out. He could number the fields in every direction, and could tell how many trees there were in the most distant clump and what excellent "liaison spots" they would make for the lovelorn kangaroo, numbats, and emu that were soon to be introduced here. But of all the views which his garden, the country, or kingdom could boast, none were to be compared with the prospect of Rosings, afforded by an opening in the trees that bordered the park nearly opposite the front of his house. It was a handsome modern building, well situated on rising ground.

From his garden, Mr. Collins would have led them round his two meadows. But the ladies, not having shoes to encounter the remains of a white frost, turned back. While Sir William accompanied him, Charlotte took her sister and friend over the house, extremely pleased to show it without her husband's help.

The house was rather small—except for Mr. Collins's disproportionately grandiose containment chamber situated near the kitchen, an addition specially built to be twice its size, and indeed the size of a dungeon, with a plethora of chains and iron padlocks to render Mr. Collins as immobile as imaginable under the dire monthly circumstances. The rest of the house was well built and convenient, with a neatness for which Elizabeth gave Charlotte all the credit. When Mr. Collins could be forgotten, there was really an air of great comfort throughout (and almost no hint of skunk odor), and by Charlotte's evident enjoyment of it, Elizabeth supposed he must be often forgotten.

She had already learnt that Lady Catherine was still in the country. While they were at dinner, Mr. Collins observed:

"Yes, Miss Elizabeth, you will have the honour of seeing Lady Catherine de Bourgh on the ensuing Sunday at church, and I need not say you will be delighted with her. She is all affability and condescension, and will include you in every invitation. Her behaviour to my dear Charlotte is charming. We dine at Rosings twice every week, and are never allowed to walk home. One of her ladyship's *several* carriages is regularly ordered for us."

"Lady Catherine is a very respectable, sensible woman indeed," added Charlotte, "and a most attentive neighbour."

"Very true, my dear, that is exactly what I say—the sort of woman whom one cannot regard with too much deference."

"I do believe I need to mention one other thing," said Charlotte to Elizabeth moments later when Mr. Collins was not paying attention, "You may be surprised, Lizzy, but since the advent of the comet and its consequent 'upset" of the male monthly routine, Lady Catherine is a bit—how shall one say—*particular* about gentlemen's cages being present *at all times* including brief visitation and extended company. She has as many cages as there are male visitors delivered into the parlor, and the dining hall, and anywhere else time is spent. It does tend to get crowded at Rosings, and a bit difficult to walk from room to room at times; and yes, I do realize it is *odd*; but, Lizzy, she did have a terrible scare once at the apex of the comet-and-full-moon. During a harmless morning call, a local squire could not help himself and *turned* into a dreadful boar (and I do mean *pig*, not an *ennui*-inducing dullard, though, the gentleman was deemed somewhat tiresome even before the incident) and he almost gutted poor Miss Anne de Bourgh . . . or possibly he was but trying to get to the cucumber sandwiches and she was unhappily in the way—"

"Oh dear! And what are Lady Catherine's views on Mr. Collins's quite extraordinary cage?"

"Mr. Collins is not allowed to even attempt to bring his travel cage indoors, for as you know it does not really *fit* . . . anywhere with a normal *door*."

"Yes—that is, no, it does not."

"Indeed not."

"Not at all." Elizabeth fought to maintain her countenance.

"Instead," continued Charlotte, with a deep breath to steady herself, but having some difficulty speaking also, "he is provided a proper guest cage—one of the many available—every time he attends Rosings . . . I do believe it is a rather good thing for all concerned."

"Yes, I agree," said Elizabeth. "Might I ask, where is that very *large* cage right now?"

"It sits near the dairy barn—Oh, hush! I convinced Mr. Collins it is altogether for the best. And cows can sometimes use it. Indeed, whenever it rains, the additional enclosure serves its purpose. And when all that Australian livestock comes—"

But neither Charlotte nor Elizabeth could contain their shaking much longer, and were obliged to hide behind napkins.

The evening was spent chiefly in talking over Hertfordshire news. Afterwards, in the solitude of her chamber, Elizabeth meditated upon Charlotte's degree of contentment and her composure in bearing with her husband, and had to admit that it was all done very well. She imagined how the rest of her visit would pass—the quiet tenor of their usual employments, the vexatious interruptions of Mr. Collins, and the gaieties of their intercourse[72] with Rosings.

About the middle of the next day, as she was in her room getting ready for a walk, a sudden noise below seemed to speak

---

[72] This is surely a scandalous thought to have and hold, and the reader is kindly begged to abstain from such unimaginable filth! Rather, one is asked to think of innocent subjects such as delicate roses and flitting butterflies.

the whole house in confusion. No, it was not yet the time of the full moon, and no one could have succumbed to the Affliction and uncontrollably *turned* in the parlor in daylight. After listening a moment while carefully testing the air for a hint of *skunk*, she heard somebody running upstairs in a violent hurry, and calling loudly after her. She opened the door and met Maria in the landing, who, breathless with agitation, cried out—

"Oh, my dear Eliza! pray make haste and come into the dining-room, for there is such a sight to be seen! Make haste!"

"Gracious! Does anyone require chains? A leash, perhaps?"

But Maria would tell her nothing more, and down they ran into the dining-room, which fronted the lane.

The wonder consisted of two ladies stopping in a low phaeton at the garden gate.

"Is this all?" cried Elizabeth. "I expected someone *eaten*, or at least that the pigs were got into the garden. Here is nothing but Lady Catherine and her daughter."

"La! my dear," said Maria, quite shocked at the mistake, "it is not Lady Catherine. The old lady is Mrs. Jenkinson, who lives with them; the other is Miss de Bourgh. Only look at her. She is quite a little creature. Who would have thought that she could be so thin and small?"

"She is abominably rude to keep Charlotte out of doors in all this wind. Why does she not come in?"

"Oh, Charlotte says she hardly ever does. It is the greatest of favours when Miss de Bourgh comes in."

"I like her appearance," said Elizabeth, struck with other ideas. "She looks sickly and cross." *Yes, she will do for him very well. She will make him a very proper wife.*

Mr. Collins and Charlotte were both standing at the gate in conversation with the ladies. And Sir William, to Elizabeth's high diversion, was stationed in the doorway, in earnest contemplation of the greatness before him, and constantly bowing whenever Miss de Bourgh looked that way.

At length there was nothing more to be said. The ladies drove on, and the others returned into the house.

Mr. Collins no sooner saw the two girls than he began to congratulate them on their good fortune. Charlotte explained that the whole party was asked to dine at Rosings the next day.

Chapter 29

Mr. Collins's triumph, in consequence of this invitation, was complete. The power of displaying the grandeur of his patroness to his visitors, and of letting them see her civility towards himself and his wife, was exactly what he had wished for.

"I confess," said he, "that, knowing her affability, I should not have been at all surprised by her ladyship's asking us on Sunday to drink tea and spend the evening at Rosings. But who could have foreseen such an attention as this? An invitation to dine, for the whole party, so immediately after your arrival!"

"I am the less surprised," replied Sir William, "from that knowledge which my situation in life has allowed me to acquire. At court, such instances of elegant breeding are not uncommon, even during the full moon."

Scarcely anything was talked of the whole day or next morning but their visit to Rosings. Mr. Collins was carefully instructing them in what they were to expect, how to maneuver "delicately, like a little lamb" around the many cages, and that the sight of such rooms, so many servants, and so splendid a dinner, might not wholly overpower them.

When the ladies were separating for the toilette, he said to Elizabeth—

"Do not make yourself uneasy, my dear cousin, about your apparel. Lady Catherine is far from requiring that elegance of dress in us which becomes herself and her daughter. I would advise you merely to put on your *best* clothes. Lady Catherine will not think the worse of you for being simply dressed. She likes to have the distinction of rank preserved."

While they were dressing, he came two or three times to their different doors, to recommend their being quick, as Lady Catherine very much objected to be kept waiting for her dinner. In regards to her ladyship, he thus terrified Maria Lucas entirely.

As the weather was fine, they had a pleasant walk of about half a mile across the park. Every park has its beauty and its prospects; and Elizabeth saw much to be pleased with, though she could not be in such raptures as Mr. Collins expected. She was also but slightly affected by his enumeration of the windows in front of the house, and what the glazing altogether had originally cost Sir Lewis de Bourgh.

When they ascended the steps to the hall, Maria's alarm increased, and even Sir William did not look perfectly calm.

Elizabeth's courage did not fail her. She had heard nothing of Lady Catherine that implied any extraordinary talent or virtue. And money or rank she could witness without trepidation.

From the entrance-hall, of which Mr. Collins pointed out, with a rapturous air, the fine proportion, the finished ornaments, and one cautionary guest cage, they followed the servants through an ante-chamber (with two more cages, albeit more genteel, of ornamental wrought iron), to the room where Lady Catherine, her daughter, and Mrs. Jenkinson were sitting. Behind them, flush against the wall, was a row of over half a dozen very fine polished iron cages, at lest ten feet in height, with insignias and embellishments, and, in places, touches of burnished gold between the thick bars and on the ornate padlocks.

Her ladyship, with great condescension, arose to receive them. And as Mrs. Collins had settled it with her husband that the office of introduction should be hers, it was performed in a proper manner, without any of those apologies and thanks which he would have thought necessary.

"Shall I avail myself—that is, shall Sir William and I both avail ourselves, Your Ladyship?" Mr. Collins thereafter uttered rapturously, pointing at the nearest cage, and bowing several times, before any other word was spoken by anyone.

"Not quite yet," was the regal answer, as the grand lady gifted them with her sharp perusal. "But, Mrs. Jenkinson, do observe them closely for any improper *signs* of the Affliction. Anything untoward, and in you go!"

Mr. Collins and Sir William—the latter in some stunned amazement—both bowed deeply in absolute acquiescence.

Indeed, in spite of having been at St. James, Sir William was so completely awed by the grandeur surrounding him, that he had but just courage enough to make a very low bow, and take his seat without saying a word—ready to spring up at a moment's notice and confine himself in the nearest cage, unasked.

Maria Lucas, frightened almost out of her senses, sat on the edge of her chair, not knowing which way to look. Only Elizabeth found herself quite equal to the scene, and could observe the three ladies before her composedly.

Lady Catherine was a tall, large woman, with strongly-marked features, which might once have been handsome. Her air was not conciliating, nor was her manner of receiving them such as to make her visitors forget their inferior rank. She was not rendered formidable by silence; but whatever she said was spoken in so authoritative a tone, as marked her self-importance, and brought Mr. Wickham immediately to Elizabeth's mind—Lady Catherine appeared to be exactly what he represented.

After examining the mother, in whose countenance and deportment she soon found some resemblance of Mr. Darcy, Elizabeth turned her eyes on the daughter. Here, she could almost have joined in Maria's astonishment at her being so thin and so small.

There was neither in figure nor face any likeness between the ladies. Miss de Bourgh was pale and sickly; her features, though not plain, were insignificant; and she spoke very little, except in a low voice, to Mrs. Jenkinson, in whose appearance there was nothing remarkable, and who was entirely engaged in listening to what she said, and placing a screen in the proper direction before her eyes.

After sitting a few minutes, they were all sent to one of the windows to admire the view. Mr. Collins attended them to point out its beauties and simultaneously make a great show of noting the closest cage, to please her ladyship. And Lady Catherine kindly informed them that it was much better worth looking at in the summer.

The dinner was exceedingly handsome, with all the servants and articles of plate that Mr. Collins had promised. And, as he had likewise foretold, he took his seat at the bottom of the table, by her ladyship's desire being the nearest to the cage "section" in that chamber, got up several times to test the door of the chosen cage and its several padlocks to make certain he could slip inside swiftly, and looked as if he felt that life could furnish nothing greater. He carved, and ate, and praised with delighted alacrity; and every dish was commended, first by him and then by Sir William, who was now enough recovered to visually claim the nearest other vacant cage for himself (together with the shortest route to make a proper retreat there) and then echo whatever his son-in-law said, in a manner which Elizabeth wondered Lady Catherine could bear.

But Lady Catherine seemed gratified by their excessive admiration, and gave most gracious smiles to both skunk and elderly panther, especially when any dish on the table proved a novelty to them.

The party did not supply much conversation. Elizabeth was ready to speak whenever there was an opening, but she was seated between Charlotte and Miss de Bourgh—the former of whom was engaged in listening to Lady Catherine, and the latter said not a word to her all dinner-time.

Mrs. Jenkinson was chiefly employed in watching the gentlemen for dangerous "signs," and noting how little Miss de Bourgh ate—pressing her to try some other dish, and fearing she was indisposed. Maria thought speaking out of the question, and the gentlemen did nothing but eat and admire.

When the ladies returned to the drawing-room, there was little to be done but to hear Lady Catherine talk, which she did without any intermission till coffee came in. She delivered her opinion on every subject in so decisive a manner, as proved that she was not used to being contradicted. She inquired into Charlotte's domestic concerns, gave her a great deal of advice as to the management of them all; told her how everything ought to be regulated in so small a family as hers, and instructed her as to the care of her cows and her poultry, segueing eventually into the integration of Australian native livestock into both herd and coop and the encouragement of their vigorous "congress" to "improve the future generations."

Elizabeth found that nothing was beneath this great lady's attention, which could furnish her with an occasion of dictating to others. In the intervals of her discourse with Mrs. Collins, she addressed a variety of questions to Maria and Elizabeth, but especially to the latter, of whose connections she knew the least, and who she observed to Mrs. Collins was a very genteel, pretty kind of girl. She asked her how many sisters she had, whether they were older or younger than herself, whether any of them were handsome and likely to be married, where they had been educated, what *beastly* flavor of Affliction did her father suffer from, what manner of metal cage and carriage he kept, and what had been her mother's maiden name.[73] Elizabeth felt all the impertinence of her questions but answered them with calm.

"Your lion father's estate is entailed on Mr. Collins. For your sake," Lady Catherine observed, turning to Charlotte, "I am glad of it; but otherwise I see no occasion for entailing estates from the female line. It was not thought necessary in Sir Lewis de Bourgh's family. Do you play and sing, Miss Bennet?"

"A little."

"Oh! then—some time or other we shall be happy to hear you. Our instrument is superior. You shall try it some day. Do your sisters play and sing?"

And then Lady Catherine proceeded to inquire and discover to her astonishment that the Bennet girls for the most part did not know at all how to play, sing, draw, had no exposure to the London masters, and had never had a governess.

"No governess! How was that possible? Five daughters brought up at home without a governess! I never heard of such a thing. Then, who taught you? You must have been neglected."

"Compared with some families, we were; but such of us as wished to learn never lacked the means. We were always encouraged to read, and had all the masters that were necessary. Those who chose to be idle, certainly might."

"Aye, no doubt; but that is what a governess will prevent, and I should have advised your mother to engage one. I always say that nothing is to be done in education without steady and regular instruction, and nobody but a governess can give it—" And Lady Catherine went on to speak of several families who thus benefited from her own recommendations.

---

[73] It has become increasingly apparent here that Lady Catherine was gathering personal information in order to open a banking account in Elizabeth Bennet's name at a financial institution, and possibly to commit identity fraud. Miss Bennet is strongly advised not to give out any personal details and to report her ladyship to the authorities.

"Does your mother herself attend to your father's confinement chamber during the indelicacy of the full moon, or does she send servants?"

"Neither, ma'am; mostly, I do it."

"What? You witness your own parent's Ordeal? How inappropriate! What happens if he were to shed his clothing?"

"I simply avert my eyes. Besides, for the most part he only drops his spectacles, and I am afraid there is no one else who is willing to do this task."

"Is his *beast* particularly gruesome?"

"On the contrary, he is quite harmless. His *lion* roars and falls asleep in minutes. I merely secure the cage."

"Well! And are any of your other sisters out, Miss Bennet?"

"Yes, ma'am, all."

"All! What, all five out at once? Very odd! The younger ones out before the elder ones are married! Your younger sisters must be very young?"

"Yes, my youngest is not sixteen. Perhaps *she* is too young to be in company. But really, ma'am, I think it would be very hard upon younger sisters, that they should not have their share of society and amusement, because the elder may not have the means to marry early. It would not promote sisterly affection."

"Upon my word," said her ladyship, "you give your opinion very decidedly for so young a person. Pray, what is your age?"

"With three younger sisters grown up," replied Elizabeth, smiling, "your ladyship can hardly expect me to own it."

Lady Catherine seemed quite astonished at not receiving a direct answer. Elizabeth suspected herself to be the first creature to have ever dared trifle with so much dignified impertinence.

"You cannot be more than twenty, I am sure, therefore you need not conceal your age."

"I am not one-and-twenty."

When the gentlemen had been allowed to join them—after first sending in a servant armed with a precautionary poker and length of chain to make sure they had not *turned* into beasts *in absentia*—and tea was over, the card-tables were placed.

Lady Catherine, Sir William, and Mr. and Mrs. Collins sat down to quadrille, at a card-table nearest the cages. And as Miss de Bourgh chose to play at cassino, the two girls had the honour of assisting Mrs. Jenkinson to make up her party.

Their table was superlatively stupid.[74] Scarcely a syllable was uttered that did not relate to the game, except when Mrs. Jenkinson expressed her fears of Miss de Bourgh's being too hot or too cold, or having too much or too little light.

A great deal more passed at the other table. Lady Catherine was speaking—stating the mistakes of the others, or relating some anecdote of herself. Mr. Collins was agreeing with everything, thanking her for every fish he won, and apologising if he won too many. Sir William did not say much. He was storing his memory with anecdotes and noble names, and once or twice glancing at the ornate vacant cages behind them.

When Lady Catherine and her daughter had played as long as they chose, the tables were broken up, the carriage was offered to Mrs. Collins, gratefully accepted and immediately ordered. The party then gathered round the fire to hear Lady Catherine determine tomorrow's weather. With the arrival of the coach, and with many speeches of thankfulness on Mr. Collins's side and as many bows on Sir William's, they departed. As soon as they had driven from the door, Elizabeth was called on by her cousin to give her opinion of all that she had seen at Rosings. For Charlotte's sake, she made it more favourable than it really was. But her commendation, though costing her some trouble, could by no means satisfy Mr. Collins, and he was very soon obliged to take her ladyship's praise into his own hands.

---

[74] As a rule, tables are not known for having much intelligence or wisdom, gentle reader. Frequently, some tables are hardly more than dull and wooden.

Chapter 30

S ir William stayed only a week at Hunsford, but his visit was long enough to convince him of his daughter's being most comfortably settled, and of her possessing such a husband and such a neighbour as were not often met with.

While Sir William was with them, Mr. Collins devoted his morning to driving him out in his gig, and showing him the country, except for the inopportune days of comet and three-quarter moon, approaching full. At such times, for caution's sake, Mr. Collins invited Sir William to join him near the barn, within his own sturdy cage alongside Mr. Collins's grand affair. There, the two gentlemen sat behind iron bars—in comfortable chairs brought inside their manly enclosures—where they sipped tea or brandy, and observed the cows and chickens directly in their midst, while Mr. Collins rapturously described the coming Australian improvements.

When Sir William went away, the whole family returned to their usual employments. Elizabeth was thankful that they did not thus necessarily see more of her cousin—the chief of the time between breakfast and dinner was now passed by him either at work in the garden or in reading and writing, and looking out of the window in his own book-room, which fronted the road.

"I do believe, when he looks out thus, he dreams of emu," said Charlotte thoughtfully.

"What in heaven's name *is* an emu?" said Elizabeth.

"Even now, I am not entirely certain," her friend replied.

The room in which the ladies sat was backwards.[75] Elizabeth had at first rather wondered that Charlotte should not prefer the better-sized dining-parlour with its pleasing aspect for common use. But she soon saw that her friend had an excellent reason—Mr. Collins would have been much less in his own apartment, had they sat in one equally lively—and she gave Charlotte credit for the arrangement.

From the drawing-room they could distinguish nothing in the lane, and were indebted to Mr. Collins for the knowledge of what carriages went along, and how often Miss de Bourgh drove by in her phaeton. He never failed to inform them of this, though it happened almost every day. She not infrequently stopped at the Parsonage, and had a few minutes' conversation with Charlotte, but was scarcely ever prevailed upon to get out.[76]

Very few days passed in which Mr. Collins or his wife, or both of them, did not walk to Rosings. Elizabeth recollected that there might be other family livings to be disposed of, and at last understood the sacrifice of so many hours.

Now and then they were honoured with a call from her ladyship, and nothing escaped her observation during these visits. She examined, looked, and advised them to do things

---

[75] Here, the astute reader might imagine that the room is somehow inverted, possibly with the floor being the ceiling, or the walls having carpet installed on them, and the ceiling possessing windows. There is simply no other sensible explanation. —Ed. *[Naturally, any other sensible explanation cannot be expected from Editorial One, also known as the Imbecile in Residence. But—I must contain myself yet again. —Ed. 2]*

[76] So the bint was a lazy cow. [My Lord, who is this? How unspeakably untoward! —Ed.] *[I would like to know also; very odd. We might have an intruder of sorts. —Ed. 2]*

differently; found fault with the decor; or detected the housemaid in negligence. Refreshment was accepted only for the sake of finding out that Mrs. Collins's joints of meat were too large for her family, even when accounting for the necessary raw slabs of steak required for lining Mr. Collins's cage.

Elizabeth soon perceived that this great lady was a most active magistrate in her own parish (the minutest concerns of which were carried to her by Mr. Collins). Whenever any of the cottagers were quarrelsome, discontented, or too poor, she sallied forth into the village to settle their differences, silence their complaints, and scold them into harmony and plenty.

The entertainment of dining at Rosings was repeated about twice a week. Without Sir William, and with only one card-table in the evening, every such event was the same as the first. Their other engagements were few, as the style of living in the neighbourhood in general was beyond Mr. Collins's reach.

This, however, was no evil to Elizabeth. She spent her time comfortably enough in pleasant conversations with Charlotte, and enjoyed the fine weather out of doors. Her favourite was a walk along a nice sheltered path near a grove, where she frequently went while the others were calling on Lady Catherine.

In this quiet way, the first fortnight of her visit soon passed away, with the comet still visible every night in the heavens. It was speculated, however, that soon it will be blessedly out of sight. Would the world then return to normal?

Easter was approaching, and the week preceding it was to bring an important addition to the family at Rosings. Elizabeth heard that Mr. Darcy was expected there shortly. And though she would have preferred to have almost anyone else instead, his coming would provide at least a fresh newcomer at their Rosings parties. Indeed, she might be amused to see Miss Bingley's hopeless designs on him. She would also observe his supposed *attentions* to his cousin, for whom he was "destined" by Lady Catherine. The latter talked of his coming with the greatest satisfaction, of his person with the highest admiration, and seemed angry that he had already been frequently seen by Miss Lucas and herself.

His arrival was soon known at the Parsonage. Mr. Collins walked the whole morning within view of the lodges opening into Hunsford Lane, in order to have the earliest glimpse. After making his bow as the carriage—followed by a conveyance bearing two elegant but discreet gentlemen's cages—turned into the Park, he hurried home with the great news.

On the following morning he hastened to Rosings to pay his respects. There were two nephews of Lady Catherine to require them, for Mr. Darcy had brought with him a Colonel Fitzwilliam, the younger son of his uncle Lord ——, and, to the great surprise of all the party, when Mr. Collins returned, the gentlemen accompanied him.

Charlotte had seen them from her husband's room, crossing the road (together with several chickens[77] that had tediously escaped again, she noted), and immediately ran to tell the girls what an honour they might expect, adding:

"I may thank *you*, Eliza, for this piece of civility. Mr. Darcy would never have come so soon to wait upon *me*."

Elizabeth had scarcely time to deny, before their approach was announced by the door-bell, and shortly afterwards the three gentlemen entered the room. Colonel Fitzwilliam, who led the way, was about thirty, not handsome, but in person and address most truly the gentleman. It was not readily apparent what *beast* he took during the full moon, but there was little doubt it was something noble, and possibly in the Great Cat family.

Mr. Darcy looked just as he had in Hertfordshire—perfectly opaque in both his person and his species of *beast*. He paid his compliments, with his usual reserve, to Mrs. Collins, and met

---

[77] Why were the chickens *and* the gentlemen crossing the road? Surely, there is some significance here.

her with every appearance of composure. Elizabeth merely curtseyed to him without saying a word.

Colonel Fitzwilliam entered into conversation directly with the readiness, pleasure, and ease of a well-bred man. But his cousin, after having addressed a slight observation on the house and garden to Mrs. Collins, sat for some time without speaking to anybody. At length, however, his civility awakened, and he inquired of Elizabeth after the health of her family. She answered him in the usual way, adding:

"My eldest sister has been in town these three months. Have you never happened to see her there?"

She was perfectly aware that he never had; but she wished to see whether he would betray any knowledge of what had passed between the Bingleys and Jane.

He looked a little confused as he answered that he had never been so fortunate as to meet Miss Bennet. The subject was pursued no farther, and the gentlemen left soon afterwards.

The moment they were out the door, Charlotte, having just received the tale from Mr. Collins, said to Elizabeth:

"He is a *swan*, Eliza! Can you imagine that? Such a refined kind of Affliction, it is nearly unheard of! Each full moon, Colonel Fitzwilliam turns into a swan!"

Chapter 31

Colonel Fitzwilliam's manners were very much admired at the Parsonage, his *swan* nature and its unusual degree of breeding thoroughly discussed, and the ladies all felt that he must add considerably to the pleasures of their engagements at Rosings.

"How does one go about restraining such an odd demon creature?" ventured Maria with curiosity.

"No chains, likely; but the cage will no doubt be required to have slim bars, set closer together," Charlotte responded. "One might think of songbirds or canaries—"

"Do you suppose he might—bite?"

"My dear, he is not a proper swan, but a *demon swan*. He might do anything," said her sister; then reconsidered frightening the girl. "On the other hand, he is likely harmless, or no worse than a swan on a lake."

"Ah! but those creatures are far from harmless," said Elizabeth with a smile. 'Though, I declare, Colonel Fitzwilliam would be as charming in his cage as he is in the drawing room."

"No doubt, the next time at Rosings, as Lady Catherine will insist upon cages so near the full moon, we will find out."

It was some days, however, before they received any invitation thither—for while there were visitors in the house, *they* could not be necessary. It was not till Easter-day that they were asked on leaving church to come there in the late afternoon. For the last week they had seen very little of Lady Catherine or her daughter. Colonel Fitzwilliam, in impeccable noble *swan* fashion, had called at the Parsonage more than once during the time, but Mr. Darcy they had seen only at church.

The invitation was accepted of course, and at a proper hour they joined the party in Lady Catherine's drawing-room. Her ladyship received them civilly, but it was plain that their company was not so sought as when she could get nobody else.

"Mr. Collins, please be so kind as to avail yourself!" said her ladyship with a barest nod, as soon as they entered. She was pointing to the third tall-and-narrow cage near the sofa, directly next to the two at present occupied by Colonel Fitzwilliam and Mr. Darcy respectively. It was still early afternoon, with nothing but the sun in the heavens, but to calm the fears of their aunt, the two gentlemen were seated in elegant chairs that had been carried *inside* the cages. They were observing the proceedings with expressions of some cool bemusement.

"Oh yes, why, with your kindest permission, yes of course, immediately!" cried Mr. Collins and rushed to the vacant cage nearest Colonel Fitzwilliam, opened the door and let himself in. "I will strive to be exceedingly diligent in attempting to control the *beastly* nature, by all the means at my disposal including the force of will, Godly forthrightness, and dedicated prayer, but if I do *turn*, I beg to reassure that I will roar most gently and discreetly, like a little lamb—"

Realizing that there was no seat inside, Mr. Collins then just as hurriedly let himself out, begging pardon of everyone around him, including the cage bars into which he bumped by accident, took hold of the nearest footstool, and brought it inside the cage, not waiting for assistance from the serving staff. Then, after fussing with the exact placement of the footstool, he rushed to shut the cage door behind himself, caught the hem of his evening jacket on the filigree metal rosette of the latch, extricated it, then tried again, caught his sleeve, apologized, struggled. . . .

Seeing the ongoing difficulty, a maid was summoned, and she liberated the portions of his clothing and padlocked the cage after Mr. Collins.

"Now then," said Lady Catherine. "We were talking of—" And she then returned to being engrossed by her nephews, speaking to them, especially to Darcy, much more than to any other person in the room.

Colonel Fitzwilliam seemed really glad to see the visitors. Anything was a welcome relief to him at Rosings; and Mrs. Collins's pretty friend had caught his fancy very much.

He now requested for his cage to be moved to the other end of the sofa (with his aunt's kind permission, and the labor of two servants) so that he could be seated by Elizabeth, and talked so agreeably through the iron bars—of Kent and Hertfordshire, of traveling, of new books and music—that Elizabeth had never been half so well entertained in that room before. Indeed, she had forgotten the peculiar presence of the bars between them, and they conversed with so much spirit and flow, as to draw the attention of Lady Catherine herself, as well as of Mr. Darcy.

His eyes had been soon and repeatedly turned towards them with a look of curiosity. Her ladyship, after a while, shared the feeling, for she did not scruple to call out:

"What is that you are saying, Fitzwilliam? What is it you are talking of? What are you telling Miss Bennet?"

"We are speaking of music, madam," said he, when no longer able to avoid a reply.

"Of music! Then pray speak aloud. It is of all subjects my delight. I must have my share in the conversation. There are few people in England who have more true enjoyment of music than myself, or a better natural taste. If I had ever learnt, I should have been a great proficient. And so would Anne, if her health had allowed her—she would have performed delightfully. How does Georgiana get on, Darcy?"

From within his cage, Mr. Darcy spoke with affectionate praise of his sister's proficiency.

"I am very glad to hear," said Lady Catherine; "and pray tell her from me, that she cannot expect to excel if she does not practise a good deal."

"I assure you, madam," he replied, "that she does not need such advice. She practises very constantly."

"So much the better. When I next write to her, I shall charge her not to neglect it on any account. I often tell young ladies that no excellence in music is to be acquired without constant practice. I have told Miss Bennet several times, that she will never play really well unless she practises more. She is very welcome to come to Rosings every day, and play on the pianoforte in Mrs. Jenkinson's room. She would be in nobody's way in that part of the house."

Within the cage, Mr. Darcy looked a little ashamed of his aunt's ill-breeding, and made no answer.

In his own cage, Mr. Collins made some inadvertent noises when his shoe buckle caught against the iron bars, and Lady Catherine immediately looked his way.

"What! What was that? Mr. Collins, is that you? Pray, is it the Affliction come upon you already? Is the comet up?"

"Oh, my dearest Lady Catherine, not at all!" he exclaimed. "Your gracious ladyship can rest assured I am indeed praying with the full force and vigor by which I have been endowed through my holy office, and thus far I have been able to hold off the unholy forces of full moon and comet—"

"Well then, it is satisfactory. I am thus relieved," replied Lady Catherine. "And, if any of you—Darcy, Fitzwilliam—start to *turn*, be sure to inform me immediately!"

When coffee was over, Colonel Fitzwilliam reminded Elizabeth of having promised to play to him; and she sat down directly to the instrument. He requested that the servants move his cage near her. This was done with much difficulty and adroit maneuvering so as not to scratch the fine polished wood of the pianoforte.

Lady Catherine listened to half a song, and then talked, as before, to her other nephew; till the latter simply opened his own apparently unlocked pen, and walked away from her—with the servants hurrying to drag the heavy and lofty cage after him.

Making his way with his usual deliberation towards the pianoforte, Darcy stationed himself so as to command a full view of the fair performer's countenance—while the harried servants now placed the cage closest to his end of the instrument and opposite of Colonel Fitzwilliam's cage location, thus blocking all means of access to and from the area—unless one was airborne.

Elizabeth thus found herself blocked off by cages on both sides, right and left. She saw what Mr. Darcy was doing, and at the first pause, turned to him with an arch smile, and said:

"You mean to frighten me, Mr. Darcy, by coming in all this state to hear me, *and* standing unrestrained, outside your cage, liable to *turn* at any moment into a savage *beast?* I will not be alarmed—even if it is the time of both full moon and comet, and your sister *does* play so well. There is a stubbornness about me that never can bear to be frightened at the will of others. My courage always rises at every attempt to intimidate me."

"I shall not say you are mistaken," he replied, stepping inside the cage for her sake, "because you could not really believe me to entertain any design of alarming—or *harming* you. As you see, I am once more safely behind cold iron bars. And I know that you find great enjoyment in occasionally professing opinions which in fact are not your own."

Elizabeth laughed heartily at this picture of herself (for indeed, she did not feel any threat from cage-free gentlemen in the daytime), and said to Colonel Fitzwilliam, "Your cousin will teach you not to believe a word I say. I am unlucky in meeting someone so able to expose my real character, where I had hoped to pass myself off with some degree of credit. Indeed, Mr. Darcy, it is ungenerous to mention all that you knew to my disadvantage in Hertfordshire—and very impolitic too—for it is provoking me to retaliate. Such *secrets* may come out as will shock your relations."

"I am not afraid of you," said he, smilingly, from his cage.

"Pray let me hear what you have to accuse him of," cried Colonel Fitzwilliam from within his. "I should like to know how he behaves among strangers."

"You shall hear then—but prepare yourself for something very *dreadful*."

Darcy watched her calmly.

"The first time of my ever seeing him in Hertfordshire was at a ball, just after a full moon—and at this ball, what do you think he did? He danced only four dances, though gentlemen were scarce; and more than one young lady was sitting down in want of a partner. Mr. Darcy, you cannot deny the fact."

"I had not at that time the honour of knowing any lady in the assembly beyond my own party."

"True; and nobody can ever be introduced in a ball-room. Well, Colonel Fitzwilliam, what do I play next? My fingers wait your orders."

"Perhaps," said Darcy, "I should have judged better, had I sought an introduction. But I am ill qualified to recommend myself to strangers."

"Shall we ask your cousin," said Elizabeth, still addressing Colonel Fitzwilliam, "why such a worldly man of sense and education, is ill qualified to recommend himself to strangers?"

"I can answer your question," said Fitzwilliam. "It is because he will not give himself the trouble."

"I certainly have not the talent which some people possess," said Darcy, "of conversing easily with those I have never seen before. Nor do I feel the need to divulge personal details."

"My fingers," said Elizabeth, "do not move over this instrument in the masterly manner which so many women's do. But then I have always supposed it is because I will not take the trouble of practising. As for withholding your *secret* self, it is surely no one's business except when it becomes everyone's."

Darcy smiled and said, "You are perfectly right. You have employed your time much better. No one admitted to the privilege of hearing you can think anything wanting. We neither of us *perform* to strangers."

Here they were interrupted by Lady Catherine, who called out to know if *anyone* was succumbing to the Affliction yet, and if not, what they were talking of.

Elizabeth immediately began playing again. Lady Catherine approached—but not too closely, for she was blocked by her nephews' cages on both sides—and, after listening for a few minutes, said to Darcy through his filigree iron bars:

"Miss Bennet would not play at all amiss if she practised more, and could have the advantage of a London master. She has a very good notion of fingering, though her taste is not equal to Anne's. Anne would have been a delightful performer, had her health allowed her to learn."

Elizabeth looked at Darcy to see his reaction to his cousin's praise. But at no moment could she discern any symptom of *love*. And from the whole of his behaviour to Miss de Bourgh, he might have just as likely married Miss Bingley.

Lady Catherine continued her remarks on Elizabeth's performance, mixed with instructions on execution and taste.

Elizabeth received them with all the forbearance of civility and the meaningful equivalent of dingoes and kangaroos. She remained at the instrument till it was time for the gentlemen to retire to their proper Ordeal rooms upstairs, and her ladyship's carriage was ready to take the rest of them home before the wicked comet and moon rose in full force in the night heavens.

Chapter 32

Elizabeth was sitting by herself the next morning, and writing to Jane while Mrs. Collins and Maria were gone on business into the village, when she was startled by a ring at the door. As she had heard no carriage, it was likely to be Lady Catherine (so she put away her half-finished letter to escape all impertinent questions). But when the door opened, to her very great surprise, Mr. Darcy alone entered the room.

He seemed astonished too on finding her alone, and apologised for his intrusion: he had assumed all the ladies were to be within.

They then sat down, and when her inquiries after Rosings were made, seemed in danger of sinking into total silence. It was absolutely necessary, therefore, to think of something, since the gentleman was so reserved that in his very *stillness* he appeared to Elizabeth to be in fact agitated.

"I trust your night's Ordeal went tolerably well, Mr. Darcy."

"Tolerably well," he replied.

"And the moon and comet did not cause you too much undue *discomfort?*"

"Not more than usual. The comet is on its last days, and should fade and altogether withdraw from the skies very soon."

"I am very relieved," said Elizabeth, "for this disturbance to everyone's daily routine in addition to all else has been quite insufferable. Indeed, Mr. Collins took most of this morning to recover from the night's dire event, and then refused to leave his enclosure so as not to 'consume the ladies with his great teeth.' Mrs. Collins could hardly convince him otherwise."

"Indeed," said Mr. Darcy.

What followed was more uncomfortable silence.

Recalling *when* she had last seen him in Hertfordshire, Elizabeth decided to ask him about their hasty departure.

"How very suddenly you all quitted Netherfield last November, Mr. Darcy! It must have been a most agreeable surprise to Mr. Bingley to see you all after him so soon. He and his sisters were well, I hope, when you left London?"

"Perfectly so, I thank you."

She found that she was to receive no other answer, and, after a short pause added:

"I think I have understood that Mr. Bingley has not much idea of ever returning to Netherfield again?"

"I have never heard him say so; but it is probable that he may spend very little of his time there in the future. He has many friends and engagements in town."

"If he means to be but little at Netherfield, it would be better for the neighbourhood that he should give up the place entirely—for then we might possibly get a settled family there."

"I should not be surprised," said Darcy, "if he were to give it up as soon as any eligible purchase offers."

Elizabeth made no answer. She was afraid of talking longer of his friend. And, having nothing else to say, she was now determined to leave the trouble of finding a subject to him.

He took the hint, and soon began with, "This seems a very comfortable house. Lady Catherine, I believe, did a great deal to it when Mr. Collins first came to Hunsford."

"I believe she did—and I am sure she could not have bestowed her kindness on a more grateful object."

"Mr. Collins appears to be very fortunate in his choice of a wife."

"Yes, indeed, his friends may well rejoice in his having met with one of the very few sensible women who would have accepted him and his *beast*, or have made him happy if they had. My friend has an excellent understanding—though I am not certain that I consider her marrying Mr. Collins as the wisest thing she ever did. She seems perfectly happy, however, and in a prudential light it is certainly a very good match for her."

"It must be very agreeable for her to be settled within so easy a distance of her own family and friends."

"I should never have considered the distance of nearly fifty miles as one of the *advantages* of the match," cried Elizabeth, "or that Mrs. Collins was settled *near* her family."

"It is a proof of your own attachment to Hertfordshire. Anything beyond the very neighbourhood of Longbourn, I suppose, would appear far."

As he spoke there was a sort of smile which Elizabeth fancied she understood. He must assume she was thinking of Jane and Netherfield, and she blushed as she answered:

"I do not mean to say that a woman may not be settled too near her family. It must all depend on the circumstances. A fortune can make the expenses of traveling unimportant. But that is not the case *here*. Mr. and Mrs. Collins have a comfortable income, but not one to allow frequent journeys—and I am persuaded my friend would not call herself *near* her family under less than *half* the present distance."

Mr. Darcy drew his chair a little towards her, and said, "*You* cannot have a right to such very strong local attachment. *You* cannot have been always at Longbourn."

Elizabeth looked surprised, and momentarily wondered if Mr. Darcy was indeed being subtly influenced by the comet in daytime—not to succumb to his *beast*, but to express some peculiar *intensity*, and speak with oddity.

The gentleman must have realized it and experienced some change of feeling. He drew back his chair, took a newspaper from the table, and glancing over it, said, in a colder voice:

"Are you pleased with Kent?"

A short dialogue on the subject of the country ensued, on either side calm and concise—and soon put an end to by the entrance of Charlotte and her sister, just returned from her walk.

The *tête-à-tête* surprised them. Mr. Darcy related the mistake which had occasioned his intruding on Miss Bennet, and after sitting a few minutes longer without saying much to anybody, went away.

"What can be the meaning of this?" said Charlotte, as soon as he was gone. "My dear, Eliza, he must be in love with you, or he would never have called us in this familiar way."

"I declare, it is the *comet* making him addled."

But when Elizabeth told of his silence, it did not seem very likely (even to Charlotte's wishes) to be the case. After various conjectures, they could at last only suppose his visit to proceed from the difficulty of finding anything to do. At this time of year all field sports were over. Within doors there was Lady Catherine, books, and a billiard-table.

But gentlemen cannot always be within doors. The two cousins found, in the pleasure of the walk to the nearby Parsonage, and the people who lived in it, a temptation to visit almost every day.

They called at various times of the morning, sometimes separately, sometimes together, and now and then accompanied by their aunt. It was plain to all that Colonel Fitzwilliam came because he had pleasure in their society. And Elizabeth was reminded by her own satisfaction in being with him, as well as by his evident admiration of her, of her former favourite George Wickham. In comparing them, she saw there was less captivating softness in Colonel Fitzwilliam's *swan* manners, but a better informed mind.

But why Mr. Darcy came so often to the Parsonage, it was more difficult to understand. It could not be for society, as he frequently sat there ten minutes together without opening his lips. He seldom appeared really animated.

Mrs. Collins knew not what to make of him. Colonel Fitzwilliam's occasionally laughing at his *stupidity*, proved that he was generally different, which her own knowledge of him could not have told her. And as she would liked to have believed this change the effect of love, and the object of that love her friend Eliza, she set herself seriously to work to find it out.

She watched him whenever they were at Rosings, and whenever he came to Hunsford; but without much success. He certainly looked at her friend a great deal, but the expression of that look was disputable. It was an earnest, steadfast gaze, but she often doubted whether there were much admiration in it, and sometimes it seemed nothing but—as Elizabeth called it—a "comet-addled" absence of mind.

She had once or twice suggested to Elizabeth the possibility of his being partial to her, but Elizabeth always laughed at the idea. And Mrs. Collins did not think it right to press the subject, from the danger of raising expectations which might only end in disappointment. For she had no doubt that all her friend's dislike would vanish, if she could suppose him to be in her power.

In her kind schemes for Elizabeth, she sometimes planned her marrying Colonel Fitzwilliam. The *swan* was beyond comparison the most pleasant man. He certainly admired her, and his situation in life was most eligible. But, to counterbalance these advantages, Mr. Darcy had considerable patronage in the church, and his cousin could have none at all.

However, Elizabeth insisted to Charlotte that Mr. Darcy surely had a dreadful *secret*.

Chapter 33

More than once did Elizabeth, in her ramble within the park, unexpectedly meet Mr. Darcy. What perverse chance brought *him*, and no one else, here? To prevent its ever happening again, she took care to inform him that it was a favourite haunt of hers.

Yet how it could occur a second time, even a third, was very odd! It seemed like willful ill-nature, or a voluntary penance. For on these occasions it was not merely a few formal inquiries and an awkward pause and then away, but he actually thought it necessary to turn back and walk with her.

He never said a great deal, nor did she give herself the trouble of talking or of listening much. But it struck her in the course of their third *rencontre* that he was asking some odd, unconnected, definitely "comet-addled" questions—about her pleasure in being at Hunsford, her love of solitary walks, and her opinion of Mr. and Mrs. Collins's happiness. When speaking of Rosings, he seemed to expect that when she came into Kent again she would be staying *there* too.

His words seemed to imply it. Could he have Colonel Fitzwilliam in his thoughts? She supposed, if he meant anything, he must mean an allusion to what might arise in that quarter. It distressed her a little, and she was quite glad to find herself at the gate in the pales opposite the Parsonage.

She was engaged one day as she walked, in perusing Jane's last letter, when, instead of being again surprised by Mr. Darcy, she saw that Colonel Fitzwilliam was meeting her. Putting away the letter immediately and forcing a smile, she said:

"I did not know before that you ever walked this way."

"I have been making the tour of the park," he replied, "as I generally do every year, and intend to close it with a call at the Parsonage. Are you going much farther?"

"No, I should have turned in a moment."

And accordingly she did turn,[78] and they walked towards the Parsonage together.

"Do you certainly leave Kent on Saturday?" said she.

"Yes—if Darcy does not put it off again. But I am at his disposal. He arranges the business just as he pleases. I am only surprised he tolerates the daytime cages so well, for one must indeed humor our aunt when under her roof."

"Ah yes, the thousand cages of Rosings. . . ."

He smiled. "You have no notion. Breakfast is often a disaster of near-colliding servants and an endless passage of dishes and platters up to the cage walls, from where one must fish out tidbits with a silver fork *through* and *between* the bars. While buttered toast poses no hardship, it is not easy to pass a thick slice of ham in this manner, nor a hearty roast. And as for cups and saucers—"

"Surely you jest! Does she not let you out to be served at least?"

Colonel Fitzwilliam laughed. "You have me, I capitulate! Yes, it is an exaggeration—but not altogether much. The cages

---

[78] Please rest assured, gentle reader, that Miss Elizabeth Bennet did not *turn* into some fiendish creature or another, for apparently ladies do not suffer the Affliction; heaven only knows why. By turning it is implied that the young lady made a turn on the path, or possibly a pirouette or two, or maybe a triple Salchow—commonly known as a sow cow. Moooo! Ahem! Begging pardon!

are required everywhere. Upon occasion Darcy simply lets himself out unasked. I notice that the servants have made it a discreet habit of not locking his cage, and Lady Catherine hardly seems to notice. She humors him in this one thing, as in most other arrangements."

"And if not able to please himself in the arrangement, he has at least pleasure in the great power of choice—he can leave Rosings anytime. I do not know anybody who seems more to enjoy the power of doing what he likes than Mr. Darcy."

"Power does have the tendency to liberate one from many things."

"Power and pride, and the keeping of secrets. I wonder if I might dare ask—or if you are even in possession of an answer—but what is Mr. Darcy's *beast?* I realize it is an impertinence to be so bold as to inquire directly, but it has become a matter of disquiet for our entire neighbourhood. No one seems to know, and it is apparently the best guarded secret in all of England!"

"Ah, my dear Miss Bennet, I am afraid the answer is indeed not mine to give, for I simply do not have it."

"Is he a rare demon *creature* of fire?"

"Your supposition is as good as anyone's. Darcy is ever silent in this regard. One wonders if he hides a dreadful thing."

"It is a pity that he has his way even in this matter!"

"He likes to have his own way very well," replied Colonel Fitzwilliam. "But so we all do. It is only that he has better means of having it than many others, because he is rich, and many others are poor. A younger son such as myself must be inured to self-denial and dependence."

"In my opinion, the younger son of an earl can know very little of either. Now seriously, when have you been prevented by want of money from going wherever you chose, or procuring anything you had a fancy for?"

"These are home questions—and perhaps I cannot say that I have experienced many such hardships. But in matters of greater weight, I may suffer from want of money. Younger sons cannot marry where they like."

"Unless they like women of fortune, which they often do."

"Our habits of expense make us too dependent, and there are not many in my rank of life who can afford to marry without some attention to money."

Is this, thought Elizabeth, *meant for me?* And she coloured at the idea; but, recovering herself, said in a lively tone, "And pray, what is the usual price of an earl's younger son? Unless the elder brother is very sickly, I suppose you would not ask above fifty thousand pounds."

He answered her in the same style, and the subject dropped. To interrupt an uncomfortable silence, she soon afterwards said:

"I imagine your cousin brought you down with him chiefly for the sake of having someone at his disposal. I wonder he does not marry, to secure a lasting convenience of that kind. But, perhaps, his sister does as well for the present, and, as she is under his sole care, he may do what he likes with her."

"No," said Colonel Fitzwilliam, "that is an advantage which he must divide with me. I am joined with him in the guardianship of Miss Darcy."

"Are you indeed? And pray what sort of guardians do you make? Does your charge give you much trouble? Young ladies of her age are sometimes a little difficult to manage, and if she has the true Darcy spirit, she may like to have her own way."

As she spoke she observed him looking at her earnestly. The manner in which he immediately asked her why she supposed Miss Darcy likely to give them any uneasiness, convinced her that she had somehow got pretty near the truth. She directly replied:

"You need not be frightened. I never heard any harm of her; and I dare say she is one of the most tractable creatures in the world. She is a very great favourite with some ladies of my acquaintance, Mrs. Hurst and Miss Bingley. I think I have heard you say that you know them."

"I know them a little. Their brother is a pleasant gentlemanlike man—he is a great friend of Darcy's."

"Oh! yes," said Elizabeth dryly; "Mr. Darcy is uncommonly kind to Mr. Bingley, and takes a prodigious deal of care of him."

"Care of him! Yes, I really believe Darcy *does* take care of him in those points where he most wants care. From something that he told me in our journey hither, I have reason to think Bingley very much indebted to him."

"What is it you mean?"

"It is a circumstance which Darcy could not wish to be generally known, because if it were to get round to the lady's family, it would be an unpleasant thing."

"You may depend upon my not mentioning it."

"What he told me was merely this: that he congratulated himself on having lately saved a friend from the inconveniences of a most imprudent marriage, but without mentioning names or any other particulars. I only suspected it to be Bingley from believing him the kind of young *tiger* to get into a scrape of that sort, and from knowing them to have been together the whole of last summer."

"Did Mr. Darcy give you reasons for this interference?"

"I understood that there were some very strong objections against the lady."

"And what arts did he use to separate them?"

"He did not talk to me of his own arts," said Fitzwilliam, smiling. "He only told me what I have now told you."

Elizabeth made no answer, and walked on, her heart swelling with indignation. After watching her a little, Fitzwilliam asked her why she was so thoughtful.

"I am thinking of what you have been telling me," said she. "Your cousin's conduct does not suit my feelings. Why was he to be the judge?"

"You are rather disposed to call his interference officious?"

"I do not see what right Mr. Darcy had to decide on the propriety of his friend's inclination, or why, upon his own judgment alone, he was to determine and direct in what manner his friend was to be happy. But," she continued, recollecting herself, "as we know none of the particulars, it is not fair to condemn him. It is not to be supposed that there was much affection in the case."

"That is not an unnatural surmise," said Fitzwilliam, "but it is a lessening of the honour of my cousin's triumph very sadly."

This was spoken jestingly. But it appeared to her so just a picture of Mr. Darcy, that she would not trust herself with an answer. She therefore abruptly changed the conversation, and talked on indifferent matters until they reached the Parsonage.

There, shut into her own room, as soon as their visitor left, she could think without interruption.

It was not to be supposed that any other people could be meant than those with whom she was connected. There could not exist in the world *two* men over whom Mr. Darcy could have such boundless influence. That he had been concerned in the measures taken to separate Bingley and Jane she had never doubted. But she had always attributed to Miss Bingley the principal design and arrangement of them.

Thus, *he* was the cause—his pride, caprice, and vanity—of all that Jane had suffered, and still continued to suffer. He had ruined every hope of happiness for the most affectionate, generous heart in the world. And no one could say how lasting an evil he might have inflicted.

The "very strong objections against the lady" probably were her having one uncle who was a country attorney, and another who was in business in London!

To Jane herself there could be no possible objection—all loveliness and goodness as she is!—her understanding excellent, her mind improved, and her manners captivating. Neither could anything be urged against her *lion* father, who, though with some peculiarities, had abilities Mr. Darcy himself need not disdain, and respectability which he will probably never reach.

When she thought of her mother, her confidence gave way a little. But she would not allow that any objections *there* had material weight with Mr. Darcy, whose pride would receive a deeper wound from the want of importance in his friend's connections, than from their want of sense.

Elizabeth concluded that he had been partly governed by this worst kind of pride, and partly by the wish of retaining Mr. Bingley for his sister.

The agitation and tears which the subject occasioned, brought on a headache. And it grew so much worse towards the evening, that, added to her unwillingness to see Mr. Darcy, it convinced her not to accompany her cousins to Rosings, where they were engaged to drink tea among the infernal cages. . . .

Mrs. Collins, seeing that she was really unwell, did not press her to go, and as much as possible prevented her husband from pressing her. But Mr. Collins could not conceal his apprehension of Lady Catherine's being rather displeased by her staying at home.

Chapter 34

When they were gone, Elizabeth, as if intending to exasperate herself as much as possible against Mr. Darcy, chose for her employment the examination of all the letters which Jane had written to her.

They contained no actual complaint, no revival of the past, no present suffering. But in almost every line of each, there was a lack of cheerfulness which used to characterise Jane's style—serene, kindly disposed towards everyone, and scarcely ever clouded. Elizabeth now noticed uneasiness in every sentence.

Mr. Darcy's shameful boast of what misery he had been able to inflict, gave her a keener sense of her sister's sufferings. It was some consolation to think that *his* visit to Rosings was to end on the day after the next—and that in less than a fortnight she should herself be with Jane again.

She could not think of Darcy's leaving Kent without remembering that his cousin was to go with him. But Colonel Fitzwilliam had made it clear he had no intentions at all. And agreeable as he was, she did not mean to be unhappy about him.

While settling this point, she was suddenly roused by the sound of the door-bell. Her spirits were a little fluttered by the idea of its being Colonel Fitzwilliam himself, who had once before called late in the evening, and might now come to inquire particularly after her.

But this idea was soon banished, and her spirits were very differently affected . . . when, to her utter amazement, she saw Mr. Darcy walk into the room.

In an hurried manner he immediately began an inquiry after her health, imputing his visit to a wish of hearing that she were better.

She answered him with cold civility.

He sat down for a few moments, and then getting up, walked about the room. Whatever his *beast*, he was moving in a manner rather demonic, confined only by a metaphysical cage.

Elizabeth was surprised, but said not a word.

After a silence of several minutes, he came towards her in an agitated manner, and thus began:

"In vain I have struggled. It will not do. My feelings will not be repressed. You must allow me to tell you how ardently I admire and love you."

Oh dear God and comet and full moon, and all of heaven!

Elizabeth's astonishment was beyond expression. She stared, coloured, doubted, and was silent.

This he considered sufficient encouragement. And the avowal of all that he felt, and had long felt for her, immediately followed. He spoke well; but there were feelings besides[79] those of the heart to be detailed. And he was not more eloquent on the subject of tenderness than of pride. His sense of her inferiority— of its being a degradation—of the family obstacles which had always opposed to inclination, were dwelt on with a warmth which seemed due to the consequence he was wounding, but was very unlikely to recommend his suit.

---

[79] It never bodes well when any feelings other than those of the heart are referred to during a gentleman's proposal. All ye gentlemen reading here, please take note!

In spite of her deeply-rooted dislike, she could not be insensible to the compliment of such a man's affection. And though her intentions did not vary for an instant, she was at first sorry for the pain he was to receive—till, roused to resentment by his subsequent language, she lost all compassion in anger.

She tried, however, to compose herself to answer him with patience, when he was going to be done. . . .

He concluded with representing to her the strength of that attachment which, in spite of all his endeavours, he had found impossible to conquer—and with expressing his hope that it would now be rewarded by her acceptance of his hand.

As he said this, she could easily see that he had no doubt of a favourable answer. He *spoke* of apprehension and anxiety, but his countenance expressed real security. Such a circumstance could only exasperate farther, and, when he ceased, the colour rose into her cheeks, and she said:

"Mr. Darcy, do you require a *cage?*"

His countenance suddenly became impossible to describe.

"No? Well, then," she continued: "In such cases as this, it is, I believe, the established mode to express a sense of obligation for the sentiments avowed, however unequally they may be returned. It is natural that obligation should be felt, and if I could *feel* gratitude, I would now thank you. But I cannot—I have never desired your good opinion, and you have certainly bestowed it most unwillingly. I am sorry to have occasioned pain to anyone. It has been most unconsciously done, however, and I hope will be, like the present full moon, of short duration. The *feelings* which have long prevented the acknowledgment of your regard, can have little difficulty in overcoming it after this explanation—unless, perhaps you *do* require a cage?"

Mr. Darcy, who was leaning against the mantelpiece with his eyes fixed on her face, seemed to catch her words with no less resentment than surprise. He paled with anger, and the disturbance of his mind was visible in every feature.

The beast in the damp dark basement was being consumed by every manner of foul vermin, and his own broken pride. . . .

He was struggling for the appearance of composure, and would not open his lips till he believed himself to have attained it.

The pause was to Elizabeth's feelings dreadful.

At length, with a voice of forced calmness, he said:

"And this is all the reply which I am to have the honour of expecting! I might, perhaps, wish to be informed why, with so little *endeavour* at civility, I am thus rejected. But it is of small importance."

"I might as well inquire," replied she, "why with so evident a desire of offending and insulting me, you chose to tell me that you liked me against your will, against your reason, and even against your character? Was not this some excuse for incivility, if I *was* uncivil? But I have other provocations. Had not my feelings decided against you—had they been indifferent, or even favourable, do you think that any consideration would tempt me to accept the man who has been the means of ruining, perhaps forever, the happiness of a most beloved sister?"

As she pronounced these words, Mr. Darcy changed colour;[80] but the emotion was short, and he listened without attempting to interrupt her while she continued:

"I have every reason in the world to think ill of you. No motive can excuse the unjust and ungenerous part you acted *there*. You dare not, you cannot deny, that you have been the principal, if not the only means of dividing them from each other—of exposing one to the censure of the world for caprice

---

[80] One is obliged to point out that upon changing color, Mr. Darcy did not turn cornflower or navy blue, chartreuse, or any shade of salad green. It is likely that he simply lightened or darkened somewhat his current hue, though if he had been exposed to excessive sun and the elements, as does a sailor, he might have become somewhat ruddy and leathery, and possibly developed jaundice and started wearing an eye patch.

and instability, and the other to its derision for disappointed hopes, and involving them both in misery of the acutest kind."

She paused, and saw with no slight indignation that he was listening with an air which proved him wholly unmoved by any feeling of remorse. He even looked at her with a smile of affected incredulity.

"Can you deny that you have done it?" she repeated.

With assumed tranquility he then replied: "I have no wish of denying that I did everything in my power to separate my friend from your sister, or that I rejoice in my success. Towards *him* I have been kinder than towards myself."

Elizabeth disdained notice of this last utterance. But its meaning did not escape, nor was it likely to conciliate her.

"But it is not merely this affair," she continued, "on which my dislike is founded. My opinion of you was decided months ago, when your character was revealed by Mr. Wickham. On this subject, what can you have to say? In what imaginary act of friendship can you here defend yourself?"

"You take an eager interest in that gentleman's concerns," said Darcy, in a less tranquil tone, and with a heightened colour.

"Who that knows what his misfortunes have been, can help feeling an interest in him?"

"His misfortunes!" repeated Darcy contemptuously; "yes, his misfortunes have been great indeed."

Before Elizabeth could respond, there was a peculiar clatter at the nearest window. A shutter slammed; then the curtain was flung aside, and then with a rush of cold air *something* large and monstrous flew into the room—

There was a great beating of powerful wings, and a breeze circulated wildly, together with a few out-flung grey feathers, and just possibly a tiny spray of liquid bird poop—

Elizabeth game a minor stifled cry, but somehow, in all her agitated state, could not help welcoming the most bizarre sight of a very familiar, very peculiar visitor in the form of a giant monstrous duck. . . .

"*What*—is that?" Darcy spoke in a clipped tone of sudden fury, forgetting his usual composure. He was being thrown off entirely by the impossible interruption—*this*, after all his roiling emotions were already turned upside down!

In the same instant, as if daring to reply to the gentleman, the monstrous *thing* gave forth a shrill, loud, terrifying screech. Then, the impossible creature rose over their heads and started circling the room.

"Wait! By all that is holy, I know that infernal bird from Netherfield!"

"Yes, Mr. Darcy, as do I. I admit, in this moment, the Brighton Duck is a rather welcome disruption."

Darcy suddenly turned to her, forgetting the monster overhead. "Is that how you see my innermost words to you? An unwelcome imposition on your time? You would rather have a duck in attendance—"

The monstrous fowl screeched again, and this time it went hurtling directly at Mr. Darcy, who put his arm up to shield his face while at the same time exclaiming in white-hot anger, "I am going—to—*kill*—this execrable wretch—"

"Oh! I suppose, in the same way this poor bird is now a wretch to you—as was Mr. Wickham?" cried Elizabeth. "Well, I shall not let you do it! Not here, not in this room, not ever!"

And heading directly to the window, she opened the curtain all the way and held the shutter wide, with trembling hands—trembling in a mixture of impossible emotion. She was filled with general indignation—not at the duck but at *Mr. Darcy*.

"Here! Begone! Shoo!" commanded Miss Elizabeth Bennet. And in a most peculiar way, the giant duck heeded her. It must have sensed her friendly intent, not to mention the unusual level of general upheaval and *intensity* in the room. Thereupon it disengaged itself from battering Mr. Darcy's upper regions and flew directly at Elizabeth—who did not even blink—and past her, and out into the open window. . . .

From the outside came one solitary trumpeting banshee cry. And it was all over.

Mr. Darcy stood, pallid one moment, and colouring in a mixture of pain and anger and bewilderment the next, while disdainfully brushing off down and duck feathers from his coat lapels and fine cravat. And he said, "You then are so blessedly certain that I caused harm to Wickham?"

"Yes, even if only judging by the amount of implacable resentment directed at a silly overgrown bird!" cried Elizabeth with energy. "You have reduced *him*—Mr. Wickham, not the duck—to his present state of comparative poverty (though, I do not expect the duck has any property either). You have withheld the advantages designed for him. You have deprived the best years of his life of that independence which was no less his due than his desert. You have done all this! and yet you can treat the mention of his misfortune with contempt and ridicule."

"And this," cried Darcy, as he walked with quick steps across the room, scattering duck feathers, "is your opinion of me! This is the estimation in which you hold me! I thank you for explaining it so fully. My faults, according to this 'calculation by duck,' are heavy indeed! But perhaps," added he, stopping in his walk, and turning towards her, "these offenses might have been overlooked, had not your pride been hurt by my honest confession of the scruples that had long prevented my forming any serious design. These bitter accusations might have been suppressed, had I, with greater policy, concealed my struggles, and flattered you into the belief of my being impelled by unqualified, unalloyed inclination. But disguise of every sort is my abhorrence. Nor am I ashamed of the feelings I related. Could you expect me to rejoice in the inferiority of your connections, so decidedly beneath my own?"

Elizabeth felt herself growing more angry every moment; yet she tried to the utmost to speak with composure. "You are mistaken, Mr. Darcy, if you suppose that the mode of your declaration affected me in any other way, than as it spared me the concern which I might have felt in refusing you, had you behaved in a more gentlemanlike manner."

She saw him start at this, but he said nothing, and she continued:

"You could not have made the offer of your hand in any possible way that would have tempted me to accept it."

Again his astonishment was obvious. And he looked at her with an expression of mingled incredulity and mortification.

"From the very beginning," she went on, "from the first moment of my acquaintance with you, your manners, impressing me with your arrogance, your conceit, your secrecy, and your selfish disdain of the feelings of others, were such as to form the groundwork of disapprobation on which succeeding events have built so immovable a dislike—and I had not known you a month before I felt that you were the *last* man in the world whom I could ever be prevailed on to marry."

"You have said quite enough, madam. I perfectly comprehend your feelings, and have now only to be ashamed of what my own have been. Forgive me for having taken up so much of your time, and accept my best wishes for your health and happiness."

And with these words he suddenly paused, and went very still, and then said haltingly: "I—I may now require a cage—"

Elizabeth watched in astonishment as the proud composed Mr. Darcy suddenly made a deep harsh sound, then doubled over, clutching his chest, and then fell forward—

He was on the floor before her, *turning*—she was quite certain of it, by the involuntary terrifying contortions of his body—and after a single loud cry, he went silent, and then, on all fours, he began to *shrink* in size.

She had never seen anything like it. The large masculine elegant shape of the gentleman was dissolving before her eyes, and the *thing* in its place barely reached the dimensions of a small fireplace log, with four short blunt appendages. One moment it seemed to be tangled in the expensive loose clothing, and then it found its way out—partially, just enough to be *seen*.

Elizabeth saw the strangest creature in the world—with webbed front legs and short hind appendages of an otter, a sleek short dark brown coat, a flat bushy tail of a beaver, and the face—oh dear God! Its muzzle was long and rounded and flat like the Brighton Duck!

But no, this *thing* that had been Mr. Darcy was definitely *not* a duck; for such was only its bill. The rest was an impossible combination of seemingly disparate creature parts, which Elizabeth just barely recalled having seen at her father's library, in a strange drawing within a natural science tome chronicling the animal species found solely within the confines of the continent of Australia!

"You—Mr. Darcy—" she whispered, putting a hand to her lips, in sudden dawning understanding of so many things. "Why, you are a *platypus!*"

The platypus Darcy scuttled about the floor at the feet of Elizabeth, dragging its clothing, and making circles in this direction and that, as though searching for something (a deep cool pond; but this she did not know).

Finally the *demon platypus* found the door, somehow pushed it open and hastily left the room. Then, Elizabeth heard *him* the next moment bumping and making fumbling knocks to open the front door—which he somehow again managed—and quit the house.

His shoes, stockings, and pants remained here, on the floor.
Dear lord in heaven!

The tumult of her mind, was now painfully great, impossible, unfathomable. She knew not how to support herself, and from actual weakness sat down and cried for half-an-hour.

Her astonishment, as she reflected on what had passed, was increased by every review of it. That she should receive an offer of marriage from Mr. Darcy! That his *beast* was not some kind of fire-breathing dragon but a duckbill platypus! That he should have been in love with her for so many months! That his admission of love and her rejection cost him his control over the *beast* and his composure! That his lofty secret was not admirable but frankly unfathomable! That he was so much in love as to wish to marry her in spite of all the objections which had made him prevent his friend's marrying her sister—and which must equally apply in his own case—all of it was almost incredible!

It was gratifying to have inspired unconsciously so strong an affection. But his shameless avowal of what he had done with respect to Jane—his unpardonable assurance and the unfeeling manner in which he had mentioned Mr. Wickham, his cruelty towards whom he had not attempted to deny—clamored to overcome the pity that his attachment had briefly excited.

But she could still pity him for one thing—the true revelation of his shameful *beastly* secret.

No, gentle reader, it did not excuse his arrogance. But it provided a profound explanation for his veneer of composure.

Mr. Darcy's pride and rigidity was a *mask*.

And now, Elizabeth knew it.

She gathered up his abandoned articles of clothing in order to discreetly put them away in her room (until there was an opportunity of returning them to their owner), and continued thus, in very agitated—nay, maddened—reflections, till the sound of Lady Catherine's carriage made her feel how unequal she was to encounter Charlotte's observation. She therefore hurried her away to her room.

Chapter 35

Elizabeth awoke the next morning to the same thoughts which had at length closed her eyes.

She could not yet recover from the shock of what had happened. It was impossible to think of anything else. Totally indisposed for employment, she resolved, soon after breakfast, to indulge herself in air and exercise.

She was proceeding directly to her favourite walk, when the recollection of Mr. Darcy's sometimes coming there stopped her. Instead of entering the park, she turned up the lane, and soon passed one of the gates into the ground.

After walking two or three times along that part of the lane, she was tempted, by the pleasant morning and greenery, to stop at the gates and look into the park. Immediately she caught a glimpse of a gentleman moving her way; and, fearful of its being Mr. Darcy, she started to retreat.

But the person who advanced was now near enough to see her. Stepping forward with eagerness, he pronounced her name.

She had turned away; but on hearing herself called by Mr. Darcy, she moved again towards the gate.

He had by that time reached it also. Holding out a letter, which she instinctively took, he said, with a look of haughty composure, "I have been walking in the grove some time in the hope of meeting you."

"Mr. Darcy . . . I have your shoes—"

"Will you do me the honour of reading that letter?"

"—and pants. What is to be done with them?"

He coloured. "Do whatever you please. Have them sent to me at Rosings. Have them discarded. Burn them. Last night—I had lost control in an unforgivable manner—I—"

"I believe, I now understand. I know what you are."

"Forgive me, but you have no notion of anything, not yet. Not until—until you read *this*."

He pointed to the letter in her hands. And then, with a flaming face and a slight bow, turned again into the plantation, and was soon out of sight.

With no expectation of pleasure, but with the strongest curiosity, Elizabeth opened the letter. To her increasing wonder, it held an envelope containing two sheets of letter-paper, written quite through, in a very close hand. The envelope itself was likewise full. Pursuing her way along the lane, she then began it. It was dated from Rosings, at eight o'clock in the morning:—

"Be not alarmed, madam, on receiving this letter, by the apprehension of its containing any repetition of those sentiments or renewal of those offers which were last night so disgusting to you. I write without any intention of paining you, or humbling myself, by dwelling on wishes which, for the happiness of both, cannot be too soon forgotten. My character requires that this letter be written and read. You must, therefore, pardon the freedom with which I demand your attention. You may bestow it unwillingly, but I demand it of your justice.

"There are three subjects of which I am compelled to speak. And of these *three*, two are offenses of a very different nature and magnitude, that you laid to my charge last night. The first was, that, regardless of the sentiments of either, I had detached Mr. Bingley from your sister. The second, that I had, in defiance of various claims, honour and humanity, ruined the immediate prosperity and prospects of Mr. Wickham—the *wolf* companion of my youth, the acknowledged favourite of my father, a young man dependent on our patronage, and brought up to expect it. The third is a subject that I must, for the sake of my own honor, reveal and explain to you, even if you do not care to know, because, now that you have seen my true *beast* nature, your portrait of it must be completed, in order to understand the full extent of the situation which you have just barely glimpsed last night during my unfortunate loss of control.

"I will therefore begin selfishly, with the third subject— the explanation of *what* I am.

"You must know, or you must have heard, that the gentlemen of the Darcy family are frequently graced by the noble Great Cat Affliction. Such was my own father, a proper *jaguar*, and his father before him a *lion*, and his, a *tiger*, in a long line of such respectable creatures of breeding. I myself was to have been a jaguar, by all signs in my boyhood—for, as you know the demon *beast* manifests at a young age in some, while in most it takes hold in early manhood. In my case, the *jaguar* started to manifest rather early, and I *felt* it stirring under my skin, flexing its claws inside my fingers, testing its incisor teeth against my jaws—forgive me for not being able to put it into better words, but it is how we experience the *beast* that shares our malleable human flesh.

"At the age of seven, just as I started to become aware of the *beast*, but before my first *transformation*, an unfortunate incident happened that changed the course of my life. We had been staying in London for the summer, and my father had taken me to see the landmarks and the various entertainment that the city offered, among them a recently opened splendid zoo, which hosted that season a newly arrived exhibit from the wilds of Australia. There, I had approached a cage enclosure of some truly rare animals swimming in a specially made pond; noting not merely their whimsical name on the placard—'duckbill platypus'— but the fact that they were by far the strangest living things

I had ever had the pleasure of encountering in my young life—an impossible egg-laying hybrid of a beaver, otter, duck, snake, amphibian, and heaven knows what else. I paused by their habitat and then remained for hours, mesmerized by the diving antics, until finally one creature approached the fence. Naturally, I stuck my hand between the bars; then reached deeper, with my fingers through the holes in the mesh below, as would any red-blooded boy filled with curiosity.

"Of what had happened next I am still not entirely certain. I believe the platypus, a male, must have felt threatened by my childish overtures, for a few paces away I noted another, likely a female, and what must have been, in the shrubbery, a hidden nest. The male defended its mate and attacked my hand; instantly I felt a sharp pain in my finger as it struck me with a venom-filled spur of its hind leg—yes, this species, it turns out, is also poisonous, but *only* the male.

"Being a little boy, I cried out and snatched my hand away. But it was swelling immediately, and in moments the finger turned an ugly violet, while the bruise and sanguine venom started to spread. I bawled, and my father soon came to fetch me. Next, from what I remember, there were apothecaries, doctors, more than one, while my head had filled with unrelenting motion, and all things started to spin—people, heavens, daylight, anxious faces. I was confused, in pain; and I remember very little from thereon.

"The next several days, I am told, were spent in a high fever, and at some point they feared for my life. My father had taken me back to our house in London, where I lay abed, burning, delirious, soaking the sheets, and eventually waning and thin from the consuming effects of the poison fever.

"A very renowned physician finally turned the course of the poison and cured me, and I convalesced for a fortnight, until I was recovered well enough to travel back to our ancestral estate Pemberley.

"It seemed soon enough, I had been cured entirely; and so it was assumed, as health returned, and color came to my cheeks. But alas! I could not speak or even properly express to anyone the one thing that was now different about me—I had stopped *feeling* the *jaguar*. Instead, I felt nothing; *nothing* at all, for months, which then turned into years.

"At the age of fourteen, my father started having me confined regularly during the full moons, in a proper gentleman's enclosure chamber, assuming that I was due to succumb to the Affliction. At sixteen, I *turned* for the first time—I remember it well, that cold indifferent light of the full moon slithering over me, and the immediate tingling lassitude over the flesh, and then a complete loss of control—a loss of humanity.

"But there was no *jaguar* coiling inside me, ready to burst out. Instead, under Selene's wicked pale fire, I was broken and reduced in every sense—body and soul—and the world instead grew large around me. I became a bizarre little oddity, my secret demon a *platypus*; and I needed the cool deep waters to surround me, in which I could drown and lose the pathetic shrunken self that was now ever to be a part of me; that had superimposed itself over my original nature.

"What you call my pride is my deepest ugly shame. I hide it well indeed, and compensate for one shortcoming by taking on another—one that, you must admit, is far more acceptable to the world at large. For, there is no censure given to pride, only distance; and such isolation is indeed a relief to me, in view of my secret burden.

"You asked me more than once, at Netherfield and elsewhere, what I was hiding; you wanted to look inside me. Last night, at long last, you witnessed it. One always wonders, had things turned out differently on that fateful day of my childhood, would I be the same man I am now? It is impossible to tell.

"But now I must relate to you the rest of it, the complete true portrait of events in all its complexity. And I shall attempt to answer both of the two grievous offences laid at my feet, in light of the intimate information I have but now imparted to you.

"I had not been long in Hertfordshire, before I saw that

Bingley preferred your elder sister to any other young woman in the country. But it was not till the evening of the dance at Netherfield that I had any apprehension of his feeling a serious attachment. I had often seen him in love before. At that ball, while I had the honour of dancing with you, I was first made acquainted, by Sir William Lucas's casual words, that Bingley's attentions to your sister had given rise to a general expectation of their marriage. He spoke of it as a certainty. From that moment I observed my friend's behaviour attentively, up to the very moments when the comet wrecked its dire havoc over the assembly. And I could then perceive that his partiality for Miss Bennet was beyond what I had ever witnessed in him. Your sister I also watched. Her look and manners were open, cheerful, and engaging as ever, but without any symptom of peculiar regard. And I remained convinced that though she received his attentions with pleasure, she did not actively invite them.

"If *you* have not been mistaken here, *I* must have been in error. You possess the superior knowledge of your sister. If so, if I have been misled by such error to inflict pain on her, your resentment has not been unreasonable. But I assert that the serenity of your sister's manner might have given the most acute observer a conviction that, however amiable, her heart was not touched. Yes, I was desirous of believing her indifferent—but my decisions are not usually influenced by my hopes or fears, but by facts. I believed her to be indifferent on impartial conviction.

"My objections to the marriage were manifold, in my own case and his. Not only the want of connection—there were other causes of repugnance; causes which, though still existing, I had myself endeavoured to forget. These causes must be stated. The objectionable situation of your mother's family was nothing in comparison to that total lack of propriety so frequently betrayed by herself, your three younger sisters, and occasionally even by your father. Pardon me. It pains me to offend you. But amidst your displeasure and concern for the defects of your relations, let it console you to know that you and your elder sister have conducted yourselves entirely without any need for censure.

From what passed that evening, my opinion of all parties was confirmed. I strengthened my resolve to preserve my *tiger* friend from what I esteemed a most unhappy connection. He left Netherfield for London, on the day following, with a plan to soon return.

"The part which I acted is now to be explained. His sisters' uneasiness matched my own; our mutual opinion soon shared, and, with no time to lose, we resolved to join him directly in London. We accordingly went—and there I took it upon myself to point out to my friend the certain evils of such a choice. I described, and enforced them earnestly. But, however this advice might have delayed his determination, it would not ultimately have prevented the marriage, had it not been seconded by the assurance that I gave of your sister's indifference.

"He had before believed her to return his affection with sincere, if not with equal regard. But Bingley has great natural modesty, with a stronger dependence on my judgment than on his own. To convince him that he had deceived himself, and persuade him against returning into Hertfordshire, was not difficult at all. I cannot blame myself for having done thus much. There is but one part of my own conduct that I dislike—it is that I concealed from him your sister's being in town. I knew it myself, as did Miss Bingley; but her brother is even yet ignorant of it. He and your sister might have met without ill consequence; but his regard was not extinguished enough for him to see her without some danger. Perhaps this deception was beneath me. It is done, however, and it was done for the best. On this subject I have nothing more to say, no other apology to offer. If I have wounded your sister's feelings, it was unknowingly done.

"With respect to that other, more weighty accusation, of having injured Mr. Wickham, I can only refute it by laying before you the whole of his connection with my family. I am ignorant of *what* exactly he accuses me; but I can summon more than one witness to substantiate my words.

"Mr. Wickham is the son of a very respectable man, a *wolf* like himself, who had for many years managed all the Pemberley estates, and whose good conduct naturally inclined my father to be of service to him. On George Wickham, his godson, his kindness was also liberally bestowed. My father supported him at school, and afterwards at Cambridge—this most important assistance being a gentleman's education. My father was fond of this young man's society and engaging manners, and had the highest opinion of him. Hoping the church would be his profession, he intended to provide for him in it.

"As for myself, it is many, many years since I first began to think of him differently. The vicious propensities—the want of principle, which he was careful to guard from those closest to him—could not escape my own observation. I was a young man of similar age who had opportunities of seeing him in unguarded moments, which the elder Mr. Darcy could not have. Here again I shall give you pain. But whatever your sentiments toward Mr. Wickham might be, it shall not prevent me from unfolding his real character—it adds even another motive.

"My excellent father died about five years ago. His attachment to Mr. Wickham was to the last so steady, that in his will he particularly recommended I promote his advancement in the best manner that his profession might allow—and if he took orders, a valuable family living was to be his as soon as it became vacant. There was also a legacy of one thousand pounds.

"His own father did not long survive mine, and within half a year, Mr. Wickham wrote to inform me that, having finally resolved against taking orders, he hoped to expect some more immediate pecuniary advantage, in lieu of the preferment, by which he could not benefit. He had some intention of studying law, and the interest of one thousand pounds would be a very insufficient support therein.

"I rather wished, than believed him to be sincere; but, at any rate, was perfectly ready to accede to his proposal. I knew that Mr. Wickham ought not to be a clergyman. The business was therefore soon settled—he resigned all claim to assistance in the church, and accepted in return three thousand pounds. All connection between us seemed now dissolved. I thought too ill of him to invite him to

Pemberley, or admit his society in town. There he chiefly lived, but his studying the law was a mere pretence—being now free from all restraint, his was a life of idleness and dissipation, including the rare perverse travesty of running *unrestrained* outside, on many nights of the full moon.

"For about three years I heard little of him. But on the decease of the incumbent of the living which had been designed for him, he wrote to me again. His circumstances, he assured me (and I had no difficulty in believing it), were exceedingly bad. He had found the law a most unprofitable study, and now resolved to be ordained, if I would present him to the living in question—of which he trusted there could be little doubt, as he was sure that I had no other person to provide for, and I could not have forgotten my revered father's intentions.

"You will hardly blame me for refusing to comply with this and every repeated entreaty. His resentment was in proportion to the distress of his circumstances—and he was doubtless as violent in his abuse of me to others as in his reproaches to myself. After this period every appearance of acquaintance was dropped. How he lived I know not. But last summer he again most painfully came to my notice.

"I must now mention a circumstance which I would wish to forget myself, and which almost nothing should induce me to unfold to any human being. Having said thus much, I feel no doubt of your *secrecy*. My sister, who is more than ten years my junior, was left to the guardianship of my mother's nephew, Colonel Fitzwilliam, and myself. About a year ago, she was taken from school, and an establishment formed for her in London. Last summer she went with the lady who presided over it, to Ramsgate. And thither also went Mr. Wickham, undoubtedly by design—for there proved to have been a prior acquaintance between him and Mrs. Younge, in whose character we were so deceived. By her connivance he so recommended himself to Georgiana—whose affectionate heart retained a strong impression of his kindness to her as a child—that she believed herself in love, and consented to an elopement.

"She was then but fifteen, which must be her excuse. Fortunately, I joined them unexpectedly a day or two before the intended elopement, and Georgiana, incapable of causing grief and offending a brother whom she almost looked up to as a father, acknowledged the whole to me. And, seeing the *state* she was in, the worst of what she described was something else altogether. It was the following—during a dangerous evening of the full moon, when proper gentlemen were undergoing the Ordeal safely in their confinement, she had been *left alone* in their residence with Mr. Wickham. While Mrs. Younge left the room, he lingered in her company till very late—with the round moon up in the heavens, with window curtains negligently (or intentionally) open to admit the dreadful light—and heedless of her safety, he *turned* in her presence.

"Yes, you are, no doubt, as shocked now as I am, writing this. I will say but one other thing and it is unspeakable. The *wolf* scratched my sister; tore her arm. He then disappeared into the night. Georgiana was left in terror, alone, and after the traitor Mrs. Younge returned too late, my sister's arm was discovered to be sanguined and the deep gash required a physician's attention and bandaging. When telling me all this, Georgiana showed me her bandage and the wound; and told me also her fears of a horrifying, unnatural *infection*.

"You may imagine what I felt and how I acted. Regard for my sister's credit and feelings and reputation prevented any public exposure—even though I was ready to hunt down this *wolf* the same night and commit murder. Instead, having no direct proof to begin even a discreet legal inquest against him other than my sister's own belated testimony (which was inadequate in such a rare and delicate situation; and the dubious physician who treated her was also suddenly 'not to be found'), I wrote to Mr. Wickham, who left the place immediately, and Mrs. Younge was of course removed from her charge. Mr. Wickham's chief object was unquestionably my sister's fortune of thirty thousand pounds. He had expected that *infecting* her would assure a bond between them. But the hope of revenging himself on me was also a strong inducement. What he did to Georgiana was beyond ordinary ruin, but a potential marring of the soul and spirit. The effect of such demonic *infection* upon a woman is, as you may know in part, entirely dire and unpredictable. Georgiana was now potentially subject to the same unspeakable curse as we all are; but as a woman, hers would have been infinitely worse, including such horrors as the inability to bear children to term. Even now, she may be ruined for motherhood. Had she been also 'ruined' by him in a more usual way, his revenge would have been complete indeed.

"As for my poor sister—Georgiana is no longer the same. For her safety and ours, she now *confines* herself each full moon, in the same manner as a gentleman. And she does not—she will not—tell me whether she suffers from the Ordeal or not. Her only consolation is to devote herself entirely to the practice of music, which soothes and calms her, and occupies the chief of her time.

"This, madam, is a faithful narrative of every event in which we have been concerned together, and of my sister's grievous secret, and my own. I hope you will acquit me henceforth of cruelty towards Mr. Wickham. I know not in what manner, under what form of falsehood he had imposed on you, but detection of the real truth could not have been in your power.

"You may possibly wonder why all this was not told you last night; but I was not then master enough of myself. Forgive me for discarding my humanity before you in the most shameful, ungentlemanlike manner possible; for cowardice; for fleeing your presence in my pitiful *platypus demon* form. For the truth of many things here related, I can appeal to the testimony of Colonel Fitzwilliam, who, from our near relationship and constant intimacy, and as one of the executors of my father's will, has been unavoidably acquainted with every particular of these transactions. The only part he does not know is my *beastly* nature; all else is within his scope. If your abhorrence of *me* should devalue *my* assertions, you may choose to confide in my cousin. To give you a chance to speak with him, I shall find some opportunity of putting this letter in your hands in the course of the morning. I will only add, God bless you.

"FITZWILLIAM DARCY"

"Naturally, I stuck my hand between the bars . . ."

Chapter 36

If Elizabeth, when Mr. Darcy gave her the letter, did not expect it to contain a renewal of his offers, she had no true notion of its contents.

But such as they were—amazing, shocking, eye-opening—she eagerly went through them. And oh! what emotion they excited!

Her feelings as she read were scarcely to be defined.

With a strong prejudice against everything he might say—against any possibility of excuse or apology—she began his account of his own childhood and the extraordinary incident with the *platypus*, followed by what had happened at Netherfield and then Ramsgate.

She read with an eagerness which hardly left her power of comprehension, and the sentences blurred before her eyes.

His belief of her sister's insensibility she instantly resolved to be false. And his account of the real objections to the match made her too angry to wish doing him justice. He expressed no regret for what he had done which satisfied her; his style was not penitent, but haughty. It was all pride and insolence, and that pride certainly bore no connection to the so-called 'veneer' that he claimed concealed his *beastly* secret.

But when this subject was succeeded by his account of Mr. Wickham—when she read attentively about events which, if true, must overthrow every cherished opinion of his worth—her feelings became even more painful and hard to define. Astonishment, apprehension, and ultimately horror, oppressed her. What he had done as *wolf* to Georgiana was a travesty! She wished to discredit it entirely, repeatedly exclaiming, "This must be false! This cannot be! This must be the grossest falsehood!"—and when she had gone through the whole letter, though scarcely knowing anything of the last page or two, put it hastily away, protesting that she would never look in it again.

In this perturbed state of mind, with restless thoughts, she walked on. But it would not do; in half a minute the letter was unfolded again, and she again began the mortifying perusal of all that related to Wickham.

The account of his connection with the Pemberley family and the kindness of the late Mr. Darcy was exactly what he had related himself. So far each recital confirmed the other. But when she came to the will, the difference was great. What Wickham had said of the living was fresh in her memory, and it was impossible not to feel that there was gross duplicity on *someone's* part. As she re-read the particulars of Wickham's resigning all pretensions to the living in lieu of receiving the sum of three thousand pounds, again she hesitated.

She put down the letter, weighed everything impartially, deliberated. But every line proved only more clearly that Mr. Darcy's conduct was entirely blameless throughout the whole.

The extravagance and general profligacy of Mr. Wickham, man and *wolf*, exceedingly shocked her. She had never heard of him before his entrance into the ——shire Militia. Of his former way of life nothing had been known in Hertfordshire but what he told himself. As to his real character, she had never wanted to inquire. His countenance, voice, and manner seemed to invoke every virtue. She tried to recollect some instance of goodness or benevolence that might rescue him from the attacks of Mr. Darcy; or atone for his described idleness and vice. But no such recollection came.

She could see him instantly before her, in every charm of air and address, the charismatic intensity of the *wolf* gaze. But she could remember no more substantial good than the general approbation of the neighbourhood, and the regard which his social powers[81] had gained him.

After pondering this, she continued to read on. The horrifying story of his designs on Miss Darcy received some confirmation from what she heard from Colonel Fitzwilliam only the morning before. In the end she was referred by Mr. Darcy's words to Colonel Fitzwilliam himself. She almost decided to ask him, but considered the awkwardness of doing so. Furthermore, Mr. Darcy would never have hazarded such a proposal, if he had not been sure of his cousin's corroboration.

She now remembered her conversation with Wickham, in their first evening at Mr. Phillips's, and was struck with the impropriety of the things he said to her, a stranger. And she wondered it had escaped her before. She remembered his indelicacy of putting himself forward, the inconsistency of his professions with his conduct, his boast of having no fear of seeing Mr. Darcy—yet he had avoided the Netherfield ball the very next week. She remembered also that only *after* the departure of the Netherfield family, did he tell his story to all, until it was discussed everywhere. He had no scruples in sinking Mr. Darcy's character despite his "respect" for the father.

How differently did everything now appear! His attentions to Miss King were now hatefully mercenary; and the mediocrity of her fortune proved but his eagerness to grasp at anything. His

---

[81] The bloke must've had several thousand Facebook friends, and spent all day spamming Twitter. What a tool! [Who is this, again? What does this mean? —Ed.] *[Whoever this intruder is, he is apparently speaking in tongues, and is thus another raving lunatic. But, it no longer surprises me. This editorial department has long since become Bedlam. —Ed. 2]*

behaviour to Elizabeth herself was disgraceful—he had either been deceived with regard to her fortune, or had been encouraging her for the sake of vanity.

Meanwhile, in farther justification of Mr. Darcy, she had to allow that Mr. Bingley was blameless in the affair. However proud and repulsive were Mr. Darcy's manners, she had never, in the whole course of their acquaintance, seen him to be unprincipled, immoral, or unjust. Among his own connections he was esteemed and valued—even Wickham had allowed him merit as a brother. And she had heard Darcy speak so affectionately of his sister as to prove him capable of *some* amiable feeling. Darcy's character and behavior (had it been indeed as Wickham described) could hardly have been concealed from the world. Also, a friendship between someone capable of such evils, and the amiable Mr. Bingley, was incomprehensible.

She grew absolutely ashamed of herself. She could think of neither Darcy nor Wickham without feeling she had been blind, partial, prejudiced, absurd.

"How despicably I have acted!" she cried; "I, who have prided myself on my discernment! Had I been in love, I could not have been more wretchedly blind! But vanity, not love, has been my folly. Pleased with the preference of one, and offended by the neglect of the other, I have courted prepossession and ignorance, and driven reason away. Till this moment I never knew myself."

From herself to Jane—from Jane to Bingley—from Bingley to the *platypus*, her thoughts flew. Mr. Darcy claimed to be totally unaware of her sister's attachment; and now she could not help remembering what Charlotte's opinion had always been. Neither could she deny the justice of his description of Jane, whose stoic feelings *seemed* vague and complacent.

When she came to that part of the letter in which her family were mentioned, her sense of shame was severe. The justice of the charge struck her too forcibly for denial.

The compliment to herself and her sister was not unfelt. It soothed, but it could not console her for his contempt toward the rest of her family. She admitted that Jane's disappointment had in fact been the work of her nearest relations. And she felt depressed beyond anything she had ever known before.

After wandering along the lane for two hours, tormented by these thoughts, fatigue, and a recollection of her long absence, made her at length return home. Elizabeth entered the house, appearing cheerful as usual, but her mood made her unfit for conversation.

She was immediately told that the two gentlemen from Rosings had each called during her absence. Mr. Darcy came only for a few minutes, to take leave—and to claim a most unusual package of items of clothing he must have somehow forgotten here.

"They were—his shoes and stockings and pants, Eliza!" whispered Charlotte. "His *pants!* What in heaven's name? How did they come to be here in the house?"

Elizabeth denied all knowledge of this, maintaining a wall of composure. "Are you certain they were not items belonging to Mr. Collins?"

"Really, would I mistake such? And if they were, *why* on earth would Mr. Darcy want them for himself?"

Again, Elizabeth could hardly find an answer.

Charlotte then added that after Mr. Darcy had gone, Colonel Fitzwilliam had been sitting with them at least an hour, hoping for her return, and almost resolving to walk after her, in his considerate, noble *swan* fashion, till she could be found.

Elizabeth could but just *affect* concern in missing him. She really rejoiced at it. Colonel Fitzwilliam was no longer an object; she could think only of her letter from the *platypus.*

Chapter 37

The two gentlemen left Rosings the next morning. Mr. Collins waited near the lodges to make them his parting obeisance. He then reported home that they appeared in good health and tolerable spirits. To Rosings he then hastened, to console Lady Catherine and her daughter (from the safe confines of a parlor cage). He returned with a message from her ladyship that she was very desirous of having them all to dine with her.

Elizabeth could not see Lady Catherine without thinking that, under different circumstances, she *might* have been presented to her as her future niece. She could not think without a smile of what her ladyship's indignation would have been. . . .

Their first subject was how the Rosings party was reduced. "I assure you, I feel it exceedingly," said Lady Catherine; "No one feels the loss of friends as I do. But I am particularly attached to these young men! As always, they were excessively sorry to go! The dear Colonel rallied his spirits tolerably till just at last; but Darcy seemed to feel it most acutely—more, I think, than last year. His attachment to *Rosings* certainly increases."

Lady Catherine observed, after dinner, that Miss Bennet seemed out of spirits, and immediately supposed that she did not want to go home again so soon—that she could be easily spared by both father and mother, and ought to stay at least two months.

"But if that is the case, you must write to your mother and beg that you may stay a little longer. Mrs. Collins will be very glad of your company, I am sure."

"I am obliged to your ladyship for your kind invitation," replied Elizabeth, "but I must be in town next Saturday."

Lady Catherine proceeded to insist, and Elizabeth proceeded to resist. This went on for quite some time.

Elizabeth concluded with: "You are all kindness, madam; but I believe we must abide by our original plan."

Lady Catherine seemed resigned. "Mrs. Collins, you must send a servant with them. I cannot bear the idea of two young women traveling post by themselves, what with that dreadful comet and the full moon! It is highly improper—and deadly! When my niece Georgiana went to Ramsgate last summer, I made a point of her having two men-servants go with her—"

"My uncle is to send a servant for us."

"Oh! Your uncle! I am glad he keeps a man-servant. Where shall you change horses? Oh! Bromley, of course. If you mention my name at the Bell, you will be attended to."

Lady Catherine had many other questions to ask about their journey, most of which she answered herself. Elizabeth felt it was lucky—with a mind so occupied, she might have forgotten where she was.

Reflection and solitary walks filled all her following days.

Mr. Darcy's letter she now knew by heart. She studied every sentence. When she remembered the style of his address, she was still full of indignation; but when she considered his strange *beastly* nature and how unjustly she had condemned and upbraided him, her anger was turned against herself; and he became the object of compassion.

His attachment excited gratitude, his general character respect, his Ordeal, some amazed pity. But she could not approve him; nor could she for a moment repent her refusal, or feel the slightest inclination ever to see him again.

In her own past behaviour, there was a constant source of vexation and regret. And in the unhappy defects of her family, a subject of yet heavier chagrin. Her father, her mother, Lydia, and Catherine. . . . In their own ways they were hopeless of remedy.

Anxiety on Jane's behalf was another prevailing concern; and Mr. Darcy's explanation, by restoring Bingley to all her former good opinion, heightened the sense of what Jane had lost.

Bingley's affection was proved sincere, and his conduct cleared of all blame. How grievous that Jane had been deprived of such happiness by the folly and indecorum of her own family!

Add to all this Wickham's dreadful character, and it was almost impossible for Elizabeth to appear cheerful at all.

Their engagements at Rosings were as frequent during the last week of her stay as they had been at first. The very last evening her ladyship again inquired minutely into the particulars of their journey, gave them directions as to the best method of packing, and was so urgent on the necessity of bringing along a spare gentleman's cage—in case a traveler succumbed to the comet's wicked influence on the road and was in urgent need of confinement—that terrified Maria begged her sister for a "tiny spare cage, one of Mr. Collins's surplus," and personally loaded it with the help of two servants, in place of her own clothes trunk (which remained behind, to be shipped separately).

Chapter 38

On Saturday morning Elizabeth and Mr. Collins met for breakfast a few minutes before the others appeared.

"I know not, Miss Elizabeth," said he, "whether Mrs. Collins has yet expressed her sense of your kindness in coming to us; but I am very certain you will not leave the house without receiving her thanks for it. The favor of your company has been much felt, I assure you. Our plain manner of living—"

Elizabeth was eager with her thanks and assurances of happiness, to prevent Mr. Collins from speaking much longer. She had spent six weeks with great enjoyment; and the pleasure of being with Charlotte, and the kind attentions she had received, must make *her* feel the obliged.

Mr. Collins was gratified, and with a more smiling solemnity replied:

"It gives me great pleasure to hear that you have passed your time at Hunsford not disagreeably. We have certainly done our best—most fortunately having it in our power to introduce you to very superior society, our connection with Rosings. Our situation with regard to Lady Catherine's family is indeed the sort of extraordinary advantage and blessing which few can boast. You see how continually we are engaged there—"

Mr. Collins went on for quite some time. Words were insufficient for the elevation of his feelings; and he was obliged to walk about the room, agitating the air somewhat with a faint aroma of *skunk*, while Elizabeth tried to unite civility and truth in a few short sentences.

"You may, in fact, carry a very favourable report of us into Hertfordshire, my dear cousin. I flatter myself at least that you will be able to do so. Lady Catherine's great attentions to Mrs. Collins you have witnessed daily. My dear Miss Elizabeth, I can from my heart most cordially wish you but equal felicity in marriage. My dear Charlotte and I have but one mind and one way of thinking. We have been designed for each other."

For Elizabeth the greatest happiness came when this conversation was interrupted by the arrival of Charlotte herself.

Poor Charlotte! it was melancholy to leave her to such eternally aromatic society! But she had chosen it with her eyes open. And though sad to see her visitors go, she did not seem to ask for compassion. Her home and her housekeeping, her parish and her poultry, and the happy promise of forthcoming Australian dingoes and kangaroos, had not yet lost their charms.

At length the chaise arrived, the trunks were fastened on, together with Maria's "surplus cage," and it was pronounced to be ready. After an affectionate parting between the friends, Elizabeth was attended to the carriage by Mr. Collins and an infinite barrage of thanks, apologies, mentions of Rosings, and best respects to all her family—including Mr. and Mrs. Gardiner, though unknown.

He then handed her in, Maria followed, and with Mr. Collins offering on their behalf to have their "grateful thanks and respects" delivered to Rosings, the carriage drove off.

"Good gracious!" cried Maria, "it seems but a day since we first came, and yet how many things have happened!"

"A great many indeed," said her companion with a sigh.

"We have dined nine times at Rosings, besides drinking tea there twice! Oh, those fancy gleaming cages in every parlor! How much I shall have to tell!"

Elizabeth thought, *And how much I shall have to conceal!*

Their journey was performed without much conversation, or any alarm; no Afflicted gentlemen requiring urgent incarceration attacked them on the road. Within four hours they reached Mr. Gardiner's house, where they were to remain a few days.

Jane looked well, and Elizabeth had little opportunity of questioning her, amidst the various engagements that her aunt had reserved for them. But Jane was to go home with her, and at Longbourn there would be leisure enough for observation.

She could hardly wait for Longbourn, to tell her sister of Mr. Darcy's proposals and his *secrets*. To know that she had the power of revealing what would so exceedingly astonish Jane, and gratify her own vanity, was such a great temptation!

Only the fear of rushing too fast to speak something of Bingley which might grieve her sister further, held her back.

Chapter 39

It was the second week in May, in which the three young ladies set out together from Gracechurch Street for the town of ———, in Hertfordshire. As they drew near the appointed inn where Mr. Bennet's carriage was to meet them, they quickly perceived both Kitty and Lydia looking out of a dining-room upstairs. These two girls had been above an hour in the place, happily employed in visiting an opposite milliner, watching the sentinel on guard (and the splendidly gleaming sentinel cage in close vicinity), and dressing a salad and cucumber.[82]

After welcoming their sisters, they triumphantly displayed a table set out with such cold meat as an inn larder usually affords, exclaiming, "Is not this nice? Is not this an agreeable surprise? And, I declare, it is not even Affliction Steak!"[83]

---

[82] The salad was scandalously in the nude, and the cucumber—begging pardon of the reader's delicate sensibilities—the cucumber required unmentionable items of attire, as do all cucumbers, merely by virtue of their existence. Ahem!

[83] Affliction Steak is the designation given to somewhat lower quality cuts of meat used by establishments specifically to stock gentlemen's cages for that delicate time of the month when slabs of rare coarse meat were deemed a necessity to placate the confined *beasts* and incidentally minimize cage interior damage as they raved within, scratching and biting at anything in reach.

"And we mean to treat you all," added Lydia, "but you must lend us the money, for we have just spent ours at that shop." Then, showing her purchases—"Look here, I have bought this hideous bonnet for scraps—"

And when her sisters abused it as sufficiently ugly, she added, "Oh! but there were several much uglier in the shop. Besides, it will not matter what one wears this summer, after the ——shire have left Meryton, and they are going in a fortnight."

"Are they indeed!" cried Elizabeth, with the greatest satisfaction.

"They are going to be encamped near Brighton with their regimental—regi-*metal*, I declare!—polished cages and chains, so it will all shine to high heaven! I do so want papa to take us all there for the summer! It would be such a delicious scheme!"

"Yes," whispered Elizabeth to Jane, "*that* would be a delightful scheme indeed, and completely do for us at once. Good Heaven! Brighton, and a whole campful of soldiers!"

"Now I have news for you," said Lydia, as they sat down at table. "Excellent news, and about a certain *wolf* we all like!"

Jane and Elizabeth looked at each other.

"Well," said Lydia, "it is about dear Wickham! There is no danger of Wickham's marrying Mary King. There's for you! She is gone down to her uncle at Liverpool. Wickham is safe."

"And Mary King is safe!" added Elizabeth; "safe from a connection imprudent as to fortune."

"I hope there is no strong regard on either side," said Jane.

"I am sure there is not on *his*," said Lydia. "He never cared three straws about her—such a nasty little freckled thing."

Elizabeth might not have used such a coarse *expression*, but had herself but recently harbored a similar coarse *sentiment*.

After they had eaten, the carriage was ordered. And after some contrivance, the whole party, with all their boxes, work-bags, parcels, surplus cage (just in case), and the unwelcome addition of Kitty's and Lydia's purchases, were seated in it.

"How nicely we are all crammed in!" cried Lydia. And then she chattered about bonnets, the amiable company at Mrs. Forster's; asked what happened to them, if they flirted with any pleasant men, whether Jane was to be an old maid; voiced her own hopes of marriage "before three-and-twenty," and before all her older sisters, adding that "Mrs. Phillips says Lizzy had better have taken Mr. Collins; but *I* do not think there would have been any fun in it, but a great deal of *skunk* hideousness!"

In such fashion did Lydia, assisted by Kitty's additions, amuse her companions all the way to Longbourn. Elizabeth listened as little as she could, but there was no escaping the frequent mention of Wickham's name.

Their reception at home was most kind. Mrs. Bennet rejoiced to see Jane in undiminished beauty, and frequently berated "the odious *moon* and *comet*" in the usual manner. And more than once during dinner Mr. Bennet said to Elizabeth, with a hint of a genuine lion purr in his voice, and an involuntary attempt to knead his plate with his fork:

"I am glad you are come back, Lizzy."

Their party in the dining-room was large, for the Lucases came to meet Maria and hear the various news. Lady Lucas was inquiring of Maria, after the welfare and poultry of her eldest daughter and whether they had already bred "those Australian emu chickens." Mrs. Bennet was busy ingesting news of the latest fashions from Jane and passing it on to the Lucases (apparently walking-shovels and cowbells were all the rage). And Lydia was talking loudly to anyone who would hear her.

"Oh! Mary," said she, "I wish you had gone with us, for we had such fun!"

Mary gravely replied that she would have preferred a book to any such amusements. But as usual Lydia did not hear a word.

In the afternoon Lydia and the rest of the girls wanted to walk to Meryton, but Elizabeth steadily opposed the scheme. It should not be said that the Miss Bennets could not be at home half a day before they were in pursuit of the officers.

There was another reason too for her opposition. She dreaded seeing Mr. Wickham again, and was resolved to avoid it as long as possible. The comfort to *her* of the regiment's approaching removal was indeed beyond expression. In a fortnight they were to go—that infernal menagerie of military gentlemen in red coats, manly steel cages, padlocks, endless lengths of chain, swords, muskets, and all—and once gone, she hoped there could be nothing more to plague her on his account.

She had not been many hours at home before she found that the Brighton scheme, which Lydia had mentioned at the inn, was under frequent discussion between her parents.

Elizabeth saw directly that her father had not the smallest intention of yielding. But his answers were at the same time so vague and equivocal, that her mother, though often disheartened, had never yet despaired of succeeding at last.

There could be no doubt—*someone* was going to Brighton eventually.

Chapter 40

Elizabeth's impatience to acquaint Jane with what had happened could no longer be overcome. The next morning she at last related to her sister the scene between Mr. Darcy and herself.

"He proposed? He is a *platypus?* He is—good heavens! I cannot even find proper words for any of this, Lizzy!"

Miss Bennet's astonishment was soon lessened by sisterly partiality—any admiration of Elizabeth was perfectly natural—and all surprise was soon lost in other feelings. She was sorry that Mr. Darcy delivered his sentiments in such a manner, but she was also grieved for his unhappiness at her sister's refusal.

"His being so sure of succeeding was wrong," said she, "but consider how much it must increase his disappointment!"

"Indeed," replied Elizabeth, "I am heartily sorry for him and his strange little *beast*. But his other feelings will probably soon drive away his regard for me. You do not blame me, however, for refusing him?"

"Blame you! Oh, no."

"But you blame me for speaking so warmly of Wickham?"

"Surely not—I do not *think* you were wrong—"

Elizabeth then related what happened the very next day. She repeated the contents of the letter as far as they concerned

George Wickham. What a stroke was this for poor Jane! that so much wickedness existed, collected in one individual! Nor did Darcy's vindication console her for such discovery.

"This will not do," said Elizabeth, seeing her struggle; "you never will be able to make *both* of them good. Take your choice. There is just enough merit between them to make *one* good man; and of late it has been shifting about pretty much. For my part, I am inclined to believe it all Darcy's."

"I do not know when I have been more shocked," said Jane. "Wickham so very bad! It is almost past belief. And poor Mr. Darcy! Dear Lizzy, only consider what he must have suffered as a boy, and as a man! Concealing his humiliating *beastly* nature from everyone all these years, and now—such a disappointment! and with the knowledge of your ill opinion, too! and having to relate such a thing of his sister, attacked by a *demon wolf!* It is really too distressing. I am sure you must feel it so."

"Oh! no, my regret and compassion are all done away by seeing you so full of both. You will do him such ample justice, now that I am growing every moment more unconcerned and indifferent. Indeed, if you lament over the platypus much longer, my heart will be as light as a feather."

"Poor Wickham! such goodness in his face and manner!"

"Unfortunately—one has got all the goodness, and the other all the appearance of it."

"I never thought Mr. Darcy so deficient in the *appearance* of it as you used to do. Even when he held himself in such rigidity to hide his *beast*, he was always rather handsome—"

"I meant to be uncommonly clever in taking so decided a dislike to him, without any reason. One may be continually abusive without saying anything just; but one cannot always be laughing at a man without once stumbling on something witty."

Elizabeth then admitted that since reading that letter she had certainly began to think differently; and oh, how she missed talking to her own sister about all of it!

"How unfortunate that you have spoken so strongly of Wickham to Mr. Darcy, for now it appears wholly undeserved."

"Certainly. But the misfortune of speaking bitterly comes from my own prejudices. Now I want your advice. Ought I tell our acquaintances in general about Wickham's *real* character?"

Miss Bennet mused. "Surely there can be no occasion for exposing him so dreadfully. What is your opinion?"

"That it ought not to be attempted. Mr. Darcy has not authorised me to make his communication public. On the contrary, everything about his sister and her possible Affliction was meant to be kept secret. And if I try to reveal the rest, who will believe me? The general prejudice against Mr. Darcy is so violent, that it would be the death[84] of half the good people in Meryton to attempt to place him in an amiable light. Wickham will soon be gone. Thus, at present I will say nothing about it."

"You are quite right. To have his errors made public might ruin him forever. Perhaps he is sorry for what he has done. . . ."

The tumult of Elizabeth's mind was allayed by this conversation with Jane. She had got rid of *two* of the dreadful secrets which had weighed on her for a fortnight. But she dared not relate the *third*—the part of Mr. Darcy's letter that explained how sincerely Jane had been regarded and valued by Bingley. Only time—and Mr. Bingley himself—might reveal that mystery.

Elizabeth was now home, and at leisure to observe the real state of her sister's spirits. In truth, Jane was not happy—she still cherished a very tender affection for Bingley.

"Well, Lizzy," said Mrs. Bennet one day, "what is your opinion *now* of this sad business of Jane's? I blame that infernal *comet*, I told my sister Phillips so the other day. Since that ball at

---

[84] Violent? Death? What, is this chick going to go all ninja on everyone? [Once again, who is this mad villain, and what chicken does he speak of? —Ed.] *[Never mind the chicken; what in heaven's name is ninja? —Ed. 2]*

Netherfield when it appeared and caused such disaster and mayhem, the gentlemen all going mad, I dare say, everything started *then*. But I cannot find out if Jane saw him in London. He is a very undeserving young man—and I do not suppose there's the least chance in the world of her ever getting him now."

"I do not believe he will ever live at Netherfield any more."

"Oh well! Nobody wants him to come. Though I shall always say he used my daughter extremely ill. Some noble *tiger* indeed! Well, my comfort is, I am sure Jane will die of a broken heart; and then he will be sorry for what he has done."

Elizabeth made no answer.

"Well, Lizzy," continued her mother, soon afterwards, "and so the Collinses live very comfortable, do they? Well, well, I only hope it will last, with him being a *skunk*, it must be tedious for her, to say the least. And what sort of table do they keep? There is nothing extravagant in *their* housekeeping, I dare say."

"No, nothing at all."

"A great deal of frugal management, depend upon it. Affliction Streak for most meals, likely. Yes, *they* will take care not to outrun their income. *They* will never be distressed for money. Well, much good may it do them!"

And Mrs. Bennet went on at length to complain about having Longbourn entailed after Mr. Bennet was dead, while Elizabeth tried not to listen.

Chapter 41

The second week of their return began. It was the last of the regiment's stay in Meryton; the endless rows of steel and iron cages were soon to be loaded on the freight carts, and all the young ladies in the neighbourhood were drooping apace.

Among the almost universal dejection, only the elder Miss Bennets were still able to eat, drink, and sleep, and pursue the usual course of their employments. Very frequently were they reproached for this insensibility by Kitty and Lydia, whose own misery was extreme.

"Good Heaven! what is to become of us? What are we to do? How can you be smiling so, Lizzy?"

Their affectionate mother shared all their grief (she had herself endured a similar occasion, five-and-twenty years ago).

"I am sure," said she, "I cried for two days when Colonel Miller's regiment went away. When his magnificent iron cage started to roll, I thought I should have broken my heart."

"I am sure I shall break *mine*," said Lydia.

"If one could but go to Brighton!" observed Mrs. Bennet.

"Oh, yes!—if one *could!* But papa is so disagreeable."

Such lamentations were heard through Longbourn House. Elizabeth tried to be diverted. But all sense of pleasure was lost in shame. She felt anew the justice of Mr. Darcy's objections, and was much disposed to pardon his interference with Bingley.

The gloom ended when Lydia received an invitation from Mrs. Forster, the wife of the colonel of the regiment, to accompany her to Brighton. This friend was a very young woman, and very recently married. A resemblance in humour and spirits had recommended her to Lydia, and the two became intimate acquaintances.

The rapture of Lydia, the delight of Mrs. Bennet, and the mortification of Kitty, were scarcely to be described. Lydia flew about the house in ecstasy, laughing and talking; whilst the luckless Kitty repined at her fate of being left behind.

"I cannot see why Mrs. Forster should not ask *me* as well as Lydia," said she. "Though I am *not* her particular friend, I have just as much right to be asked, for I am two years older."

In vain did Elizabeth attempt to make her reasonable, and Jane to make her resigned. Elizabeth considered this invitation as the death warrant of all common sense. And she could not help secretly advising her father not to let Lydia go. She reminded him of all the improprieties of Lydia's behaviour, the disadvantage from the friendship of such an equally silly woman as Mrs. Forster, and the probability of her being yet more imprudent with such a companion at Brighton, where the *moon* was going to be dangerously full during the most of it, and both temptations and *threats* must be greater than at home.

He heard her attentively, and then said:

"Lydia will never rest until she has exposed herself in some public place or other. Might as well have her to do it with as little expense or inconvenience to her family as possible."

"If you were aware," said Elizabeth, "of the very great disadvantage to us all which must arise from the public notice of Lydia's imprudent manner—nay, which has already arisen from it—I am sure you would judge differently."

"Already arisen?" repeated Mr. Bennet. "What, has she frightened away some of your lovers? Come, let me see the list of pitiful fellows who have been kept aloof by Lydia's folly."

"Indeed you are mistaken. I have no such injuries to resent. It is not of particular, but of general evils, which I am now complaining. Our respectability in the world must be affected by the wildness of Lydia's character. If you, my dear father, will not take the trouble of checking her exuberant spirits, she will soon be beyond help. She will, at sixteen, be the most determined flirt that ever made herself or her family ridiculous. Kitty is also in danger, and will follow wherever Lydia leads. Vain, ignorant, idle, and absolutely uncontrolled! Oh! my dear father, they will be censured and despised wherever they are known, and their sisters will be involved in the disgrace!"

"Do not make yourself uneasy, my love," said Mr. Bennet with affection. "Wherever you and Jane are known you must be respected and valued, despite having *three* very silly sisters. We shall have no peace at Longbourn if Lydia does not go to Brighton. Let her go, then. Colonel Forster is a sensible man, and will keep her out of any real mischief. And she is luckily too poor to be an object of prey to anybody. The menagerie of officers will find women better worth their notice."

With this answer Elizabeth was forced to be content. But her own opinion was the same, and she left him disappointed.

Had Lydia and her mother known of her talk with her father, their indignation would have been boundless. In Lydia's imagination, a visit to Brighton comprised every possibility of earthly happiness. She saw, with the creative eye of fancy, the streets of that gay[85] bathing-place covered with delightfully *beastly* officers and their polished confinement and cutlery, all radiant in the sun. She saw herself the object of attention, to tens

---

[85] Oh most delightful reader, pray, be not confounded by any notions of Oscar Wilde's sort of liaisons going on at Brighton. The only danger to one's virtue in Brighton comes from a certain infernal duck.

and to scores of them, each in possession of Great Cat, wolf, bear, and other noble *beast* varieties. She saw all the glories of the camp—its tents and cages stretched forth in beauteous uniformity of lines and metal bars, crowded with the young and the gay,[86] and dazzling with scarlet. And, to complete the view, she saw herself seated beneath a tent, handling lengths of chain and tenderly flirting with at least six officers at once. . . .

Elizabeth was now to see Mr. Wickham for the last time. Having been frequently in company with him since her return, agitation was pretty well over. She had even learnt to detect in his "gentleness" an affectation, and beneath it, a dangerous dark *wolf*. He seemed inclined to renew his attentions, and it only served to provoke her. She lost all concern for him and his frivolous gallantry.

On the regiment's last day at Meryton, he dined, with other officers, at Longbourn. Elizabeth was not disposed to part from him in good humour. When he inquired as to her time at Hunsford, she mentioned Colonel Fitzwilliam's and Mr. Darcy's having both spent three weeks at Rosings.

He looked surprised, displeased, alarmed; but with a returning *wolfish* smile replied that he had formerly seen the Colonel often, observed that he was very gentlemanlike, and asked how well she liked him.

Her answer was warmly in his favour.

With an air of indifference he soon afterwards added: "His manners are very different from his cousin's."

"Yes, but I think Mr. Darcy improves upon acquaintance."

"Indeed!" cried Mr. Wickham with a look which did not escape her. "And pray, may I ask?—" But checking himself, he added, in a gayer tone, "Has he deigned to add aught of civility to his ordinary style?—for I dare not hope," he continued in a more serious tone, "that he is improved in essentials."

---

[86] Once more, o gracious reader, we know not what is to be said at such a juncture; even though there is nothing wrong with that juncture. Ahem!

"Oh, no!" said Elizabeth. "In essentials, I believe, he is very much what he ever was."

While she spoke, Wickham could not be sure of her meaning. There was something new in her countenance that made him listen with anxious attention.

"I did not mean," said Elizabeth, "that his *mind* or his *manners* were in a state of improvement, but that—from knowing him better—his disposition was better understood."

Wickham's alarm increased. For a moment he was silent; then, shaking off his anxiety, he said in the gentlest manner:

"You, who know my feeling towards Mr. Darcy, will readily comprehend how I must rejoice that he is wise enough to assume even the *appearance* of what is right. His pride may be of service, but it can only deter him from foul misconduct. I fear that his 'cautiousness' is merely adopted on his visits to his aunt—he stands much in awe of her good opinion and judgment. His fear of her has always operated when they were together. And he very much desires a match with Miss de Bourgh."

Elizabeth could not repress a smile at this, but she answered only by a slight inclination of the head. The rest of the evening passed with the *appearance*, on his side, of usual cheerfulness, but with no further attempt to distinguish Elizabeth. They parted at last with mutual civility, and possibly a mutual desire of never meeting again.

When the party broke up, Lydia returned with Mrs. Forster to Meryton, from whence they were to set out early the next morning. Upon separation, the family farewells were noisy. Kitty shed tears (from vexation and envy). Mrs. Bennet was diffuse in her good wishes for the felicity of her daughter. And in the clamorous happiness of Lydia, the more gentle adieus of her two oldest sisters were barely heard.

Chapter 42

Had Elizabeth's opinion of conjugal felicity been drawn from her own family, she could not have formed a very pleasing opinion.

Her father, captivated by youth and beauty, had married a woman whose weak mind had very early in their marriage put an end to all real affection. Respect, esteem, and confidence had vanished forever, and so did his views of domestic happiness.

But Mr. Bennet, the somewhat redolent *lion*, was not of a disposition to seek comfort for the disappointment in any of those pleasures that console the unfortunate for their folly or vice. He found enjoyment in the country and books. His wife's ignorance and folly also contributed to his amusement. This is not the sort of happiness a man would wish to owe to his wife; but a true leonine philosopher benefits from what is at hand. . . .

Elizabeth had never been blind to the impropriety of her father's behaviour as a husband. But she respected his abilities, was grateful for his affectionate treatment of herself, and tried to forget that continual breach of conjugal obligation and decorum which exposed his wife to the contempt of her own children.

But she had never felt so strongly as now the disadvantages of the children of so unsuitable a marriage.

Elizabeth had rejoiced over Wickham's departure but she had no other reason to enjoy the loss of the regiment. The comet was almost gone from the skies, and with it the danger of sudden daytime *turnings* dwindled to naught. Meanwhile, with the military gentlemen gone, their parties were now less varied than before, and her mother and sister constantly bemoaned the dullness of everything around them, throwing a real gloom over their domestic circle. And, though Kitty might in time regain her natural degree of sense, since the disturbers[87] of her brain were removed, her other sister, Lydia, was likely to be hardened in all her folly by the double danger of a watering-place[88] and a camp.

Upon the whole, Elizabeth found that many social events to which she had been looking forward with anticipation, gave her little to no pleasure. Her tour to the Lakes was now the object of her happiest thoughts.

When Lydia went away she promised to write very often and very minutely to her mother and Kitty. But her letters were always long expected, and always very short. Those to her mother contained little else than that they were just returned from the library, where such and such *wolf* or *panther* officers had attended them, mentions of beautiful ornaments, new gowns, parasols—all which she took no time to describe, being obliged to hurry away with Mrs. Forster—they were going off to the camp to observe the movement and readying of regimental cages

---

[87] It is important to reassure that Kitty's brain itself was not removed, only the disturbers of it. "Disturbers" of a brain are small goblins and gnome-like unnatural creatures found infesting domiciles in the country, and they thrive within the vacant brains of young ladies who are not otherwise exercising their reasoning faculties. Symptoms of such an infestation include restlessness, an affinity for the color pink, and excessive attention to ribbons, lace, and any visiting gentlemen.

[88] One is reassured that Brighton is a genuine watering place because there is water there; which one might use to water things such as plants and persons needing to be watered.

for the approaching full moon, etc. In her letters to her sister, there was still less—only underlined words and innuendoes.

After the first fortnight or three weeks of her absence, health, good humour, and cheerfulness began to reappear at Longbourn. The families who had been in town for the winter came back again, the wicked *comet* was at last gone entirely, and summer finery and summer engagements arose.

Mrs. Bennet was restored to her usual querulous serenity. And Kitty was so much recovered as to be able to enter Meryton without tears. Elizabeth could only hope that by the following Christmas she might be reasonable enough not to mention an officer more than once a day—unless, by some cruel and malicious arrangement at the War Office, another regiment should be quartered in Meryton.

The time fixed for the beginning of their northern tour was now fast approaching. Within a fortnight, a letter arrived from Mrs. Gardiner, informing that Mr. Gardiner would be prevented by business from setting out till a fortnight later in July, and must be in London again within a month. Since that left too short a period for them to travel so far, they were obliged to give up the Lakes, and substitute a shorter tour—no farther northwards than Derbyshire. In that county there was enough to be seen to occupy their three weeks; and to Mrs. Gardiner it had a peculiarly strong attraction. The town where she had formerly passed some years of her life (and where they were now to spend a few days) was a great object of her curiosity.

Elizabeth was excessively disappointed—she had set her heart on seeing the Lakes. But eventually she was reconciled to the new itinerary and satisfied; and all was soon right again.

With the mention of Derbyshire, it was impossible for her to see the word without thinking of Pemberley and its *platypus* owner. "But surely," said she, "I may enter his county without impunity, and without his perceiving me."

Thus, another four weeks passed before Mr. and Mrs. Gardiner, with their four children, appeared at Longbourn. The children, two girls of six and eight years old, and two younger boys who had not yet experienced their first Ordeal, were to be left under the care of their sweet and loving cousin Jane, who was the general favourite.

The Gardiners stayed only one night at Longbourn, and set off the next morning with Elizabeth in pursuit of novelty and amusement.

It is not the object of this work to give a description of Derbyshire, nor of any of the remarkable places through which their route thither lay. A small part of Derbyshire is all the present concern. To the little town of Lambton, the scene of Mrs. Gardiner's former residence they bent their steps, after having seen all the principal wonders of the country. And within five miles of Lambton, Elizabeth found from her aunt that Pemberley was situated.

It was not in their direct road, nor more than a mile or two out of it. Mrs. Gardiner expressed an inclination to see the place again. Mr. Gardiner declared his willingness, and Elizabeth was applied to for her approbation.

"My love, should not you like to see a place of which you have heard so much?" said her aunt.

Elizabeth was distressed. She felt that she had no business at Pemberley. She preferred to decline, saying she was tired of seeing "great houses."

Mrs. Gardiner however said it was not merely a fine house, but the grounds were delightful, with some of the finest woods in the country.

Elizabeth said no more—but her mind could not acquiesce. The possibility of meeting Mr. Darcy, while viewing the place, instantly occurred. It would be dreadful!

She blushed at the very idea, and thought it would be better to speak openly to her aunt than to run such a risk. She finally decided that openness would be her last resort, after inquiries.

Accordingly, when she retired at night, she asked the chambermaid whether Pemberley was at present occupied by its owner. A most welcome negative followed—and her alarms now being removed, she was at leisure to feel a great deal of curiosity to see the house herself.

The next morning, she answered with a proper air of indifference that she had not really any dislike to the scheme.

To Pemberley, therefore, they were to go.

Chapter 43

As they drove along, Elizabeth watched for the first appearance of Pemberley Woods with some perturbation. And when at last they turned in at the lodge, her spirits were in a high flutter.

The park was very large, with great variety of ground. They entered it and drove for some time through a beautiful wood.

Elizabeth's mind was too full for conversation, but she saw and admired every remarkable view. They gradually ascended for half-a-mile, and then found themselves at the top where the wood ceased, and the eye was instantly caught by Pemberley House, situated on the opposite side of a valley.

It was a large, handsome stone building, standing well on rising ground, and backed by a ridge of high woody hills. In front, a stream of some natural importance was swelled into greater, but without any artifice. Its banks were neither formal nor falsely adorned. Elizabeth was delighted, and for some reason suddenly imagined the *demon platypus* cajoling in these cool waters under a full moon . . . and then in her mind's eye the vision transformed to the slim powerful human shape of the man himself, rising out of the water, dripping wet, and for some reason still in his fine shirtsleeves. . . .

She had never seen a place for which nature had done more, or where natural beauty had been so untainted by awkward taste. They were all warm in their admiration. And at that moment she felt that to be mistress of Pemberley might be something!

They descended the hill, crossed the bridge, and drove to the door. And here, all her apprehension of meeting its owner returned. She dreaded lest the chambermaid had been mistaken. On applying to see the place, they were admitted into the hall; and Elizabeth, as they waited for the housekeeper, had leisure to wonder at her being where she was.

The housekeeper came; a respectable-looking elderly woman, much less fine, and more civil, than expected. They followed her into the dining-parlour—large, well-proportioned, handsomely fitted up.

Elizabeth, after surveying it, went to a window to enjoy its prospect. The hill, crowned with wood, which they had descended, was a beautiful object. Every disposition of the ground was good; and she looked on the whole scene, the river, the trees scattered on its banks and the winding of the valley, as far as she could trace it, with delight.

As they passed into other rooms, from every window there were beauties to be seen. The lofty, handsome rooms held furniture suitable to the fortune of its proprietor. And Elizabeth admired his taste—it was neither gaudy nor uselessly fine; with less splendour and more real elegance than that of Rosings.

And of this place, thought she, *I might have been mistress! With these rooms I might now have been familiarly acquainted as my own, rejoiced in them, welcomed my uncle and aunt as visitors. But no,*—recollecting herself—*that could never be; my uncle and aunt would have been lost to me; I should not have been allowed to invite them.*

This was a lucky recollection—it saved her from regret.

She longed to inquire of the housekeeper whether her master was really absent, but had not the courage for it. Instead, the question was asked by her uncle. Mrs. Reynolds replied that he was, adding, "But we expect him to-morrow, with a large party of friends."

Oh, how Elizabeth rejoiced that their own journey had not been delayed a day!

Her aunt now called her to look at a picture, the likeness of Mr. Wickham, among other miniatures, over the mantelpiece. Even now, there was a shadow of the *wolf* in his eyes.

Her aunt asked her, smilingly, how she liked it. The housekeeper told them it was a picture of a young gentleman, the son of her late master's steward, who had been brought up by him at his own expense. "He is now gone into the army," she added; "but I am afraid he has turned out very wild."

Mrs. Gardiner looked at her niece with a smile, but Elizabeth could not return it.

"And that," said Mrs. Reynolds, pointing to another of the miniatures, "is my master—and very like him. It was drawn at the same time as the other—about eight years ago."

"I have heard much of your master's fine person," said Mrs. Gardiner, looking at the picture; "it is a handsome face. But, Lizzy, you can tell us whether it is like or not."

Mrs. Reynolds's respect for Elizabeth seemed to increase on this intimation of her knowing her master.

"Does that young lady know Mr. Darcy?"

Elizabeth coloured, and said: "A little."

"And do not you think him a very handsome gentleman, ma'am?"

"Yes, very handsome."

"I am sure I know none so handsome; but in the gallery upstairs you will see a finer, larger picture of him than this. This room was my late master's favourite room, and these miniatures are just as they used to be then. He was very fond of them."

This explained why Wickham was still shown among them.

Mrs. Reynolds then directed their attention to one of Miss Darcy, drawn when she was only eight years old.

"And is Miss Darcy as handsome as her brother?" said Mrs. Gardiner.

"Oh! yes—the handsomest young lady that ever was seen; and so accomplished!—She plays and sings all day long. In the next room is a new instrument just come down for her—a present from my master. She comes here to-morrow with him."

Mr. Gardiner, easy and pleasant, in typical canine manner, encouraged her by his questions and remarks. Mrs. Reynolds had evidently great pleasure in talking of her master and his sister.

"Is your master much at Pemberley during the year?"

"Not so much as I could wish, sir. He may spend half his time here. Miss Darcy is always down for the summer months."

Except, thought Elizabeth, *when she goes to Ramsgate and gets mauled by a wolf. . . .*

"If your master would marry, you might see more of him."

"Yes, sir; but I do not know when *that* will be. I do not know who is good enough for him."

Mr. and Mrs. Gardiner smiled. Elizabeth could not help saying, "It is very much to his credit that you should think so."

"I say no more than the truth, and everybody will say that knows him," replied Mrs. Reynolds.

Elizabeth listened with increasing astonishment as the housekeeper added, "I have never known a cross word from him in my life, and I have known him since he was four years old."

This was extraordinary praise—most opposite to her ideas. That he was not a good-tempered man had been her firmest opinion. And now her keenest attention was awakened. She longed to hear more, and was grateful to her uncle for saying:

"There are very few people of whom so much can be said. You are lucky in having such a master."

"Yes, sir, I know I am. If I were to go through the world, I could not meet with a better. But I have always observed, that they who are good-natured when children, are good-natured when they grow up. And he was always the sweetest-tempered, most generous-hearted boy in the world."

Elizabeth almost stared at her. *Can this be Mr. Darcy?*

"His father was an excellent man," said Mrs. Gardiner.

"Yes, ma'am, that he was indeed, a noble jaguar; and his son will be just like him—just as affable to the poor."

"So the younger Mr. Darcy is a jaguar, then?" inquired her uncle casually.

"To be sure, it is sometimes rumored, sir; but I will not stake my word on it, for the master keeps his *beast* a close secret, more than anything. It is no doubt a noble *beast*; it has to be," the housekeeper replied with a warm measure of pride.

Elizabeth listened, wondered, doubted; was impatient for more. Mrs. Reynolds could not interest her in other pictures, room dimensions, and furniture costs—all was recited in vain.

Mr. Gardiner, amused by the kind of family prejudice to which he attributed her excessive praise of her master, soon led again to the subject. And she dwelt with energy on Darcy's many merits as they proceeded up the great staircase.

"He is the best landlord and master," said she, "that ever lived. All of his tenants and servants can only give him praise. Some people call him proud; but I never saw anything of it. It is only because he does not rattle away like other young men."

In what an amiable light does this place him! thought Elizabeth. *And yet, a strange little platypus in a great big man.*

"This fine account of him," whispered her aunt as they walked, "is inconsistent with his behaviour to poor Wickham."

"Perhaps we might be deceived."

On reaching the spacious lobby above they were shown into a pretty sitting-room, more elegant than the apartments below; and were informed that it was newly decorated for Miss Darcy, who had taken a liking to the room when last at Pemberley.

"He is certainly a good brother," said Elizabeth, as she walked towards one of the windows.

Mrs. Reynolds anticipated Miss Darcy's delight, when she should enter the room. "And this is always the way with him," she added. "Whatever can give his sister any pleasure is sure to be done in a moment. There is nothing he would not do for her."

The picture-gallery, and several principal bedrooms, were all that remained to be shown. In the former were many good paintings; but Elizabeth knew nothing of it. She instead turned to look at some crayon drawings[89] of Miss Darcy's, whose subjects were usually more interesting, and also more intelligible.

In the gallery there were many family portraits. But Elizabeth walked in quest of the only face whose features would be known to her. At last it arrested her—and she beheld a striking resemblance to Mr. Darcy, with such a *secret* smile over the face as she remembered to have sometimes seen when he looked at *her*. She stood several minutes before the picture, in earnest contemplation, and returned to it again before they quitted the gallery. Mrs. Reynolds informed them that it had been taken in his father's lifetime.

There was at this moment, in Elizabeth's mind, a more gentle sensation towards Mr. Darcy than she had ever felt. The commendation of Mrs. Reynolds was no trifle—what praise is more valuable than the praise of an intelligent servant? How many people's happiness were in his guardianship! How much pleasure or pain, good or evil was it in his power to bestow!

And as Elizabeth stood before the canvas on which he was represented, fixing his smiling secret eyes upon herself, she thought of his regard with a deeper sentiment of gratitude than it had ever raised before. She remembered its warmth, and softened its impropriety of expression and odd platypus ending.

When all of the open parts of the house had been seen, they returned downstairs, and, taking leave of the housekeeper, were consigned over to the gardener, who met them at the hall-door.

---

[89] Miss Darcy did not draw portraits with her crayons, because one cannot draw anything worth a damn with crayons; likely she did scrawl some large-headed stick people or stick ducks, then added a zigzag tree, a house with a chimney, and a sun with five rays sticking out.

As they walked across the hall towards the river, Elizabeth turned back to look again. Her uncle and aunt stopped also. And while the former was conjecturing as to the date of the building, the *owner* of it himself suddenly came forward from the road, which led behind it to the stables.

Mr. Darcy!

They were within twenty yards of each other. And so abrupt was his appearance, that it was impossible to avoid his sight.

Their eyes instantly met. And the cheeks of both were overspread with the deepest blush. Darcy absolutely started, and for an instant seemed immovable from surprise (Elizabeth feared on his behalf that he might lose control again, in the same manner as before, and *turn* before all witnesses). But shortly recovering himself, he advanced towards the party, and spoke to Elizabeth—if not in terms of perfect composure, at least of perfect civility.

She had instinctively turned away. But stopping on his approach, she received his compliments with an embarrassment impossible to be overcome. For once her heart beat so fast that she felt a flutter—almost, as if there had been a full moon, and she was a *man*, and a transformation, a *something* was upon her!

Had his resemblance to the picture they had just seen, been insufficient to assure the other two that they now saw Mr. Darcy, the gardener's expression of surprise, on beholding his master, immediately told it. They stood a little aloof while he was talking to their niece—who, astonished and confused, scarcely dared lift her eyes to his face, and knew not what answer she returned to his civil inquiries after her family.

Amazed at the alteration of his manner since they last parted, every sentence that he uttered was increasing her embarrassment. And every idea of the impropriety of her being found here recurred to her mind. These few minutes were some of the most uncomfortable in her life.

Nor did he seem much more at ease. When he spoke, his accent had none of its usual sedateness. And he repeated the *same* inquiries, so often, and in so hurried a way, as plainly spoke the distraction of his thoughts.

"Miss Bennet, at what time did you leave Longbourn?"

"Just a few days ago, I believe, that is—ten o'clock—"

"And how are you enjoying your stay in Derbyshire?"

"Very well, sir. And how are *you*—enjoying your—?"

"Yes, thank you. Might I inquire after your parents?"

"They are quite well, thank you."

"And when did you leave Longbourn?"

"I believe it was around ten in the morning—or nine?"

"How well do you like your parents—that is, *Derbyshire?*"

"Very well, I believe—ten in the morning—"

"And your parents and sisters are all quite well?"

"Yes, all, very well, thank you all—thank *you.*"

"When was it that you left Longbourn?"

"Derbyshire is, thank you, very amiable, in the morning—"

This nightmare went on for quite some time.

At last every idea seemed to fail him, and every reply failed her. After standing a few moments in abject stupidity, without saying a word, he suddenly recollected himself, and took leave.

Her uncle and aunt then joined her, and expressed admiration of his figure. But Elizabeth heard not a word. Her mind, faculties—indeed, all reason—were equally flooded. Contemplating her own stupidity, she followed them in silence.

She was overpowered by shame and vexation. Her coming there was the most unfortunate, ill-judged thing in the world! How it must appear to him! In what a disgraceful light! As if she had *purposely thrown herself in his way* again!

Oh! why did she come? And why did he come a day early? Had they been only ten minutes sooner in leaving—

She blushed again and again over the perverseness of the meeting. And his behaviour, so strikingly altered—what could it mean? Amazing that he should even speak to her!—but to speak with such civility (to be sure, it was stumbling and rather imbecile, but it was *civil* nevertheless); to inquire after her family! Never had she seen him so undignified, gentle, as on this unexpected meeting. What a contrast with Rosings Park, when he handed her his letter!

They had now entered a beautiful walk by the side of the water, but it was some time before Elizabeth was sensible of any of it. She answered her uncle and aunt mechanically;[90] looked, but did not see the sights before her. Her thoughts were all fixed on Pemberley House, where Mr. Darcy now was. She longed to know what was passing through his mind—and whether, in defiance of everything, she was still dear to him. . . .

Perhaps he had been civil only because he felt at ease. Yet there had been *that* in his voice which was *not* like ease (if speaking abject nonsense was any indication). Did he feel pain or pleasure in seeing her? It was certainly not composure.

They entered the woods, and bidding adieu to the river,[91] ascended some of the higher grounds. Mr. Gardiner expressed a wish of going round the whole park, but feared it might be too far for a walk. With a triumphant smile they were told that it was ten miles round.

It settled the matter; and they started to return the same way they had come. Elizabeth longed to explore, but Mrs. Gardiner was rather tired and thought only of returning to the carriage. Their progress was slow, for Mr. Gardiner was very fond of fishing, and often stopped to watch for trout in the nearby water.

---

[90] Regardless of what this might suggest, it is unlikely that Miss Elizabeth Bennet was at any point employed as a mechanic. The delicate reader is reassured that neither steam engines nor tiny delightful clockwork mechanisms were ever repaired by this young lady's skilled but gentle hand.

[91] To be sure, the river does not require an adieu since it is incapable of replying in the manner of a lady or gentleman. A river is neither a lady nor a gentleman, o most erudite reader. The Gardiners and Miss Bennet must have been mistaken when they attempted to converse with it.

Whilst wandering on in this slow manner, they were again surprised—and Elizabeth's astonishment was equal to the first—by the sight of Mr. Darcy approaching them.

This time Elizabeth was at least more prepared for the encounter, and resolved to appear calm and not to babble.

When he approached, she saw that he had lost none of his recent civility. Imitating his politeness, she began to volubly admire the beauty of the place. But she had not got beyond the words "delightful," and "charming," when it occurred to her that any praise of Pemberley coming from *her* might be misconstrued. Her colour changed, and she said no more.

Mrs. Gardiner was standing a little behind; and on her pausing, Darcy asked Elizabeth if she would do him the honour of introducing him to her friends. This was a stroke of civility for which she was quite unprepared—she could not suppress a smile that he now sought the acquaintance of those very people against whom his pride had revolted in his offer to herself.

He will be surprised, she thought, *when he learns who they are. My uncle is a dog! But he takes them for people of fashion.*

The introduction, however, was immediately made. And as she named their relationship to herself, she stole a sly look at him, to see how he bore it, expecting he would decamp as fast as he could from such disgraceful companions.

That he was *surprised*, was evident. However, instead of turning his back on them and going away, the *platypus* entered into conversation with Mr. Gardiner. Elizabeth was pleased; indeed, felt triumph that he would see she had some relations for whom there was no need to blush. She listened most attentively to all that passed between them, and gloried in every word of her uncle, which marked his intelligence, taste, or good manners.

The conversation soon turned to fishing. And Mr. Darcy invited him, with the greatest civility, to fish there as often as he chose while he continued in the neighbourhood, offering to supply him with fishing tackle, and pointing out those parts of the stream where there was usually most sport.

Elizabeth again imagined the small *beast* swimming in the moonlight. . . . And then, superimposed in her mind's eye, came the sleek form of the human gentleman, in a decidedly wet shirt.

Mrs. Gardiner, walking arm-in-arm with Elizabeth, gave her a look expressive of wonder.

No! Does she know I am thinking of the demon platypus? Elizabeth blushed; then recollected that her aunt knew nothing.

Elizabeth said nothing also. Meanwhile it gratified her exceedingly—Darcy's hospitality had to be a compliment to herself. Her astonishment, however, was extreme. *Why is he so changed?* She thought it could not be for *her*—for *her* sake that his manners were thus softened. But, how could it be?

It is impossible that he should still love me.

After walking some time in this way, the two ladies in front, the two gentlemen behind, they descended to the brink of the river for the better inspection of some curious water-plant. Mrs. Gardiner, fatigued by the exercise of the morning, found Elizabeth's arm inadequate support, and consequently preferred her husband's. And so it was that Mr. Darcy took her place by her niece, and they walked on together.

After a short silence, Elizabeth first spoke. She wished him to know that she had been assured of his absence before she came to the place. "Your housekeeper," she added, "informed us that you would certainly not be here till to-morrow, and that you were not immediately expected in the country."

He acknowledged the truth of it, and said that business with his steward was his reason for arriving a few hours before the rest of his traveling party. "They will join me early to-morrow," he continued, "and among them are Mr. Bingley and his sisters."

Elizabeth answered only by a slight bow, thinking back to the last time when Mr. Bingley's name had been mentioned between them. Mr. Darcy's mind was similarly engaged.

"There is one other person in the party," he continued, "who particularly wishes to be known to you. Will you allow me to introduce my sister to you during your stay at Lambton?"

The surprise of such an application was great indeed. Elizabeth immediately felt that whatever desire Miss Darcy might have of being acquainted with her must be the work of her brother. And it was gratifying to know that his resentment had not made him think really ill of her.

They now walked on in silence, each of them deep in thought. Elizabeth was not comfortable (that was impossible); but she was flattered and pleased. His wish of introducing his sister to her was a compliment of the highest kind. They soon outstripped the others, and when they had reached the carriage, Mr. and Mrs. Gardiner were half a quarter of a mile behind.

He then asked her to walk into the house—but she declared herself not tired, and they stood together on the lawn in awkward silence. She wanted to talk, but there seemed to be an embargo on every subject. At last they spoke of traveling—while in the minds of both for some reason stood only the full moon . . . and pale human or *beast* shapes sliding through cool watery depths.

Yet time (and her aunt) moved slowly—and Elizabeth's patience and ideas were nearly worn out before the *tête-à-tête* was over. On Mr. and Mrs. Gardiner's coming up they were all pressed to go into the house for some refreshment. But this was declined, and they parted with utmost politeness. Mr. Darcy handed the ladies into the carriage. And when it drove off, Elizabeth saw him walking slowly towards the house.

The observations of her uncle and aunt now began. They pronounced Mr. Darcy to be infinitely superior to anything they had expected—"Perfectly well behaved, polite, unassuming."

"There *is* something a little stately in him, to be sure," replied her aunt, "but it is confined to his air, and is not unbecoming. I can now say with the housekeeper, that though some people may call him proud, I have seen nothing of it."

"I was quite surprised—his behaviour to us was more than civil; it was really attentive; and there was no necessity for such attention. His acquaintance with Elizabeth was very trifling."

"To be sure, Lizzy," said her aunt, "he is not so handsome as Wickham. Or, rather, he has not Wickham's smoldering *wolf* countenance, for his features are perfectly good. But how came you to tell me that he was so disagreeable?"

Elizabeth excused herself as well as she could, and admitted that she liked him better now than before.

"But perhaps he may be a little whimsical in his civilities," replied her uncle. "Remind me, what is his *beast*? A jaguar, is it not? Or some other fine Great Cat? And as for whimsy, all your great men often are. Therefore I shall not take him at his word about coming here and fishing, as he might change his mind, and warn me off his grounds."

Elizabeth *knew* that they had entirely misunderstood his character, but said nothing.

"From what we have seen of him," continued Mrs. Gardiner, "I really should not have thought that he could have behaved so cruelly to anyone as he has to poor Wickham. He has not an ill-natured look—regardless, I venture, of the phase of the moon—indeed, his *beast* might not be quite that wicked! On the contrary, there is something pleasing about his mouth when he speaks; and a dignity in his countenance that suggests a fine heart. The good housekeeper did give him a most flaming character—as though he were a rare *fire dragon!* I could hardly keep from laughing. But he is obviously a liberal master, and *that* in the eye of a servant comprehends every virtue."

Elizabeth felt herself called on to say something in vindication of his behaviour to Wickham. She therefore told them, as carefully as she could, that according to Darcy's relations in Kent, he was capable of very different actions—his character was not so faulty, nor Wickham's so amiable. In confirmation of this, she related the unhappy particulars of all the financial transactions in which they had been connected.

Mrs. Gardiner was surprised and concerned. But as they were now approaching spots familiar to her, every thought gave way to the charm of recollection of younger days spent in this neighborhood. She was too busy pointing out all things to her husband to think of anything else. Fatigued as she had been by the morning's walk, they had no sooner dined than she set off again in quest of her former acquaintances. The evening was spent in this happy manner.

The occurrences of the day were too full of interest to leave Elizabeth much attention for any of these new friends.

She could do nothing but think, and wonder, of Mr. Darcy's civility, and, above all, of his wishing her to be acquainted with his charming, vulnerable, and possibly *demon-infected* sister.

Chapter 44

Elizabeth had settled it that Mr. Darcy would bring his sister to visit her the day after she arrived at Pemberley.

She was consequently resolved not to be out of sight of the inn the whole of that morning. But instead, on the very morning after their arrival at Lambton, these visitors came.

Elizabeth and her uncle and aunt had been out walking with some of Mrs. Gardiner's old-time friends, and were just returning to the inn for dinner, when the sound of a carriage drew them to a window.

A gentleman and a lady in a curricle drove up the street. Elizabeth immediately recognized the livery, guessed what it meant, and surprised her relations by acquainting them with the honour which she expected.

Her uncle and aunt were all amazement. And her embarrassment as she spoke, coupled with the circumstance itself—and many of the circumstances of the preceding day— opened to them a new idea on the business.

Nothing had ever suggested it before, but they felt that there was no other way of accounting for such attentions from such a quarter than by supposing a *partiality* for their niece. . . .

While these newly-born notions were passing in their heads, Elizabeth's agitation was at every moment increasing.

She was quite amazed at her own discomposure. Mostly she dreaded that, from his partiality to her, Darcy should have exaggerated her virtues to his sister. She was more than anxious to please Georgiana, yet afraid of failing.

Elizabeth retreated from the window, afraid of being seen. As she paced the room, trying to compose herself, she saw such looks of inquiring surprise in her uncle and aunt as made everything worse.

Miss Darcy and her brother appeared, and this formidable introduction took place. With astonishment Elizabeth saw that her new acquaintance was at least as embarrassed as herself.

Since her being at Lambton, she had heard that Miss Darcy was exceedingly *proud*. But it took only a few minutes to convince her that she was only exceedingly *shy*—it was difficult to obtain even a word from her beyond a monosyllable.

Miss Darcy was tall, and on a larger scale than Elizabeth. And, though little more than sixteen, her figure was formed, and her appearance womanly and graceful. She was less handsome than her brother. But there was sense and good humour in her face, and her manners were perfectly unassuming and gentle.

Elizabeth, who had expected to find in her the same acute sentiments as in Mr. Darcy, was much relieved by the difference. And she was also unable to discern—however closely she looked—any symptoms of the Affliction in her person, or any strange "wildness," or unnatural *wolf* affectation.

They had not long been together before Mr. Darcy told her that Bingley was also coming to visit. And she had barely time to express her satisfaction, when Bingley's quick *tiger* step was heard on the stairs, and in a moment he entered the room.

All Elizabeth's anger against him had been long done away. Even if she felt any, it would have fallen before the unaffected warmth with which Mr. Bingley expressed himself on seeing her again. He inquired in a friendly way after her family, and was filled with the same good-humoured ease as always.

To Mr. and Mrs. Gardiner he was equally interesting. They had long wished to see him. Indeed, the whole party before them excited a lively attention. The suspicions which had just arisen of Mr. Darcy and their niece, made them observe each closely. And they were soon convinced that at least *one* was in love. Of the lady's sensations they remained a little in doubt. But it was evident that the gentleman was overflowing with admiration.

Elizabeth, on her side, had much to do—to ascertain the feelings of her visitors; to compose her own, and to make herself agreeable to all. Fortunately, they were all prepossessed in her favour. Bingley was ready, Georgiana was eager, and Darcy determined, to be pleased.

In seeing Bingley, her thoughts naturally flew to her sister. And, oh! how ardently did she long to know whether *his* were directed in a like manner! Sometimes, it seemed, he talked less than before. And once or twice, as he looked at her, it was as if he was looking for a resemblance to Jane. But, though this might be imaginary, his behaviour to Miss Darcy (who had been set up as a rival to Jane) was perfectly indifferent—no looks, no particular regard. Nothing occurred between them that could justify the hopes of his sister.

On this point Elizabeth was soon satisfied. And ere they parted, he seemed instead to show a tender recollection of Jane, and a wish of her mention. While others were talking together, he observed in a tone of real regret, that it "was a very long time since he had had the pleasure of seeing her;" and, before she could reply, he added, "We have not met since the 26th of November, when we were all dancing together at Netherfield."

Elizabeth was pleased to find his memory so exact. And afterwards he took occasion to ask her whether *all* her sisters were at Longbourn. The question came with a meaningful look.

It was not often that she could turn her eyes on Mr. Darcy himself. But, whenever she did catch a glimpse, she saw an expression of complaisance, and a tone so far removed from *hauteur* or disdain, that she was convinced of a long-term improvement of his manners.

When she saw him thus seeking the acquaintance and courting the good opinion of people with whom any intercourse[92] a few months ago would have been a disgrace—and recollected their last lively and disastrous scene in Hunsford Parsonage—the change was so great, that she could barely hide her astonishment. Neither in the company of his dear friends at Netherfield, nor his dignified relations at Rosings—never had she seen him so desirous to please; free from self-consequence, *secret* aloofness, or unbending reserve, as now. The subjects of his present kind attentions would have drawn down the ridicule and censure of the ladies both of Netherfield and Rosings.

Their visitors stayed with them above half-an-hour. When they arose to depart, Mr. Darcy called on his sister to join him in expressing their wish of seeing Mr. and Mrs. Gardiner, and Miss Bennet, to dinner at Pemberley, before they left the country.

Miss Darcy, with a shy diffidence that suggested she was unaccustomed to giving invitations, readily obeyed.

Mrs. Gardiner looked at her niece, wondering how *she*, whom the invitation most concerned, felt disposed—but Elizabeth had turned away. She assumed that this studied avoidance was the result of discomfiture rather than refusal. And since her husband, fond of society in true *great dane* fashion, displayed a willingness to accept it, she ventured to confirm their attendance, and the day after the next was fixed on.

Bingley expressed great pleasure in the certainty of seeing Elizabeth again, having still many inquiries to make after all their Hertfordshire friends. Elizabeth sensed that he wished to speak of her sister, and was pleased. Thus, she found herself, when their visitors left them, able to think of the last half-hour

---

[92] Such dreadful notions are not implied at all, o most delicate reader! Mr. Darcy is certainly *not* looking to engage in lewd and scandalous behaviour with multiple persons!

with some satisfaction. Eager to be alone, and fearful of inquiries or hints from her uncle and aunt, she stayed with them only long enough to hear their favourable opinion of Bingley, and then hurried away to dress.

But she had no reason to fear Mr. and Mrs. Gardiner's curiosity—it was not their wish to force her confession. It was evident that she was much better acquainted with Mr. Darcy than expected. And it was evident that he was very much in love with her. They saw much to interest, but nothing to justify inquiry.

Of Mr. Darcy it was now a matter of anxiety to think well; and there was no fault to find. They could not be untouched by his politeness. Indeed, *this* version of his character would not have been recognized by anyone in Hertfordshire. The Gardiners were happily willing to believe the housekeeper, trusting the authority of a servant who had known him since he was four years old. Neither had their Lambton friends anything to say that was not of a positive nature. They had nothing to accuse him of but pride—which he had. It was acknowledged, however, that he was a liberal man, and did much good among the poor.

The travelers soon found however that Wickham was not held there in much estimation. His interactions with the son of his patron were imperfectly understood. But it was a well-known fact that, when he left Derbyshire, he had also left many debts behind him, which Mr. Darcy afterwards discharged.

As for Elizabeth, her thoughts were at Pemberley. The evening seemed long, but was not enough to determine her feelings towards *one* in that mansion. And she lay awake two whole hours endeavouring to make them out.

She certainly did not hate him. No; hatred had vanished long ago, from the moment she had seen him *turn* into the pitiful little *demon platypus* creature, so that she was now ashamed of ever feeling a dislike against him. . . .

The respect of his valuable qualities, though at first unwillingly admitted, had for some time ceased to be repugnant to her. And it was now heightened by the discovery of his disposition shown in so amiable a light. But above all, above respect and esteem, there was a motive within her of goodwill which could not be overlooked.

It was gratitude—gratitude, not merely for having once loved her, but for loving her still well enough to forgive all the petulance and acrimony of her manner in rejecting him, and all the unjust accusations accompanying her rejection.

He who (she had thought) would avoid her as his greatest enemy, seemed, on this accidental meeting, most eager to preserve the acquaintance. Without any indelicate display, or any peculiarity of manner (except for that initial effusion of babbling), he was soliciting the good opinion of her friends. And he was bent on making her known to his sister!

Such a change in such a proud man invoked astonishment and gratitude—for to love, *ardent love*, it must be attributed. And its pleasing impression on her was to be encouraged. She respected, she esteemed; she was grateful to him. She felt a real interest in his welfare . . . and in his *beast*. And she only wanted to know how far she wished that welfare to depend upon herself—how far for the happiness of both should she employ the power (which her fancy told her she still possessed) of bringing on her the *renewal* of his addresses.

It had been settled in the evening between the aunt and the niece that such a striking civility as Miss Darcy's in coming to see them so early on the very day of her arrival at Pemberley ought to be imitated by some exertion of politeness on their side. And thus they decided to visit her at Pemberley the following morning. Elizabeth was pleased; though when she asked herself the reason, she had very little to say in reply.

Mr. Gardiner, meanwhile, left them soon after breakfast, for a fishing engagement with the gentlemen at Pemberley.

Chapter 45

Elizabeth was convinced that Miss Bingley's dislike of her had originated in jealousy. She could not help wondering how unwelcome her appearance at Pemberley must be to her. How much civility to expect on that lady's part?

On reaching the house, they were shown through the hall into the saloon,[93] whose northern aspect rendered it delightful for summer. Its windows admitted a most refreshing view of the high woody hills behind the house.

In this house they were received by Miss Darcy, who was sitting there with Mrs. Hurst and Miss Bingley, and the lady with whom she lived in London. Georgiana's reception of them was very civil, but mixed with embarrassment, shyness, and the fear of doing wrong. It was easy to imagine how this made her wrongfully appear proud and reserved. Mrs. Gardiner and her niece, however, did her justice, and pitied her.

---

[93] Although handsomely situated in Great Britain and not in the American Wild West, apparently Pemberley housed a disreputable saloon filled with cowboys, gunfighters, gamblers, carpetbaggers, desperados, gold prospectors, working ladies, and many other persons with crooked, gold, and rotten teeth. There was also an untuned pianoforte with missing ivories, and an old toothless drunk who played it every night, and never allowed Miss Georgiana Darcy near it.

By Mrs. Hurst and Miss Bingley they were noticed only by a curtsey. They were seated, and an awkward pause followed. It was first broken by Mrs. Annesley, a genteel, agreeable-looking woman, whose endeavour to introduce some kind of discourse proved her to be more truly well-bred than either of the others. Between her and Mrs. Gardiner, with occasional help from Elizabeth, the conversation was carried on.

Miss Darcy looked as if she wished for courage enough to join in it; and sometimes did venture a short sentence when there was least danger of its being heard.

Elizabeth soon saw that she was herself closely watched by Miss Bingley. Indeed, she could not speak a word, especially to Miss Darcy, without calling her attention. This would not have prevented her from trying to talk to the latter, but they were seated at a distance. However, filled with her own thoughts, Elizabeth was not sorry to be spared the necessity of speaking.

She expected every moment that some of the gentlemen would enter the room. She wished and feared that the master of the house might be amongst them. . . . And whether she wished or feared it most, she did not know.

After a quarter of an hour without hearing Miss Bingley's voice, Elizabeth suddenly received from her a cold inquiry after the health of her family. She answered with equal indifference and brevity, and the others said no more.

The next variation was produced by the entrance of servants with cold meat, cake, and a variety of all the finest fruits in season. But this did not take place till after a significant look and smile from Mrs. Annesley to Miss Darcy, to remind her of her duties as hostess. There was now employment for the whole party—for though they could not all talk, they could all eat; and the beautiful pyramids[94] of grapes, nectarines, and peaches soon collected them round the table.

While everyone was thus engaged, Elizabeth felt the gentle and quiet approach of Georgiana Darcy, who paused at her side with a small dish of fruit and other delights, and pretending to nibble on something, addressed her thus:

"Miss Bennet, might I have the honour of conversing with you privately? There is a small room just around the corner on the right of the hall. Would you do me the kindness of following me there? Now, I shall walk out first, and I beg you to follow a few moments later?"

Her curiosity engaged, Elizabeth nodded. And as promised, Miss Darcy took her leave, saying to the room in general she will return briefly.

Miss Bennet waited as asked, then also made her excuses for a powder room visit, and then slipped into the hallway, where she soon discovered the room in question.

Georgiana was within, and after closing the door behind them she came forward, her hands reaching out to grasp those of her guest, and wearing an expression of such trust that Elizabeth felt her heart swell with a sentiment she could hardly describe.

"Dear Miss Bennet! I thank you kindly! And—I presume you can guess why I must thus speak with you. My brother has told me *everything*—no need to fear, I will not make excuses for his behavior or repeat any offers he has made that might be unpleasant to you. I merely need to ask you, as the only other female of my acquaintance who now knows my plight—except for the awful Mrs. Younge who is now gone—Miss Bennet, I must ask what you think of my *condition*."

Elizabeth coloured. She certainly did not expect this sudden turn of conversation, nor the young lady's directness. "Miss

---

[94] Whilst there are in fact rumored to be Egyptian pyramids at an estate called Mansfield Park, there may also be such similar ancient structures at Pemberley, in addition to the western saloon.

Darcy," she began. "First, I would make my most profound reassurances to you that there is nothing in what I have been told of your misfortune that would ever make me think less of you; and, to the contrary, your situation has engaged my deepest sympathies. But now I must ask you, and beg forgiveness in advance—have you in fact *turned?*"

Miss Darcy's countenance was turbulent, her eyes downcast, as she spoke in the barest whisper: "No; I have not—not yet." And then she added with a passion, "But oh! I can feel the *beast!* It is just under the skin, so close to the surface, pushing at my defenses, and all it would take for me is to let go but one time, and I shall be lost. It seems it would take but a single breath, an exhalation. . . ."

For a long moment, Elizabeth knew not how to answer. "I wish I had more knowledge and comprehension of this; for the Affliction is not something we females have much experience with—if any. To be honest, this is the first that I am hearing of such a thing as your—plight."

Georgiana began to pace, and sometimes wrung her hands. "Maybe it was a mistake to disturb your pleasurable visit with all *this*, Miss Bennet," she cried. "Oh, how I do regret making you think on this sorry, horrible—"

"Nay; not at all!" Elizabeth hurried to reassure. And then she probed her memory in search of anything that might be of assistance, remembering suddenly an old rhyme, or possibly a silly story her own mother had spoken to her once, when she, a young girl, had first brought up the subject:

"A woman does not *turn*, does not fear the odious moon, nor does she suffer from the Affliction," her mother had said casually, "because a woman *loves*."

"What does it mean? Does not a gentleman love also?"

But her mother was very busy and made no answer.

And when Elizabeth had tried to question further, plying Mrs. Bennet with both subtle and forthright questions, she was met either with avoidance or with an unusual—unusual for her loquacious mother—amount of silence. It was as though Mrs. Bennet was unwilling, or unable, to impart to her anything more.

But now, this notion, this one simple sentence spoken to a little girl, had crept into Elizabeth's mind. Miss Darcy had no mother to discuss such things or to impart the necessary maternal wisdom, and Mrs. Annesley, though a lovely woman, was only a companion with whom such extreme intimacies might not be tested. And so she approached Georgiana, and in turn took her cold trembling hands into her own.

"Miss Darcy . . ." she said, "will you trust me now? I believe—I think I *know*, and can help you."

Georgiana raised her gaze; Elizabeth looked at her warmly, and she said: "Your brother, Mr. Darcy, has an unusual secret. I have seen the *creature* he turns into—"

"The *platypus!*" exclaimed Georgiana with delight, "Yes, I have seen it! It is so odd, and decidedly impossible, and funny!"

"Then you and I, Miss Darcy, are possibly the only two alive who have witnessed it. I mention it now, because your brother seems to have an unusual amount of control over the *act* of transformation itself; more so than is normal in a man."

"Yes, I do believe it is so. It is because of how he too had been *infected* as a young boy; or, should I say, poisoned."

"And has he tried assisting you with your own control?"

"Why, no; we have not spoken of it since the incident."

"Miss Darcy, believe me when I say, he is dreadfully concerned! For, he does not *know* if you have been truly infected or not, if you have *turned* or not. He knows nothing, only tortures himself with suppositions! I believe he can be of such great help to you, if only you would speak to him plainly!"

"Oh, but I cannot! I cannot face him and speak of this—"

"Then, face *me*," said Elizabeth.

Georgiana looked up, for the first time meeting the other's gaze directly. Her hands, still held in Elizabeth's own, were trembling.

"And, now, Miss Darcy, I am going to ask you something impossible. I beg you to *let go* of whatever inner hold you presently have on the *beast*, and simply *turn*—right now, right this instant!"

Georgiana drew back. "What? Oh—oh, no! Good Lord, Miss Bennet, you cannot mean—"

"Did you feel an attachment for the man who harmed you so wickedly, and put you in such danger from his *wolf?*"

"Yes, I—"

"Did you love him?"

"Yes—no—I don't know! This is terrible, why do you ask me such things?"

Elizabeth felt her own cheeks blazing from what she had suddenly conceived in that most peculiar moment.

"When you decide for yourself whether you had even for a moment loved Wickham—forgive me for even mentioning his name—then your fledgling *beast* will no longer have control over you."

The younger lady thought, then exclaimed, "I did *not* love him, no. . . . There was some infatuation at one point, warm sentiments, but never love."

"I am glad," replied Elizabeth. "For in that case, I harbour a brave supposition that you may soon be freed of any traces of this so-called 'infection.' Now I beg you try, as I say, to *turn*. Only, instead of his *wolf* taking over you, you take over *it*. And fear not for my own sake; I know you will not harm me."

Miss Darcy nodded, then, with a sudden quick breath—an exhalation, as though indeed requiring an active *resignation* of will—she released Elizabeth's supporting hands, stood back, and tightly closed her eyes.

And thus, Elizabeth observed a curious, impossible sight.

The air between them seemed to warp, as though from the heat of a fireplace. . . . And Miss Georgiana Darcy gave a single muffled cry, then stumbled, clutching her breast, and suddenly the edges defining her shape seemed to blur. . . .

There was no sound of bones breaking. No moans or inhuman roars of a monster *demon* asserting itself. Instead, there was the barest flicker, a mere *shadow* of the *wolf*. In a blink it came—and was gone.

And then, with a hard snap, as though pulled back by an invisible force, Georgiana spread her arms wide, moved them apart and simultaneously threw her head back, so that her pretty coiffed hair broke out of its careful dressing and streamed behind her in golden waves.

And before Elizabeth's amazed gaze, the streaming waves of hair turned into waves of *fire* . . . and plumes.

The womanly shape was gone, replaced by the outline of a great, golden, burning, winged creature—a bird.

The *firebird* was golden-scorching-white. It had a smooth elegant beak, a wingspan greater than a swan, and a tail that was as long as that of a peacock, except it was a flaming waterfall. And yet—the creature's scalding delicate outline was etched in flickering cold-burning flames, each tiny feather defined by a spark that harmlessly scattered around the room, disappearing into nothing, harming nothing with its effervescent faerie light.

The bird gave one delicate cry, lovely as a crystal flute. It beat its fire wings and rose to the ceiling like a small sun, as Elizabeth observed it with wonder.

And in the next instant, the *firebird* descended, light as a dream, and folded its wings, and again transformed into the womanly shape of Miss Darcy, somewhat *en déshabillé*.

Miss Darcy gave a cry of delight, and then came forward to embrace Elizabeth.

"Oh, Miss Bennet!" she said, "I am indeed free of the *wolf!* Instead, I can now be *anything!*"

They returned to the saloon moments later—separately, to throw off undue speculation, especially from Miss Bingley—after Elizabeth helped Georgiana tidy her attire and pin up her hair. Original worry was now coupled with exultation, and both the ladies had high color in their cheeks for different reasons. Miss Darcy seemed as though she had truly come alive, and her natural shyness, though still present, had partly given way to a barely repressed chaotic vivacity.

Elizabeth meanwhile, could hardly repress her own joyful smile on her younger friend's behalf. What a wonder she had just been witness to!

However, the moment she stepped back into the saloon, the recent miracles were strongly overshadowed by an old familiar anxiety, because Mr. Darcy soon entered the room.

He had been with Mr. Gardiner and several other gentlemen, by the river, and had left him only on learning that the ladies of the family intended a visit to Georgiana that morning. No sooner did he appear than Elizabeth wisely resolved to be perfectly easy and unembarrassed (a difficult feat), because she saw that the suspicions of the whole party were awakened against them—all eyes watched his behaviour when he first came into the room.

No one was more curious than Miss Bingley, in spite of her smiles. Jealousy had not yet made her desperate, and her attentions to Mr. Darcy were by no means over.

Miss Darcy, on her brother's entrance, quickly glanced at Elizabeth with a fleeting smile, and then exerted herself much more to talk. Elizabeth saw that he was anxious for his sister and herself to get acquainted—not knowing to what extent they already were—and encouraged conversation on both sides.

Miss Bingley saw all this likewise; and, in the imprudence of anger, said with sneering civility:

"Pray, Miss Eliza, are not the ——shire Militia removed from Meryton? They must be a great loss to *your* family."

In Darcy's presence she dared not mention Wickham's name. But Elizabeth instantly knew she referred to him, and it gave her a moment's distress. To repel the ill-natured attack, she answered the question in a tolerably detached tone.

While she spoke, an involuntary glance showed her Darcy, with a heightened complexion, earnestly looking at her, and his sister unable to lift up her eyes. Had Miss Bingley known what pain she was then giving her beloved friend, she would have refrained from the hint. But she had merely intended to discompose Elizabeth, to make her betray a sensibility which might injure her in Darcy's opinion, and, perhaps, to remind him how her family were "connected" with that corps.

Not a syllable had ever reached her of Miss Darcy's meditated elopement, nor of the *infection* received from the *wolf*. To no creature had it been revealed, except to Elizabeth. And from all Bingley's connections her brother was particularly anxious to conceal it, for various reasons.

Elizabeth's composed behaviour, however, soon quieted his emotion. And as Miss Bingley, vexed and disappointed, dared not refer more directly to Wickham, Georgiana also recovered in time. Although neither Wickham nor his *beast* had any hold on her any longer (as of only a half an hour ago), any revelation of the incident was still a cause for scandal.

Meanwhile, her brother, whose eye she feared to meet, seemed to scarcely remember Georgiana. Instead, he was focused on Elizabeth—the opposite of Miss Bingley's intent.

Their visit did not continue long after. While Mr. Darcy attended them to their carriage, Miss Bingley vented her feelings in criticisms on Elizabeth's person, behaviour, and dress.

But Georgiana would not join her. Her brother's recommendation was enough to ensure her favour, but in truth, the lovely and amiable Elizabeth had just helped change her life.

When Darcy returned to the saloon, Miss Bingley could not help repeating to him what she had been saying to his sister.

"How very ill Miss Eliza Bennet looks this morning, Mr. Darcy!" she cried; "I never in my life saw anyone so much altered as she is since the winter. She is grown so brown and coarse! Louisa and I were agreeing, we could not recognize her."

Mr. Darcy coolly replied that he perceived no other alteration than her being rather tanned from summer travel.

"For my own part," she rejoined, "I never could see any beauty in her. Her face is too thin; her complexion has no brilliancy; and her features are not at all handsome. Her nose lacks character. Her teeth are just tolerable. And as for her eyes, which have sometimes been called so *fine*, I could never see anything extraordinary in them. They have a sharp, shrewish look, which I do not like. And in her air altogether there is a self-sufficiency without fashion, which is intolerable."

Certain that Darcy admired Elizabeth, this was not the best way for Miss Bingley to recommend herself. But angry people are not always wise. He looked somewhat nettled, but was resolutely silent. Determined to make him speak, she continued:

"I remember, when we first knew her in Hertfordshire, how amazed we all were to find that she was a reputed beauty. And I particularly recollect your saying one night, after they had dined at Netherfield, '*She* a beauty!—I should as soon call her mother a wit.' But afterwards she seemed to improve on you, and I believe you thought her rather pretty at one time."

"Yes," replied Darcy, unable to contain himself any longer, "but *that* was only when I first saw her, for it is many months since I have considered her as one of the handsomest women of my acquaintance."

He then went away, and Miss Bingley was left to all the satisfaction of having forced him to say what gave no one any pain but herself.

As they returned, Mrs. Gardiner and Elizabeth talked of their visit, but not of Mr. Darcy. They talked of his sister, his friends, his house, his fruit—of everything but himself—even though, both longed to know what the other thought of him.

And now, in addition to all else, Elizabeth longed to know—what would Darcy think of the *firebird* Georgiana?

Chapter 46

Elizabeth had been disappointed in not finding a letter from Jane on their first arrival at Lambton; and this disappointment recurred each morning. But on the third morning she received two letters from her at once.

They had just been preparing to walk as the letters came in. Her uncle and aunt set off by themselves, leaving her to enjoy them in quiet. Elizabeth started with the one written five days ago. The beginning contained an account of all their usual country engagements. But the latter half, dated a day later, and written in evident agitation, gave more important intelligence. It was to this effect:

"Since writing the above, dearest Lizzy, something has occurred of a most unexpected and serious nature. But, not to alarm you—be assured that we are all well. What I have to say relates to poor Lydia. An express came at twelve last night, just as we were all gone to bed, from Colonel Forster, to inform us that she was gone off to Scotland with one of his officers—Wickham! Imagine our surprise. To Kitty, however, it does not seem so wholly unexpected.

"I am very, very sorry. So imprudent a match on both sides! But I am willing to hope the best, and that his character has been misunderstood. Thoughtless and indiscreet I can easily believe him, but this step (and let us rejoice over it) marks nothing bad at heart. His choice is disinterested at least, for he must know my father can give her nothing.

"Our poor mother is sadly grieved and mentions the 'odious moon' in every other sentence. My father bears it better. How thankful am I that we never let them know what has been said against him; we must forget it ourselves.

"They were off Saturday night about twelve, at the height of the full moon—as is conjectured, after some kind of upheaval at the camp having to do with unlocked cages and several *turned* officers on the loose, *bears*, *panthers*, a pack of *hyenas*—but were not missed till yesterday morning at eight. My dear Lizzy, they must have passed within ten miles of us—not the *hyenas*, but the couple.

"Colonel Forster gives us reason to expect him here soon. Lydia left a few lines for his wife, informing her of their intention. I must conclude this note, for I cannot be long away from my poor mother. I am afraid you will not be able to make it out; I hardly know what I have written."

Scarcely knowing what she felt, Elizabeth finished this letter and instantly seized the other. Written a day later than the conclusion of the first, it read as follows:

"By this time, my dearest sister, you have received my hurried letter; I wish this may be more intelligible. But my head is so bewildered that I cannot be coherent. Dearest Lizzy, I hardly know what I would write, but I have bad news for you, and it cannot be delayed. Imprudent as the marriage between Mr. Wickham and our poor Lydia would be, we are now anxious to be assured it has taken place, for there is reason to fear they are *not* gone to Scotland.

"Colonel Forster came yesterday, having left Brighton the day before. Though Lydia's short letter to Mrs. F. gave them to understand that they were going to Gretna Green, something was dropped by Denny expressing his belief that W. never intended to go there, or to marry Lydia at all, which was repeated to Colonel F., who, instantly taking the alarm, set off from B. intending to trace their route. He did trace them to Clapham, but no further—they removed into a hackney coach, and dismissed the chaise from Epsom. All that is known after this is, that they were seen to continue the London road.

"I know not what to think. After making every possible inquiry on that side London, Colonel F. came into Hertfordshire, anxiously checking all the turnpikes in case Wickham had *turned*, had gotten himself loose from his cage by accident (naturally!), and ran wild in the countryside—it being the full moon, still—and at inns in Barnet and Hatfield, but without success—no such people had been seen to pass through, and no *wolf* run amok.

"With the kindest concern he came on to Longbourn (Colonel F, not the *wolf*), and broke his apprehensions to us in a manner most creditable to his heart. I am sincerely grieved for him and Mrs. F., but no one can blame them.

"Our distress, my dear Lizzy, is very great. My father and mother believe the worst, but I cannot think so ill of him. It is possible they married privately in town rather than pursue their first plan. And even if *he* could form such an unlikely design against a young woman of Lydia's connections, can I suppose her so lost to everything? Impossible! I grieve to find, however, that Colonel F. is not disposed to depend upon their marriage—he shook his head when I expressed my hopes, and said he feared W. was not a man to be trusted.

"My poor mother is really ill, and keeps her room. And as to my father, I never in my life saw him so affected, and he has been roaring in his cage every night of the Ordeal. Poor Kitty has anger for having concealed their attachment; but as it was a matter of confidence, one cannot wonder.

"I am truly glad, dearest Lizzy, that you have been spared something of these distressing scenes. But now, as the first shock is over, I long for your return! I am not so selfish, however, as to press for it. Adieu! And yet—circumstances are such that I cannot help earnestly begging you all to come here as soon as possible. I know my dear uncle and aunt so well, that I am not afraid of requesting it, though I have still something more to ask of the former. My father is going to London with Colonel Forster instantly, to try to discover her. What he means to do I know not. But his excessive distress will not allow him to be careful, and Colonel Forster is obliged to be at Brighton again to-morrow evening—to deal with the effects of the previously mentioned *upheaval* at the camp, since certain persons have been harmed by the *beasts* released from their cages (yes, now it comes to light, it was intentionally done!). Thus, my uncle's advice and assistance would be crucial. He will comprehend what I feel, and I rely upon his goodness."

"Oh! where, where is my uncle?" cried Elizabeth, darting from her seat as she finished the letter, eager to follow him, without losing precious time. But as she reached the door, it was opened by a servant, and Mr. Darcy appeared.

Her pale face and impetuous manner made him start. Before he could recover himself to speak, she, in whose mind all was superseded by Lydia's situation, breathlessly and hastily exclaimed, "I beg your pardon, but I must leave you. I must find Mr. Gardiner this moment; I have not an instant to lose!"

"Good God! what is the matter?" cried he, with more feeling than politeness; then recollecting himself, "I will not detain you a minute. But let me, or let the servant go after Mr. and Mrs. Gardiner. You are not well enough to go yourself."

Elizabeth hesitated. But her knees trembled under her. Calling back the servant, therefore, she requested unintelligibly that he fetch his master and mistress home instantly.

She then sat down, unable to support herself. She looked so miserably ill, that it was impossible for Darcy to leave her, or to refrain from saying, in a tone of gentleness and commiseration, "Let me call your maid. Is there nothing you could take to give you present relief? A glass of wine; shall I get you one? You are very ill."

"No, I thank you," she replied, trying to recover herself. "There is nothing the matter with me. I am quite well; I am only distressed by some dreadful news from Longbourn."

She burst into tears as she alluded to it, and for a few minutes could not speak another word.

Darcy, in wretched suspense, could only say something indistinctly of his concern, and observe her in compassionate silence. He had come to thank her for the *miracle* she had helped Georgiana achieve—but this was not the time to mention it.

At length Elizabeth spoke again. "I have just had a letter from Jane, with such dreadful news. It cannot be concealed from anyone. My younger sister has left all her friends—has eloped; has thrown herself into the power of—of Mr. Wickham. They are gone off together from Brighton during the full moon. *You* know him too well to doubt the rest. She has no money, no connections, nothing that can tempt him to—she is lost forever."

Darcy was fixed in astonishment.

"When I consider," she added in a yet more agitated voice, "that I might have prevented it! I, who knew what he was. Had I but explained some part of it only—some part of what I learnt, to my own family! Had his character been known, this could not have happened. But it is all—all too late now!"

"I am grieved indeed," cried Darcy; "grieved—shocked. But is it certain—absolutely certain?"

"Oh, yes! They left Brighton together on Sunday night, with the wicked moon on-high, with half the military set loose from their *beastly* cages, and were traced almost to London, but not beyond. They are certainly not gone to Scotland."

"And what has been done, or attempted, to recover her?"

"My father is gone to London, and Jane has written to beg my uncle's immediate assistance. And we shall be off, I hope, in half-an-hour. But nothing can be done—I know very well that nothing can be done. How is such a *wolf* to be worked on? How are they even to be discovered? I have no hope. It is horrible!"

Darcy shook his head in silent acquiescence.

"When *my* eyes were opened to his real character—Oh! had I known what I ought to do! But I was afraid of doing too much. Wretched, wretched mistake!"

Darcy made no answer. He seemed scarcely to hear her, and was walking up and down the room in earnest meditation, his brow contracted, his air gloomy.

Elizabeth understood. Her power was sinking—everything *must* sink under such a proof of family weakness and disgrace. She did not blame him. But it increased her distress, and clarified her own wishes—never had she so honestly felt that she could have loved him, as now, when all love must be vain.

But Lydia—the humiliation, the misery she was bringing on them all—soon swallowed up every private care. Elizabeth covered her face with her handkerchief, and was lost to everything else. After several minutes, she was recalled by the voice of Mr. Darcy, full of compassion and restraint.

"I am afraid you have been long desiring my absence, nor have I any excuse to prolong my stay, only concern. Would to Heaven that I could do anything that might offer consolation! But I will not torment you with vain wishes, which may seem purposely to ask for your thanks. This unfortunate affair will, I fear, prevent my sister's having the pleasure of seeing you at Pemberley to-day."

"Oh, yes. Be so kind as to apologise for us to Miss Darcy. Say that urgent business calls us home immediately. Conceal the unhappy truth as long as possible. I would never willingly quench her newly achieved joyful *fire*. . . ."

He readily assured her of his secrecy; again expressed his sorrow for her distress, wished it a happier conclusion than there was reason to hope. And, with one serious, *intense* parting look, he went away.

As he quitted the room, Elizabeth felt how improbable it was that they should ever see each other again on such terms of cordiality. And as she thought in retrospective over the whole of their contradictory acquaintance, she sighed at the perverseness of those feelings which now desired it, and formerly would have rejoiced in its termination.

If gratitude and esteem are good foundations of affection, Elizabeth's change of sentiment will be neither improbable nor faulty. She saw him go with regret. And in this early example of what Lydia's infamy must produce, she found additional anguish as she reflected on that wretched business.

Never, since reading Jane's second letter, had she entertained a hope of Wickham's meaning to marry her. Surprise was the least of her feelings. After the first letter, she was astonished that Wickham should marry a girl without money. How Lydia could ever have attached him was incomprehensible. But for an "attachment" of another sort she might have sufficient charms. And though not deliberately eloping without the intention of marriage, it was clear that silly Lydia was easy prey.

Elizabeth had never perceived, while the regiment was in Hertfordshire, that Lydia had any partiality for the *wolf*. But she was convinced that Lydia wanted only encouragement to attach herself to *anybody*. Sometimes one officer, sometimes another, had been her favourite, as their attentions raised them in her opinion. Indeed, there had been *hyenas*, a *bear* or two, canines, Great Cats of every flavor, and even a *hedgehog*. Her affections had been continually in flux, but never without an object. The mischief of neglect and mistaken indulgence towards such a girl—oh! how acutely did she now feel it!

Elizabeth was wild to be at home—to share with Jane in the cares, in a family so deranged, a father absent, a mother incapable of exertion, and requiring constant attendance. And though, surely, nothing could be done for Lydia, her uncle's help just now seemed of the utmost importance.

Mr. and Mrs. Gardiner had hurried back in alarm, supposing by the servant's account that their niece was taken suddenly ill. Instead, she communicated the news, reading the two letters aloud with trembling energy.

Though Lydia had never been a favourite with them, Mr. and Mrs. Gardiner were deeply afflicted. Not Lydia only, but all were concerned in it. And after the first exclamations of surprise and horror, Mr. Gardiner promised every assistance in his power. Elizabeth thanked him with tears of gratitude; and everything relating to their journey was speedily settled.

They were to be off as soon as possible. "But what is to be done about Pemberley?" cried Mrs. Gardiner. "John told us Mr. Darcy was here when you sent for us; was it so?"

"Yes; and I told him we should not be able to keep our engagement. *That* is all settled."

"What is all settled?" repeated the other, as she ran into her room to prepare. "And are *they* upon such terms as for her to disclose the real truth? Oh, that I knew how it was!"

But in the hurry and confusion of the following hour, Elizabeth had no leisure to be idle, despite her wretchedness. She had her share of business as well as her aunt. There were notes to be written to all their friends at Lambton, with false excuses for their sudden departure. An hour was sufficient to complete everything.

Mr. Gardiner settled his account at the inn. Their boxes were packed, his efficient gentleman's travel cage loaded. Nothing remained to be done but to go.

And Elizabeth, after all the misery of the morning, found herself seated in the carriage, and on the road to Longbourn.

Chapter 47

"I have been thinking it over again, Elizabeth," said her uncle, as they drove from the town; "and it appears very unlikely that any young man should form such a design against a girl who is not unprotected or friendless, and who was actually staying in his colonel's family. Thus, I am inclined to hope the best. Knowing that her friends would step forward, could he expect to be noticed again by the regiment, after such an affront to Colonel Forster? His temptation is not adequate to the risk!"

"Do you really think so?" cried Elizabeth, brightening up for a moment.

"Upon my word," said Mrs. Gardiner, "I begin to be of your uncle's opinion. It is really too great a violation of decency, honour, and interest. I cannot think so very ill of Wickham. Can you yourself, Lizzy, believe him capable of it?"

"Not, perhaps, of neglecting his own interest—but of every other neglect I can believe him capable."

"In the first place," replied Mr. Gardiner, "there is no absolute proof that they are not gone to Scotland."

"Oh! but they removed from the chaise into a hackney coach! And, no traces of them were found on the Barnet road."

"Well, then—suppose they are in London, for the purpose of concealment. It is likely that with little money they decided to be married in London rather than in Scotland."

"But why all this secrecy? Why any fear of detection? Why must their marriage be private? According to his friend Denny, he never intended to marry her. Wickham will never marry a woman without some money. *He cannot afford it.* And what claims has Lydia—beyond youth, health, and good humour—that could make him forego marrying well? I know not what the effects of disgrace in the corps might mean to him. Meanwhile, Lydia has no brothers to step forward. And he might imagine my indolent, inattentive father would do little to nothing but roar."

"But can you think that Lydia is so lost as to consent to live with him on any terms other than marriage?"

"It does seem, and it is most shocking indeed," replied Elizabeth, with tears in her eyes, "that Lydia's virtue should raise doubt. Perhaps I am not doing her justice. But she is very young and naturally lively. She has never been taught to think on serious subjects, only amusement and vanity. Since the —— shire were first quartered in Meryton, nothing but love, flirtation, and officers with their various *beasts* and sparkling regimental cages have been in her head. And we all know that Wickham has every *wolfish* charm that can captivate a woman."

"But Jane," said her aunt, "does not think so very ill of Wickham as to believe him capable of the attempt."

"Of whom does Jane ever think ill? But Jane knows, as well as I do, what Wickham really is. We both know that he has been profligate in every sense of the word. He has neither integrity nor honour. He is as false and deceitful as he is insinuating."

"And do you really know all this?" cried Mrs. Gardiner, highly curious as to the manner of her knowing.

"I do indeed," replied Elizabeth, colouring. "I told you, the other day, of his infamous behaviour to Mr. Darcy. And you yourself heard how Wickham spoke of the man who had behaved with such liberal forbearance towards him. And there are other circumstances which I am not at liberty to relate—but his lies about the whole Pemberley family are endless. From what he said of Miss Darcy I was prepared to see a proud, reserved, disagreeable girl. Yet he knew to the contrary himself, that she was amiable and unpretending."

"But does Lydia know nothing of this? Can she be ignorant of what you and Jane seem so well to understand?"

"Oh, yes!—that, that is the worst of all. Till I was in Kent, and saw so much both of Mr. Darcy and his relation Colonel Fitzwilliam, I was ignorant of the truth myself. And when I returned home, the ——shire was about to leave Meryton, so neither Jane nor I thought it necessary to make our knowledge public. And even when it was settled that Lydia should go with Mrs. Forster, the necessity of opening her eyes to his character never occurred to me. That *she* could be in any danger from him never entered my head."

"When they all removed to Brighton, you had no reason to believe them fond of each other?"

"Not the slightest. I can remember no symptom of affection on either side. When first he entered the corps, Lydia was ready enough to admire him; but so we all were. Every girl in or near Meryton was out of her senses about this *wolf* for the first two months. But he never distinguished *her* by any particular attention. Consequently, after a moderate period of extravagant and wild admiration, her fancy for him gave way. And others of the regiment, who treated her with more distinction and had better chains, padlocks, and cages, again became her favourites."

The painful subject of Lydia occupied them during the whole of the journey. From Elizabeth's thoughts it was never absent. In anguish and self-reproach, she could find no forgetfulness, not even when she thought in sudden keen moments of the curious gentleman *platypus* and his *firebird* sister.

They traveled as quickly as possible, sleeping one night on the road, and reached Longbourn by dinner-time the next day.

The little Gardiners met them on the steps of the house. When the carriage drove up, joyful surprise lit up their faces.

Elizabeth jumped out; and, after giving each of them a hasty kiss, hurried into the vestibule, where Jane immediately met her.

They embraced affectionately, whilst tears filled the eyes of both. Elizabeth immediately asked whether anything had been heard of the fugitives.

"Not yet," replied Jane. "But now that my dear uncle is come, I hope everything will be well."

"Is my father in town?"

"Yes, he went on Tuesday, as I wrote you word."[95]

"And have you heard from him often?"

"We have heard only twice. He wrote me a few lines on Wednesday to say that he had arrived safely, and to give me his directions,[96] which I particularly begged him to do. He merely added that he should not write again till he had something of importance to mention."

"And my mother—how is she? How are you all?"

"My mother is tolerably well; though her spirits are greatly shaken. She is upstairs and will have great satisfaction in seeing

---

[95] Despite what she says here, Miss Jane Bennet likely wrote not just one word but several words. It is possible she wrote the word "word" over and over again, repeatedly; but it is likely not the case, in this particular case.

[96] It must be explained that Mr. Bennet had a curiously tedious habit of giving directions to various British travel destinations and points of arrival at random, and to random individuals. He sometimes included detailed itineraries and alternate routes, and had sent not one but several dozen hapless travelers to the Tower of London, Vauxhall, Stonehenge, York Minster, Stratford-upon-Avon, Edinburgh Castle, and Buckingham Palace, when all they wanted was the nearest roadside inn. In this instance, since they were pressed for time, Jane Bennet begged her father *not* to engage in this behavior, and that it would suffice if he merely sent his present address.

you all. She does not yet leave her dressing-room, but often points at the window, and makes observations about the *moon*. Mary and Kitty, thank Heaven, are quite well."

"But you—how are you?" cried Elizabeth. "You are pale!"

Her sister, however, assured her she was perfectly well. And their conversation (while Mr. and Mrs. Gardiner were engaged with their children) now ended because of the approach of the whole party. Jane ran to her uncle and aunt, and welcomed and thanked them both, with smiles and tears.

When they were all in the drawing-room, the questions were repeated, and they soon found that Jane had no intelligence[97] to give. Hope, however, had not yet deserted her; she still expected that it would all end well.

Mrs. Bennet, to whose apartment they all repaired,[98] received them with tears and lamentations of regret, invectives against the villainous conduct of Wickham and all the heavenly *luminaries*, and complaints of her own sufferings and ill-usage; blaming everybody but herself.

"If I had been able," said she, "to carry my point in going to Brighton, with all my family, *this* would not have happened. But poor dear Lydia had nobody to take care of her. Why did the Forsters ever let her go out of their sight? I am sure there was some great neglect on their side, for she is not the kind of girl to do such a thing if well looked after. I always thought they were unfit to have the charge of her; but I was overruled, as I always am. Poor dear child! And now here's Mr. Bennet gone away, and I know he will fight Wickham in the horrid cage, his *lion*

---

[97] The astute reader notices by now that it is very possible that Jane Bennet was a covert operative; indeed, a spy for the British Crown, gathering intelligence and feeding it back to her superiors in the Royal Cabinet.

[98] Mrs. Bennet felt the need for someone to repair her apartment, hence, this mass excursion to her quarters. Likely, she required new wallpaper and flooring.

against the younger *wolf*, and then he will be killed, and what is to become of us all? The Collinses will turn us out before he is cold in his grave, Longbourn will smell like *skunk*, and if you are not kind to us, brother, I do not know what we shall do."

They all exclaimed against such terrific ideas. And Mr. Gardiner, in proper *great dane* fashion, after general assurances of his canine affection for her and all her family, told her that he meant to be in London the very next day, and would assist Mr. Bennet in every way to recover Lydia.

"Do not give way to useless alarm," added he; "though it is right to prepare for the worst, it is not a certainty. They left Brighton but a few days ago, and soon we may gain news of them. Till we know that they are not married, and have no design of marrying, let us not give up. As soon as I get to town I shall make my brother come home with me to Gracechurch Street. There we may consult together as to what is to be done."

"Oh! my dear brother," replied Mrs. Bennet, "that is exactly what I could most wish for. And now do, when you get to town, find them, wherever they may be. And if they are not married already, *make* them marry! And as for wedding clothes, tell Lydia she shall have as much money as desired, after they are married. And, above all, keep Mr. Bennet from fighting! Lock him up in his cage, if needed! If he roars, rattles the bars, put another Affliction Steak in there, a bowl of fresh cream, and he will compose himself eventually. Tell him what a dreadful state I am in, frighted out of my wits—and have such tremblings, such flutterings, all over me—such spasms in my side and pains in my head, and such beatings at heart, that I can get no rest by night—what, with the *odious moon* gloating down at us—nor by day. And tell my dear Lydia not to order her clothes till she has seen me, for she does not know the best warehouses—"

But Mr. Gardiner assured her of his earnest endeavours and then recommended moderation in both hopes and fears. When dinner was served, they all left her again to vent her feelings on the housekeeper and the moon outside the windows.

Though her brother and sister did not feel there was occasion for such a *seclusion* from the family, they did not attempt to oppose it—Mrs. Bennet could not hold her tongue before the servants waiting at the dinner table, and it was better that only *one* trustworthy servant knew, than the whole lot.

In the dining-room they were soon joined by Mary and Kitty. One came from her books, and the other from her toilette. The faces of both, however, were tolerably calm; and no change was visible in either, except more fretfulness than usual in Kitty. As for Mary, she whispered to Elizabeth, with a countenance of grave reflection, soon after they were seated at table, something about "stemming the tide of malice," and "sisterly consolation."

When Elizabeth did not reply, she added, "Unhappy as the event must be for Lydia, we may draw from it this useful lesson: that loss of virtue in a female is irretrievable! One false step involves her in endless ruin. Her reputation is no less brittle than it is beautiful. And she cannot be too much guarded in her behaviour towards the Afflicted sex."

Elizabeth lifted up her eyes in amazement, but was too much oppressed to make any reply. Mary, however, continued to console herself at length with other such moral extractions.

In the afternoon, the two elder Miss Bennets had a half-an-hour to themselves; and Elizabeth took the opportunity for more inquiries. "What did Colonel Forster say? Had they any suspicions before the elopement took place?"

"Colonel Forster did own that he had noted some partiality, especially on Lydia's side, but nothing to give him any alarm."

"And was Denny convinced that Wickham would not marry? Did he know of their intending to go off? Had Colonel Forster seen Denny himself?"

"Yes; but, when questioned by *him*, Denny denied knowing anything of their plans, and would not give his real opinion."

"And till Colonel Forster came himself, not one of you entertained a doubt, I suppose, of their being really married?"

"How was it possible that such an idea should enter our brains? I felt a little uneasy—fearful of my sister's happiness with him. My father and mother knew nothing of his conduct; only felt it was an imprudent match. Kitty, knowing more than the rest of us, triumphantly admitted that Lydia had told of her plans in her last letter. She had known, *for weeks*, of their being in love with each other. But not before they went to Brighton."

"And did Colonel Forster appear to think well of Wickham himself? Does he know his real character?"

"I must confess that he did not speak so well of Wickham as before. He believed him to be imprudent and extravagant—and somehow responsible for the disastrous camp incident of the many unlocked cages and officer *hyenas* and *bears* on the loose on that night of the full moon, when they eloped—not the *hyenas* and *bears* eloped, but Wickham and Lydia. Also, Wickham left Meryton greatly in debt."

"Oh, Jane, had we been less secret, had we told what we knew of him, this could not have happened!"

"Dreadful Secrets are indeed at fault," replied her sister. "But to expose the former faults of anyone seemed unjustifiable. We acted with the best intentions."

Jane then took, from her pocket-book, Lydia's note to Mrs. Forster that Colonel Forster had brought to show them, and gave it to Elizabeth. These were the contents:

"MY DEAR HARRIET,

"You will laugh when you know where I am gone, and I cannot help laughing myself at your surprise to-morrow morning, as soon as I am missed. I am going to Gretna Green, and if you cannot guess with who, I shall think you a simpleton, for there is but one man in the world I love, and he is an angel—when he is not a *wolf*. I should never be happy without him, so think it no harm to be off. You need not tell anyone at Longbourn of my going, if you prefer, for it will make the surprise the greater, when I write to them and sign my name 'Lydia Wickham.' What a good joke it will be! I can hardly write for laughing. But oh! Speaking of grand jokes, I must tell you *this* one—we ran about the camp, opening all the regiment cages, *every one of them*, and I was not afraid in the least, since the silly old moon was still hidden and no one had *turned* yet, and mostly because my dearest *wolf* was at my side to protect me. And then—oh, but pray make my excuses to Pratt for not keeping my engagement with him to-night; and tell him we will dance at the next ball we meet, with great pleasure. I shall send for my clothes when I get to Longbourn. Good-bye. Give my love to Colonel Forster. I hope you will drink to our good journey.

> "Your affectionate friend,
>
> "LYDIA BENNET."

"Oh! thoughtless, thoughtless Lydia!" cried Elizabeth when she had finished it. "What a letter is this, to be written at such a moment! But at least it shows that *she* was serious on the subject of marriage. Whatever else the *wolf* might persuade her to, it was not on her side a *scheme* of infamy. But oh, *she* had opened those cages! My poor father! how he must have felt!"

"I never saw anyone so shocked. He could not speak a word for full ten minutes, and for a moment it seemed his *beast* was coming! My mother was taken ill immediately, and the whole house in such confusion!"

"Oh! Jane," cried Elizabeth, "was there a servant who did not know the whole story before the end of the day?"

"I do not know. But to be guarded at such a time is very difficult. My mother was in hysterics, and though I tried to help her, I am afraid the horror of what might happen took from me my own faculties."

"Your attendance upon her has been too much for you. You do not look well. Oh that I had been with you!"

"Mary and Kitty have been very kind; but I did not think it right for either of them. Kitty is slight and delicate; and Mary studies so much, that her hours of repose should not be broken in on. My aunt Phillips came to Longbourn on Tuesday, after my father went away; and she was of great use and comfort to us all. And Lady Lucas has been very kind; and offered her services."

"She had better have stayed at home," cried Elizabeth; "perhaps she *meant* well, but in misfortune, it is better not to see neighbours. Assistance is impossible; condolence insufferable. Let them triumph over us at a distance, and be satisfied."

Jane then told of the measures their father had taken: "He meant to go to Epsom, where they last changed horses. His principal object must be to discover the number of the hackney coach that took them from Clapham. It had come with a fare from London, with one gentleman's *regimental* cage that had to be unloaded and then loaded again. And he thought that the circumstance of a gentleman and lady's removing from one carriage into another might be noticed. In short, he was in such a hurry to be gone, and his spirits so greatly discomposed, that I had difficulty in finding out even so much as this."

Chapter 48

The whole party hoped for a letter from Mr. Bennet the next morning, but there was none. His family knew him to be, on all common occasions, a most negligent correspondent (except when there was an opportunity to give someone unwanted directions); but this time they had hoped for exertion.

They were forced to conclude that he had no good news to send. And Mr. Gardiner waited only for that day's letters (or lack of such) before he set off.

When he was gone, they were certain at least of receiving constant information of what was going on. Their uncle also promised to prevail on Mr. Bennet to return to Longbourn promptly, to the great consolation of his sister, who considered it as the only security for her husband's not being killed savagely in a *beastly* cage duel.

Mrs. Gardiner and the children were to remain in Hertfordshire a few days longer, to help her nieces. She assisted with Mrs. Bennet, and was a great comfort. Their other aunt also visited frequently, with the design of cheering them up—though, as she always reported some fresh instance of Wickham's folly, she left them more dispirited than ever.

All Meryton now strove to blacken the lupine man who, but three months before, had been almost an angel of light. He was declared to be in debt to every tradesman in the place, and his intrigues (all honoured with the title of seduction) had been extended into every family. Everybody declared that he was the wickedest young man in the world, and they had always distrusted the appearance of his goodness.

Elizabeth did not credit above half of what was said, but believed enough. And Jane, who believed still less of it, became almost hopeless.

Mr. Gardiner left Longbourn on Sunday; on Tuesday his wife received a letter from him. It told them that, on his arrival, he had immediately found out his brother, and persuaded him to come to Gracechurch Street; that Mr. Bennet had been to Epsom and Clapham, before his arrival, but without gaining any satisfactory information; and that he was now determined to inquire at all the hotels in town. Mr. Gardiner himself did not expect any success from this measure, but meant to assist Mr. Bennet in pursuing it. He added that Mr. Bennet seemed wholly disinclined at present to leave London and promised to write again very soon. There was also a postscript to this effect:

"I have written to Colonel Forster to desire him to find out, if possible, from some of the young man's intimates in the regiment, whether Wickham has any relations or connections who would be likely to know in what part of town he has now concealed himself. At present we have nothing to guide us. Colonel Forster will do everything in his power. But, perhaps, Lizzy could tell us better than anyone what relations he has."

Elizabeth understood from whence this deference to her authority proceeded. But she had never heard of his having had any relations, except a father and mother, both of whom had been dead many years.

Every day at Longbourn was now a day of anxiety. But the most anxious part of each was when the post was expected. The arrival of letters was the grand object of every morning's impatience. And every day was expected to bring some important news.

But before they heard again from Mr. Gardiner, a letter arrived addressed to their father, from a different quarter—from Mr. Collins!—which, as Jane had received directions to open all that came for him in his absence, she accordingly read. And Elizabeth, who knew what curiosities his letters always were, looked over her shoulder, inhaled carefully (in case of a whiff of *skunk*) and read it likewise. It was as follows:

"MY DEAR SIR,

"I feel myself called upon, by our relationship, and my situation in life, to condole with you on the grievous affliction you are now suffering under—not the demon Affliction of the flesh and spirit caused by the wicked moon, but an even more dire affliction of circumstances, of which we were yesterday informed by a letter from Hertfordshire.

"Be assured, my dear sir, that Mrs. Collins and myself sincerely sympathise with you and all your respectable family, in your present bitterest distress proceeding from a cause which no time can remove. No arguments shall be wanting on my part that can alleviate so severe a misfortune—or that may comfort you, under a circumstance that must be the most afflicting to a parent's mind. The death of your daughter would have been a blessing in comparison. And it is to be more lamented, because there is reason to suppose (as my dear Charlotte informs me) that this licentious behaviour in your daughter is the result of a faulty degree of indulgence. For the consolation of yourself and Mrs. Bennet, I am inclined to think that her own disposition must be naturally bad, or she could not be guilty of such an enormity, at so early an age.

"Howsoever that may be, you are grievously to be pitied—in which opinion I am not only joined by Mrs. Collins, but likewise by Lady Catherine and her daughter. They agree with me in fearing that this false step in one daughter will be injurious to the fortunes of *all the others*— for who, as Lady Catherine herself says, will connect themselves with such a family?

"This leads me moreover to reflect, with augmented satisfaction, on a certain *event* of last November. For had it been otherwise, I must have been involved in all your sorrow and disgrace. Let me then advise you, dear sir, to console yourself as much as possible, to throw off your unworthy child from your affection for ever, and leave her to reap the fruits of her own heinous offense.

"I am, dear sir, etc., etc."

Mr. Gardiner did not write again till he had received an answer from Colonel Forster. And then he had nothing of a pleasant nature to send.

Wickham did not have a single relative with whom he kept up any connection, and it was certain that he had no near one living. His former acquaintances had been numerous; but since the militia, he did not remain on friendly terms with any of them. No one could give any news of him. And in the wretched state of his own finances, there was a very powerful motive for secrecy, in addition to his fear of discovery by Lydia's relations, for he had left considerable gaming debts behind him.

Colonel Forster believed that more than a thousand pounds would be necessary to clear his expenses at Brighton. Wickham owed a good deal in town, but his debts of honour were still more formidable. Mr. Gardiner did not attempt to conceal these particulars from the Longbourn family.

Jane heard them with horror. "A gamester!" she cried. "This is wholly unexpected. I had no idea!"

Mr. Gardiner added in his letter, that they might expect to see their father at home on the following day. Disheartened by the ill-success of all their endeavours, he had yielded to his brother-in-law's entreaty that he would return to his family, and leave it to him to continue their pursuit.

When Mrs. Bennet was told of this, she did not express so much satisfaction as her children expected, considering what her anxiety for his life had been before.

"What, is he coming home without poor Lydia?" she cried. "He must not leave London before he has found them! Who else is to fight Wickham in the cage, and make him marry her?"

As Mrs. Gardiner began to wish to be at home, it was settled that she and the children should go to London, as Mr. Bennet came from it. The coach, therefore, took them, and brought its master back to Longbourn.

Mrs. Gardiner went away still perplexed about Elizabeth's relationship with her lofty Derbyshire friend. Darcy's name had never been voluntarily mentioned before them by her niece; and the kind of half-expectation which Mrs. Gardiner had formed, had ended in nothing. Elizabeth had received no letter since her return that could come from Pemberley.

The present unhappy state of the family rendered any other excuse for her low spirits unnecessary. Elizabeth, by now well acquainted with her own feelings, was perfectly aware that, had she known nothing of Darcy's various secrets, she could have borne the dread of Lydia's infamy somewhat better.

When Mr. Bennet arrived, he had all the appearance of his philosophic composure. He said as little as usual; made no mention of the business, and it was some time before his daughters had courage to speak of it.

It was not till the afternoon, when he joined them at tea, that Elizabeth ventured to express her sorrow for what he endured.

"Say nothing of that," he replied. "Who should suffer but myself? It has been my own doing, and I ought to feel it."

"You must not be too severe upon yourself, father."

"No, Lizzy, let me once in my life feel how much I have been to blame. I am not afraid of being overpowered by the impression. It will pass away soon enough."

"Do you suppose them to be in London?"

"Yes; where else can *wolves* be so well concealed?"

"And Lydia used to want to go to London," added Kitty.

"She is happy then," said her father dryly; "and her residence there will probably be of some duration."

Then after a short silence he continued:

"Lizzy, I bear you no ill-will for being justified in your advice to me last May, which shows some greatness of mind."

They were interrupted by Miss Bennet, who came to fetch her mother's tea.

"This is a parade," he cried, "which gives such an elegance to misfortune! Another day I will do the same; I will sit in my library, in my nightcap and powdering gown, or perhaps in the cage upstairs, roaring and clamoring regardless of the moon's or my own phase—indeed, *barking*, for a change—and give as much trouble as I can. Or, I may defer it all till Kitty runs away."

"I am not going to run away, papa," said Kitty fretfully. "If I should ever go to Brighton, I would behave better than Lydia."

"*You* go to Brighton! I would not trust you so near it as Eastbourne for fifty pounds! No, Kitty, I have at last learnt to be cautious, and you will feel the effects of it. No officer is ever to enter into my house again, nor even to pass through the village. Any regimental cages shall be bludgeoned and driven off with cudgels. Balls will be absolutely prohibited, unless you stand up with one of your sisters. And you are never to stir out of doors till you can prove that you have spent ten minutes of every day in a rational manner."

Kitty, who took all these threats in a serious light, began to cry.

"Well, well," said he, "do not make yourself unhappy. If you are a good girl for the next ten years, I will take you to a review at the end of them, allow a ball, and you might then be granted one dance with an amiable civilian *hedgehog*."

Chapter 49

Two days after Mr. Bennet's return, as Jane and Elizabeth were walking together in the shrubbery behind the house, they saw the housekeeper coming fast towards them.

"Dear madam," cried Mrs. Hill, "there is an express come for master from Mr. Gardiner! He has been here this half-hour, and master has had a letter!"

Away ran the girls, too eager to reply, through the vestibule into the breakfast-room; from thence to the library. Their father was in neither. They were on the point of seeking him upstairs with their mother, when they were met by the butler, who said:

"If you are looking for my master, ma'am, he is walking towards the little copse."

Upon this information, they instantly passed through the hall once more, and ran outside across the lawn after their father.

Jane, who was not so light nor so much in the habit of running as Elizabeth, soon lagged behind, while her sister, panting for breath, came up with him, and eagerly cried out:

"Oh, papa, what news—what news? Have you heard from my uncle?"

"Yes I have had a letter from him by express."

"Well, and what news does it bring—good or bad?"

"What is there of good to be expected?" said he, taking the letter from his pocket. "But perhaps you would like to read it."

Elizabeth impatiently caught it from his hand. Jane now came up.

"Read it aloud," said their father, "for I hardly know myself what it is about."

> *"Gracechurch Street, Monday, August 2.*
>
> "MY DEAR BROTHER,
>
> "At last I am able to send you some tidings of my niece, and such as, upon the whole, I hope it will give you satisfaction. Soon after you left me on Saturday, I was fortunate enough to find out in what part of London they were. The particulars I reserve till we meet; it is enough to know they are discovered. I have seen them both—"

"Then it is as I always hoped," cried Jane; "they are married!"

Elizabeth read on:

> "I have seen them both. They are *not* married, nor can I find there was any intention of being so. But if you are willing to perform the engagements which I have ventured to make on your side, I hope it will not be long before they are.
>
> "All that is required of you is, to assure to your daughter, by settlement, her equal share of the five thousand pounds secured among your children after the decease of yourself and my sister; and, moreover, to allow her, during your life, one hundred pounds per annum. These are conditions which, considering everything, I had no hesitation in complying with. I shall send this by express, to quickly have your answer. Mr. Wickham's circumstances are not so hopeless as they are generally believed to be. I am happy to say there will be some little money, even when all his debts are discharged, to settle on my niece, in addition to her own fortune.

"If you send me full powers to act in your name throughout the whole of this business, I will immediately give directions for preparing a proper settlement. There will not be the smallest occasion for your coming to town again. Therefore stay quiet at Longbourn, and depend on my diligence and care. Send back your answer as fast as you can, and be careful to write explicitly. We have judged it best that my niece should be married from this house, of which I hope you will approve. She comes to us to-day. I shall write again as soon as anything more is determined on. Yours, etc.,

"EDW. GARDINER."

"Is it possible?" cried Elizabeth, when she had finished. "Can it be possible that he will marry her?"

"Wickham is not so undeserving, then, as we thought him," said her sister. "My dear father, I congratulate you."

"And have you answered the letter?" cried Elizabeth.

"No; but it must be done soon."

"Oh! my dear father!" she cried, "then do come back and write immediately. Consider how important every moment is in such a case."

"Let me write for you," said Jane, "if you dislike the trouble yourself."

"I dislike it very much," he replied; "but it must be done."

And so saying, he turned back with them, and walked towards the house.

"And may I ask—" said Elizabeth; "but the terms, I suppose, must be complied with."

"Complied with! I am only ashamed of his asking so little."

"And they *must* marry! Yet he is *such* a man!"

"Yes, yes, they must marry; nothing else to be done. But two things I want to know—how much money your uncle has laid down to bring it about; and how am I ever to pay him."

"Money! My uncle!" cried Jane, "what do you mean, sir?"

"I mean, that no *wolf* in his senses would marry Lydia on so slight a temptation as one hundred a year during my life, and fifty after I am gone."

"That is very true," said Elizabeth; "though it had not occurred to me before. His debts to be discharged, and something still to remain! Oh! it must be my uncle's doings! Generous, good man, I am afraid he has distressed himself. A small sum could not do all this."

"No," said her father; "Wickham's a *beastly* fool if he takes her with less than ten thousand pounds. I should be sorry to think so ill of him, in the very beginning of our relationship."

"Ten thousand pounds! Heaven forbid! How is half such a sum to be repaid?"

Mr. Bennet made no answer, and each of them, deep in thought, continued silent till they reached the house. Their father then went on to the library to write, and the girls walked into the breakfast-room.

"And they are really to be married!" cried Elizabeth, as soon as they were by themselves. "How strange this is! And for *this* we are to be thankful. That they should marry, small as is their chance of happiness, and wretched as is his character, we are forced to rejoice. Oh, Lydia!"

"I comfort myself with thinking," replied Jane, "that he would not marry Lydia if he had not a real regard for her. Though our kind uncle has done something towards clearing him, I cannot believe it was ten thousand pounds. He has children of his own! How could he spare even half the sum?"

"If one might learn what Wickham's debts have been," said Elizabeth, "and how much is settled on our sister, we shall know exactly what Mr. Gardiner has done for them, since Wickham has not sixpence of his own. The kindness of my uncle and aunt can never be requited."

"We must endeavour to forget all that has passed on either side," said Jane: "I hope and trust they will yet be happy. His consenting to marry her is a proof that he is come to a right way of thinking. Their mutual affection will steady them. They will settle quietly, and live in a rational manner, all past forgotten."

"Their conduct has been such," replied Elizabeth, "as neither you, nor I, nor anybody can ever forget."

It now occurred to the girls that their mother was in all likelihood perfectly ignorant of what had happened. They went to the library, therefore, and asked their father whether he would not wish them to make it known to her. He was writing and, without raising his leonine head, coolly replied:

"Just as you please."

"May we take my uncle's letter to read to her?"

"Take whatever you like, and get away."

Elizabeth took the letter from his writing-table, and they went upstairs together. Mary and Kitty were both with Mrs. Bennet.

The letter was read aloud. Mrs. Bennet could hardly contain herself. As soon as Jane had read Mr. Gardiner's hope of Lydia's being soon married, her joy burst forth, and every following sentence added to its exuberance, until she was in a violent state of delight. Her daughter, to be married! She was undisturbed by fears for her felicity, and had entirely forgotten her misconduct.

"My dear, dear Lydia!" she cried. "This is delightful indeed! She will be married at sixteen! I shall see her again! My good, kind, *loyal dog* brother! Oh, I knew he would manage everything! How I long to see her and dear *wolf* Wickham too! But the clothes, the wedding clothes! I will write to my sister Gardiner about them directly. Lizzy, my dear, run down to your father, and ask him how much he will give her. Stay, stay, I will go myself. Ring the bell, Kitty, for Hill. I will put on my things in a moment. My dear, dear Lydia! How merry we shall be together when we meet! And to think I was so despairing that I had once today hoped you were married to that Collins *skunk!*"

Her eldest daughter tied to lessen the violence of these transports, by reminding her of their obligations to Mr. Gardiner.

"For we must attribute this happy conclusion," she added, "in a great measure to his kindness. We are persuaded that he has pledged himself to assist Mr. Wickham with money."

"Well," cried her mother, "it is all very right; who should do it but her own uncle? If he had not had a family of his own, I and my children must have had all his money. It is the first time we have ever had anything from him, except a few presents. Well! I am so happy! I shall have a daughter married! Mrs. Wickham! How well it sounds! She will get to tend to her own gentleman's cage—and a great big *wolf*, no less! And she, only sixteen! My dear Jane, I am in such a flutter, that I will dictate, and you write, these things should be ordered immediately—"

She proceeded to dictate the calico, muslin, and cambric, but Jane persuaded her to wait till her father could be consulted. One day's delay, she observed, would not matter.

"I will go to Meryton," said Mrs. Bennet, happily forgetting the order, "as soon as I am dressed, and tell the good news to my sister Philips. And as I come back, I can call on Lady Lucas and Mrs. Long. Kitty, run down and order the carriage. An airing would do me a great deal of good! Here comes Hill! My dear Hill, have you heard the good news?"

Mrs. Hill began instantly to express her joy. Elizabeth received her congratulations with the rest, and then, sick of this folly, took refuge in her own room, to think.

Poor Lydia's situation must, at best, be bad enough. But that it was no worse, she had to be thankful.

And though neither rational happiness nor worldly prosperity could be expected for her sister, considering what they had feared only two hours ago, Elizabeth felt all the contradictory advantages of what they had gained. . . .

Among other things, a *wolf* brother-in-law.

Chapter 50

M r. Bennet had often wished that, instead of spending his whole income, he had laid by an annual sum for the better provision of his wife and children. He now wished it more than ever. Had he done his duty in that respect, Lydia need not have been indebted to her *great dane* uncle. The satisfaction of prevailing on one of the most worthless young men in Great Britain to be her husband might then have rested in its proper place.

He was seriously concerned that such a pitiful cause should be forwarded at the sole expense of his brother-in-law, and was determined to discharge the obligation as soon as he could.

When first Mr. Bennet had married, economy was held to be perfectly useless, for, of course, they were to have a son, a proper *lion* like his father. The son was to join in roaring (or napping) in a fine cage alongside him on full moon nights, and in cutting off the entail, as soon as he should be of age, and the widow and younger children would be provided for.

Five daughters successively entered the world, but yet the *lion* cub was to come. And Mrs. Bennet, for many years after Lydia's birth, had been certain that he would. This event had at last been despaired of, but it was then too late to begin saving.

Mrs. Bennet had no turn for economy, and her husband's love of independence had alone prevented their exceeding their income.

Five thousand pounds was settled on Mrs. Bennet and the children. But in what proportions it should all be divided, depended on the will of the parents. Lydia's share was now to be given out, and Mr. Bennet agreed to the proposal before him. In his reply letter, he delivered his grateful acknowledgment for the kindness of his brother, his perfect approbation of all that was done, and his willingness to fulfill his obligations.

He had never supposed that, could Wickham be prevailed on to marry his daughter, it would be done with so little inconvenience to himself. That it would also be done with such trifling exertion on his side, was another welcome surprise; for his wish was to have as little trouble in the business as possible.

When the first transports of cage-rattling rage were over, he naturally returned to all his former *lion* indolence. His letter was soon dispatched. He begged to know further particulars of what he was indebted to his brother, but was too angry with Lydia to send any message to her.

The good news spread quickly through the house, and through the neighbourhood. To be sure, it would have made for better conversation had Miss Lydia Bennet returned to town directly; or been secluded from the world in some distant farmhouse, visited by none and haunted by a monstrous duck.

But there was much to be talked of her marriage. And the presently good-natured wishes that had come from all the spiteful old ladies in Meryton lost no spirit in this change of circumstances—with Wickham for a husband, her misery was considered certain, and tongues could gleefully roll.

It was a fortnight since Mrs. Bennet had been downstairs. But on this happy day she again took her seat at the head of her table.

No shame dampened her triumph. The marriage of a daughter—the first object of her wishes since Jane was sixteen—

was now being accomplished. She was engrossed in dreams of elegant nuptials, fine muslins, new carriages, servants, and a proper residence for her daughter and her *wolf*.

Her husband allowed her to talk on without interruption, evaluating the merits of fine local estates, while the servants remained. But when they had withdrawn, he said: "Mrs. Bennet, before you take any or all of these houses for your son and daughter, let us come to a right understanding. Into *one* house in this neighbourhood they shall never have admittance. I will not encourage their impudence, by receiving them at Longbourn."

A long, harrowing dispute followed. But Mr. Bennet was firm. Mrs. Bennet found, with amazement and horror, that her husband would not advance a guinea to buy clothes for his daughter. Mrs. Bennet could hardly comprehend it. That his anger could be carried to such a point! She was more distressed at her daughter's lack of new clothes for her nuptials, than about the shame of her eloping with Wickham.

Elizabeth was now most heartily sorry that she had made Mr. Darcy acquainted with their fears for her sister. For since there was to be marriage, the earlier unsavorable details need not have been revealed.

She had no fear of him spreading it any farther. There were few people on whose *secrecy* she would depend more. But, at the same time, there was no one whose knowledge of her sister's weakness would have mortified her so much.

At any rate, there seemed a gulf impassable between them. Even if Lydia's marriage had been proper, Mr. Darcy would never connect himself with a family where he must be related to Mr. Wickham.

From such a connection she could not wonder that he would shrink. The wish of procuring her regard (which she had assured herself of his feeling in Derbyshire) could not survive such a blow as this. She was humbled, she was grieved; she repented, though she hardly knew of what. She became jealous of his esteem, when she could no longer hope to be benefited by it. She was haunted by visions of him—the sleek little *platypus* waddling to the banks of the deep pond before Pemberley House, entering the still waters under the cool silver moonlight, and then emerging, pale, well-formed, *human*, in wet shirtsleeves . . . or sometimes without anything at all. . . . She wanted to hear of him—man or *demon monotreme*[99]—when there seemed the least chance of gaining intelligence. She was convinced that she could have been happy with him, when it was no longer likely they should meet.

What a triumph for him, she thought, if he only knew that the proposals which she had proudly spurned only four months ago, would now have been most gladly and gratefully received! He was generous, no doubt; but while he was mortal, there must be a triumph.

She began now to comprehend that he was exactly the man who, in disposition and talents, would most suit her. His understanding and temper, though unlike her own, would have answered all her wishes. Even his curious *beast* would have been a constant source of wonder for her. It was a union that must have been to the advantage of both—by her ease and liveliness, his mind might have been softened, his manners improved, his *platypus* reconciled; and from his judgment, information, and knowledge of the world, she must have received benefit of greater importance.

But no such happy marriage could now teach the admiring multitude what connubial felicity really was. A union of a different sort (and precluding the possibility of the other) was soon to be formed in their family.

---

[99] A *monotreme*, gentle reader, is a rare sort of mammal that lays eggs instead of giving birth to little ones. Which makes one ponder, if Mr. Darcy and Miss Bennet were to breed, would there be eggs? —Ed. *[Oh, dear God in heaven! Miss Bennet is not the one who is the platypus! How <u>could</u> there be eggs? But, what am I saying; how <u>any</u> of this absurdity be in any sense or degree even subject to rational discussion? Oh, woe! —Ed. 2]*

How Wickham and Lydia were to survive monetarily, she could not imagine. But little permanent happiness could belong to a couple only brought together because their passions were stronger than their virtue.

M r. Gardiner soon wrote again to his brother. To Mr. Bennet's acknowledgments he replied that he was eager to promote the welfare of his family; and entreated that the subject never be mentioned again. His letter was to inform them that Mr. Wickham had resolved on quitting the militia.

> "It was greatly my wish that he should do so," he added, "as soon as his marriage was fixed. I think you will agree, the removal from that corps is highly advisable, both on his account and my niece's, in particular after that dire *incident* at Brighton with the unlocked cages and *beasts* on the loose—three *hyenas* at least were implicated in terrorizing a spinster and her small pug, though blessedly the pug drove them off bravely (and neither it nor the lady suffered more than emotional damage). It is Mr. Wickham's intention to go into the regulars. Among his former friends, there are still some who might assist him in the army. He has the promise of an ensigncy in General ———s' regiment, now quartered in the North. It is an advantage to have it so far from here. He promises fairly, upon his *wolf's* honor. And I hope among different people, they will both be more prudent. I have written to Colonel Forster, to request that he will satisfy the various Brighton creditors of Mr. Wickham, with assurances of speedy payment (for which I have pledged myself). And will you carry similar assurances to his creditors in Meryton? He has given in all his debts—I hope he has not deceived us. All will be completed in a week. They will then join his regiment, unless they are first invited to Longbourn; and I understand from Mrs. Gardiner, that my niece is very desirous of seeing you all before she leaves the South. She is well, and begs to be dutifully remembered to you and her mother.—Yours, etc.,
>
> "E. GARDINER."

Mr. Bennet and his daughters saw all the advantages of Wickham's removal from the ——shire as clearly as Mr. Gardiner. But Mrs. Bennet was not so well pleased with it. Lydia's being settled in the North, just when she had expected most pleasure and pride in her company (for she had not given up her plan of their residing in Hertfordshire), was a severe disappointment. Besides, it was such a pity that Lydia should be taken from her familiar regiment where she was acquainted with everybody, such as her favorite Mrs. Forster.

Lydia's request of being admitted into her family again before she set off for the North, received at first an absolute negative. But Jane and Elizabeth, who wished for her sake that she should be noticed on her marriage by her parents, urged Mr. Bennet so persuasively to receive her and her lupine husband at Longbourn, as soon as they were married, that he was prevailed on to agree. And their mother had the satisfaction of knowing that she would be able to show her married daughter in the neighbourhood before she was banished to the North.

When Mr. Bennet wrote again to his brother, therefore, he sent his permission for them to come. And it was settled, that as soon as the ceremony was over, they should proceed to Longbourn.

Elizabeth was surprised, however, that Wickham himself should consent to such a scheme. And any meeting with him was the last object of her wishes.

Chapter 51

Their sister's wedding day arrived; and Jane and Elizabeth felt for her probably more than she felt for herself. The carriage was sent to meet them at ——, and they were to return in it by dinner-time. Their arrival was dreaded by the elder Miss Bennets, and Jane especially, who assigned Lydia her own sensibilities, and was wretched on her behalf.

They came. The family were assembled in the breakfast room to receive them. Smiles decked the face of Mrs. Bennet as the carriage drove up to the door. Her husband looked impenetrably grave; her daughters, alarmed, anxious, uneasy.

Lydia's voice was heard in the vestibule. The door was thrown open, and she ran into the room. Her mother stepped forwards, embraced her, and welcomed her with rapture; gave her hand, with an affectionate smile, to Wickham, who followed his lady; and wished them both joy.

Their reception from Mr. Bennet was not quite so cordial. His countenance rather gained in austerity; and he scarcely opened his lips. The easy assurance of the young couple was enough to provoke the *lion* in him into a grim state indeed.

Elizabeth was disgusted, and even Jane was shocked. Lydia was Lydia still—untamed, unabashed, wild, noisy, and fearless. She turned from sister to sister, demanding their congratulations;

and when at length they all sat down, looked eagerly round the room, and observed, with a laugh, that it was a great while since she had been there.

Wickham was not at all more distressed than Lydia. But his manners were always so pleasing, that—had his character and his marriage been exactly what they ought—his smiles and easy address would have delighted them all.

Elizabeth had not before believed him quite equal to such assurance. But she sat down, resolving never to underestimate the impudence of an impudent man. *She* blushed, and Jane blushed. But the cheeks of the two who caused their confusion suffered no variation of colour.

There was no want of discourse. The bride and her mother could not talk fast enough. And Wickham, who happened to sit near Elizabeth, began inquiring after his acquaintance in that neighbourhood, with a good-humoured ease which she was unable to match in her replies. The newlyweds seemed to have the happiest memories in the world. Nothing of the past was recollected with pain; and Lydia brought up subjects that her sisters would not have alluded to for the world.

"Only think of its being three months," she cried, "since I went away. It seems but a fortnight! Good gracious! When I went away, I had no more idea of being married till I came back again—though I thought it would be very good fun if I was."

Her father lifted up his eyes. Jane was distressed. Elizabeth looked expressively at Lydia.

But she, who never heard nor saw anything she did not choose, gaily continued, "Oh! mamma, do the people hereabouts know I am married to-day? I was afraid they might not; and we overtook William Goulding in his curricle, so I was determined he should know it, and so I let down the side-glass next to him, and took off my glove, and let my hand just rest upon the window frame, so that he might see the ring, and then I bowed and smiled like anything."

Elizabeth could bear it no longer. She got up, and ran out of the room; and returned no more, till she heard them passing through the hall to the dining parlour. She then joined them soon enough to see Lydia, with anxious parade, walk up to her mother's right hand, and hear her say to her eldest sister, "Ah! Jane, I take your place now, and you must go lower, because I am a married woman!"

It was not to be supposed that time would give Lydia that embarrassment which she lacked. Her ease and good spirits *increased*. She longed to see Mrs. Phillips, the Lucases, and all their other neighbours, and to hear herself called "Mrs. Wickham" by each of them. And in the meantime, she went after dinner to show her ring, and boast of being married, to Mrs. Hill and the two housemaids.

At one point, as the hand with the ring was being admired, Elizabeth noticed that Lydia's *other* hand, just above the wrist, bore a small inconspicuous bandage that was neatly covered by her sleeve lace.

A dark terrible suspicion immediately entered Elizabeth. Thoughts of Georgiana Darcy's similar plight came to plague her. Indeed, Lydia had put herself in the exact same position, by being alone with the *wolf* when the moon was full. . . .

Those unlocked regimental cages! Elizabeth thought. *That evil night when they eloped, did not Wickham* turn *also, and was there not a strong chance that he somehow scratched or otherwise* infected *her foolish younger sister?*

Elizabeth discreetly approached Lydia, and during a pause in happy chatter, took her by that very hand and, pressing it, whispered, "Where and how did you get hurt? What happened?"

Lydia turned at her touch, and momentarily her smiling face showed a pause of true uncertainty—the first such moment in their whole visit.

"Oh," she said. "It is nothing, just a tiny scratch! It is all perfectly healed now. My dear Wickham and I were having such a delight, when we eloped, after we had run all around the camp with all the *panthers* and *bears* and *hyenas* pouncing about everywhere—just like at that crazy ball at Netherfield, such terrible fun!—I saw him *turn*, and oh! he made such a pretty *wolf*! I even tried to pet his silvery fur, and he let me; and then, oh, he growled a bit, and turned his head suddenly, and I dare say it was an accident, but his sharp teeth tore my hand a bit, right on top there. But I did not mind, because he then licked it so gently, that I knew all would be well after—"

"Good lord, Lydia!" Elizabeth exclaimed. "Do you know what this means? That you are *infected* and will now have to suffer the gentleman's Affliction! That you will *turn*, every full moon, into a female *demon wolf*!"

But Lydia giggled, and put her hand to her lips, and she said in a loud whisper, "I *know*! Is it not just a wonder? I cannot wait till the first full moon! But, oh! do hush, Lizzy, I do not want to tell my mother or the others just yet; let it be a surprise! Oh, I shall be alongside my dearest husband in his confinement chamber, and we shall both *turn* every month together!"

Elizabeth was stunned. There were simply no words to utter at this. But, as she did not reply immediately, Lydia had already turned away from her and was laughing with Kitty and her mother about something else.

And then, it occurred to Elizabeth, *on some strange remote level, Lydia must truly love him.*

But what of Wickham? Did he intentionally *infect* her, with the notion of having her more under his control as a result? Or was he merely being a thoughtless *wolf* without a care?

There were no immediate answers to be had.

"Well, mamma," said Lydia, when they were all returned to the breakfast room, "and what do you think of my husband? Is not he a charming man? I am sure my sisters must all envy me. I only hope they may have half my good luck. They must all go to Brighton. That is the place to get husbands. What a pity it is, mamma, we did not all go."

"Very true; and if I had my will, we should. But my dear Lydia, I don't like your going such a way off. Must it be so?"

"Oh, lord! yes;—there is nothing in that. I shall like it of all things. You must all come down and see us. We shall be at Newcastle all the winter, there will be some balls, and I will take care to get good partners for all my sisters. And when you go away, leave my sisters behind—I shall get husbands for them before the winter is over!"

"I thank you for my share of the favour," said Elizabeth; "but I do not particularly like your way of getting husbands."

Their visitors were not to remain above ten days with them. Mr. Wickham had received his commission before he left London, and he was to join his regiment at the end of a fortnight.

No one but Mrs. Bennet regretted that their stay would be so short. She made the most of it by visiting about with her daughter, and having very frequent parties at home. These parties were acceptable to all—to avoid a family circle was even more desirable to such as did think, than such as did not.

Wickham's affection for Lydia was just what Elizabeth had expected—not equal to Lydia's for him. She was certain that their elopement had been brought on by the strength of her love, rather than by his. And now it was certain that his flight was rendered necessary by distress of circumstances. He was not the young man to resist an opportunity of having a companion, and in particular, ensuring that she would be bound to him not only by affection but Affliction.

Lydia was exceedingly fond of him. He was her dear Wickham on every occasion; no one was to be put in competition with him. He did everything best in the world; and she was sure he would "kill" more Affliction Steaks in the cage than any other, and now she was to be there, *inside* with him.

One morning, soon after their arrival, as Lydia was sitting with her two elder sisters, she said to Elizabeth:

"Lizzy, I never gave *you* an account of my wedding, I believe. You were not by, when I told mamma and the others all about it. Are not you curious to hear how it was managed?"

"No really," replied Elizabeth; "I think there cannot be too little said on the subject."

"La! You are so strange! But I must tell you how it went off. We were married at St. Clement's, because Wickham's lodgings were in that parish. And it was settled that we should all be there by eleven o'clock. My uncle and aunt and I were to go together; and the others were to meet us at the church. Well, Monday morning came, and I was in such a fuss! I was so afraid that something would happen to put it off, and then I should have gone quite distracted. And there was my aunt, all the time I was dressing, preaching and talking away just as if she was reading a sermon. However, I did not hear above one word in ten, for I was thinking of my dear Wickham and how he had been all silvery-furred in the *moonlight!* I longed to know whether he would be married in his blue coat."

"Well, and so we breakfasted at ten as usual; I thought it would never be over; for my doggish uncle and aunt were horrid unpleasant all the time I was with them. I did not once put my foot out of doors! Not one party, or scheme, or anything. To be sure London was rather thin, but the Little Theatre was open. Well, and so just as the carriage came to the door, my uncle was called away upon horrid business. Well, I was so frightened I did not know what to do, for my uncle was to give me away; and if we were beyond the hour, we could not be married all day. But, luckily, he came back again in ten minutes' time, and then we all set out. However, I recollected afterwards that if he had been delayed, the wedding need not be put off, for Mr. Darcy might have done as well."

"Mr. Darcy!" repeated Elizabeth, in utter amazement.

"Oh, yes!—he was to come there with Wickham, you know. But gracious me! I quite forgot! I ought not to have said a word about it. I promised them so faithfully! What will Wickham say? It was to be such a *secret!*"

"If it was to be secret," said Jane, "say not another word."

"Oh! certainly," said Elizabeth, though burning with curiosity; "we will ask you no further questions."

"Thank you," said Lydia, "for if you did, I should certainly tell you all, and then my dear *wolf* would be angry."

On such encouragement to ask, Elizabeth was forced to put it out of her power, by running away.

But to live in ignorance on such a point was impossible—or at least it was impossible not to try for information. Mr. Darcy had been at her sister's wedding! It was the *last* place he would be! Rapid, wild conjectures hurried into her brain; but she was satisfied with none. Possibilities that best pleased her (placing his conduct in the noblest light) seemed most improbable.

She could not bear such suspense. And hastily seizing a sheet of paper, she wrote a short letter to her aunt, to request an explanation of what Lydia had let slip.

"You may readily comprehend," she added, "what my curiosity must be to know how a person unconnected with any of us, and a stranger to our family, should have been amongst you at such a time. Pray write instantly, and let me understand it! Lydia seems to think it necessary that it remains a secret. . . . My dear aunt, I beg you, do not oblige me to resort to tricks and stratagems to find it out!"

Chapter 52

Elizabeth had the satisfaction of receiving an answer to her letter as soon as she possibly could. She was no sooner in possession of it than, hurrying into the little copse, where she was least likely to be interrupted, she sat down on a bench and prepared to be happy—for the length of the letter convinced her that it did not withhold any secrets.

"Gracechurch street, Sept. 6.

"MY DEAR NIECE,

"I have just received your letter, and shall devote this whole morning to answering it, as I foresee that a *little* writing will not comprise what I have to tell you. I must confess myself surprised by your question—I had not imagined such inquiries to be necessary on *your* side. If you do not choose to understand me, forgive my loving impertinence. Your uncle is as much surprised as I am— and nothing but the belief of your being a party concerned would have allowed him to act as he has done. But if you are really innocent and ignorant, I must be more explicit.

"On the very day of my coming home from Longbourn, your uncle had a most unexpected visitor. Mr. Darcy called, and was shut up with him several hours. He came to tell Mr. Gardiner that he had found out where your sister and Mr. Wickham were, and that he had seen and talked with them both. He left Derbyshire only one day after ourselves, and came to town with the resolution of hunting[100] for them. The motive professed was his conviction of its being his fault that Wickham's worthlessness had not been so well known as to make it impossible for any young woman of character to love or confide in him. He generously blamed his own mistaken pride, having thought it beneath him to lay Wickham's private actions open to the world. The wolf's character was to speak for itself. He called it, therefore, his duty to step forward, and remedy an evil that had been brought on by himself. If he *had another* motive, I am sure it would never disgrace him. He had been some days in town, before he was able to discover them. But he had something to direct his search, which was more than *we* had.

"There is a lady, it seems, a Mrs. Younge, who was some time ago governess to Miss Darcy, and was dismissed from her charge on some cause of disapprobation. She then took a large house in Edward-street, and has since maintained herself by letting lodgings. This Mrs. Younge was, he knew, intimately acquainted with Wickham. And Mr. Darcy went to her for news of him as soon as he got to town. But it was several days before he could get from her what he wanted. She would not betray her trust without bribery and corruption, for she really *did* know where they were. Wickham indeed had gone to her on their first arrival in London—since it was the full moon and he needed proper containment quarters, with vulnerable Lydia in his company—and had she been able to receive them into her house, they would have taken up their abode with her. At length, however, Mrs. Younge procured the wished-for direction. They were in —— street. Darcy saw Wickham, and afterwards insisted on seeing Lydia. His first object with her had been to persuade her to quit her present

---

[100] Mr. Darcy was known to hunt birds, as other gentlemen; but he was also a clandestine bounty hunter, and had more than a dozen times captured renowned ruffians and villains for a tidy sum each, which partially accounted for his family fortune. He liked to supplement his income in this manner every summer. At other times he liked to pan for gold in the Americas.

disgraceful situation, and return to her friends, offering his assistance, as far as it would go. But he found Lydia absolutely resolved on remaining where she was. She cared for none of her friends, wanted no help, would not hear of leaving Wickham—and, here, I must relate some shocking intelligence—she had apparently been next to Wickham when he was running loose in *beast* form, and had somehow received a scratch or bite on her forearm! You have my deepest sympathies on this, my dearest Lizzy, because such a supernatural *infection* for a female can result in a great deal of little-known harm. I know not what you may tell your mother on this, but in any case. . . . Lydia was sure they should be married some time or other, and it did not much signify when. Since such were her feelings, it only remained, Mr. Darcy thought, to secure and expedite a marriage, which, in his very first conversation with Wickham, he learnt had never been *his* design. Wickham confessed having to leave the regiment, on account of some debts of honour; and scrupled not to lay all the ill-consequences of Lydia's flight on her own folly alone. He meant to resign his commission immediately. As to his future situation, he must go somewhere—he did not know where—with nothing to live on.

"Mr. Darcy asked him why he had not married Lydia at once. Though Mr. Bennet was not rich, he would have been able to do something for him, and his situation must have been benefited by marriage. But he found that Wickham still cherished the hope of making his fortune in a finer marriage.

"They met several times, for there was much to be discussed. At one point, apparently, with your uncle present for the first time, the two young men had locked themselves in a room together, and there were some minutes, Mr. Gardiner suspects, where there had been the possibility of violence; or at least some unusual gentlemanly altercation—loud knocks and noises, and the fierce, wild sounds of two angry *demon beasts* fighting, not unlike what happens within a confinement chamber during the full moon. . . . Indeed, highly peculiar and unusual! There was even one extremely loud wolfish howl of pain, followed by many knocks on the walls (of bodies thrown), and more wolf snarling—whatever the other *beast* had been, it was impossible to tell, for *he* remained unusually quiet throughout, and all the recognizable vocalizations were lupine and one-sided.

"When it was over, Wickham emerged with a disheveled appearance, and an arm bandaged hastily in some lace. Mr. Darcy followed him, looking impeccable, as though nothing had happened. Mr. Gardiner, who happened to witness this portion only, was duly impressed—indeed, whatever Mr. Darcy's *beast* happens to be, it is a remarkably powerful specimen to have so managed to subdue a fully-grown *demon wolf!* And, as a result of such 'negotiation,' Wickham, who of course wanted more than he could get, was reduced to be reasonable.

"Everything being settled between *them*, Mr. Darcy's next step was to make your uncle fully acquainted with the agreed-on details, and they again both returned to Gracechurch street, leaving Wickham in his own residence to nurse his wounds. Immediately after, Mr. Gardiner was about to inform your father of the satisfactory news—but Mr. Bennet had already gone to his separate lodgings, and would quit town the next morning. Mr. Darcy did not judge your father to be a person whom he could so properly consult as your uncle, and therefore readily postponed that meeting. He did not leave his name the previous times he called, and thus Mr. Bennet never knew of his involvement.

"On Saturday Mr. Darcy came again. Your father was gone, your uncle at home, and they had a great deal of talk together.

"They met again on Sunday, and then *I* saw him too. It was settled by Monday, and the express was sent off to Longbourn. But our visitor was very obstinate. I fancy, Lizzy, that obstinacy is the real defect of his character, after all. He has been accused of many faults at different times, but *this* is the true one. Nothing was to be done that he did not do himself; though I am sure your uncle would most readily have settled the whole.

"They battled it together for a long time (with no *beastly* fur flying, I must add, unlike that other time with Darcy and

Wickham)—which was more than either the gentleman or lady concerned in it deserved. But at last your uncle was forced to yield—which went sorely against the grain. Indeed, your letter this morning gave him great pleasure, because an explanation would have required him to give the praise and credit for all the endless expenses to Mr. Darcy, where it was due. But, Lizzy, this must go no farther than yourself, or Jane at most.

"You know pretty well, I suppose, what has been done for the young people. His debts are to be paid, considerably more than a thousand pounds, another thousand in addition to her own settled upon *her*, and his commission purchased. The reason why all this was to be done by him alone, was given above. It was owing to him, to his *secrecy*, reserve, and want of proper consideration, that Wickham's character had been so misunderstood, and consequently that he had been so liberally received in society. Perhaps there was some truth in *this*—though I doubt whether *anybody's* reserve can be answerable for the event. But in spite of all this fine talking, my dear Lizzy, you may rest assured that your uncle would never have yielded, if we had not given him credit for *another interest* in the affair.

"When all this was resolved on, Mr. Darcy returned again to his friends, who were still staying at Pemberley. But it was agreed that he should be in London once more for the wedding, and all money matters would then be completed.

"I believe I have now told you everything. Since you tell me you are unaware of all of this, it must come as a great surprise. I hope at least it will not afford you any displeasure. Lydia came to us; and Wickham had constant admission to the house. *He* was exactly what he had been in Hertfordshire. But I would not tell you how little I was satisfied with *her* behaviour while she staid with us, if Jane's last letter had not described her similar conduct on coming home—and therefore this can give you no fresh pain. I talked to her repeatedly in the most serious manner, representing to her all the wickedness of what she had done, and all she had brought on her family. I am sure she did not listen. I was sometimes quite provoked, but then I recollected my dear Elizabeth and Jane, and for their sakes had patience with her.

"Mr. Darcy was punctual in his return, and as Lydia informed you, attended the wedding. He dined with us the next day, and was to leave town again on Wednesday or Thursday. Will you be very angry with me, my dear Lizzy, if I take this opportunity of saying how much I like him? His behaviour to us, his understanding and opinions, have been as pleasing as when we were in Derbyshire. He lacks nothing but a little more liveliness, and *that*, if he marry *prudently*, his wife may teach him. I thought him very sly— he hardly ever mentioned your name. But slyness seems the fashion.

"Pray forgive me if I have been very presuming, or at least do not punish me so far as to exclude me from Pemberley. I shall never be quite happy till I have been all round the park. A low phaeton, with a nice little pair of ponies, would do nicely!

"Yours, very sincerely,

"M. GARDINER."

The contents of this letter threw Elizabeth into a flutter of spirits. Difficult to determine whether pleasure or pain bore the greatest share. . . .

The vague suspicions of what Mr. Darcy might have been doing to forward her sister's match, were proved beyond their greatest extent to be true! He had followed them purposely to town, he had taken on himself all the trouble and mortification attendant on such a research—including asking assistance from a woman whom he despised; and frequently meeting, persuading, and finally bribing the hateful man whom he always most wished to avoid!

He had done all this for a silly girl whom he could neither regard nor esteem.

But no, her heart whispered, *he had done it for her.*

But this hope was shortly checked by other considerations. Surely her vanity was insufficient, when required to depend on his affection for her—a woman who had already refused him—in order to overcome abhorrence against dealing with Wickham. Brother-in-law of Wickham! Every kind of pride must revolt from the connection with the *wolf*. And if she understood correctly, there had even been some kind of battle in which his little *platypus* prevailed over the *wolf*, behind locked doors, to the point of wounding him! Elizabeth could not imagine how it had happened, and to what end?

He had done so much! Though she would not place herself as his principal inducement, she could, perhaps, believe that remaining partiality for her was involved. It was exceedingly painful, to know that they were under obligations to a person who could never receive a return. They owed the restoration of Lydia, her character, everything, to the gentleman *platypus*.

Oh! how heartily did she grieve over every ungracious sensation she had ever encouraged, every saucy speech she had ever directed towards him!

For herself, she was humbled; but she was proud of him. Proud, that in a cause of compassion and honour, he had been able to get the better of himself—his secret shame of his *beast*, odd insecurity, and infinite complexity of stubborn character. She read over her aunt's commendation of him again and again. It was hardly enough; but it pleased her. She was even pleased to find that both her aunt and uncle had been persuaded that affection and confidence existed between Mr. Darcy and herself.

She was roused from her bench, and her reflections, by someone's approach. And she saw Wickham.

Having just read her aunt's account, she knew enough to look directly at his hands and arms to see if there were any scars remaining of a supernatural battle. Indeed, his right arm, covered by jacket sleeve, showed the end of a fading dark gash, which disappeared under the cuff—if she had not known to look, she would never have noticed.

Well! Mr. Darcy had marked you rather effectively! she could not help the gleeful thought. *Brave little platypus!*

"I am afraid I interrupt your solitary ramble, my dear sister?" said he, not noticing her brief glance at his telltale scar.

"You certainly do," she replied with a smile; "but the interruption is not unwelcome."

"I should be sorry indeed, if it were. We were always good friends; and now we are better."

"True. Are the others coming out?"

"I do not know. Mrs. Bennet and Lydia are going in the carriage to Meryton. And so, my dear sister, I find, from our uncle and aunt, that you have actually seen Pemberley."

She replied in the affirmative.

"I almost envy you the pleasure, and yet it would be too much for me, else I would stop by it on my way to Newcastle. And you saw the old housekeeper, I suppose? Poor Reynolds, she was always very fond of me. But of course she did not mention my name to you."

"Yes, she did. She said that you were gone into the army, and, she was afraid, had—not turned out well. At such a distance as *that*, you know, things are strangely misrepresented."

"Certainly," he replied, biting his lips. Elizabeth hoped she had silenced him; but he soon afterwards said:

"I was surprised to see Darcy in town last month. We passed each other several times. I wonder what he can be doing."

"Perhaps preparing for his marriage with Miss de Bourgh," said Elizabeth. "It must be something particular."

"Undoubtedly. Did you see him while you were at Lambton? I understood from the Gardiners that you had."

"Yes; he introduced us to his sister. I like her very much."

"I have heard, indeed, that she is uncommonly improved. When I last saw her, she was not very promising. I am very glad you liked her. I hope she will turn out well."

"I dare say she will. She has got over the most trying age."

"Did you go by the village of Kympton? It is the living which I ought to have had. A most delightful parsonage!—It would have suited me in every respect."

"No—but, how should you have liked making sermons?"

"Exceedingly well. I should have considered it as part of my duty. Now, a *wolf* ought not to repine—but it would have been such a thing for me! The quiet life would have answered all my ideas of happiness! But it was not to be. . . . Did Darcy mention the circumstance, when you were in Kent?"

"I have heard from *as good* authority, that it was left you conditionally only, and at the will of the present patron."

"You have! Yes, there was something in *that.* I told you so from the first, you may remember."

"I *did* hear, too, that there was a time, when sermon-making was not so palatable to you as it seems to be at present—that you actually declared your resolution of never taking orders, and that the business had been compromised accordingly."

"You did! And it was not wholly without foundation. You may remember what I told you, when first we talked of it—"

They were now almost at the door of the house (for she had walked fast to get rid of him). And unwilling, for her sister's sake, to provoke him, she only said in reply, with a good-humoured smile:

"Come, Mr. Wickham, we are brother and sister, you know. Do not let us quarrel about the past. In future, I hope we shall be always of one mind."

She held out her hand.

He kissed it with affectionate lupine gallantry, though he hardly knew how to look, and they entered the house.

Chapter 53

Mr. Wickham was so perfectly "satisfied" with their conversation that he never brought up the subject again. Elizabeth was pleased to find that she had said enough to keep him quiet.

The day of his and Lydia's departure soon came, and Mrs. Bennet was forced to submit to at least a year's separation.

Lydia and her mother cried and exclaimed random things at each other, at the *odious moon*, and promised to write often.

"But you know married women have never much time for writing!" Lydia cried. "My sisters may write to *me*. They will have nothing else to do. Whilst I—I will now spend all this time tending to my dear Wickham's cage!"

And at the next full moon, you might even be joining him inside that cage . . . thought Elizabeth with annoyance.

Mr. Wickham's adieus were much more affectionate than his wife's. He smiled, looked handsome, and said many pretty things.

"He is as fine a wolfish fellow," said Mr. Bennet, as soon as they were out of the house, "as ever I saw. He simpers, and smirks, and makes love to us all. I am prodigiously proud of him. I defy even Sir William Lucas himself to produce a more valuable son-in-law. This one's cage is polished to a gleam!"

Speaking of gleam—the loss of her daughter made Mrs. Bennet very dull for several days.

"There is nothing so bad," said she, "as parting with one's friends. One seems so forlorn without them."

"This is the consequence, madam, of marrying[101] a daughter," said Elizabeth. "It must make you better satisfied that your other four are single."

"It is no such thing! Lydia does not leave me because she is married, but only because her husband's regiment happens to be so far off. Else, she would not have gone so soon."

But Mrs. Bennet's sad condition was shortly relieved, and her mind agitated with hope, by an article[102] of news which then began to be in circulation. The housekeeper at Netherfield had received orders to prepare for the arrival of her master, who was coming down in a day or two, to shoot there for several weeks. Mrs. Bennet was quite in the fidgets. She looked at Jane, and smiled and shook her head by turns.

"Well, well, and so Mr. Bingley is coming down, sister," said Mrs. Bennet to Mrs. Phillips who first brought the news. "Not that I care about it. The *tiger* is nothing to us, and I am sure *I* never want to see him again. But, he is welcome to come to

---

[101] One hurries to reassure that here it is never implied that Mrs. Bennet marries her own daughter! That would be an abomination and a travesty! — Ed. *[And on that wretched note, we pass our hundredth footnote. —Ed. 2]*

[102] The article was published, o astute reader, by none other than Mrs. Bennet herself. There is no doubt the esteemed matron was trying her hand at literary expression; and raw and unadulterated publication was her primary goal, regardless of sense, purpose, and propriety. To see her name—or rather, her anonymous, gender ambiguous initials—in print, was the culmination of many years of actively exercising and engaging her verbal faculties via unfettered speech. And as everyone knows, words require an eventual outlet of another sort; logorrhea is a harsh mistress; and one thing leads to another, and you have a book in you, and then before you, and then on some hapless acquisitions editor's desk—Ahem!

Netherfield. Who knows what *may* happen? But—we will not mention a word. And so, is it quite certain he is coming?"

"You may depend on it," replied the other, "for Mrs. Nicholls told me so. He comes down on Wednesday or Thursday. She was going to the butcher's, she told me, to order in some meat on Wednesday, and she has got three couple of ducks just fit to be killed, but the butcher complained that every time he made the attempt, he was thwarted by some kind of monstrous *duck* on the loose—rumor has it, *unnatural*, and a notorious killer—and I declare, it had flown at him, screeching all godawful-like—"

Miss Jane Bennet had not been able to hear of Bingley's coming without changing colour. It was months since she had mentioned his name to Elizabeth. But now, as soon as they were alone together, she said:

"I saw you look at me to-day, Lizzy, when my aunt told us of the news; and I know I appeared distressed—but only for a moment. I do assure you that the news does not affect me. I am glad that he comes alone; because we shall see the less of him. I only dread other people's remarks."

Elizabeth did not know what to make of it. After seeing Bingley in Derbyshire, she still thought him partial to Jane. Did he come *with* his friend's permission, or was he bold enough to come without it?

In spite of what Jane declared, Elizabeth could easily see that her spirits were affected—she was more disturbed than ever.

"As soon as ever Mr. Bingley comes, my dear," said Mrs. Bennet to her spouse, as she did a twelvemonth ago, "you will wait on him of course."

"No, no. You forced me into visiting him last year, and promised he should marry one of my daughters. But it ended in nothing, except a bothersome comet come to plague us for many months, together with my fool cousin, who mercifully plagued us only for a se'nnight. And thus, I will not be sent on a fool's errand again to court similar misfortune; and that, right before the *fool's* moon."

His wife artfully represented to him how absolutely necessary such an attention would be from all the neighbouring gentlemen, on Bingley's returning to Netherfield.

"'Tis an *etiquette* I despise," said Mr. Bennet. "If he wants our society, let him seek it. He knows where we live. I will not run after my neighbours every time they go away and come back again. Besides, I hear there is a *monster* formed like a duck causing terror in these parts. Why venture outside and risk it?"

"What? Gracious, what duck, Mr. Bennet? Well, all I know is, it will be abominably rude if you do not wait on him. But, that shan't prevent my asking him to dine here, with Mrs. Long and the Gouldings—so there will be just room at table for him."

Meanwhile, the day of Mr. Bingley's arrival drew near.

"I begin to be sorry that he comes at all," said Jane to her sister. "I *could* see him with perfect indifference, but I can hardly bear to hear it thus perpetually talked of. My mother means well. But she does not know—no one can know—how much I suffer from what she says. Happy shall I be, when his stay at Netherfield is over!"

"I wish I could say anything to comfort you," replied Elizabeth; "but it is wholly out of my power."

Mr. Bingley arrived. Mrs. Bennet, with the assistance of servants, contrived to have the earliest tidings of it. She counted the days that must intervene before their dinner invitation could be sent; hopeless of seeing him before. But on the third morning after his arrival in Hertfordshire, she saw him, from her dressing-room window, enter the paddock and ride towards the house.

Surely, at last, the *tiger* was coming!

Her daughters were eagerly called to partake of her joy. Jane resolutely kept her place at the table. But Elizabeth, to satisfy her mother, went to the window. She looked . . . and saw

Mr. Darcy with him. And, with her knees gone weak, she sat down again by her sister. Her heart was beating very fast. . . .

The *tiger* and the *platypus!*

"There is some gentleman with him, mamma," said Kitty. "La! it looks just like that man that used to be with him before. Mr. what's-his-name. That tall, proud *secretive* man."

"Good gracious! Mr. Darcy!—and so it does! Well, any friend of Mr. Bingley's will always be welcome here. But otherwise I must say that I hate the very sight of him."

Jane looked at Elizabeth with surprise and concern. She knew but little of their meeting in Derbyshire, and therefore felt for the awkwardness which must attend her sister, in seeing him almost for the first time after receiving his explanatory letter.

Both sisters were uncomfortable enough. Each felt for the other, and for themselves. And their mother talked on—of her dislike of Mr. Darcy, and her resolution to be civil to him only as Mr. Bingley's friend—without being heard by either.

But Elizabeth had additional reasons for uneasiness, unsuspected by Jane (to whom she had never yet had courage to show Mrs. Gardiner's letter, or to relate her own absolute change of sentiment towards Darcy).

To Jane, he could be only a man whose proposals she had refused; a man who, since childhood, was harboring a peculiar *platypus demon* that shaped his adult character with additional complexity; and whose merit she had undervalued. But to Elizabeth, he was the person to whom the whole family were indebted, and whom she herself regarded with an interest—if not quite so tender, then at least as equitable as what Jane felt for Bingley. Her astonishment at his coming—to Netherfield, to Longbourn, and voluntarily seeking her again—was immense.

The colour which had left her face, returned briefly with an additional glow, and a smile of delight added lustre to her eyes, as she wondered that his affection and wishes must still be unshaken. But she would not be sure. . . .

Let me first see how he behaves, she thought.

She sat intently at work, striving to be composed, and without daring to lift up her eyes. Anxious curiosity made her glance at the face of her sister as the servant was approaching the door. Jane looked a little paler than usual, but more sedate than Elizabeth had expected. On the gentlemen's appearing, her colour increased. Yet she received them with tolerable ease and perfect propriety.

Elizabeth said as little to either as civility would allow. And she sat down again to her work, with an uncommon eagerness. She had ventured only one glance at Darcy. He looked serious, as usual—more as he used to look in Hertfordshire, than as she had seen him at Pemberley. But, perhaps in her mother's presence he could not be what he was before her uncle and aunt. It was a painful, but a likely conjecture.

Bingley looked both pleased and embarrassed, and in a most feline manner seemed ready to rub himself against furniture, and knead the upholstery. He was received by Mrs. Bennet with a degree of civility which made her two daughters ashamed, especially when contrasted with the cold and ceremonious politeness of her curtsey and address to his friend.

Elizabeth in particular, who knew that her mother owed to the latter the preservation of her favourite daughter from dire infamy, was hurt and distressed.

Darcy, after inquiring of her about Mr. and Mrs. Gardiner— a question which she could not answer without confusion—said scarcely anything. He was not seated by her; perhaps that was the reason of his silence. But it had not been so in Derbyshire. There he had talked to her friends. But now several minutes elapsed without bringing the sound of his voice. When occasionally, unable to resist curiosity, she raised her eyes to his face, she as often found him looking at Jane as at herself, and frequently on the ground. More thoughtfulness and less anxiety to please, than when they last met, were plainly expressed. She was disappointed (and angry with herself for being so).

Could I expect it to be otherwise! Yet why did he come?

She was in no humour for conversation with anyone but himself. But to him she had hardly courage to speak.

She inquired after his sister, but could do no more. And his reply could have been read as meaningful, for it included a subtle mention of "joyful freedom, akin to fiery birds in flight."

Meanwhile, Mrs. Bennet gently reproached Mr. Bingley for being away for such a long time, and he readily agreed to it.

"I began to be afraid you would never come back again. People *did* say you meant to quit the place entirely; but I hope it is not true. A great many changes have happened in the neighbourhood, since you went away. Miss Lucas is married and settled. And one of my own daughters. I suppose you have heard of it—indeed, you must have seen it in the papers. It was in *The Times* and *The Courier*, though it only said, 'Lately, George Wickham, Esq. to Miss Lydia Bennet,' without mention of her father, her residence, the gentleman's *beast*, or anything. Did you see it?"

Bingley replied that he did, and made his congratulations. Elizabeth dared not lift up her eyes. How Mr. Darcy looked, therefore, she could not tell.

"It is a delightful thing to have a daughter well married," continued her mother, "but at the same time, Mr. Bingley, it is very hard to have her taken such a way from me, to Newcastle, and there they are to stay however long. His regiment is there; for I suppose you have heard of his leaving the ——shire, and being gone into the regulars. Thank Heaven; he has *some* friends, though perhaps not so many as he deserves."

Elizabeth, who knew this to be levelled at Mr. Darcy, was in such misery of shame, that she could hardly keep her seat. It made her obliged to speak, and she asked Bingley whether he meant to stay in the country. A few weeks, he believed.

"When you have killed all your own birds, Mr. Bingley," said her mother, "I beg you will come here, and shoot as many as you please on Mr. Bennet's manor. I am sure he will be vastly happy to oblige you. There is some breed of *monstrous duck* purported to be on the loose all over the neighborhood, I am told. Or is it a single duck? I declare, it is all rather unclear."

At the mention of *ducks*, Mr. Bingley paled, while Mr. Darcy's colour rose. Both recalled the incident at Netherfield. And Mr. Darcy also painfully recalled the incident at Hunsford.

Elizabeth's misery increased, at such unnecessary officious attention to Bingley. At that instant, she felt that years of happiness could not make Jane or herself amends for moments of such painful confusion.

The first wish of my heart, she thought, *is to never see either of them again! Their society can afford no pleasure that will atone for such wretchedness as this!*

Yet the misery (for which years of happiness were to offer no compensation) was soon relieved from observing how much the beauty of her sister re-kindled the admiration of her former tigrine lover.

When first he came in, he had barely spoken to her. But every minute seemed to give her more of his attention. He found her as handsome as she had been last year—as good natured, and as unaffected, though not quite so chatty. . . .

Jane was anxious that no difference should be perceived in her at all, and thought she talked as much as ever. But she was trying so hard, that she did not realize when she was silent.

When the gentlemen rose to go, Mrs. Bennet invited them to dine at Longbourn in a few days time.

"You are quite a visit in my debt, Mr. Bingley," she added, "for last winter you promised to take a family dinner with us, as soon as you returned. I have not forgot; and was so disappointed that you did not come back and keep your engagement."

Bingley looked a little silly, and said something about having been prevented by business. They then went away.

Mrs. Bennet had been strongly tempted to ask them to stay to dine that same day. But nothing less than two courses could have been good enough for such two lofty men.

Chapter 54

As soon as they were gone, Elizabeth walked out to recover (or further deaden) her spirits in solitude. Mr. Darcy's behaviour astonished and vexed her.

Why, if he came only to be silent, grave, and indifferent, mused she, *did he come at all?*

She could settle it in no way that gave her pleasure.

He is still amiable and pleasing to my uncle and aunt—and why not to me? If he fears me, why come hither? If he no longer cares for me, why be silent? Teasing, teasing, strange platypus man! I will think no more about him . . . in the moonlight. . . .

Her resolution was for a short time kept by the approach of her sister, who joined her with a cheerful look—Jane was far better satisfied with their visitors.

"Now," said she, "that this first meeting is over, I feel perfectly easy. I know my own strength, and I shall never be embarrassed again by his coming. When he dines here on Tuesday, it will be publicly seen that we meet only as common and indifferent acquaintances."

"Yes, very indifferent indeed," said Elizabeth, laughingly. "Oh, Jane! take care. I dare say, the *tiger* is on the prowl!"

"My dear Lizzy, you cannot think me so weak, as to be in danger now?"

"I think you are in very great danger of making him as much in love with you as ever."

They did not see the gentlemen again till Tuesday, with the moon bright and *wickedly* full each night, and everyone properly confined afterwards. Mrs. Bennet, in the meanwhile, was giving way to all the happy schemes, which Mr. Bingley's good humour and politeness, in half an hour's visit, had revived.

On Tuesday there was a large party assembled at Longbourn. And the two most anxiously expected, to the credit of their punctuality as sportsmen, arrived in very good time.

When they repaired to the dining-room, Elizabeth eagerly watched whether Bingley would take the place—which, in all their former parties, had belonged to him—by her sister. Her prudent mother, having the same idea, did not invite him to sit by herself. On entering the room, he seemed to hesitate. But Jane happened to look round, and happened to smile: it was decided. He placed himself by her.

Elizabeth triumphantly looked towards Mr. Darcy. He bore it with noble indifference, and she would have imagined that Bingley had received his sanction to be happy, had she not seen his eyes likewise turned towards Mr. Darcy, with an expression of half-laughing alarm.

During dinner, Bingley's behaviour to her sister showed only a slightly more guarded admiration. Elizabeth was sure that Jane's happiness, and his own, would be speedily secured. She was pleased to see this, for she was in no cheerful humour. Mr. Darcy was almost as far from her as the table could divide them, seated next to her mother—a situation giving pleasure to neither.

She was not near enough to hear, but noticed they barely spoke to each other, remaining formal and cold. Her mother's ungraciousness was painful to Elizabeth. Oh, how she would have given anything to tell him how his kindness was appreciated by at least *some* of the family!

She hoped that the evening would afford some opportunity of bringing them together for a private conversation. The period in the drawing-room, before the gentlemen came, was so wearisome that she almost became uncivil. She looked forward to their entrance as her one chance of pleasure for the evening.

"If he does not come to me *then*," she muttered, "I shall give him up forever."

The gentlemen came. But, alas! the ladies had crowded round the table, where Miss Bennet was making tea, and Elizabeth pouring out the coffee, in so close a confederacy that there was not a single vacancy near her which would admit of a chair. And on the gentlemen's approaching, one of the girls spoke teasingly that, considering the dangers of the full moon, the gentlemen were unwanted so nearby, being all "unstable and liable to *turn* at any moment."

Thus, Darcy walked away to another part of the room. Elizabeth followed him with her eyes, envied everyone to whom he spoke, had scarcely patience enough to help anybody to coffee; and then was enraged against herself for being so silly!

A man once refused! How could I ever be foolish enough to expect a renewal of his love? Is there a gentleman who would allow the weakness of a second proposal to the same woman?

She was a little revived, however, by his bringing back his coffee-cup himself. And she seized the opportunity of saying:

"Is your sister at Pemberley still?"

"Yes, she will remain there till Christmas," he replied softly with a look of intense eyes. "I am pleased to report that she *burns* with new life, and your wise counsel has given her *wings*."

"I am so glad. . . ."

Elizabeth felt her breath catch in her throat. But she could think of nothing else to say. Surely if he wished to converse with her, and persisted, he might have better success. He stood by her, however, for some minutes, in strange profound silence. And, at last, when someone else addressed Elizabeth, he walked away.

When the tea-things were removed, and the card-tables placed, the ladies all rose. Elizabeth hoped he would then join her. But he fell a victim to her mother's rapacity for whist players, and was seated with the rest of the party.

She now lost every expectation of pleasure. They were confined for the evening at different tables, and she could only hope that his eyes were so often turned towards her side of the room, as to make him play as unsuccessfully as herself.

Mrs. Bennet had designed to keep the two Netherfield gentlemen to supper. But it *was* the full moon, the gentlemen all fragile and high-strung, and therefore their carriage was ordered, for a timely return to take their own confinement for the night's Ordeal. Thus, she had no opportunity of detaining them.

"Well girls," said she, as soon as they were left to themselves, "What say you to the day? I think everything has passed off uncommonly well! The dinner was as well dressed as any I ever saw. The venison was roasted to a turn. The soup was fifty times better than at the Lucases' last week. Even Mr. Darcy acknowledged that the partridges were remarkably well done (and I suppose he has two or three French cooks at least). And, my dear Jane, I never saw you look in greater beauty. Indeed, even Mrs. Long said, 'Ah! Mrs. Bennet, we shall have her at Netherfield at last.' Mrs. Long is as good a creature as ever lived, even with all those *hyenas* in the family, poor dear—and her nieces are very well behaved girls, and not at all handsome: I like them prodigiously."

Mrs. Bennet, in short, was in very great spirits. She had seen enough of Bingley's behaviour to Jane, to be convinced that she would get him at last. And her expectations were such that she was disappointed at not seeing him there again the next day, to make his proposals.

"It has been a very agreeable day," said Jane to Elizabeth. "The party was so amiable. I hope we may often meet again."

Elizabeth smiled.

"Lizzy, you must not! You must not suspect me. It mortifies me. I assure you that I have now learnt to enjoy his conversation without having a wish beyond it. I am perfectly satisfied that he never had any design of engaging my affection. It is only that he is blessed with such great, pleasing, *cat* sweetness of address—"

"You are very cruel," said Elizabeth. "You will not let me smile, and are provoking me to it every moment."

"How hard it is to be believed!"

"And how impossible!"

"But why should you wish to persuade me that I feel more than I acknowledge?"

"That is a question which I know not how to answer. Forgive me—but if you persist in indifference, do not make me your confidante! There—the pale orb outside the window is round and wicked and, as my father calls it, entirely 'fool'—talk to Selene instead!"

Chapter 55

A few days after this visit, Mr. Bingley called again, alone. Mr. Darcy had left that morning for London, but was to return in ten days time. Bingley sat with them above an hour, and was in remarkably good spirits. Mrs. Bennet invited him to dine with them. But he confessed himself engaged elsewhere.

"Next time," said she, "I hope we shall be more lucky."

He expressed his happiness at calling on them early at the next opportunity.

"Can you come to-morrow?"

Yes, he had no engagement at all for to-morrow. And her invitation was accepted with alacrity.

He came, and in such very good time that the ladies were none of them dressed. In ran Mrs. Bennet to her daughters' room, in her dressing gown, and with her hair half finished, crying out, "My dear Jane, make haste and hurry down! He is come—Mr. Bingley is come! He is, indeed! Make haste, make haste! Here, Sarah, come to Miss Bennet this moment, and help her on with her gown. Never mind Miss Lizzy's hair—"

"We will be down as soon as we can," said Jane; "but I dare say Kitty is readier than either of us; she went half an hour ago."

"Oh! hang[103] Kitty! what has she to do with it? Come be quick, be quick! Where is your sash, my dear?"

But when her mother was gone, Jane would not be prevailed on to go down without one of her sisters.

The same anxiety to get them by themselves was visible again in the evening. After tea, Mr. Bennet retired to the library, as was his custom, especially on a night of the Ordeal, and Mary went up stairs to her instrument. Two obstacles of the five being thus removed, Mrs. Bennet sat looking and winking at Elizabeth and Catherine for a considerable time, without making any impression on them. Elizabeth would not observe her; and when at last Kitty did, she very innocently said, "What is the matter mamma? What do you keep winking at me for? What am I to do? Is there something in your eye?"

"Nothing child, nothing! I did not wink at you." Mrs. Bennet then sat still five minutes longer. But unable to waste such a precious occasion, she suddenly got up, and saying to Kitty, "Come here, my love, I want to speak to you," took her out of the room.

Jane instantly cast a look at Elizabeth that spoke her distress at such premeditation, and her entreaty that *she* would not give in to it. In a few minutes, Mrs. Bennet half-opened the door and called out:

"Lizzy, my dear, I want to speak with you! Your father will soon need assistance with his chains and padlocks!"

Elizabeth was forced to go.

"We may as well leave them by themselves you know;" said her mother in the hall. "Kitty and I are going upstairs."

---

[103] Pray, o gentlest of readers, do not fear! Mrs. Bennet does not intend to hang, or in any way murder, her own daughter. She is merely speaking in a manner conducive to metaphor and exaggeration, and who can blame her? Therefore, may we all "hang" Kitty, and Mary and, what the deuce, Lydia too, indeed!

Elizabeth made no attempt to reason with her mother, but remained quietly in the hall, till she and Kitty were out of sight, then returned into the drawing-room.

Mrs. Bennet's schemes for this day were ineffectual. Bingley was every thing that was charming, except the professed lover of her daughter. His ease and cheerfulness rendered him a most agreeable addition to their evening party. And he bore with the ill-judged officiousness of the mother, and patiently heard all her silly remarks.

He scarcely needed an invitation to stay for supper; and before he went away to confine himself against the rising moon, an engagement was formed, for his coming next morning to shoot with her husband as soon as Mr. Bennet was well enough to be let out of his Affliction room.

After this day, Jane said no more of her indifference. And Elizabeth went to bed in the happy belief that all must speedily be concluded—unless Mr. Darcy returned to provide some new, perchance *metaphysical* obstacle. Seriously, however, she felt sure that all this must have taken place with Darcy's approval.

Bingley was punctual to his appointment. And he and Mr. Bennet spent the morning together, as planned, both freshly recovered from their *beastly* night (and both being Great Cats, rather ravenous for hunting in any sense). The latter was much more agreeable than his companion expected. There was nothing of presumption or folly in Bingley that could provoke his ridicule, disgust him into silence, or offend his sensitive feline olfactory senses. And so, Mr. Bennet was more communicative, and less eccentric, than the other had ever seen him.

Bingley, of course, returned with him to dinner. And in the evening Mrs. Bennet again went to work to get everybody away from him and her daughter. Elizabeth, who had a letter to write, went into the breakfast room for that purpose soon after tea. Since the others were all going to sit down to cards, she could not be needed to thwart her mother's less-than-tactful schemes.

But on returning to the drawing-room, when her letter was finished, she saw, to her infinite surprise, there was reason to fear that her mother had been too ingenious for her. . . .

On opening the door, she perceived her sister and Bingley standing *together* over the hearth, as if engaged in earnest conversation. One window had been throw open, the curtains blowing in the breeze; and on the floor and furniture, were scattered several dove-grey feathers. . . . And had this not been suspicious enough, the faces of both, as they hastily turned round and *moved away from each other*, would have told it all. Their situation was already awkward. But *hers*, she thought, was still worse! Not a syllable was uttered by either. . . .

Elizabeth was on the point of going away again, when Bingley—who, like Jane, had sat down—suddenly rose, and whispering a few words to her sister, ran out of the room, as though his *tiger* was giving chase to a wildebeest of the Serengeti. . . .

Jane could not hide her exuberant joy from Elizabeth. And instantly embracing her, she acknowledged that she was the happiest creature in the world.

"'Tis too much!" she added, "by far too much! I do not deserve this happiness!"

Elizabeth's congratulations were given with a fiery delight, which words could but poorly express. And every sentence was a fresh source of happiness to Jane.

"I must go instantly to my mother!" she cried. "I would not on any account trifle with her affectionate solicitude; or allow her to hear it from anyone but myself. He is gone to my father already—oh, would that both of them do not *turn* into their cats from joy! Oh! Lizzy, to know that what I have to relate will give such pleasure to all my dear family! how shall I bear so much happiness!"

She then hastened away to her mother.

Elizabeth, left by herself, now smiled at the rapidity and ease with which an affair of so many months of suspense and vexation was finally settled, in a single night of the "fool" moon.

And this, mused she, *is the end of Darcy's anxious circumspection! of Miss Bingley's falsehood and contrivance! the happiest, wisest, most reasonable end!*

In a few minutes she was joined by Bingley, whose conference with her father had been short and to the purpose.

"Where is your sister?" said he hastily, opening the door. He was visibly agitated in the manner of an ecstatic feline, kneading everything he could put his hands on, including the hapless door handle, and almost making purring sounds deep in his throat.

"With my mother up stairs. She will be down in a moment, I dare say. Mr. Bingley—are you well? Do you—by any chance require a *cage?*"

But he then shut the door, and, coming up to her, claimed the good wishes and affection of a sister. Elizabeth honestly and heartily expressed her delight in the prospect of their new relationship. They shook hands with great cordiality (Elizabeth had to extricate hers gently because he was starting to knead her knuckles). And then, till her sister came down, she had to listen to all he had to say of his own happiness, and of Jane's endless perfections.

It was an evening of uncommon delight to them all. Miss Bennet had a glow of such sweet animation to her face, as made her look handsomer than ever. Kitty simpered and smiled, and hoped her turn was coming soon (even if only with a *hedgehog*). Mrs. Bennet gave her consent and spoke her approbation in such warm terms that seemed to her hardly enough—though she talked to Bingley of nothing else for half an hour. And when Mr. Bennet joined them at supper, his purring voice and manner plainly showed how really happy he was.

Not a word, however, passed his lips in allusion to it, till their visitor took his sudden hasty leave for the night—almost forgetting it was time to be incarcerated for the Ordeal. But as soon as he was gone, Mr. Bennet turned to his daughter.

"Jane, before I retire and lock myself up amongst Affliction Steak, I congratulate you. You will be a very happy woman."

Jane went to him instantly, kissed him, and thanked him for his goodness.

"You are a good girl;" he replied, "and I am greatly pleased that you will be so happily settled. I have not a doubt of your doing very well together. Your tempers are by no means unlike, for in many ways you are a gentle *tigress*. You are each of you so fiercely complying, that nothing will ever be resolved on; so easy, that every servant will cheat you; and so generous, that you will always exceed your income."

"Exceed their income! My dear Mr. Bennet," cried his wife, "what are you talking of? Why, the dear *tiger* has over five thousand a year!" Then addressing her daughter, "Oh! my dear Jane, I am so happy! I shan't get a wink of sleep all night. I knew it must be so, at last. I was sure you could not be so beautiful for nothing! As soon as he first came into Hertfordshire last year, I thought the two of you should end up together. Oh! he is the handsomest young man that ever was seen!"

Wickham, Lydia, were all forgotten. Jane was now, beyond competition, her favourite child. At that moment, she cared for no other. . . .

Meanwhile, Jane's younger sisters soon began to show interest in the material objects of her happiness, which she might in future be able to dispense. Mary petitioned for the use of the library at Netherfield. And Kitty begged very hard for a few balls there every winter.

Bingley, from this time, was of course a daily visitor at Longbourn; coming frequently before breakfast, and always remaining till late after supper—especially on those days it was

safely after the full moon—unless some barbarous neighbour
had given him a dinner invitation he could not refuse.

Elizabeth now had little time for talks with her sister—for
while he was present, Jane had no attention for anyone else.

"He has made me so happy," said she, one evening, "by
telling me that he was totally *ignorant* of my being in town last
spring! He was not avoiding me—he really did not *know!*"

"I suspected as much," replied Elizabeth. "But how did he
account for it?"

"It must have been his sisters' doing. They were certainly
not partial to his acquaintance with me—which I cannot wonder
at, since he might have chosen so much more advantageously.
But when they see that their brother is happy with me, they will
learn to be contented, and we shall be on good terms again—
though we can never be what we once were to each other."

"That is the most unforgiving speech," said Elizabeth, "that
I ever heard you utter. Good girl! It would vex me, indeed, to see
you again the dupe of Miss Bingley's pretended regard."

"Would you believe it, Lizzy, that when he went to town
last November, he really loved me, and nothing but a belief of
my indifference would have prevented his return!"

"A little mistake to be sure; but a credit to his modesty."

This naturally introduced a panegyric from Jane on his
diffidence, and the little value he put on his own good qualities.
Elizabeth was pleased he had not revealed the interference of his
friend. For, though Jane had the most generous and forgiving
heart in the world, it must prejudice her against Mr. Darcy.

"I am the most fortunate creature that ever existed!" cried
Jane. "Oh! Lizzy, if I could but see *you* as happy! If there *were*
but such another *tiger* for you!"

"If you were to give me forty such *tigers*, nay, an entire
zoo, I never could be so happy as you. Till I have your
disposition and goodness, I never can have your happiness. No,

let me shift for myself. Perhaps, if I am very lucky, I may yet meet another *skunk*."

Chapter 56

One morning, about a week after Bingley's engagement with Jane had been formed, as he and the females of the family were sitting together in the dining-room, they heard the sound of a carriage. A chaise and four was driving up the lawn.

It was too early in the morning for visitors. And besides, the equipage did not belong to any of their neighbours. The horses were post. And neither the carriage, nor the livery of the servant looked familiar. Bingley instantly prevailed on Miss Bennet to avoid the tediousness of some visitor, and walk away with him into the shrubbery. They both set off. The remaining three were left in the room, till the door was thrown open and their visitor entered. It was none other than Lady Catherine de Bourgh.

They all expected to be surprised. But their astonishment was beyond measure. At least the grand lady was perfectly unknown to Mrs. Bennet and Kitty, but Elizabeth was stunned.

She entered the room with a particularly ungracious air, made no other reply to Elizabeth's salutation than a slight inclination of the head, and sat down without saying a word. Elizabeth mentioned her name to her mother on her ladyship's entrance, though no request of introduction had been made.

Mrs. Bennet, all amazement, though flattered by having a guest of such high importance, received her with the utmost politeness. After sitting for a moment in silence, her ladyship said very stiffly to Elizabeth,

"I hope you are well, Miss Bennet. That lady, I suppose, is your mother."

Elizabeth replied very concisely that she was.

"And *that* I suppose is one of your sisters."

"Yes, madam," said Mrs. Bennet, delighted to speak to Lady Catherine. "She is my youngest girl but one. My youngest of all is lately married, and my eldest is out walking with a young man who will soon become a part of the family."

"You have a very small park here," returned Lady Catherine after a short silence.

"It is nothing in comparison of Rosings, my lady, I dare say; but I assure you it is much larger than Sir William Lucas's."

After enduring a lofty comment about the "inconvenient sitting room," Mrs. Bennet replied the best she could, then added:

"May I take the liberty of asking your ladyship whether you left Mr. and Mrs. Collins well?"

"Yes, very well. I saw them the night before last."

Elizabeth now expected that she would produce a letter for her from Charlotte—the only probable motive for her calling. But no letter appeared, and now she was completely puzzled.

Mrs. Bennet begged her ladyship to take some refreshment. But Lady Catherine not very politely declined eating anything; and then, rising up, said to Elizabeth:

"Miss Bennet, there seemed to be a prettyish kind of a little wilderness on one side of your lawn—rather Australian from a distance, if one squints the eye. I should be glad to take a turn in it, if you will favour me with your company."

"Go, my dear," cried her mother, "and show her ladyship about the different walks!"

Elizabeth obeyed, and running into her own room for her parasol, attended her noble guest downstairs. As they passed through the hall, Lady Catherine opened the doors into the dining-parlour and drawing-room, pronounced them both decent looking, and walked on.

Her carriage remained at the door, and Elizabeth saw that her waiting-woman was in it. They proceeded in silence along the gravel walk that led to the copse. Elizabeth was determined to make no effort for conversation with a woman who was now more than usually insolent and disagreeable.

How could I ever think her like her nephew? she thought.

As soon as they entered the copse, Lady Catherine said: "You can be at no loss, Miss Bennet, to understand the reason of my journey hither. Your own heart, your own conscience, must tell you why I come."

Elizabeth looked with unaffected astonishment.

"Indeed, you are mistaken, madam. I have not been at all able to account for the honour of seeing you here."

"Miss Bennet," replied her ladyship angrily, "I am not to be trifled with. A report of a most alarming nature reached me two days ago. Not only is your sister on the point of being most advantageously married, but you, Miss Elizabeth Bennet, are to be, in all likelihood, soon afterwards united to my own nephew, Mr. Darcy! Though I *know* it must be a scandalous falsehood, I instantly resolved on setting off for this place, that I might make my sentiments known to you."

"If you believed it impossible to be true," said Elizabeth, colouring with astonishment and disdain, "I wonder you took the trouble of coming so far."

"I insist that you, *at once*, have such a report universally contradicted."

"Your coming to Longbourn," said Elizabeth coolly, "will be rather a confirmation of it—if, indeed, such a report existed."

"If! Do you pretend to be ignorant of it? Has it not been industriously circulated by yourselves and spread abroad?"

"I never heard that it was."

From the corner of her eye, Elizabeth noticed a large flying *object* approach from out of the overhanging trees, beating extraordinary massive wings. . . .

"And can you declare, that there is no *foundation* for it?"

"I do not pretend to possess equal frankness with your ladyship. *You* may ask questions which *I* shall not choose to answer."

As she spoke, the flying monstrous *thing* suddenly was very close, was almost overhead, and Elizabeth recognized a very familiar, very peculiar giant *duck*.

"This is not to be borne! Miss Bennet, I insist on being satisfied. Has my nephew, made you an offer of marriage?"

The duck replied instead, by uttering an ear-splitting *hell-shriek* worthy of a demonic unholy apparition. For the first time, Lady Catherine took note, and visibly started, raising her hand before her eyes to shield them from the sun as she momentarily looked on-high.

"What in heaven's name is that displeasing noisome bird? Never mind—has my nephew made you an offer?"

"Your ladyship has declared it to be impossible. And that, I believe, is the Brighton Duck."

"It ought to be impossible, while he retains the use of his reason!" continued the lady. "But *your* arts and allurements may, in a moment of infatuation, have made him forget what he owes to himself and to all his family. You may have drawn him in."

Overhead, the dark oversized shadow of the *duck* hurtled closely by, just missing Lady Catherine's splendid hat and its upraised crown of blossoms and jeweled feathers.

"Why, this thing is insupportable!" said her ladyship. "Miss Bennet, why is it flying so close by us? Is it a common occurrence? Have your family *bred* ducks to be thus grievously inclined? But never mind yet again—have you bewitched my nephew?"

"If I have, I shall be the last person to confess it. And no, despite what you might think, duck breeding is not our pastime."

"Miss Bennet, do you know who I am? I have not been accustomed to such language as this!"

The monstrous duck screeched yet again, this time just alongside Lady Catherine's right ear, narrowly passing between Elizabeth and herself.

"Oh!" cried the lady, fanning her hands before her face. "Fie! this needs to stop; what does the bird want? Why, pray, is it here?"

"I am afraid I have not the faintest notion, not being in the habit of communing with birds, and thus have no answer."

"Insolent girl! I am almost the nearest relation Darcy has in the world, and am entitled to know all his dearest concerns."

"But you are not entitled to know *mine*; nor will such behaviour as this, ever induce me to be explicit."

The Brighton Duck rose higher and perched momentarily on a tall branch of the nearest tree. From there it observed the discourse, apparently biding its time.

"Let me be rightly understood. This match, to which you presume to aspire, can never take place. Never! Mr. Darcy is engaged to *my daughter*. Now what have you to say?"

"Only this; that if he is so, you can have no reason to suppose he will make an offer to me."

Lady Catherine hesitated for a moment, looked up once at the *duck* roosted overhead, and then replied:

"The engagement between them is of a peculiar kind. From their infancy, they have been intended for each other. It was the favourite wish of *his* mother, as well as of hers. While in their cradles, we planned the union! It will *not* be prevented by a young woman of inferior birth! Do you pay no regard to propriety? Have you not heard me say that from his earliest hours he was destined for his cousin?"

"Yes, and I had heard it before. But what is that to me? If there is no other objection to my marrying your nephew, I shall certainly not be kept from it. If Mr. Darcy is neither by honour nor inclination confined to his cousin, why is not he to make another choice? And why may not I accept him?"

"Because honour, decorum, prudence, nay, interest, forbid it! You will be censured, slighted, and despised, by everyone connected with him. Your alliance will be a disgrace; your name will never even be mentioned by any of us."

The duck made another ear-rending screech; then beat its wings, scattering leaves and several feathers, and was airborne once more. It flew up, and then suddenly dove down directly at Lady Catherine's hat. . . .

The good lady made a sound not unlike the creature at present roosting on her headdress.

"God help me! Miss Bennet, *assist me immediately!*"

Elizabeth got up in haste and tried to shoo the duck away, but it clung to the milliner's delight that was her ladyship's intricate head covering.

"The parasol! Use the parasol, stupid girl!" shrieked Lady Catherine. "Do it this instant, strike!"

To be sure, this was enough to give Elizabeth pause. But she took up her parasol, carefully closed it, so that it became a long object, and then gently prodded with the pointed end at the Brighton Duck, as though it were a regimental sword (to clarify, it is the parasol being employed as the sword; not the duck)—*very gently*, so as not to actually harm the unusual creature, or damage the hat, or heaven forbid, strike the lady on the head. . . .

"More, more!" her ladyship cried, using her hands in vain to dislodge the thing on her head, "Strike harder! This is infernal! Oh, but that I were in your place, I would undoubtedly strike with all precision and forcefulness necessary to remove the fiend!"

"I beg pardon, madam, I would rather not damage your ladyship's—attire," replied Elizabeth, making vague motions with the end of the parasol—when in the next instant the duck apparently grew bored with its resting spot and suddenly released the hat. With a sweep of grandiose wings it was aloft once more, and circling them overhead at a great height.

Lady Catherine's hat was a scandalous mess of broken feathers and torn jeweled fabric.

The lady herself got up at this point, continuing to beat at her own head, and exclaim. "This is an outrage! What kind of horrid savage birds do you keep, Miss Bennet! You must control them immediately!"

"There is only one bird," replied Elizabeth, calmly adjusting her rumpled parasol and opening it once again, "and I am afraid it is quite beyond my or anyone's control."

Lady Catherine resembled a somewhat battered stormcloud (if a stormcloud wore a hat with crushed feathers and torn fabric roses). But she now continued with her original discourse nevertheless. "Heed me now, ungrateful girl. You will be shunned. You will be hated and disdained!"

"These are heavy misfortunes," replied Elizabeth. "But the wife of Mr. Darcy must have such extraordinary sources of happiness, that she could have no cause to repine."

"Obstinate, headstrong girl! I am ashamed of you! Is this your gratitude for my attentions to you last spring? Let us sit down again. Miss Bennet, I came here with determined purpose; nor will I be dissuaded from it, regardless of savage fauna. I am not in the habit of brooking disappointment."

Overhead, the Brighton Duck came in for another pass, but this time it did not alight, and merely whistled by her ladyship's disgraced headgear.

"I *will not* be interrupted!" exclaimed Lady Catherine, seeming to address the *duck* directly, then turned back to Elizabeth. "Hear me in silence! My daughter and my nephew are descended from noble lines; from respectable, honourable, ancient families. Their fortune on both sides is splendid. They are destined for each other! But you? If you were sensible of your own good, you would not wish to quit the sphere in which you have been brought up."

"In marrying your nephew, I should not consider myself as quitting that sphere. He is a gentleman; I am a gentleman's daughter; so far we are equal."

"True. You *are* a gentleman's daughter. But who was your mother? Who are your uncles and aunts? *Dogs* and *bears?* A mangy *wolf*, perchance? Do not imagine me ignorant!"

"Whatever my connections may be," said Elizabeth, "if your nephew does not object, they can be nothing to *you*."

"Tell me once for all, are you engaged to him?"

The Brighton Duck made a horrific screech and another aerial pass between them.

"I am not. . . ."

Lady Catherine seemed pleased. She deliberately picked off a single gray feather from her sleeve.

"And will you promise me, never to enter into such an engagement?"

"I will make no promise of the kind."

"Miss Bennet I am shocked and astonished! I expected to find a more reasonable young woman. But do not deceive yourself into a belief that I will ever recede. I shall not go away till you have given me the assurance I require—"

"And I certainly *never* shall give it!" exclaimed Elizabeth, frustrated to the breaking point.

In that moment the monstrous *duck* overhead made another intricate maneuver, and then with a plop, it let go of *unspeakable matter* of a liquid nature. . . .

It came down, not unlike sudden unsavory rain.

The liquid bombardment landed on Lady Catherine—first her hat, then her shoulders and then her lap, so that the pale splatters ended decorating the fine expensive garment in an entirely unplanned and odious fashion.

"Oh! Oh! *Oh!*" screeched her ladyship, rising up for the second time; then sitting down again in stunned outrage.

For once Elizabeth ignored the interruption, and spoke as though nothing was the matter. "I am not to be intimidated. Allow me to say, Lady Catherine, that your arguments have been frivolous and ill-judged. I do indeed apologise profusely for this misfortunate and entirely accidental *drenching*. But you have widely mistaken my character, if you think I can be worked on by such persuasions as these. How far your nephew might approve of your interference in his affairs, I cannot tell. But you have certainly no right to concern yourself in mine. I must beg, therefore, to be importuned no farther on the subject."

"Not so hasty, if you please. I am by no means done!" cried Lady Catherine, simultaneously talking and attempting to clean herself with a handkerchief; dripping and yet relentless. "To all the objections I have still another to add—your youngest sister's infamous elopement. I know it all—that the young man's marrying her was a patched-up business, at the expense of your father and uncles. And is such a girl to be my nephew's sister? Is her husband, the wolfish son of his late father's *wolf* steward, to be his brother? Heaven and earth! Are the shades of Pemberley to be thus polluted?"

"You can now have nothing further to say," Elizabeth resentfully answered. "You have insulted me in every possible method. And you appear to be in need of a change of attire. I must beg to return to the house."

And she rose as she spoke. Lady Catherine rose also, and they turned back. To say that her ladyship—with a scandalous broken hat, drenched in unspeakable bird matter—was "highly incensed" was an understatement. However, that all of this had so little effect on her single-minded purpose, spoke much of her rather indomitable spirit.

"You have no regard, then, for the honour and credit of my nephew! Unfeeling, selfish girl!"

"Lady Catherine, I have nothing further to say."

"You are then resolved to have him?"

"I have said no such thing. I am only resolved to act in a manner which will constitute my happiness."

"An outrage! Horrid, obstinate, insufferable girl!"

In this manner Lady Catherine talked on, with the Brighton Duck still following them and circling above at a distance, till they were at the door of the carriage (from within, the waiting-woman stared at her patroness, and her condition of dress, in abject horror). Then, turning hastily round—and sending splatters of bird *matter* in every direction—she added, "I take no leave of you, Miss Bennet. I send no compliments to your mother. You deserve no such attention. I am most seriously displeased!"

Elizabeth made no answer; and without attempting to persuade Lady Catherine to return into the house, walked quietly into it herself.

From the outside came one more infernal *banshee* screech. For a moment, it was unclear if it were her ladyship or the *duck*.

Elizabeth heard the carriage drive away as she proceeded up stairs. Her mother impatiently met her, to ask why Lady Catherine would not come in again and rest herself.

"She did not choose it," said her daughter, "she would go."

"She is a very fine-looking woman, and her calling here was prodigiously civil! She only came, I suppose, to tell us the Collinses were well, being on her way elsewhere. I suppose she had nothing particular to say to you, Lizzy?"

Elizabeth was forced to give into a little falsehood here.

For, to acknowledge the substance of their conversation was impossible.

"Use the parasol, stupid girl!" shrieked Lady Catherine.

Chapter 57

The discomposure of spirits which this extraordinary visit threw Elizabeth into, could not be easily overcome. She could not stop thinking of it for many hours.

Lady Catherine had actually taken the trouble of this journey from Rosings, for the sole purpose of breaking off her supposed engagement with Mr. Darcy. Elizabeth was at a loss to imagine where her ladyship had received this report, unless it was some kind of nonsense from Mr. Collins.

In pondering Lady Catherine's expressions, however, she could not help feeling some uneasiness as to the possible consequence of this encounter. It occurred to Elizabeth that she might attempt to interrogate and influence her nephew. And how *he* might respond to the notion of a connection with her, she dared not pronounce.

If he had been wavering before as to what he should do, the advice and entreaty of so near a relation might settle every doubt. In that case the gentleman *platypus* would return no more.

If he gives Bingley an excuse for not keeping his promise to return to Netherfield within a few days, she thought, *I shall know how to understand it. I shall then give up every expectation, and soon cease to regret him at all.*

The surprise of the rest of the family, on hearing who their visitor had been, was very great. But they supposed the same reasons for the visit as Mrs. Bennet. And Elizabeth was spared from many questions on the subject.

The next morning, her father came out of his library with a letter in his hand.

"Lizzy," said he, "I was going to look for you; come into my room."

She followed him thither, curious to know what he had to tell her, and if it was connected with the letter he held. What if the missive was from Lady Catherine?

She followed her father to the fireplace, and they both sat down.[104]

He then said: "I have received an astonishing letter this morning. And it principally concerns you! Indeed, I did not know that I had *two* daughters on the brink of matrimony. Let me congratulate you on a very important conquest."

The colour now rushed into Elizabeth's cheeks in the instantaneous conviction of its being a letter from Mr. Darcy himself. And she was unsure whether to be pleased that he explained himself at all, or offended that his letter was not addressed to her.

Her father continued: "You look conscious. Young ladies have great penetration in such matters as these—but I think I may defy even *your* sagacity, to discover the name of your admirer. This letter is from Mr. Collins. Pray, do not attempt to sniff the paper."

"From Mr. Collins! and what can *he* have to say?"

---

[104] At this junction—and also juncture—it is necessary to reassure that when Mr. Bennet and Elizabeth approached the fireplace, they did not in fact sit down *in* it, only beside it. Furthermore, there was no fire lit at present, so even if they *had* decided to sit within the fireplace, they would have been perfectly unharmed, though they might have injured their heads by knocking them against the brickwork overhead.

"He begins with congratulations on the approaching nuptials of my eldest daughter—of which, it seems, he has been told by some of the good-natured, gossiping Lucases. I shall not sport with your impatience. What relates to yourself, is as follows: 'Having thus offered you the sincere congratulations of Mrs. Collins and myself on this happy event, let me now add a short hint on the subject of another; of which we have been advertised by the same authority. Your daughter Elizabeth, it is presumed, will not long bear the name of Bennet, and the chosen partner of her fate may be reasonably looked up to as one of the most illustrious personages in this land.'

"Can you possibly guess, Lizzy, who is meant by this?" 'This young gentleman is blessed, in a peculiar way, with every thing the heart of mortal can most desire,—splendid property, noble kindred, *beastly* pedigree, and extensive patronage. Yet in spite of all these temptations, let me warn of what evils you may incur by accepting this gentleman's proposals, which, of course, you will be inclined to do immediately.'

"Have you any idea, Lizzy, who this gentleman is? But now it comes out:

"'My motive for cautioning you is as follows. We have reason to imagine that his aunt, Lady Catherine de Bourgh, does not look on the match with a friendly eye.'

"*Mr. Darcy*, you see, is the man! Now, Lizzy, I think I *have* surprised you. Could he, or the Lucases, have pitched on any less likely man within the circle of our acquaintance? Mr. Darcy, who never looks at any woman but to see a blemish, and who probably never looked at you in his life! It is admirable!"

Elizabeth tried to join in her father's pleasantry, but could only force one reluctant smile. Never had his *lion* wit been directed in a manner so little agreeable to her.

"Are you not diverted?"

"Oh! yes. Pray read on."

"'After I mentioned the likelihood of this marriage to her ladyship last night, she immediately expressed what she felt on the occasion—she would never give her consent to what she termed so disgraceful a match. I thought it my duty to give the speediest intelligence of this to my cousin, that she and her noble admirer may not run hastily into a marriage which has not been properly sanctioned.' Mr. Collins moreover adds, 'I am truly rejoiced that my cousin Lydia's sad business has been so well hushed up. I must not, however, neglect the duties of my station, and declare my amazement at hearing that you received the young couple into your house. It was an encouragement of vice! You ought certainly to forgive them, as a Christian, but never to admit them in your sight, or allow their names to be mentioned in your hearing.' *That* is his notion of Christian forgiveness! The rest of his letter is only about his dear Charlotte's situation, and his expectation of a young olive-branch—and also some large livestock packages from Australia. But, Lizzy, you look as if you did not enjoy it. You are not going to be *missish*, I hope, and pretend to be affronted at an idle report. For what do we live, but to make sport for our neighbours, and laugh at them in our turn?"

"Oh!" cried Elizabeth, "I am excessively diverted. But it is so strange! And Charlotte, in the family way! And shipments from Australia!"

"Yes—*that* is what makes it amusing. Had they fixed on any other man it would have been nothing. But *his* perfect indifference, and *your* pointed dislike, make it so delightfully absurd! Much as I abominate letters, I would not give up Mr. Collins's correspondence for anything. Nay, when I read a letter of his, I cannot help giving him the preference even over Wickham, much as I value the impudence and hypocrisy of my son-in-law. And pray, Lizzy, what said Lady Catherine about this report? Did she call to refuse her consent?"

To this question his daughter replied only with a laugh.

Oh, but Elizabeth had never been more at a loss to disguise her feelings! It was necessary to laugh, when she would rather have cried. . . .

Chapter 58

Instead of receiving a letter of excuse from his friend, as Elizabeth expected, Mr. Bingley was able to bring Darcy with him to Longbourn before many days had passed after Lady Catherine's visit.

The gentlemen arrived early. And, before Mrs. Bennet could tell Darcy of their having seen his aunt (which her daughter dreaded), Bingley, who wanted to be alone with Jane, proposed their all walking out.

It was agreed to. Mrs. Bennet was not in the habit of walking. Mary could never spare time. But the remaining five set off together.

Bingley and Jane, however, soon allowed the others to outstrip them. They lagged behind, while Elizabeth, Kitty, and Darcy were to entertain each other. Very little was said by either. Kitty was too much afraid of him to talk. Elizabeth was secretly forming a desperate resolution; and perhaps he might be doing the same.

They walked towards the Lucases, because Kitty wished to call upon Maria. And as Elizabeth saw no occasion for making it a general concern, when Kitty left them she went boldly on with *him* alone. Now was the moment for her resolution to be executed, and, while her courage was high, she immediately said:

"Mr. Darcy, I am a very selfish creature. And, for the sake of giving relief to my own feelings, I care not how much I may be wounding yours. I can no longer help thanking you for your impossible kindness to my poor sister. Ever since I have known it, I have been most anxious to acknowledge my deep gratitude. And if the rest of my family knew, theirs would be boundless."

"I am exceedingly sorry," replied Darcy, in a tone of surprise and emotion, "that you have ever been informed of what may have given you uneasiness. I did not think Mrs. Gardiner was so little to be trusted."

"You must not blame my aunt. Lydia's thoughtlessness first betrayed to me that you had been involved. And, of course, I could not rest till I knew the particulars. Let me thank you again and again, in the name of all my family, for that generous compassion which induced you to take so much trouble, and bear so many mortifications, for the sake of locating them."

"If you *will* thank me," he replied, "let it be for yourself alone. I shall not deny that the wish of giving happiness to you added force to my actions. But your *family* owes me nothing. Much as I respect them, I thought only of *you*."

Elizabeth was too much embarrassed to say a word. The sun was bright through the lattice of trees, and a light breeze swept the leaves into cascades of gentle whispers. A tiny remote speck of a bird glided far overhead, looking remotely familiar.

After a short pause, her companion added, "You are too generous to trifle with me. If your feelings are still what they were last April, tell me so at once. *My* affections and wishes are unchanged, but one word from you will silence me on this subject forever."

Elizabeth, feeling all the more than common awkwardness and anxiety of his situation, now forced herself to speak. And immediately (though not very fluently) she gave him to understand that her sentiments had undergone so material a change, since the period to which he alluded, as to make her receive with gratitude and pleasure his present assurances.

The happiness that this reply produced was such as he had probably never felt before. And he expressed himself on the occasion as sensibly and as warmly as a man violently in love can be supposed to do.

"Dearest Elizabeth!" he said, "There is something different with the world; can you suddenly feel it?"

Had Elizabeth been able to encounter his eye, she might have seen how well the expression of heartfelt delight, diffused over his face, became him. But, though she could not look, she could listen . . . and he told her of feelings that proved how important she was to him, and made his affection every moment more valuable.

Overhead, a very great dark speck of a bird circled nearer and nearer, and then alighted on a nearby large branch with a wild beating of dove-grey wings.

Elizabeth looked up to see the monstrous Brighton Duck observing her from its perch with one unblinking wise eye. It appeared to have no intention of moving (or screeching, or doing anything else highly untoward).

"I know that ridiculous duck!" said Darcy suddenly. "It was there with us that first time also. In my bitterness and broken pride I wanted to shoot it. But now—"

"—but now it makes my heart soar," completed Elizabeth.

"Elizabeth—my love," said he, "I—"

She finally looked up, meeting his earnest eyes directly for the first time since their mutual confession.

"I—" said Mr. Darcy, "I cannot help it now; my will is all yours. I think I might again require a cage. . . ."

"Oh dear!" she managed to exclaim, as her lover suddenly began to *turn* right before her eyes. The wind blew, the air shimmered, he fell forward and then *dissolved*. . . .

Moments later, the little *platypus* creature with webbed feet, a dark brown coat of waterproof fur, a thick tail, and a ridiculous duck bill, was crawling on the floor before her, in a puddle of elegant gentleman's clothes.

Elizabeth felt her heart break. It was an equal measure of sympathy mingled with compassion, and with *something* for which she had no words, and had never felt before.

And suddenly, as the sun shone warmly from above, and the leaves fluttered in smooth motion, leaving lacework shadows, she felt a moment of overwhelming vertigo, a *letting go*—and she too felt her own *self* dissolving.

The world quickly rose up all around her, and she was suddenly swooning, falling, shrinking. Her hands shortened and became little webbed appendages, and her face elongated, until she felt the long duck snout—and immediately lost her bonnet. She struck her furry tail from side to side, freeing herself from her gown and petticoats. . . . And now she was a perfectly well-formed, odd little female *creature*, of a slightly lighter yellow-brown with just a tinge of bronze.

With one tiny cry she moved toward the other *platypus*, and the two of them touched skins. . . .

From overhead the Brighton Duck observed them with a dignified nonchalance that can only be expressed by a fellow creature. Then, it beat its grandiose wings, and silently shot up into the burning sky.

Time seemed measureless. But eventually they became once more *human*, self-aware, and rational enough to hastily put on their discarded clothing; their backs modestly turned to each other, their cheeks aflame.

"How is it that you can *become* the same creature as myself?" he asked in wonder. "Without a scratch, a bite, a breath of harm?"

"I believe it is a Dreadful Secret," she replied with a subtle smile. "My mother had revealed some of it once, but I think we all come to know it only when we ourselves begin to *love*."

"It is true, then," he whispered, "Georgiana, able to rise above the 'natural order' of the curse was not an anomaly—"

"I think," mused Elizabeth, "that the 'curse' of the Affliction had fallen upon the *men* because they, for the most part, took their capacity for love for granted. Thus, the demon nature took its hold, and manifested every fool—pardon me— *full* moon, because, deep in their hearts the men permitted it to be. The women, however—the so-called fairer sex, have never quite forgotten how to love. We are 'fair' indeed, for in our unconditional regard we are just, and everyone knows that Lady Justice is blind. And as such, there was no need for supernatural intervention for us, for transformation or punishment. We, women, were ever blind in love, for we closed our eyes to the ephemeral veneer of evil (that so easily seduces men), and saw in our beloved only the eternal, steady, inner shining light. Indeed, the more I think of it, the more I believe there is no punishment at all, for *either* sex—only a self-inflicted state of *wilderness*, a loss of personal control and yes, responsibility, that the men allow themselves each moon. . . ."

Then they walked on, without knowing in what direction. There was too much to be thought, and felt, and said.

Elizabeth soon learnt that they were indebted for their present *understanding* to the efforts of his aunt, who did call on him in London, and there related her journey to Longbourn, its motive, and the substance of her conversation with Elizabeth. Lady Catherine dwelled emphatically on every expression of the latter, which denoted her "perverseness and assurance." This was told Darcy in the belief that it might assist her endeavours. But, unluckily for her ladyship, its effect was the opposite.

"It taught me to hope," said he, "as I had scarcely ever allowed myself to hope before. I knew that, had you been absolutely, irrevocably decided against me, you would have acknowledged it to Lady Catherine, frankly and openly."

Elizabeth coloured and laughed as she replied, "Yes, you know enough of my frankness to believe me capable of *that*. After abusing you so abominably to your face, I could have no scruple in abusing you to all your relations."

"What did you say of me, that I did not deserve? For, though your accusations were formed on mistaken premises, my behaviour to you at the time had merited the severest reproof. It was unpardonable. And then I lost control so shamefully and *turned* before your eyes."

"We will not quarrel for the greater share of blame," said Elizabeth.

"I cannot be so easily reconciled to myself," he replied. "Your reproof, I shall never forget: 'had you behaved in a more gentlemanlike manner.' Those were your words. You cannot know how they have tortured me—"

"Oh! do not repeat what I then said. These recollections will not do at all. I assure you that I have long been most heartily ashamed of it."

They spoke of Darcy's letter, and how it had served to change Elizabeth's feelings.

"The letter, perhaps, began in bitterness, but it did not end so. But think no more of the letter," she said. "The feelings of the person who wrote, and the person who received it, are now so widely different from what they were then."

"And yet," he said, "painful recollections will intrude. I have been a selfish being all my life. As a child I was taught what was *right*, but I was not taught to correct my temper. I was given good principles, but left to follow them in pride and conceit. Unfortunately an only son, I was spoilt by my parents, who, though good themselves, taught me to be selfish and overbearing—to care for none beyond my own family circle; to think meanly of all the rest of the world, of their sense and worth compared with my own. The unfortunate incident with the platypus that poisoned me when I was a child, only served to enhance my sense of bitter isolation. Such I was, from eight to eight and twenty; and such I might still have been but for you, dearest, loveliest Elizabeth! What do I not owe you! You taught me a lesson! By you, I was properly humbled. And by you, I was *raised* up again, into the light."

They spoke of many things then—of nuances and moments, and details that defined the progress of their complex and gradual love.

He then told her of Georgiana's delight in her acquaintance, and then her amazement and sublime exultation at the *ability* that Elizabeth had brought out in her.

"My golden burning sister now flies like a sun each morning! She is a joy, and her practicing of music has become once again what it must be, not a dutiful escape, but a delight!"

After walking several miles in a leisurely manner, and too busy to know anything about it, they found at last, on examining their watches, that it was time to be at home.

"What could have become of Mr. Bingley and Jane!" was a question that introduced the discussion of *their* affairs. Darcy admitted he was delighted with their engagement.

"You had given your permission. I guessed as much," said Elizabeth. And though he exclaimed at the term, she found that it had been pretty much the case.

"On the evening before my going to London," said he, "I made a confession to him, which I ought to have made long ago. I told him of all that had occurred to make my former interference in his affairs absurd and impertinent. His surprise was great. But he has since forgiven me."

Elizabeth could not help smiling. But before saying something overly teasing, she checked herself. He had yet to learn to be laughed at, and it was rather too early to begin.

They continued the conversation till they reached the house.

Chapter 59

"My dear Lizzy, where can you have been walking to?" was a question which Elizabeth received from Jane as soon as she entered their room, and from the others when they sat down to table. She replied that they had "wandered about." She coloured as she spoke. But it did not awaken a suspicion of the truth.

The evening passed quietly, unmarked by anything extraordinary. The moon's phase was now past the danger point of fullness, so there was no longer a rush to retire early, and no thoughts of cages.

The acknowledged lovers talked and laughed, the unacknowledged were silent. Darcy was not of a disposition in which happiness overflows in mirth—particularly after his single extraordinary loss of composure and *platypus* outburst this afternoon. And Elizabeth, agitated and confused, rather *knew* that she was happy than *felt* herself to be so. She was still numb from the intensity of the day, the afterglow of her *transformation* filling her flesh and all her senses with a wild *otherness*, and a newfound freedom and awareness. And yet, she was now painfully aware of the ordinary reality. For, besides the immediate embarrassment, there were other evils before her. She imagined what would be felt in the family when her situation became known. She was aware that no one liked Darcy but Jane; and feared that it was a dislike which not all his fortune and consequence might do away.

At night she opened her heart to Jane, who was absolutely incredulous here.

"You are joking, Lizzy. This cannot be!—engaged to Mr. Darcy! No, you shall not deceive me. It is impossible."

"This is a wretched beginning indeed! My sole dependence was on you—nobody else will believe me, if you do not. Yet, indeed, I am in earnest. He still loves me, and we are engaged."

Jane looked at her doubtingly. "But—I know how much you dislike him!"

"You know nothing of the matter. *That* is all to be forgot. Perhaps I did not always love him so well as I do now—but then, I did not know how to *love* at all."

Miss Bennet still looked all amazement. Elizabeth again, and more seriously assured her of its truth.

"Good Heaven! can it be really so! Yet now I must believe you," cried Jane. "My dear, Lizzy, I would congratulate you—but are you quite certain that you can be happy with him?"

"There can be no doubt of that. It is settled between us already, that we are to be the happiest couple in the world. But are you pleased, Jane? Shall you like to have such a brother?"

"Very, very much. Nothing could give either Bingley or myself more delight. But, will you tell me how long you have loved him?"

"It has been coming on so gradually, that I hardly know when it began. But I believe I must date it from my first seeing him as the strange little *platypus*. And then seeing his beautiful grounds at Pemberley certainly added to the appeal—not to mention his propensity for finding himself clad in wet shirts!"

Another entreaty that she would be serious, however, produced the desired effect. And she soon satisfied Jane by her solemn assurances of attachment. When convinced on that article, Miss Bennet had nothing further to wish.

"Now I am quite happy," said she, "for you will be as happy as myself. But Lizzy, you have been very sly with me. How little did you tell me of what passed at Pemberley and Lambton!"

Elizabeth told her the motives of her secrecy. She had been unwilling to mention Bingley. And the unsettled state of her own feelings had made her equally avoid the name of his friend. But now she would no longer conceal Darcy's share in Lydia's marriage. All was acknowledged, and half the night spent in conversation.

"Good gracious!" cried Mrs. Bennet, as she stood at a window the next morning, "if that disagreeable Mr. Darcy is not coming here again with our dear Bingley! What can he mean by being so tiresome as to be always coming here? Lizzy, you must walk out with him again, that he may not be in Bingley's way."

Elizabeth could hardly help laughing at so convenient a proposal. Yet she was really vexed that her mother should be always giving him such an epithet.

As soon as they entered, the gentleman *tiger* looked at her so expressively, and shook hands with such warmth, as left no doubt of his being aware of their secret good news. And he soon afterwards said aloud, "Mrs. Bennet, have you no more lanes hereabouts in which Lizzy may lose her way again to-day?"

Darcy professed a great curiosity to see the view from Oakham Mount, and Elizabeth silently consented. As she went up stairs to get ready, Mrs. Bennet followed her, saying:

"I am quite sorry, Lizzy, that you should be forced to have that disagreeable man all to yourself. But I hope you will not mind, for Jane's sake. And there is no occasion for talking to him, except just now and then. So, do not put yourself to inconvenience."

During their walk, it was resolved that Mr. Bennet's consent should be asked in the course of the evening. Elizabeth reserved to herself the application for her mother's. She could not determine how her mother would take it. But whether she were violently set against the match, or violently delighted, it was certain that her manner would be equally ill adapted to do credit to her sense.

In the evening, soon after Mr. Bennet withdrew to the library, she saw Mr. Darcy rise also and follow him, and her agitation on seeing it was extreme. Elizabeth did not fear her father's opposition, but he was going to be made unhappy. And that it should be through his favourite child, was a wretched reflection.

She sat in misery till Mr. Darcy appeared again, when, looking at him, she was a little relieved by his smile. In a few minutes he approached the table where she was sitting with Kitty. And, while pretending to admire her work, he whispered, "Go to your father, he wants you in the library."

Her father was walking about the room, looking grave and anxious. "Lizzy," said he, "what are you doing? Are you out of your senses, to be accepting this man? Have not you always hated him?"

She assured him of her attachment to Mr. Darcy.

"Or, in other words, you are determined to have him. He is rich, to be sure, and you may have more fine clothes and fine carriages than Jane. But will they make you happy?"

"Have you any other objection," said Elizabeth, "than your belief of my indifference?"

"None at all. We all know him to be a proud, unpleasant sort of man; but this would be nothing if you really liked him."

"I do, I do like him," she replied, with tears in her eyes, "I love him. I *turned*, father! I *turned* into his *beast*. Indeed you do not know what he really is."

"Lizzy!" said her father, "You *have!*" He paused, suddenly unable to speak from sentiment, while Elizabeth noticed liquid gathering in his eyes.

"You have . . ." repeated Mr. Bennet, with sudden complete understanding. It seemed that he was remembering something fine, delicate and infinitely *precious* in his own long-gone past. . . . And then, swiftly composing himself, he continued, "Then I am *glad*, for I have given him my consent. He is the kind of man, indeed, to whom I should never dare refuse anything. And I now give it to *you*, seeing you are indeed resolved on having him."

Elizabeth, still more affected, was earnest and solemn in her reply. And at length, by repeated assurances that Mr. Darcy was really the object of her choice, and by explaining the gradual change in her estimation of him—and the reasons behind it—she convinced her father.

"Well, my dear," said he, when she ceased speaking, "I have no more to say. If this be the case, he deserves you. I could not have parted with you, my Lizzy, to anyone less worthy. But, tell me, is he perchance a Great Cat? What mysterious *beast* does he harbour?"

"I shall tell you one day, father," she answered with a smile.

To complete the favourable impression, she then told him what Mr. Darcy had voluntarily done for Lydia. Her father heard her with astonishment.

"This is an evening of wonders, indeed! And so, Darcy did everything; made up the match, gave the money, paid the fellow's debts, and got him his commission! I shall offer to pay him to-morrow. But he will rant and storm about his love for you, and there will be an end of the matter, I venture to guess."

Further lightening an already jovial mood, he then recollected her embarrassment a few days before, on his reading Mr. Collins's letter. . . . And after laughing at her some time, he allowed her at last to go—saying, as she quitted the room, "If any young *tigers, wolves,* or decidedly civilian *hedgehogs* come for Mary or Kitty, send them in, for I am quite at leisure!"

Elizabeth's mind was now relieved from a very heavy weight. And, after half an hour's quiet reflection in her own room, she was able to join the others with tolerable composure.

The evening passed tranquilly away. There was no longer anything to be dreaded.

When her mother went up to her dressing-room at night, she followed her, and made the important communication.

Its effect was most extraordinary. For on first hearing it, Mrs. Bennet sat quite still, and unable to utter a syllable. Nor was it under many, many minutes that she could comprehend what she heard. She began at length to recover, to fidget about in her chair, get up, sit down again, wonder, and bless herself.

"Good gracious! Lord bless me! Mr. Darcy! Who would have thought it! And is it really true? Oh, my sweetest Lizzy! How rich and how great you will be! What pin-money, what jewels, what carriages you will have! Jane's is nothing to it! Such a charming man! So handsome! So tall! Oh, my dear Lizzy! Pray apologise for my having disliked him so much before—" And then, muttering about "three daughters married" and "ten thousand a year," Mrs. Bennet apparently had indeed gone distracted. . . .

Elizabeth quietly tiptoed out of the room. But, in minutes, her mother followed her.

"My dearest child!" she cried, "I can think of nothing else! Ten thousand a year, and very likely more! 'Tis as good as a Lord! But my dearest love, tell me what dish Mr. Darcy is particularly fond of, that I may have it to-morrow! What is his *beast*, a Great Cat? Does he perchance like dishes of creamy milk to be stirred in—"

This was a sad omen of what her mother's behaviour to the gentleman himself might be. But the morrow passed off much better than she expected. For Mrs. Bennet luckily stood in such awe of her intended son-in-law that she ventured not to speak to him, unless it was in her power to offer him any attention, or mark her deference for his opinion.

Elizabeth had the satisfaction of seeing her father taking pains to get acquainted with him. And Mr. Bennet soon assured her that Darcy was rising every hour in his esteem, "even if he were not a Great Cat—as he could *tell*."

"I admire all my three sons-in-law highly," said he. "Wickham, perhaps, is my favourite; but I think I shall like *your* husband quite as well as Jane's."

Chapter 60

Elizabeth's spirits soon again rose to playfulness. She wanted Mr. Darcy to admit the moment he had fallen in love with her.

"I cannot fix on the hour, or the spot, or the look, or the words, which laid the foundation," he said, looking at her warmly. "It is too long ago. I was in the middle before I knew that I *had* begun. And then, I knew my control over the *beast* was sorely tested in your company, so it was as good an indication as any."

"My beauty you had early withstood, and as for my manners—Now be sincere; did you admire me for my impertinence?"

"For the liveliness of your mind, I did."

"You may as well call it impertinence. The fact is, you were sick of civility, of deference, of officious attention. And you were disgusted with keeping *secrets* and holding back."

They talked at length, offering up memories of their various encounters, back and forth, remembering each glimmer, each spark, each contrary and intriguing word and glance that came to glitter between them.

"That ball at Netherfield, when the comet first appeared, and all the gentlemen lost control over their demons," she recalled, "I remember you calling out to me—was it to run or approach?"

He laughed. "I know not what I called out. I was on the verge of falling to the darkness. But you were the only one I could think of, even then. I knew I could not help you myself, for fear of revealing my useless little *beast*—"

"Useless? I beg to differ, sir! It is the same *beast* that defeated Mr. Wickham's *wolf!*"

And then he told her of that encounter, which Mr. Gardiner had only witnessed on the other side of a closed door.

"We fought, indeed—after my words had proved inadequate. His *wolf*—all silver-grey fur, dripping ivory fangs and green-eyes—was called up easily, regardless of the moon being out; for, as you might have noticed over the course of these events, we men do not require the excuse of the moon to allow our demons freedom over us. But of course, if the truth of this were to be known, we would all be restrained with chains, and locked up in cages, permanently.

"In short—we fought, and my *platypus*, being half his size, could have no chance in heaven of winning—if it were not for the venom. I struck the *wolf* with my poison spurs, in the same manner as the platypus in the zoo had struck me as a child. I snagged the wolf's paw. He howled in pain, snarled, drew back, and our struggle ceased in that instant, for the poison took immediate effect. . . .

"Now, this is not something widely known, not even by your uncle and aunt, but Wickham took to bed afterwards. He had become ill, in the same manner as myself when a child, except he was older and stronger, and had received the poison when in *demon wolf* form. For that reason his illness was brief and his recovery much shorter that my own.

"However, things were different between us, and my influence had changed him in a manner hardly imaginable, indeed, in a more-than-ordinary 'persuasive' sense. Suffice it to say, he is no longer a *wolf.*"

"*What?*" Elizabeth exclaimed, with dawning understanding. "He is—you mean he is now—"

"A *demon duckbill platypus*."

Elizabeth had never yet had a chance to answer Mrs. Gardiner's long letter; but now, having such welcome news to communicate, she immediately wrote her a happy reply, part of which was as follows:

> "I thank you, again and again, dear aunt, for *not* going to the Lakes. How could I be so silly as to wish it! Your idea of the ponies is delightful. We will go round the Park at Pemberley every day. *Yes*, I am the happiest creature in the world! I am happier even than Jane; she only smiles, I laugh, and I *transform*. Mr. Darcy sends you all the love in the world that he can spare from me. You are all to come to Pemberley at Christmas. Yours, etc."

Mr. Darcy's letter to Lady Catherine was in a different style. And still different from either was what Mr. Bennet sent to Mr. Collins, in reply to his last.

> "DEAR SIR,
>
> "I must trouble you once more for congratulations. Elizabeth will soon be the wife of Mr. Darcy. Console Lady Catherine as well as you can. But, if I were you, I would stand by the nephew. He and his *beast* have more to give.
>
> "Yours sincerely, etc."

Miss Bingley's congratulations to her brother, on his approaching marriage, were all that was affectionate and insincere. She wrote even to Jane on the occasion, to express her delight, and repeat all her former professions of regard.

Jane was not deceived, but she was affected; and could not help writing her a much kinder answer than was deserved.

The joy that Miss Georgiana Darcy expressed on receiving similar information, was as sincere as her brother's in sending it. Four sides of paper were insufficient to contain all her delight and all her earnest desire of being loved by her new sister. And her letter, when unfolded, contained a strange insert of several cobweb-fine golden bird feathers that floated in the lightest breeze, and, under a certain light, appeared to be on *fire*. . . .

Before any answer could arrive from Mr. Collins, or any congratulations to Elizabeth from his wife, the Longbourn family heard that the Collinses themselves had come to Lucas Lodge.

The reason of this sudden removal was soon evident. Lady Catherine had been rendered so exceedingly angry by her nephew's letter, that Charlotte—really rejoicing in the match—was anxious to get away till the storm was blown over.

At such a moment, the arrival of her friend was a sincere pleasure to Elizabeth—though in the course of their meetings she must sometimes think the pleasure dearly bought, when she saw Mr. Darcy exposed to all the parading and obsequious civility of her husband (not to mention the accompanying pernicious and ever-present whiff of *skunk)*. He bore it, however, with admirable calmness (and an occasional, discreet usage of a handkerchief and snuff box).

Darcy could even listen to Sir William Lucas, when he complimented him on carrying away "the brightest jewel of the country," and expressed his hopes of their all meeting frequently at St. James's, with very decent composure. Mrs. Phillips's vulgarity was a greater tax on his forbearance. Elizabeth did all she could to shield him from the frequent notice of either, and was ever anxious to keep him to herself (and to those of her family with whom he might converse without mortification).

Thus, she looked forward with delight to the time when they should be removed from society so little pleasing to either, to all the comfort and elegance of Pemberley.

Chapter 61

Happy for all her maternal feelings was the day on which Mrs. Bennet got rid of her two most deserving daughters. With what delighted pride she afterwards visited "Mrs. Bingley," and talked of "Mrs. Darcy," may be guessed.

Dear Reader, I wish I could say, for the sake of her family, that the accomplishment of her most earnest desire in the establishment of so many of her children made her a sensible, amiable, well-informed woman for the rest of her life. Alas! it was not so. Though, perhaps it was lucky for her husband, that she still was occasionally nervous and invariably silly, and could thus provide him with reliable fodder for amiable sport.

However, there were occasions when Mr. Bennet recalled the earlier dreaming days when she had *transformed* for him. . . .

Mr. Bennet missed his second daughter exceedingly. He delighted in going to Pemberley, especially when he was least expected.

Mr. Bingley and Jane remained at Netherfield only a twelvemonth. He bought an estate in a neighbouring county to Derbyshire, and Jane and Elizabeth, in addition to every other source of happiness, were within thirty miles of each other.

Kitty, to her very material advantage, spent the chief of her time with her two elder sisters. In society so superior to what she had generally known, her improvement was great. Removed from the influence of Lydia's example, she became, by proper attention and management, less irritable, less ignorant, and less insipid. And though Mrs. Wickham frequently invited her to come and stay with her, with the promise of balls and young military men, her father would never consent to her going.

Mary was the only daughter who remained at home; and she was necessarily drawn from the pursuit of accomplishments by Mrs. Bennet's being quite unable to sit alone. Mary was obliged to mix more with the world, but she could still moralize over every morning visit. Here, she soon discovered that the admiring attentions of an erudite *bovine*, *ursine*, or even a well-read *hyena* were a thing not entirely displeasing.

As for Wickham and Lydia, their characters suffered no revolution from the marriage of her sisters. The newly forged *platypus* was convinced that Darcy might yet be prevailed on to make his fortune.

The congratulatory letter which Elizabeth received from Lydia on her marriage bore an entirely non-veiled request for monetary assistance, and concluded with "but however, do not speak to Mr. Darcy about it, if you had rather not."

As it happened that Elizabeth had *much* rather not, she endeavoured in her answer to put an end to every entreaty and expectation of the kind. However, through putting aside a bit here and there in her own private expenses, she frequently sent them what help she could.

Though Darcy could never receive *him* at Pemberley, yet, for Elizabeth's sake, he assisted him further in his profession. Lydia was occasionally a visitor there, when her husband was gone to enjoy himself in London or Bath. And with the Bingleys they frequently staid so long, that even Bingley's good humour was overcome, and he talked of giving them a hint to be gone.

Miss Bingley was very deeply mortified by Darcy's marriage. But as she thought it advisable to retain the right of visiting at Pemberley, she dropt all her resentment; was fonder than ever of Georgiana, almost as attentive to Darcy as heretofore, and paid off every arrear[105] of civility to Elizabeth.

Pemberley was now Georgiana's home; and the attachment of the sisters was exactly what Darcy had hoped to see. Georgiana had the highest opinion in the world of Elizabeth; though at first she often listened with an astonishment bordering on alarm at her lively, sportive, manner of talking to her brother. He, who had always inspired in herself a respect which almost overcame her affection, she now saw the object of open pleasantry. By Elizabeth's instructions, she began to comprehend that a woman may take liberties with her husband which a brother will not always allow in a sister more than ten years younger than himself.

Lady Catherine was extremely indignant on the marriage of her nephew. In her reply she sent him language so very abusive, especially of Elizabeth, that for some time all intercourse[106] was at an end. But at length, by Elizabeth's persuasion, Darcy was prevailed on to overlook the offence, and seek a reconciliation. And, after a little further resistance on the part of his aunt, her resentment gave way, either to her affection for him, or her curiosity to see how his wife conducted herself. And she condescended to wait on them at Pemberley.

---

[105] Dear reader, here Miss Bingley is apparently paying off Elizabeth Bennet via some manner of installment plan. If she forfeits—nay; what is the word?—defaults even on a single payment, it is the sad fate of a debtor's prison that awaits the elegant lady. —Ed. *[And on that dulcet note, this being our last wretched footnote in this monstrously wretched affair, I might bid the fair reader a blessed adieu, and remove myself to imbibe port and absinthe, and continue to get thoroughly sloshed. Adieu, fair muse, adieu! —Ed. 2]*

[106] Gracious! And just when we were about to have our last footnote, one comes upon such a scandalous unspeakable thing, not to be ignored! Cleanse your eyes, your mind, your very spirit of such filth, fair reader! Make haste! And whatever you do, do *not* think of England!

Charlotte, meanwhile, corresponded with her dear friend quite often. In the most recent letter she at last had the pleasure of describing a long awaited event—no, not her own happy increase in the family (that was yet to come), but a dearly awaited shipment of livestock crates from Australia:

> "You can imagine Mr. Collins's happiness, Lizzy—nay, you cannot, for it was equalled only by the rapidity with which he proceeded to make arrangements and thorough preparations to begin the process of Australian breeding.
>
> "The crates, bearing within the different animal varieties, were unloaded and opened one by one. The first, upon opening, released two pairs of rather large kangaroo or possibly wallaroo. The kangaroos, sensing freedom, immediately engaged their powerful haunches and sprang forth, hopping all over the yard, and scattering my chickens. Needless to say, Mr. Collins bravely gave chase, brandishing a specially ordered 'training stick.' But in moments, bouncing mightily, the kangaroos fled into the shrubbery.
>
> "Next to be released was the emu. The *emu*, my dear Lizzy, is a large brownish-feathered flightless bird, vaguely similar to our own local turkey, but much larger—and when I say *larger*, it is closer to this wild creature called an ostrich that I have never in my entire life seen before, nor do I ever want to see again. Needless to say, there was a tussle; the 'training stick' was employed to no end. One thing led to another; the emu gave chase, and Mr. Collins fled into the shrubbery. . . ."

Elizabeth shared the letter with Darcy, and they pondered the images it invoked with some astonishment.

And speaking of correspondence—with the Gardiners, they were always on the most intimate terms. Darcy, as well as Elizabeth, really loved them. And they were both ever sensible of the warmest gratitude towards the persons who, by bringing her into Derbyshire, had been the means of uniting them.

At some point, when a certain full moon was approaching, Elizabeth made an interesting suggestion to her beloved. This time, she ventured, instead of using his splendid confinement chamber on the second floor of Pemberley house next to their bedroom, they might consider braving the night and the stars and the pale moon above, and allow the Affliction to take its natural hold directly by the deep lovely pond. . . .

"If you prefer, Mr. Darcy, I can yet again go into your Ordeal chamber and tub with you. We can go into the cage together and *turn*. Or we can go before the still waters of the pond, and face the moonlight together. And maybe this time, with the pale magical light upon us, our hands clasped, and our spirits soaring, we will both remain *human*."

THE END

APPENDIX

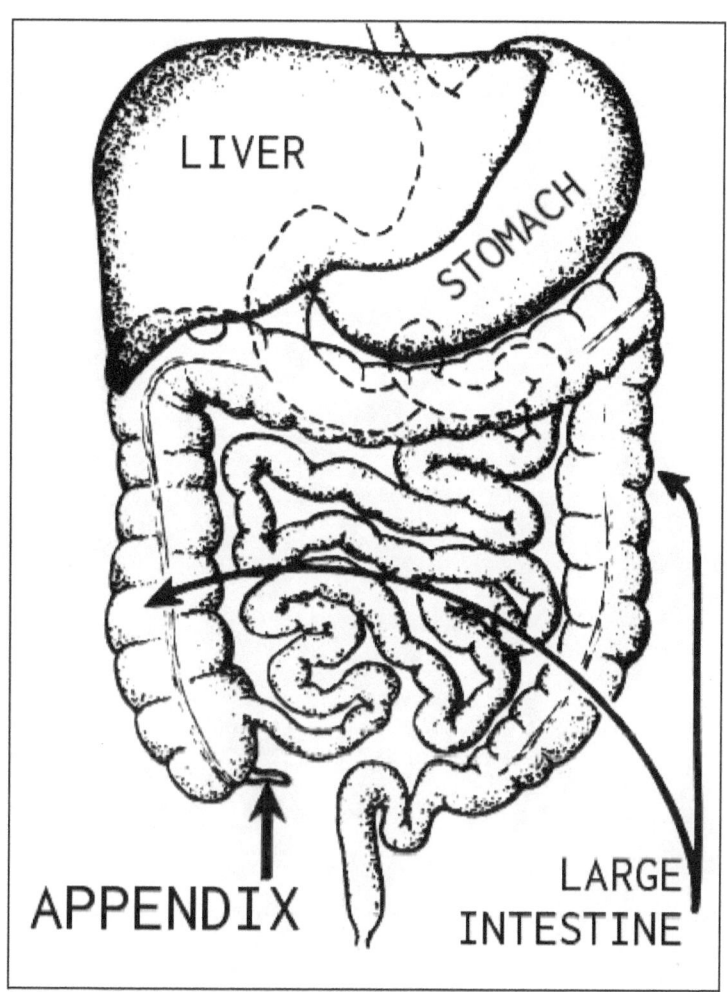

Figure 1

APPENDIX 2

Figure 2: Platypus Plumbing

Author's After-Note

GENTLE READER—

No, this is not *she,* but the other—the shameless harridan who
has taken it upon herself to take up pen and mangle Miss
Austen's deathless (but never *undead*), perfectly civil,
delightfully romantic, pointedly sarcastic, and by all accounts
immortal prose, with the crass additions of her own fired
imagination.

To parody the most popular novel in the world is a nigh-
impossible task—until one adds in supernatural wonders, the
entirety of the wild animal kingdom of Australia, and throws in a
comet for good measure!

The Great Comet of 1811 was an amazing coincidence to
the real historical timeline of the events described herein, seen
blazing in the heavens for approximately 260 days, and being at
its brightest in October of that year, just a month before the ball
at Netherfield. One can only thank the stars for such serendipity!

Meanwhile, I humbly beg a thousand pardons of Miss
Austen's noble shade—and all the noble shades of Pemberley
that shall remain delightfully unpolluted—and trust you have
enjoyed the northern tour through this menagerie of absurdities
and droll amusements, never intended to offend but instead to
soothe any gentleman's pride and diffuse any lady's prejudice.

Yours, in All Amiability,
THE HARRIDAN.

Vera Nazarian
June, 2012

About the Harridan

Vera Nazarian immigrated to the USA from the former USSR as a kid, sold her first story at the age of 17, and since then has published numerous works in anthologies and magazines, and has seen her fiction translated into eight languages.

She made her novelist debut with the critically acclaimed arabesque "collage" novel *Dreams of the Compass Rose*, followed by epic fantasy about a world without color, *Lords of Rainbow*. Her novella *The Clock King and the Queen of the Hourglass* from PS Publishing (UK) with an introduction by **Charles de Lint** made the *Locus* Recommended Reading List for 2005. Her debut short fiction collection *Salt of the Air*, with an introduction by **Gene Wolfe**, contains the 2007 Nebula Award-nominated "The Story of Love." Recent work includes the 2008 Nebula Award-nominated, self-illustrated baroque fantasy novella *The Duke In His Castle*, science fiction collection *After the Sundial* (2010), **Jane Austen** parodies *Mansfield Park and Mummies* (2009) and *Northanger Abbey and Angels and Dragons* (2010), *The Perpetual Calendar of Inspiration* (2010), and this literary curiosity that you now hold in your hands. . . .

Vera recently relocated from Los Angeles to the East Coast. She lives in a small town in Vermont, and uses her Armenian sense of humor and her Russian sense of suffering to bake conflicted pirozhki and make art.

In addition to being a writer and award-winning artist, she is also the publisher of Norilana Books.

Official website:
www.veranazarian.com